# BRER RABBIT
## STORY COLLECTION

**Look out for all of these enchanting story collections by**

*Enid Blyton*

# Enid Blyton

# BRER RABBIT

## STORY COLLECTION

Hodder
Children's
Books

# HODDER CHILDREN'S BOOKS

First published in Great Britain in two separate volumes as *Enid Blyton's Brer Rabbit Book* (1948) by Latimer House and *Brer Rabbit's a Rascal* (1965) by Dean
This edition published in 2016 by Hodder and Stoughton

3 5 7 9 10 8 6 4 2

Text and illustrations copyright © Hodder and Stoughton
Enid Blyton's signature is a Registered Trademark of Hodder and Stoughton

A CIP catalogue record for this book is available from the British Library.

ISBN 978-1-444-93022-1

Typeset in ConcordeBE by
Avon DataSet Ltd, Bidford on Avon, Warwickshire
Printed and bound in Great Britain by Clays Ltd, St Ives plc

The paper and board used in this book are made from wood
from responsible sources.

Hodder Children's Books
An imprint of
Hachette Children's Group
Part of Hodder and Stoughton
Carmelite House
50 Victoria Embankment
London EC4Y 0DZ

An Hachette UK Company
www.hachette.co.uk
www.hachettechildrens.co.uk

# CONTENTS

THE
BRER
RABBIT
Book

# CONTENTS

# Brer Rabbit's Pond

At the back of Brer Rabbit's house was a round pond. Sometimes, when it got very dirty with leaves falling into it, Brer Rabbit cleaned it out.

One time he cleaned it out beautifully, and then he stood and sighed by the edge of his empty pond.

'If only the rain would come and fill it!' he groaned to himself. 'If the rain doesn't come I'll have to fill my big watering-can fifty times and carry it from the tap to the pond!'

Well, the rain didn't come. The sun shone out, and the sky was as blue as forget-me-nots. Not a rain-cloud was to be seen!

'It's no good!' said Brer Rabbit at last. 'I'll have to fill the pond myself.' So he picked up his big watering-can and filled it at the tap by the side of his house.

He dragged it to the pond and emptied the water in – slishy-sloshy, slishy-sloshy! It made a lovely noise. Brer Terrapin came by, and looked over the wall when he heard the noise.

'My!' he said to Brer Rabbit, 'that's a fine game you're having this morning! It's fun to play with water like that. Let me have a turn.'

'You can't drag my big watering-can along, old slow-coach!' said Brer Rabbit. But Brer Terrapin soon showed him that he could! He balanced the big can on his back and walked slowly to the pond. He stood with his back to the pond and jerked the can. It poured all the water out at once.

'My, but it's heavy!' panted Brer Terrapin. 'I guess you've got a hard job this morning, Brer Rabbit. Why don't you get your friends to come along and help you?'

'Huh! As if Brer Fox and Brer Wolf would fill my pond for me!' said Brer Rabbit.

'You let me manage things for you,' said Brer Terrapin with a sly grin. 'You let me manage things, Brer Rabbit. You've always been a good friend to me, and if you'll let me have a swim in your pond now and again, I'll just see if I can't get you a bit of help this morning!'

'All right, Brer Terrapin, you try,' said Brer Rabbit, and he watched Brer Terrapin crawling out of his gate.

Well, Brer Terrapin, he went down the road, and soon he met Brer Fox.

'Heyo, old shellyback, where have you been this long time?' said Brer Fox.

'Oh, I've just come from Brer Rabbit's,' said Brer Terrapin. 'And my, he gave me such a treat! He let me help him pour water into his pond! It went slishy-sloshy, slishy-sloshy into the empty pond, a real treat to see it! It's fun to play with water, isn't it, Brer Fox? But it's no use *you* going along to Brer Rabbit's, for I don't suppose he'll give you a treat like that. It's only because I'm a friend of his.'

'Well, I'm a friend of his too!' said Brer Fox. 'Haven't I known him for years and years? My, I guess we've done more things together than any other creatures in the world. If I want to pour water into his pond, I just *know* he'd let me!'

'All right, you go and see, Brer Fox,' said Brer Terrapin, putting his head inside his shell to grin to himself. 'You go and see!'

So Brer Fox went along to Brer Rabbit's, and he soon heard Brer Rabbit singing, 'Hi ho! Hi ho!' and he heard the sound of water splashing merrily into the pond.

'Heyo, Brer Rabbit!' yelled Brer Fox. 'You seem

to be mighty busy this morning. That's a fine job you're doing.'

'Oh, a mighty fine job!' said Brer Rabbit, winking to himself. 'A job that everyone would like to do, Brer Fox. I just gave Brer Terrapin a turn at it, because he's a very old friend of mine, and I like giving him a treat.'

'Well, I'm an old friend of yours too,' said Brer Fox. 'You let me have a turn as well, Brer Rabbit. I don't like Brer Terrapin going around saying he's the only friend of yours that helps you with your pond. You let me have a turn too.'

'Why, Brer Fox, I'd be pleased to,' said Brer Rabbit. 'Yes, yes, you have a turn – have two turns – have ten turns if you want to! I'm not one to be selfish. No – if my friends want a share in my pleasures, they are welcome to them. You take the can, Brer Fox, and have a good time!'

So Brer Fox dragged the heavy can to and fro a good many times, whilst Brer Rabbit sat on the warm sunny wall and smoked his pipe and talked.

Now it wasn't long before Brer Bear and Brer Wolf came along and looked over the wall too.

'Heyo, Brer Rabbit,' said Brer Bear. 'We've just met Brer Terrapin, and he's been a-boasting and a-bragging that you've let him fill up your pond because he's such an old friend of yours. And he said he was mighty certain you wouldn't give anyone else that treat – and here we see Brer Fox playing with the water too!'

'Oh, Brer Bear,' said Brer Rabbit politely, 'that's too bad of Brer Terrapin to go around saying I won't give any of my friends but him a chance to play with my pond. Brer Fox, he came along and said just the same thing – and I'm giving him a treat too! If you want to join in, you just say the word. I'm not the man to stop anyone having a good time!'

Well, by this time Brer Fox was nearly worn out with carrying the heavy can. So he spoke up at once.

'And I'm not the man to be selfish either. I'll let Brer Bear and Brer Wolf have a turn now. That's only fair!'

So Brer Wolf and Brer Bear came in at the gate and set to work to fill the can and empty the water into the pond. My, but it was nearly full now! It only needed about four more cans and it would overflow.

Cousin Wildcat looked over the wall and grinned. Brer Rabbit hopped off to the garden-seat, for he didn't trust Cousin Wildcat's claws.

'Heyo, Brer Rabbit,' said Cousin Wildcat. 'I just heard from Brer Terrapin that you've got Brer Fox and Brer Wolf and Brer Bear doing all your hard work for you. Ah, you're a smart one, Brer Rabbit, no doubt about that! But you don't catch me coming along and carrying your heavy cans for you all morning long. No – my brains are as good as yours *any* day, Brer Rabbit!'

Brer Fox, Brer Wolf, and Brer Bear stood and stared in surprise. Then they turned their eyes on Brer Rabbit, who began to feel mighty uncomfortable. But he put a bold face on it and spoke up well.

'Brer Fox! Brer Wolf! Brer Bear! Are you going to stand there, and let Cousin Wildcat make out I've tricked you, when all you've been doing is to have a treat? You go for him right now, and make him say he's sorry!'

So Brer Fox, Brer Wolf, and Brer Bear jumped over the wall and chased Cousin Wildcat right into the middle of the wood. He fled up a tree and laughed at them. 'Go and ask Brer Terrapin!' he cried. 'Maybe you'll believe *him*!'

But when the three of them hunted for Brer Terrapin, he was nowhere to be found! He was having a fine swim in Brer Rabbit's nice full pond –

and every now and again he would come up to the top and wink his eye at Brer Rabbit. Then down he'd go to the bottom – ker-blinkety-blunk!

# Brer Fox and the White Plums

It happened one morning that Brer Rabbit was going through the woods, and he ran bang into old Brer Fox. Brer Fox took hold of Brer Rabbit and looked at him.

'I feel mighty hungry, Brer Rabbit,' said Brer Fox.

'Huh, Brer Fox,' said Brer Rabbit, trying to wriggle away, 'I don't feel hungry myself because I've just been eating a whole lot of white plums.' And then Brer Rabbit smacked his lips together and licked his mouth as if he could still taste something nice.

'Brer Rabbit, what in the name of goodness are white plums?' said Brer Fox, astonished, 'and how is it I've never seen any?'

'I don't know why you've never seen any,' said Brer Rabbit. 'Some folks see straight, some see crooked, some see one thing and some see another. I saw those white plums, and more than that, I ate

15

them all up! I ate all that were on one tree, but I expect there are a lot more round about.'

Old Brer Fox's mouth began to water.

'Come on, Brer Rabbit, come on!' he said. 'Show me where those white plums grow!'

Brer Rabbit hung back as if he didn't want to take Brer Fox. Brer Fox dragged him forward. 'Come on, Brer Rabbit, come on!'

But still Brer Rabbit hung back. Then he said, 'Hoo, Brer Fox! You want to get me in the middle of the wood all alone and do something to me. You want to take me out there and scare me.'

Old Brer Fox, he held up his hands and cried, 'I declare to goodness, Brer Rabbit, I wouldn't think of such a thing. Whatever makes you think that? Come on, Brer Rabbit, and let's go and get those white plums.'

'Hoo, Brer Fox, you play so many tricks on folks that I'm afraid to go anywhere alone with you,' said Brer Rabbit.

'I won't scare you or do you any harm, Brer Rabbit,' promised Brer Fox. So they set out for the middle of the woods, and Brer Rabbit brought Brer Fox to a wild walnut tree. The walnuts were as green as could be, but in the bright sunshine they shone pale and white. The tree was loaded down with unripe nuts. Brer Fox looked astonished.

'Are those white plums?' he said. 'It's funny I didn't know that before.'

Old Brer Rabbit, he scratched himself and said, 'Those are the plums. They may not be as ripe as those I had for my breakfast, but those are white plums as sure as anything. There are red plums, and purple plums, and yellow plums, but these plums are white ones.'

'How can I get them?' said Brer Fox.

'You'll have to do as I did, Brer Fox,' said Brer Rabbit.

'What's that?' asked Brer Fox.

'You'll have to climb up for them, Brer Fox.'

'How can I climb a tree like that?' said Brer Fox, looking up the tall, straight trunk in dismay.

'Oh, grab with your hands, hold tight with your legs and I'll push you behind,' said Brer Rabbit.

Well, Brer Fox began to climb, and Brer Rabbit, he began to push till, sure enough, Brer Fox got to where he could grab up and catch the lowest branch of the tree. He heaved himself up and there he was! He climbed on up, he did, till he came to where he could reach a green walnut. He picked it and put it into his mouth whole. He chewed it hard – and then, bless gracious, if Brer Fox didn't forget all his manners! The fruit was so bitter and so hard that Brer Fox nearly fell out of the tree.

He shouted 'Ow!' and spat the walnut out of his mouth as if it was poison, and he made such a face that Brer Rabbit had to have a fit of coughing to hide his grins and giggles.

'You'd better come down, Brer Fox, if the white plums aren't ripe,' he shouted up at last. 'Come down and we'll go somewhere else.'

Brer Fox started down the tree, and he got along well enough till he came to the lowest branch again. When he got there he stopped. He didn't see how he was going to get down the long trunk. He had no claws to cling by, like Cousin Wildcat, and he hadn't much leg either, to hold on with.

Brer Rabbit kept on shouting, 'Come on down!' and Brer Fox kept trying to think how to get down.

'Oh, do come on, Brer Fox,' said Brer Rabbit. 'I pushed you up, didn't I, and if I was anywhere near you I'd push you down too! Come on!'

Brer Fox sat clinging to the lowest bough and looked mighty scared. He wasn't used to climbing trees. By and by Brer Rabbit stood a little way off from the tree and said, 'If you'll jump out this way, Brer Fox, I'll catch you.'

Brer Fox looked down and he looked all round,

and he still looked mighty scared. Brer Rabbit came a little bit closer and shouted, 'Hop right down here, Brer Fox, and I'll catch you.'

Well, he kept on like this till by and by Brer Fox

made up his mind to jump into Brer Rabbit's arms – and what's more, Brer Fox meant to get hold of old Brer Rabbit, too, and tell him what he thought of his white plums! But he didn't say that – no, he kept quiet, and just thought of a few things he'd say to old Brer Rabbit.

So Brer Fox jumped straight at Brer Rabbit, but just as he jumped Brer Rabbit hopped out of the way, yelling, 'Ow! Ow! Excuse me, Brer Fox! I trod on a thorn! Excuse me, Brer Fox! I trod on a thorn!'

And old Brer Fox, he hit the ground like a sack of potatoes, and all his breath was knocked out of him. When he got up he counted all his legs and his tail to see if they were still there, and then he sat down and licked himself hard.

As for Brer Rabbit, he was nowhere to be seen; but I guess it will be a long time before Brer Fox goes looking for white plums again!

# The Wonderful Tar-Baby

One day, after Brer Rabbit had tricked Brer Fox with the calamus root, Brer Fox went to work and got some tar and mixed it with turpentine, and made a thing he called a tar-baby.

The tar-baby was like a little black man, and looked very funny. Brer Fox took his tar-baby, gave it a hat and set it by the lane. Then he hid himself in some bushes to see what would happen.

He didn't have to wait long, because by and by Brer Rabbit came along, galloping down the road, lippity, clippity, just as saucy as a jay-bird. Brer Fox lay low. Brer Rabbit came prancing along till he spied the tar-baby, and then he sat up on his hind legs in astonishment. The tar-baby sat there, and Brer Fox, he lay low.

'Morning!' said Brer Rabbit to the tar-baby. 'Nice weather today!

The tar-baby said nothing, and Brer Fox, he lay low.

'How are you feeling this fine day?' said Brer Rabbit.

Brer Fox winked to himself and lay low, and the tar-baby said nothing at all.

'What's the matter with you? Are you deaf?' said Brer Rabbit. 'Cos if you are, I can shout louder.'

The tar-baby stayed still, and Brer Fox, he lay low. Brer Rabbit got angry.

'You're stuck-up, that's what you are!' said Brer Rabbit 'and I'm going to cure you, that's what I'm going to do!'

Brer Fox sort of chuckled inside himself, but the tar-baby said nothing.

'I'm going to teach you how to talk to nice people if it's my last act!' said Brer Rabbit. 'Now just you listen to me – if you don't take off your hat and say, "How do you do?" to me, I'm a-going to hit you into the middle of next week!'

The tar-baby stayed still, and Bear Fox, he lay low.

Brer Rabbit kept on telling the tar-baby to be polite, and the tar-baby kept on saying nothing, so presently Brer Rabbit drew back his fist and hit the tar-baby on the side of the head – blip! And that's just where he made a mistake. His fist stuck in the tar-baby, and he couldn't pull it loose. The tar held him. But the tar-baby stayed still, and Brer Fox, he lay low.

'If you don't let me loose, I'll hit you again,' said Brer Rabbit, and with that he hit out with his other hand – and that stuck too! The tar-baby said nothing, and Brer Fox, he lay low.

'Turn me loose, or I'll kick the stuffing out of

you!' said Brer Rabbit, but the tar-baby, she said nothing at all. She just held on, and then Brer Rabbit kicked out at her with all his might – and his feet stuck too. Brer Fox still lay low.

Then Brer Rabbit squealed out that if the tar-baby didn't turn him loose, he would butt her so hard she would go lop-sided.

And then he butted her – blip! And his head stuck too. Then Brer Fox, he strolled out of the bushes, looking as innocent as a day-old lamb.

'How do you do, Brer Rabbit?' said Brer Fox. 'You look sort of stuck-up this morning!' And then Brer Fox rolled on the ground and laughed and laughed till he couldn't laugh any more.

'I expect you'll have dinner with me *this* time, Brer Rabbit!' he said. 'I've got some calamus root for you, and I'm not going to take any excuse. You've just got to come to dinner with me this time!'

Old Brer Fox rolled on the ground again and laughed till he cried. 'Well, I expect I've got you this time, Brer Rabbit,' he said. 'Maybe I haven't, but I think I have! You've been running round here cheeking me for a mighty long time, but I expect you won't do it any more. You've been dancing about and bouncing around until you think you're the biggest person here. And you are always somewhere that you've got no business to be,' said Brer Fox. 'Who asked you to come and talk to this tar-baby? And who stuck you up where you are? Nobody in the world!'

Brer Rabbit said nothing. He just stayed stuck and thought hard.

'You just threw yourself at that tar-baby without waiting to be invited,' said Brer Fox. 'And there you are, and there you'll stay till I fix up a wood-pile and set it alight, because I'm going to cook you this day, sure enough!' said Brer Fox.

Then Brer Rabbit talked mighty humbly:

'I don't care what you do with me, Brer Fox,' he said, 'so long as you don't fling me in that brier-bush. Cook me, Brer Fox, but don't fling me in that brier-bush!'

'It's too much trouble to make a fire,' said Brer Fox. 'I think I'll have to hang you.'

'Hang me as high as you please, Brer Fox,' said Brer Rabbit, 'but for goodness' sake don't fling me in that brier-bush!'

'I haven't got any string,' said Brer Fox, 'so I expect I'll have to drown you.'

'Drown me as deep as you please, Brer Fox,' said Brer Rabbit, 'but don't fling me in that brier-bush!'

'There's no water near,' said Brer Fox, 'so I expect I'll have to skin you.'

'Skin me all you like, Brer Fox,' said Brer Rabbit, 'but please, please don't fling me in that brier-bush!'

Well, Brer Fox wanted to hurt Brer Rabbit just as much as ever he could, so he thought he *would* fling him into the prickly brier-bush! He caught him by the hind legs and slung him right in the middle of the brier-bush – blim!

There was a great to-do when Brer Rabbit hit the bush, and Brer Fox sort of hung around to see what would happen. By and by he heard somebody calling him, and away up the hill he saw Brer Rabbit sitting cross-legged on a log, combing the tar out of his fur with a wood-chip.

Then Brer Fox knew he had been badly tricked. Of course, Brer Rabbit had to be saucy, and he shouted out:

'I was bred and born in a brier-bush, Brer Fox – bred and born in a brier-bush!' And with that he skipped off just as lively as a cat on hot bricks!

# Brer Rabbit Gets a Riding-Horse

Brer Rabbit stayed in his house till the tar from the tar-baby rubbed off his fur, but it wasn't many days before he was galloping up and down the place the same as ever, and perhaps a little cheekier than before.

Well, the tale about how Brer Rabbit got stuck in the tar-baby soon got round, and everyone laughed to hear it. Miss Meadows and the girls, who were great friends of Brer Rabbit, heard the tale too – and when Brer Rabbit paid them a visit, Miss Meadows asked him about it, and the girls began to giggle.

But Brer Rabbit sat up just as cool as a cucumber, and let them giggle.

By and by he crossed his legs and winked his eye slowly. Then he said:

'Ladies, Brer Fox was my daddy's riding-horse for thirty years; maybe more, but thirty years anyhow!' Then he bowed politely, put on his hat, and marched off as stiff and straight as a walking-stick.

Well, the next day Brer Fox went calling on Miss Meadows and the girls, and as soon as he began to laugh about Brer Rabbit being stuck up in the tar-baby, Miss Meadows told him what Brer Rabbit had said.

'Brer Rabbit says you were his daddy's riding-horse for thirty years,' she said. 'Well, well, fancy you being ridden by a rabbit, Brer Fox!'

Brer Fox snapped his jaws and looked mighty angry to hear such a thing. He stood up to go, and said:

'Ladies, just wait till I get hold of Brer Rabbit! I'll make him chew up his words, sure enough!' And with that off Brer Fox marched.

And when he got to the main road he shook the dew off his tail and made straight for Brer Rabbit's house. When he got there, Brer Rabbit was expecting him, and the door was shut fast.

Brer Fox knocked – blim, blam! Nobody answered. Brer Fox knocked again – blim, blam! Still nobody answered. Then he knocked a third time – blim, blam!

Brer Rabbit called out in a mighty weak voice:

'Is that you, Brer Fox? I want you to run and fetch the doctor. The dish of parsley I ate this morning is making me feel bad. Do, please, Brer Fox, ran quickly!' said Brer Rabbit.

'I've come for you,' said Brer Fox. 'There's going to be a party up at Miss Meadows'. All the girls will be there, and I promised that I'd fetch you. The girls said it wouldn't be a proper party unless you were there, and they made me fetch you.'

'I'm too sick to come,' said Brer Rabbit.

'You're all right!' said Brer Fox. 'A party will put you right, Brer Rabbit. It's what you're needing.'

'I'm not needing anything,' said Brer Rabbit in a weak voice. 'You just go away, Brer Fox. You make me feel worse.'

'You're bound to feel bad if you go and shut yourself up on a fine day like this,' said Brer Fox. 'Come along with me, and smell what a fine day it is.'

'The day smells all right,' said Brer Rabbit. 'It's you that doesn't smell so good to me, Brer Fox.'

'The girls will be mighty sorry if I go back without you,' said Brer Fox.

'I can't walk, I'm so weak,' said Brer Rabbit.

'Well, I'll carry you,' said Brer Fox.

'How?' said Brer Rabbit.

'In my arms,' said Brer Fox.

'You'll drop me,' said Brer Rabbit.

'I won't,' said Brer Fox.

'Well,' said Brer Rabbit, after a bit, 'I'll come with you if you'll carry me on your back, Brer Fox.'

'That's all right with me,' said Brer Fox at once. 'Come on, Brer Rabbit, or the party will be over.'

'I can't ride on your back unless I have a saddle to sit on,' said Brer Rabbit. 'I'd be slipping off all the time.'

'I'll get you a saddle,' said Brer Fox.

'It's no good me sitting in a saddle unless I've some reins to hold on by,' said Brer Rabbit.

'Well, I'll get a bridle,' said Brer Fox.

'I won't ride you unless you wear blinkers,' said Brer Rabbit. 'If you don't wear blinkers, Brer Fox, you'll be shying at the tree-stumps along the road, and I'll fall off.'

'I'll get some blinkers,' said Brer Fox.

'You get all those things and I'll go to the party,' said Brer Rabbit.

'Now, see here, Brer Rabbit,' said Brer Fox, 'I'll just carry you to the lane outside Miss Meadows' house, but you must get down and walk the rest of the way.'

'That suits me all right,' said Brer Rabbit, and

then Brer Fox ran to fetch the saddle, the reins, and the blinkers.

Now Brer Rabbit knew quite well that Brer Fox meant to take him to Miss Meadows' and make him tell them it wasn't true that Brer Fox had been his daddy's riding-horse, and he made up his mind to trick Brer Fox. By the time he had combed his hair and twisted up his whiskers along came Brer Fox with the saddle and bridle on, looking as smart as a circus pony. He trotted up to the door and stood pawing the ground and champing the bit in his mouth like a proper horse. Brer Rabbit got on his back and they ambled off.

Brer Fox couldn't see him behind him, because he was wearing blinkers over his eyes, but by and by he felt Brer Rabbit lift up one of his feet.

'What are you doing, Brer Rabbit?' he said.

'Just pulling up my sock, Brer Fox, just pulling up my sock,' said Brer Rabbit.

By and by Brer Rabbit lifted up the other foot.

'What are you doing now, Brer Rabbit?' said Brer Fox.

'Just scratching my toe, Brer Fox, just scratching my toe,' said Brer Rabbit.

But all the time, gracious goodness, Brer Rabbit was putting on sharp spurs, and when they got close to Miss Meadows', where Brer Rabbit should have got off, Brer Rabbit slapped the spurs into Brer Fox's skin, and my word, didn't Brer Fox gallop along! Every time he slowed down, Brer Rabbit just stuck those spurs into him again, and Brer Fox let out a yell and galloped on at top speed.

When they got to the house, Miss Meadows and the girls were sitting outside on the verandah, and instead of stopping at the gate, Brer Rabbit rode right through it, and up to the horse-rack. He jumped off Brer Fox, threw the reins over the horse-rack, and ambled into the house grinning all over his face.

He shook hands with everyone, and sat down to smoke a big cigar. Then he took the cigar out of his mouth, puffed out a cloud of smoke, and said:

'Ladies, didn't I tell you Brer Fox was the riding-horse for our family? He's not so fast now as he was, but I dare say he'll get better after I've ridden him for a month or two!'

And then Brer Rabbit grinned, and the girls giggled, and Miss Meadows said what a fine pony Brer Fox was. Brer Fox was hitched tightly to the horse-rack and couldn't loose himself.

'You just wait till you ride me home, Brer Rabbit!' said Brer Fox, gritting his teeth. 'You just wait!'

# Brer Rabbit is in a Hole

Well, you remember that old Brer Rabbit had ridden Brer Fox up to Miss Meadows' house, saddle and bridle and all, and hitched him to the post there. Everyone laughed and talked and sang and then at last the time came to go home.

'Well, it's time I was a-going,' said Brer Rabbit. 'My horse will be pawing the ground to bits, soon, if I don't go out to him. Good-bye, Miss Meadows, good-bye, girls, and thanks for a wonderful party. It was real kind of Brer Fox to fetch me along!'

Brer Rabbit went to the horse-rack, where Brer Fox was tied, walking as though he owned the whole world. He jumped on to Brer Fox's back and rode off, waving his hat to the girls.

Brer Fox didn't say anything at all. He just tore off and kept his mouth shut, and Brer Rabbit sort of felt there was trouble coming. So he held on to the reins tightly and waited to see what old Brer Fox was going to do.

Brer Fox ambled on till he got into the long lane, out of sight of Miss Meadows' house, and then he just went wild! He ripped and he roared, he snorted and cavorted, he reared and he bucked!

He was trying to fling Brer Rabbit off his back. But he might just as well have tried to fling off his own shadow. Every time he humped himself up, Brer Rabbit slapped the spurs into him, and there they went, up and down, up and down! Brer Fox fairly tore up the ground, and he jumped so high and he jumped so fast that he nearly snatched his own tail off!

They kept on like this, till by and by Brer Fox lay down on the ground and rolled over. This sort of unsettled Brer Rabbit, and he fell off – but by the time Brer Fox was up on his feet again, Brer Rabbit was rushing through the wood faster than a racehorse!

Brer Fox set out after him, and he went so fast that he caught him up, and Brer Rabbit only just had time to get into a hollow tree. The hole he shot in by was too small for Brer Fox, and he had to lie down and rest and get his breath again.

Well, while Brer Fox was lying there, all out of

breath, Brer Buzzard came flapping along, and saw Brer Fox stretched out on the ground. Brer Buzzard flew down beside him and looked at him. Then he shook his wings sadly, put his head on one side and said:

'Brer Fox is dead, and I'm so sorry.'

'No, I'm not dead,' said Brer Fox. 'I've got old Brer Rabbit shut up in here, in this hollow tree, and I'm going to get him this time, if it takes till Christmas!'

Then, after some more talking, Brer Fox made a bargain with Brer Buzzard, and Brer Buzzard promised to watch the hole and keep Brer Rabbit there whilst Brer Fox went to fetch his axe. So Brer Fox galloped off, and Brer Buzzard took up his stand by the hole.

By and by, when everything was still, Brer Rabbit sort of scrambled round close to the hole and shouted out:

'Brer Fox! Oh, Brer Fox!'

Brer Fox had gone, and nobody said anything. Then Brer Rabbit squealed out as if he were mad.

'You needn't talk unless you want to, Brer Fox,' he said. 'I know you're there, and I don't care if you are! I just want to tell you that I wish old Brer Turkey Buzzard was here!'

Then Brer Buzzard tried to talk like Brer Fox. 'What do you want with Brer Buzzard?' he said.

'Oh, nothing in particular, except that there's the fattest grey squirrel in here that ever I saw,' said Brer Rabbit, 'and if Brer Turkey Buzzard was around he'd be mighty glad to get him!'

'How could Brer Buzzard get him?' said Brer Buzzard.

'Well, there's a little hole round on the other side of the tree,' said Brer Rabbit, 'and if Brer Buzzard was here so that he could stand just there, I'd drive out that squirrel to him.'

'Drive him out,' said Brer Buzzard, hopping round to the other side of the tree, 'drive him out, and I'll see that Brer Buzzard gets him!'

Then Brer Rabbit kicked up such a noise, just as if he were really driving out a squirrel, and when he heard old Brer Buzzard going round the tree to get the squirrel, Brer Rabbit dashed out of the hole and raced for home!

Well, when Brer Buzzard saw Brer Rabbit rushing off, he felt mighty lonesome, but he had promised Brer Fox that he'd stay, and he thought he would hang round and see what Brer Fox would say when he found Brer Rabbit was gone. He didn't have to wait long, because by and by

Brer Fox came galloping through the woods with his axe on his shoulder.

'How's Brer Rabbit getting on, Brer Buzzard?' said Brer Fox.

'Oh, he's in there,' said Brer Buzzard. 'He's mighty still, though. I expect he's taking a nap.'

'Then I'm just in time to wake him up,' said Brer Fox. And with that he threw off his coat and grabbed his axe. He brought it down on the tree-trunk – pow! And every time he struck the tree with the axe – pow! – Brer Buzzard did a little dance and shouted out:

'Oh, he's in there, Brer Fox. He's in there, sure enough!'

And every time a chip flew off, Brer Buzzard would jump and dodge and shout, 'He's in there, Brer Fox. I just heard him. He's in there, sure enough!'

And Brer Fox, he lammed away at that hollow tree, till by and by, after he had almost cut the tree through he stopped to get his breath – and he saw Brer Buzzard laughing at him behind his back. And straight away, Brer Fox knew something was up. But Brer Buzzard, he kept on shouting:

'He's in there, Brer Fox. He's in there! I've just seen him!'

Then Brer Fox pretended that he was peeping
into the tree, and he said: 'Come here, Brer Buzzard,
and see if this is Brer Rabbit's foot hanging down!'
And Brer Buzzard came stepping up and stuck

his head in at the hole; and no sooner had he done that, than Brer Fox grabbed him. Brer Buzzard scrambled round and flapped his wings, but it was no use. Brer Fox had got him fast.

Then Brer Buzzard squealed out loudly, 'You let me alone, Brer Fox. Turn me loose! Brer Rabbit will get out! You've nearly cut the tree through. A few more cuts and you'll have Brer Rabbit!'

'I'm nearer to you, Brer Buzzard, than I'll be to Brer Rabbit today!' said Brer Fox. 'What did you trick me for?'

'Let me alone, Brer Fox,' said Brer Buzzard. 'My old woman's waiting for me. Brer Rabbit's in there!'

'There's a bunch of his fur on that blackberry bush,' said Brer Fox. 'That's the way he went, Brer Buzzard.'

Then Brer Buzzard told Brer Fox all about it. 'And Brer Rabbit's the greatest rascal that ever lived!' he said.

'That's neither here nor there, Brer Buzzard,' said Brer Fox. 'I left you to watch this hole and I left Brer Rabbit in there. I come back and I find you at the hole and Brer Rabbit gone. I'm going to make you pay for it. I'm going to fling you on a wood-pile and burn you up!'

'If you fling me on the fire, Brer Fox, I'll fly away!' said Brer Buzzard.

'Well, then, I'll settle you right now!' said Brer Fox, and he grabbed Brer Buzzard by the tail to dash him to the ground – but it was just about the time of year when the tail feathers of buzzards drop out, and Brer Buzzard sailed up into the air like a balloon, leaving a few feathers in Brer Fox's hand!

'You've given me a good start, Brer Fox!' shouted Brer Buzzard, and Brer Fox had to sit there and watch him fly out of sight!

# Poor Sis Cow!

After Brer Rabbit had escaped out of the hollow tree, he went skipping along home, just as saucy as a jay-bird. He went galloping along, he did, but he felt mighty tired out and stiff in his joints, and he was dying for something to drink.

By and by, when he was almost home, he spied old Miss Cow feeding in a field, and he thought he'd see if she would give him a drink. Brer Rabbit had a feeling that Miss Cow wouldn't give him any milk at all because she had said no often enough, even when Brer Rabbit's old woman was sick. But never mind – Brer Rabbit was going to try again!

He danced up to the fence and called out loudly to Miss Cow:

'Howdy, Sis Cow!'

'Why, howdy, Brer Rabbit!' said Miss Cow.

'How are you these days?' said Brer Rabbit.

'Oh, so-so, just so-so,' said Miss Cow. 'How's yourself, Brer Rabbit?'

'Oh, I'm just so-so myself, Sis Cow,' said Brer Rabbit. 'Not too bad but not too grand either!'

'How are your folks?' said Miss Cow.

'Just middling, Sis Cow,' said Brer Rabbit. 'How's Brer Bull getting on?'

'Bellowing as usual,' said Miss Cow.

Then Brer Rabbit looked at a tree near by. 'There are some mighty nice apples up this tree, Sis Cow,' said Brer Rabbit, 'and I'd like mighty well to have some!'

'How are you going to get them?' asked Miss Cow.

'Well, I thought I might ask you to butt your head against the tree and shake some down for me,' said Brer Rabbit.

Well, Miss Cow thought she might as well do it as not, so she marched up to the apple-tree. She hit it a rap with her horns – blam!

But those apples were as green as grass, and not one dropped off the tree! Then Miss Cow butted the tree again – blim! Not an apple dropped. Then Miss Cow backed away a little, took a run, and knocked the apple-tree hard – blip! No apples dropped, not even a tiny one.

Then Miss Cow backed off a little further, hoisted her tail over her back, and ran at the tree again – kerblam! And she came so fast, and she came so hard that one of her horns went right into the trunk, and there she was, stuck fast! She couldn't go forwards and she couldn't go backwards.

This was exactly what Brer Rabbit was waiting for, and he no sooner saw old Miss Cow all stuck up than he began to grin and rub his hands in joy.

'Come and help me out, Brer Rabbit,' said Miss Cow.

'I can't climb, Sis Cow,' said Brer Rabbit, 'but I'll run and tell Brer Bull to help you.'

And with that Brer Rabbit set out for his home, and it wasn't long before he came back again with his old woman and all his children – and every single one of his family was carrying a pail! The big ones had big pails and the little ones had little pails.

They all surrounded Miss Cow, and they milked her till she hadn't a drop of milk left. The big ones got their pails full, and the little ones got their pails full too. When they had got enough Brer Rabbit said:

'I wish you mighty well, Sis Cow. I'm afraid you'll have to camp out all night, but it doesn't look like rain, so maybe you'll be all right.'

Then off he went home, he and all his family carrying their pails so as not to spill a drop.

Well, Miss Cow, she stood there, she did, and tried to think how to get loose. She pulled and she jerked at her horn, but it was jammed too tightly in the tree to come out. But at last, when she jerked it mighty hard, just before day, she got it loose.

She grazed round in the field a bit, for she was hungry. Old Miss Cow thought that Brer Rabbit would soon be hopping along that way to see how she was getting on, and she thought she would lay a trap for him.

'I'll stick my horn back into the hole just before Brer Rabbit comes along,' thought Miss Cow. 'Then he'll think I'm still stuck fast, and he'll come up to me – and won't I kick out at him and won't I chase him round the field and stick my horn into him! I'll teach you to trick old Sis Cow, Brer Rabbit, so I will!'

Well, just about sunrise what did old Miss Cow do but march up to the apple-tree and stick her horn back into the hole, just as she had planned. But she didn't do it quite soon enough! Brer Rabbit had come hopping quietly along, and he was in a corner of the field, watching her.

Brer Rabbit was surprised to see Sis Cow loose – and even more surprised to see her sticking her horn back into the tree!

'Heyo !' he said to himself. ' What's all this going on? Just wait a minute, and I'll find out!'

He crept out of the field and went back down the road a little way. By and by he came along – lippitty-clippitty-lippitty-clippitty – galloping down the main road.

'Morning, Sis Cow,' said Brer Rabbit. 'How do you feel this morning?'

'Poorly, Brer Rabbit, poorly,' said Miss Cow. 'I haven't had any rest all night. I can't get my horn out of the tree. But if you'll come and catch hold of my tail, Brer Rabbit, I reckon maybe I can get my horn out!'

Then Brer Rabbit came a little closer, but he didn't come *too* close!

'I think I'm near enough, Sis Cow,' said Brer Rabbit. 'I'm a mighty little man, and if I come any nearer you might trample on me. You do the pulling out, Sis Cow, and I'll do the shouting!'

Then Miss Cow pulled out her horn in a rage and tore after Brer Rabbit. Down the road they went, Brer Rabbit with his ears laid back, and Miss Cow with her head down and her tail up. Brer Rabbit ran fast and by and by he darted into a brier-patch. By the time Miss Cow came along he had his head sticking out, and his eyes looked as big as saucers.

'Heyo, Sis Cow!' said Brer Rabbit, not looking a bit like himself. 'Where are you going?'

'Hallo, Brer Big-Eyes,' said Miss Cow. 'Have you seen Brer Rabbit go by?'

'He's just this minute passed,' said Brer Rabbit, 'and he looked mighty sick, Sis Cow.'

When she heard that, Miss Cow tore off down the road as if the dogs were after her – and Brer Rabbit, he just lay down there in the brier-patch and rolled and laughed till his sides hurt him. He simply *had* to laugh. Fox after him, Buzzard after him, Cow after him – and they hadn't caught him yet!

# Mr Lion's Soup

Once Mr Lion put on his tall hat, reached for his stick, and set out to have his dinner at Brer Possum's Hotel. He felt hungry, and he made up his mind to have a really good dinner.

'I'll have oxtail soup!' said Mr Lion to himself, as he walked along, swishing off the daisy-heads with his stick, which was very wrong of him. 'Yes, oxtail soup, rich and thick and tasty. Aha!'

He reached Brer Possum's Hotel and went up the steps. As soon as the hall-porter saw him he rushed to greet him, for Mr Lion was a very honoured customer. If people didn't pay attention to him, he got very angry, so the waiters flocked round him, and Brer Possum himself helped him off with his coat.

'Give me the best table,' said Mr Lion in his growly voice. So they gave him the best table, and he sat down, tucking his tail neatly under the chair.

'What will you have to eat, Mr Lion, sir?' asked Brer Possum, beckoning to Brer Hare, Brer Raccoon, and Brer Hedgehog, all waiters.

'Bring me some oxtail soup,' said Mr Lion in a very commanding sort of voice.

Brer Possum flew to tell the cook to make some oxtail soup. Very soon it was ready. It was poured into a silver tureen, and taken to Mr Lion's table. He sniffed at it as it was poured into his soup-plate.

'It smells good,' he said.

'It *is* good,' said Brer Hare, the waiter, waiting for Mr Lion to begin tasting it. But Mr Lion didn't. He sat there, and didn't taste it at all.

'What's the matter, Mr Lion?' asked Brer Hare, seeing a frown beginning to come on Mr Lion's great forehead.

'I can't eat this soup,' said Mr Lion.

'Oh, sir!' said Brer Hare, alarmed. 'I hope it's good! Is it too hot?'

'I don't know,' said Mr Lion. 'I can't eat it.'

Brer Hare flew to get Brer Raccoon, and took him over to Mr Lion's table. Brer Raccoon bowed anxiously before the great Mr Lion.

'What is the matter, sir?' he asked.

'I can't eat this *soup*!' said Mr Lion.

'Has it too much pepper in it?' asked Brer

Raccoon anxiously. 'The cook does sometimes use the pepper-pot too much.'

'I don't know,' said Mr Lion. 'All I know is that I can't eat my soup!'

Brer Raccoon flew to get Brer Hedgehog. 'He says he can't eat his soup,' said Brer Raccoon, nodding his head backwards towards Mr Lion. 'What are we to do?'

'I'd better go and see if it's got too much onion in,' said Brer Hedgehog, dropping his napkin in his hurry, and tripping over his prickles. 'He doesn't like onion.'

So he scampered to Mr Lion's table and bowed low. 'Mr Lion, sir,' he said, 'I'm sorry to hear about this. Has your soup got too much onion in?'

'I don't know,' said Mr Lion, in a rage. 'I tell you I can't eat my soup!'

'Well, I'll fetch Brer Possum,' said poor Brer Hedgehog, in a panic, and he shot off to get the master of the hotel. Brer Possum was horrified to hear that Mr Lion couldn't eat his soup, and he hurried at once to his table.

'I'm sorry the soup is not to your liking,' he said. 'Do tell me what is wrong, Mr Lion. You didn't find a fly in it, I hope, or a caterpillar?'

'No,' growled Mr Lion, looking fiercer than ever.

'Well, has it too much salt in it?' asked Brer Possum, shivering with fear, for he knew Mr Lion's habits when he was displeased.

'I don't know,' said Mr Lion. 'All I say is – I can't – eat – my – SOUP!'

'Well, sir, I'll fetch the cook who made it,' said Brer Possum, trembling. 'It was Brer Raccoon's old woman who made it. Just wait a minute and I'll get her.'

In a few moments Brer Raccoon's wife came shuffling along, looking very scared indeed, twisting up the corners of her apron, and looking ready to cry, for she was very much afraid of Mr Lion.

'Good morning, sir,' she said, dropping a curtsey. 'I hear you can't eat the soup I made.'

'No, I can't possibly,' said Mr Lion gloomily.

'But, sir, it's made of the very best ox-tail that ever was,' said Brer Raccoon's old woman eagerly. 'And I didn't put much onion into it, and only a little pepper and salt, and it was nice and hot when it left my kitchen.'

'All the same, I can't eat it,' said Mr Lion, still more gloomily.

'Well, let me take it away and bring you another kind,' said Mrs Raccoon, and she stretched out her paw to take the plate. But Mr Lion shouted at her so loudly, and showed his teeth so fiercely, that she backed away in alarm.

'Leave my soup!' shouted Mr Lion. 'I want to eat it, but I can't. I HAVEN'T GOT A SPOON!'

Well, well, well! Just to think of that! Brer Raccoon got him a spoon, and Brer Hedgehog gave him one, and Brer Possum and Brer Hare did too. They were all so pleased to find that nothing was really wrong with the soup. As for silly old Mr Lion, he only had himself to blame if the soup was cold!

# Oh, Brer Rabbit!

One day, after Brer Fox had been doing all he could to catch Brer Rabbit, and Brer Rabbit had been doing all he could to stop him, Brer Fox said to himself that he'd play a trick on Brer Rabbit.

And no sooner had he said the words than Brer Rabbit came lolloping up the road looking as plump and as fat as a blackbird in spring.

'Half a minute, Brer Rabbit!' said Brer Fox.

'Can't stop, Brer Fox,' said Brer Rabbit, going a bit faster.

'I want to have a talk with you, Brer Rabbit,' said Brer Fox.

'All right, Brer Fox but you'd better shout to me from where you are. I'm not coming any nearer,' said Brer Rabbit.

'I saw Brer Bear yesterday,' said Brer Fox, 'and he said he was shocked because you and I don't make friends and live in peace, and I told him that I'd see about it.'

Then Brer Rabbit scratched one of his ears with his hind foot sort of doubtfully, and said, 'Right you are, Brer Fox. Suppose you drop round tomorrow and take dinner with me. We don't have anything fancy at our house, but I expect my old woman and the children can scramble round and get something to fill you up.'

'Fine!' said Brer Fox.

'Then I'll see you tomorrow,' said Brer Rabbit.

Next day Brer Rabbit and old Miss Rabbit got up early, before day, and got some cabbages and corn and sparrow-grass, and fixed up a splendid dinner.

By and by one of the little rabbits, playing out in the backyard, came running in, shouting, 'Oh, Ma! Oh, Ma! I saw Mr Fox a-coming!'

And then Brer Rabbit, he took his children by their ears and made them sit down, and then he and Miss Rabbit waited about for Brer Fox. And they kept on waiting, but Brer Fox didn't come.

After a while Brer Rabbit went to the door and peeped out – and what do you think he saw? Why, sticking out from behind the corner was the tip-end of Brer Fox's tail!

'So Brer Fox is a-hiding there, ready to jump out on us!' said Brer Rabbit, with a grin. He shot indoors and sat down. He put his paws behind his ears and began to sing:

> *'I won't go out this morning,*
> *I don't like getting shocks,*
> *'Cos where you see a tail,*
> *You're sure to find a fox!'*

Then Brer Rabbit and old Miss Rabbit and all the little rabbits grinned at one another and ate up the dinner as fast as they could.

Next day Brer Fox sent Brer Mink to say that he was sorry he hadn't come to dinner the day before, but he was too ill to come, and please would Brer Rabbit come and take dinner with him! Brer Rabbit said yes, he would.

So by and by, when the sun was high in the sky, Brer Rabbit brushed his fur well, and wandered off down to Brer Fox's house. When he got there he heard somebody groaning, and he peeped in at the door and there he saw Brer Fox sitting up in a rocking-chair all wrapped up in flannel, and looking mighty weak.

Brer Rabbit looked all round, but he didn't see

any dinner. The dish-pan was on the table, and close by was a large carving knife.

'Looks as if you're going to have chicken for dinner, Brer Fox,' said Brer Rabbit.

'Yes, Brer Rabbit, all nice and fresh and tender,' said Brer Fox.

Then Brer Rabbit pulled at his whiskers and said, 'You haven't got any calamus root, have you, Brer Fox? You know I just simply can't eat chicken unless it's seasoned with calamus root.'

And with that Brer Rabbit shot out of the door and dodged into some bushes. He sat there, hidden, waiting and watching to see what Brer Fox would do.

He hadn't watched very long before he saw

Brer Fox fling off his flannel and creep out of the house, ready to pounce on Brer Rabbit when he came back.

'So that's his little game!' grinned Brer Rabbit to himself. He sat a little longer, and then he shouted loudly:

'Oh, Brer Fox! I'll just put the calamus root out here on this tree-stump! You'd better come and get it whilst it's fresh!'

And then Brer Rabbit galloped off home. So Brer Fox didn't catch him after all – and he's not going to either!

# Brer Rabbit Lays in his Winter Stores

Now one time the winter set in very early, and the creatures couldn't seem to find enough to eat. Brer Fox got as thin as a broom handle, and Brer Rabbit was just a bag of bones.

One day they met in the road and began to talk.

'Bad times, Brer Rabbit, bad times,' said Brer Fox.

'You've nothing to grumble at, Brer Fox,' said Brer Rabbit. 'You've got a horse and cart, and I've got nothing except my old wheelbarrow!'

'What's the use of a horse and cart?' said Brer Fox. 'You just tell me that, Brer Rabbit – what's the use of a horse and cart when you've got nothing to carry in it? Why, I used to go to the town and bring back my cart full of food – but now the horse is lazing in the field and the cart is lying idle in the shed.'

'That's bad,' said Brer Rabbit. 'Why don't you sell your horse and cart, Brer Fox, and buy food with the money? I'm surprised that a clever man like you hasn't thought of that before.'

Well, Brer Fox thought it over and he reckoned it was a mighty good idea. Having a horse and cart wouldn't help him if he was dying of hunger!

'Well,' said Brer Fox, 'that's a good idea, Brer Rabbit – but if I go to town and sell my horse and cart to buy food, I'll have no cart to bring it home in and no horse to pull it! So I'd be no better off than before!'

'Well, Brer Fox,' said Brer Rabbit, 'I don't mind giving you a hand over this. I'll lend you my wheelbarrow to bring your shopping home in. We can put the wheelbarrow in the cart when we set out, and after you've sold your horse and cart, you can buy food with the money and put it into my barrow. We can take turns in wheeling it home!'

'That's mighty good of you, Brer Rabbit,' said Brer Fox. 'I'll do that. Meet me at the corner of the road tomorrow morning and we'll set off for town.'

So the next morning the two of them set off in the cart. Brer Fox clucked to his horse and they galloped into the town. Pretty soon Brer Fox had sold the horse and cart and had money to jingle in his pockets.

My, the food he bought! It just made old Brer

Rabbit's mouth water, so it did! A sack of rice, a sack of corn, a sack of coffee, a sack of turnips – it was a wonder it all went into the barrow!

'You take a turn at wheeling the barrow first,

Brer Rabbit,' said Brer Fox. 'My arms ache from driving the horse.'

Brer Rabbit lifted the handles of the barrow. My, but it was heavy! Brer Rabbit puffed and panted and Brer Fox grinned to see him. Brer Fox walked fast and Brer Rabbit couldn't keep up with him. He did his best, but Brer Fox always seemed to manage to keep so far ahead that Brer Rabbit couldn't shout loudly enough to him to make him hear.

Well, at last Brer Rabbit's arms were aching so much that he had to put the barrow down.

'Heyo, Brer Fox!' he yelled. 'You come along back here! It's your turn now!'

Brer Fox went skipping along in front and didn't so much as turn his head.

'Brer Fox! BRER FOX! You come along back here!' yelled Brer Rabbit. 'I'm not going to wheel your food all the way home. You give me my share for helping you, and I'll take it and go.'

Brer Fox heard that all right. He turned round and grinned at Brer Rabbit.

'The food's mine!' he shouted. 'I may give you a handful of rice, Brer Rabbit, but that's all you'll get! Aha! Some one else can play tricks, as well as you!'

Brer Rabbit thought mighty hard, he did. Then he shouted to Brer Fox.

'All right, Brer Fox. Just give me my handful of rice and I'll be off. But you might pop into Brer Bear's house just over there and ask him for a little bag to put my rice in. I can't carry it in my paws very well.'

So Brer Fox, grinning to himself and feeling mighty pleased with things, bopped along to Brer Bear's house and borrowed the smallest bag he could.

Now as soon as Brer Fox was out of sight, Brer Rabbit took hold of the sack of rice and pulled it out of the barrow. He hid it under a bush, but before he left it there he put his hand in at the top and got a handful of rice grains out. He ran back to the barrow and then set off in the opposite direction, dropping the rice as he went. Then back he went to the barrow again and sat down by it, pretending to cry.

By and by Brer Fox came back with a small bag, and when he got there he saw Brer Rabbit crying. My, but he was boo-hooing!

'In the name of goodness, Brer Rabbit, what's the matter?' said Brer Fox.

'Matter enough, matter enough!' said Brer Rabbit. 'I wish you'd stayed here instead of going off, Brer Fox.'

'What's up then, Brer Rabbit?'

'Oh, a man came, Brer Fox, and stole your lovely bag of rice!' sobbed Brer Rabbit. 'I ran after him but he went too fast for me.'

'Which way did he go, Brer Rabbit?'

'There's the way he went, Brer Fox, there's where he dropped the rice out of the sack as he ran. If you're quick, Brer Fox, you'll catch him!'

Brer Fox dropped the bag he carried and tore off, hoping to catch the man that Brer Rabbit spoke of. He was hardly out of sight when Brer Rabbit caught hold of the bag of coffee and carried that away to the bush and hid it too. He put his hand into the top of the sack, took out some coffee beans, ran back to the barrow, and then set off in the other direction, dropping the beans as he went. It looked just as if some one had run there with a sack, dropping beans out of it as he ran!

After a while, back came Brer Fox, a-puffing and a-panting. He hadn't seen any man at all. Brer Rabbit shouted to him.

'You haven't come a minute too soon, Brer Fox! While you were gone another man came and carried off the coffee. See, that's the way he went, Brer Fox, and if you're quick, you'll catch him!'

Well, Brer Fox set off again as fast as he could,

and he ran and ran, but he didn't see any man at all. Whilst he was gone Brer Rabbit carried off the sack of corn, and sprinkled some grains in the opposite direction again. Then Brer Fox came back, shouting that he hadn't seen anyone – and Brer Rabbit yelled to him to say that another man had been and had carried off the corn.

Well, this suddenly seemed mighty strange to Brer Fox – all these men coming by that way, in a lonely place, and stealing out of his barrow. He wondered if maybe Brer Rabbit was up to one of his tricks, so when he ran off, pretending to chase the man again, he didn't go very far, but turned round and crept back to see what Brer Rabbit was doing.

And he was just in time to see Brer Rabbit pulling at the sack of turnips in his barrow! Well, Brer Fox was mighty tired with running hither and thither and backwards and forwards, but he felt so mad when he saw what Brer Rabbit was up to that he dashed up to him and shouted at him.

'What are you going to do with that sack of turnips?' he yelled.

Brer Rabbit put the sack down and looked very upset. He looked at Brer Fox as if he felt mighty sorry for folks who asked such foolish questions. He shook his head, he did, and said:

'Well, well, well! Who'd have thought Brer Fox would have come yelling at me like this, when any one would guess I was just a-carrying it off to save for him, so's no man could steal it?'

But this sort of talk didn't deceive Brer Fox, and he snarled so fiercely that Brer Rabbit thought it would be better to run – and run he did, with Brer Fox at his tail, between the trees. And at last Brer Rabbit came to a hollow tree and in he went!

Well, old Brer Buzzard was a-sailing round in the air, and Brer Fox called to him.

'Just you watch this hole for me, Brer Buzzard,' said Brer Fox. 'I'm a-going to fetch some fire to smoke old Brer Rabbit out!'

Well, Brer Fox set off, and Brer Buzzard settled down beside the hole – and after a bit Brer Rabbit sang out, 'I've got the better of you, Brer Buzzard! I surely have!'

'How's that, Brer Rabbit?' said Brer Buzzard.

'Because I can see you and you can't see me!' said Brer Rabbit, in his most cheeky voice.

With that Brer Buzzard stuck his head in the hole of the tree and looked up to see Brer Rabbit, and no sooner did he do this than Brer Rabbit flung a handful of sand down into his eyes.

Poor Brer Buzzard! He blinked and he winked

but he couldn't get the sand out – so down to the stream he flew to wash his eyes. And whilst he was gone Brer Rabbit came down out of the hollow tree, and raced back to the barrow.

It wasn't long before he had taken the sacks of corn, rice, and coffee out from under the bush where he had hidden them, popped them into the barrow with the sack of turnips, and trundled away merrily to his home.

And my, didn't Brer Fox shake his fist when he passed by Brer Rabbit's house the next day and smelt fried rice cakes and fresh coffee! Ah, it's no use trying to trick Brer Rabbit!

# Brer Wolf Tries to Grow Horns

It came about one day that all the creatures that had horns made up their minds to meet together and have a talk about how to take care of themselves – because the creatures that had teeth and claws were snatching the horned animals round every corner!

So the horned animals sent out word all round the countryside, and planned a meeting in the woods. When the day came, what a large crowd of them there was! They stamped through the bushes, they bellowed and they mooed, they grunted and they snorted. My, it was a fine crowd that met together that day!

Mr Bull, he was there, and he took the head of the meeting. Mr Steer was there, stamping his hoof. Miss Cow was there, whisking her tail round. Mr Billy Goat was there, wagging his beard and talking away to Miss Cow. Mr Unicorn was there, with his great long horn sticking right up into the air. Mr Benjamin Ram was there, with his fiddle. And Old Man Rhinoceros was there too, taking up a mighty lot of room.

There were lots more, too many to tell, for they came in crowds. Old Brer Wolf, he heard about this meeting and he made up his mind he'd go along and see what it was all about – and maybe sneak off with one of Mr Benjamin Ram's children.

But he didn't know how to go without being known as Brer Wolf. Any creature there without horns would be noticed at once and sent away with a horn in his side if he wasn't careful! So Brer Wolf sat down and thought hard. He meant to go to that meeting – but how could he go there unnoticed?

Pretty soon he grinned to himself and went out to the woods. He cut himself two crooked sticks and tied them on his head! The sticks looked just like horns – and my, but Brer Wolf looked a mighty strange creature! He set off to the meeting, and mixed with all the crowd.

Now as he went to the meeting Brer Rabbit saw him – and he sprang aside into the bushes quickly when he saw a creature looking like Brer Wolf, yet carrying horns on his head! 'My!' said Brer Rabbit to himself, 'if it isn't enough that Brer Wolf's got claws and teeth – and now he's got horns as well. I wonder why.'

Well, Brer Rabbit didn't mean to let Brer Wolf out of his sight, so he went after him, hiding in the bushes all the way. And pretty soon he came to the meeting too, but as he had no horns on his head Brer Rabbit kept in the bushes, and lay there without moving even an ear.

When Brer Wolf got to the meeting Mr Bull saw him.

'Who are you?' said Mr Bull, in surprise, for he had never seen a creature quite like Brer Wolf before.

'Baa-aa-aa!' said Brer Wolf. 'I'm little Sooky Calf.'

Well, Mr Bull looked at Brer Wolf very hard over the tops of his spectacles, and Brer Wolf he put down his head and made little bleating noises as best as he could. But just then someone called Mr Bull away, and Brer Wolf took his place among the crowd, sniffing and smelling every one.

By and by the creatures began talking and telling each other of the bad ways of toothed and clawed animals. Whilst all this was going on, a big horse-fly came sailing around, and Brer Wolf quite forgot that he was supposed to be a horned creature, and he did what no horned animal ever does – he snapped at that fly!

All this time Brer Rabbit had been hiding in the bushes watching Brer Wolf, and when he saw Brer Wolf snap at the horse-fly he laughed out loud.

Mr Bull heard the laugh and he bellowed out angrily:

'Who's that laughing away, and showing bad manners at this meeting?'

Nobody answered at all, and there was a silence. Then Brer Rabbit shouted out:

'Oh, *kittle-kattle, kittle-kattle, where are your eyes?*
*Whoever saw a Sooky Calf snapping at flies?'*

The horned animals all looked at one another and wondered what this meant. Brer Wolf felt mighty angry with Brer Rabbit, but he couldn't do a thing about it.

Before very long something bit Brer Wolf on the back of his neck, and before he knew what he was doing he sat right down and scratched himself well with his hind foot – a thing that no cow or bull ever did!

Well, Brer Rabbit shouted with laughter once more to see him, and disturbed the meeting again.

Mr Bull bellowed away in anger – and as soon as he had stopped and there was a dead silence, Brer Rabbit sang out at the top of his voice again:

*'Scritchum-scratchum, look at his paws,*
*See that Sooky Calf scratching with claws!'*

Brer Wolf was mighty scared, but it didn't seem as if any of the horned creatures knew what Brer Rabbit meant, for they took no notice of him at all.

Brer Wolf sat down on the ground behind Mr Benjamin Ram, hoping that Mr Ram would hide him well from Mr Bull's eye. He put his long tail out behind him, and Sis Cow stepped on it by mistake. Brer Wolf gave a yell, and Brer Rabbit gave a great shout of laughter again.

'Who's that a-laughing and a-spoiling the meeting?' roared Mr Bull. Nobody spoke a word – and then old Brer Rabbit he shouted loudly again from where he was hidden in the bushes:

*'Rinkum, sinkum, ride him on a rail,*
*That Sooky Calf's got a long, bushy tail!'*

Brer Wolf crouched down behind Mr Benjamin Ram and tried to hide his tail. Nobody seemed to take much notice of him – except Mr Bull – and he had his eye on Brer Wolf all right! Yes – Brer Wolf noticed that Mr Bull was looking straight at him, and he didn't like it a bit. He felt mighty scared!

The meeting went on, but Brer Wolf felt more and more scared because he saw Mr Bull edging nearer and nearer to him through the crowd. And Brer Rabbit, he wasn't going to be quiet, not he! He shouted out at the top of his voice:

*'One and one never can make six,*
*Sticks aren't horns, and horns aren't sticks!'*

And just about then Mr Bull saw that Brer Wolf's horns weren't horns at all but two bits of crooked stick! He roared in a rage and ran straight at Brer Wolf. He put down his head, he did, and he ran at Brer Wolf like a thunderbolt.

Brer Wolf gave a yelp and tore away. Mr Bull grazed his horns against Brer Wolf's sides and gave him two good cuts. My, how Brer Wolf jumped!

He rushed away from the meeting, and he was so mad with Brer Rabbit that he reckoned he would pretend that the wounds Mr Bull had given him had killed him. So he sent word round that he was dead.

Well, Brer Rabbit thought it might well be so, for he had seen Mr Bull's horns going straight at Brer Wolf. And he thought he would pop round to Brer Wolf's house and see if he really was dead. But he remembered how Brer Wolf had tried to trick him that way before, and he didn't go inside the house – he only put his head round the door and peeped in.

Brer Rabbit saw some of the other creatures there, and he said 'howdy' to them. Then he said, 'Poor Brer Wolf! So Mr Bull killed him! Dear, dear!

Tell me, folks, has Brer Wolf grinned yet?'

'No, Brer Wolf hasn't grinned,' said the creatures there. 'Whyever should he grin, Brer Rabbit?'

'Ah,' said Brer Rabbit, 'wolves are strange creatures, folks. They aren't dead till they grin. You tell me when Brer Wolf grins and I'll know he's dead for good.'

Well, when Brer Wolf heard this, he wanted Brer Rabbit to think he was dead, so he grinned from ear to ear! And then, of course, Brer Rabbit knew he was alive all right, and he picked up his hat and stick and ran off for home – and every now and again he would sit down and laugh fit to kill himself!

# Brer Rabbit Meets His Match

One time Brer Rabbit and Brer Turkey Buzzard thought they could go shares together. They dug up a field and planted their seed, and they weeded and they watered and their crops grew mighty well.

Brer Buzzard was pleased and he told Brer Rabbit that when they sold their crop there would be a mighty lot of money between the two of them.

Well, Brer Rabbit gathered in the crop and he set off to sell it. Brer Buzzard let him do the selling for he hadn't much head for that sort of thing. But there was a great shock for Brer Buzzard the day he asked Brer Rabbit for his share of the money.

'Brer Buzzard, I'm mighty sorry, but I've got bad news for you,' said Brer Rabbit, looking sad and solemn. 'That crop of ours wasn't any good at all when it came to selling.'

'It looked mighty good in the field,' said Brer Turkey Buzzard, puzzled.

'Yes, it did so,' said Brer Rabbit. 'But it fetched no money at all, Brer Buzzard, except what it cost me to sell it. I'm in a bad way, I am, Brer Buzzard, with the winter coming on, and children to feed, and no money in my pocket.'

Brer Buzzard flew off, and he sat in a tree and thought hard. He made up his mind to watch Brer Rabbit carefully, and if he saw him spending money and acting gay and cheerful, Brer Buzzard reckoned he would know Brer Rabbit had deceived him over the crops.

But Brer Rabbit, he went about with a long face, and moped round till nobody liked him about. All the same, Brer Buzzard knew how tricky Brer Rabbit could be, and he didn't just believe that things were so bad as Brer Rabbit made out.

So he thought a bit more and at last he got a plan. One day he flew along to where Brer Rabbit was sitting, and shouted to him:

'Brer Rabbit! I've got a bit of luck! I've been across the river, and let me tell you there's fine rich gold-mines over there!'

'What, just across the river?' said Brer Rabbit.

'That's right,' said Brer Buzzard. 'You come with me, Brer Rabbit. I'll scratch in the mines and you can grabble, and between the two of us we'll

76

get enough gold to set us up properly. I'm sorry for you, Brer Rabbit, these days – you go around looking so sad and solemn. You come and share this bit of luck with me!'

'I'd like to come,' said Brer Rabbit, 'but it beats me how I'll get across the river, Brer Buzzard. Every time I get my foot wet all my family catch cold!'

'That's too bad, Brer Rabbit,' said Brer Buzzard. 'I guess I'll have to go alone.'

'How are you going to cross the river?' said Brer Rabbit.

'Oh, I shall fly,' said Brer Buzzard, and he spread his big wings.

'Wait a minute, Brer Buzzard,' said Brer Rabbit. 'Can't you carry me across, so's I could come with you?'

'Well, I dare say I could,' said Brer Buzzard, and he squatted down on the ground so that Brer Rabbit could get on his back. Then he spread his wings and rose up in the air.

But instead of flying right across the river Brer Buzzard flew to an island in the middle of it – and on this island was a tall pine-tree, and Brer Buzzard went and perched on the very topmost bough. There he sat, with Brer Rabbit clinging to his back, just about the scaredest rabbit in the whole world!

Well, as soon as Brer Rabbit found himself there he knew quite well that Brer Buzzard was tricking him, and he was mighty frightened. But he didn't show it. He spoke up kindly to Brer Buzzard.

'Whilst we're resting here, Brer Buzzard, and seeing you've been so kind to me, I've got some good news to tell you. I've got a gold-mine of my own, one that I made myself, and it wouldn't be a bad idea to go and see my mine before we bother about the one over the river.'

Then old Brer Buzzard he laughed till he shook, and Brer Rabbit felt sure he would fall off and drown in the deep water running all round.

'Hold on, Brer Buzzard!' he shouted. 'Don't flap your wings when you laugh, because if you do I shall drop off, and my gold-mine won't do you any good, and neither will yours do *me* any good!'

'I'm a-going to flap my wings and shake my tail and laugh till I fall off the branch myself,' said old Brer Buzzard. 'My, this is the best joke I've had for years, Brer Rabbit, so it is! You did me out of my fair share of money when you sold our crops, Brer Rabbit, and now I'm going to do you! Ho, ho, you thought I had a gold-mine across the river. But I haven't. I'm just a-going to laugh some more and then I'm flying off and leaving you here to study how to make crops pay next year!'

'Oh, Brer Buzzard, don't do that,' said Brer Rabbit. 'Pray don't do that. I'll give you some of my own money, so I will. I told you I had a gold-mine I'd made myself, didn't I? Well, I'll show you where it is.'

'Yes, and that gold-mine of yours is made out of my money,' said Brer Buzzard. 'No, Brer Rabbit, you're a robber and a man that plays tricks on everyone. I guess folks would be pleased if I let you drop into the river right now.'

'Don't you do that or you won't get any of your money or mine either,' begged Brer Rabbit.

'Where have you hidden the money?' said Brer Buzzard. 'Now you tell me the truth, Brer Rabbit, or I'll fly off and leave you.'

'It's buried in the field by my house,' said Brer Rabbit. 'You fly with me there, Brer Buzzard, and I'll show you.'

Well, Brer Buzzard had seen Brer Rabbit's field all dug up some days back, and he guessed Brer Rabbit was speaking the truth for once in a way. So he believed him, and told him to hold tight and he'd fly with him back to the field. Off they went, Brer Rabbit all of a shake in case Brer Buzzard should drop him by mistake.

Well, when they got to the field, Brer Rabbit turned up the earth and there was the money hidden in a box! Brer Buzzard took nearly all of it and left Brer Rabbit just a bit. As for Brer Rabbit, he had had such a scare that he didn't say a word when he saw old Brer Buzzard flying off, squawking in glee.

Poor Brer Rabbit! He walked weak in the knees for a whole month afterwards!

# Brer Rabbit Gets
# Brer Fox's Dinner

Now, after Brer Rabbit had built a steeple on his house, all the other creatures felt as if they wanted to do something to their houses too. Brer Bear put a new cellar under his, and Brer Wolf put up new window-blinds. Some chose one thing and some chose another, but old Brer Fox he took it into his head to nail new shingles on to his roof.

Brer Rabbit heard about this, and what must he do but run round and see how old Brer Fox was getting on. When he got near Brer Fox's house, he heard a mighty lamming and a blamming, and lo and behold, there was Brer Fox sitting a-straddle on the top of his roof, nailing on wooden shingles as hard as he could.

Brer Rabbit smelt something nice and he let his eye wander round Brer Fox's garden a bit. He saw Brer Fox's dinner sitting in a corner by the fence in a dinner-pail, neatly covered up. It looked so nice

81

that Brer Rabbit's mouth began to water when he saw it, and he said to himself that he really *must* eat that dinner before he went away from there!

Then Brer Rabbit shouted up to Brer Fox, 'How are you doing, Brer Fox?'

'I'm too busy to talk,' said Brer Fox.

'What are you doing up there?' said Brer Rabbit.

'Putting a new roof on my house before the rain comes,' said Brer Fox, hammering away.

'What time is it, Brer Fox?' asked Brer Rabbit.

'It's working-time with me, that's what it is,' said Brer Fox, lamming away at his roof.

'Don't you want any help?' shouted Brer Rabbit.

'I could do with some,' said Brer Fox, 'though I don't know where in the name of goodness I'm going to get any!'

With that Brer Rabbit sort of pulled at his whiskers. Then he said, 'I used to be a mighty handy man with a hammer, Brer Fox, and I'm not too proud now to climb up and help you.'

'I'm mighty much obliged,' said Brer Fox. And no sooner had he said that than Brer Rabbit snatched off his coat, leapt up the ladder, and sat down to hammer on shingles. And he put on more shingles in an hour than Brer Fox put on in two.

Oh, he was a clever fellow, Brer Rabbit was!

There wasn't any kind of work that Brer Rabbit couldn't do, and do it better than any one else too.

He nailed on shingles till he got tired, Brer Rabbit did, and all the time he was thinking how to get Brer Fox's dinner. Maybe Brer Fox would offer to share it with him – and maybe he wouldn't! Brer Rabbit nailed and nailed. He would nail one row and Brer Fox would nail one row. He caught up Brer Fox and passed him – caught him up and passed him again, till by and by, whilst he was a-nailing, Brer Fox's tail got in his way.

Brer Fox was working just above Brer Rabbit, and his tail hung down on to Brer Rabbit's row of shingles. Brer Rabbit couldn't see what he was doing, so he pushed Brer Fox's tail out of the way.

'I don't know what in the name of goodness folks have such long tails for!' he said to himself.

Soon Brer Fox's tail got in Brer Rabbit's way again. He pushed it to the side. It came back again. He pushed it away. But he hadn't more than pushed it away before it came back again.

Well, this made Brer Rabbit mighty mad. How can a man nail shingles on a roof if a big tail is in the way all the time? 'If this tail doesn't get out of my way I'll have to do something about it,' said Brer Rabbit to himself. And at that, down came the tail again and nearly knocked Brer Rabbit's hammer out of his hand.

Well, there was only one thing to do – and Brer Rabbit did it. He nailed Brer Fox's tail to the roof, and then he went on working, glad that the tail wasn't in his way any more. Well, they nailed and they nailed – and bless gracious, it wasn't long before Brer Fox tried to move along, and found that he couldn't! He dropped everything and squalled out:

'Lawks-amussy, Brer Rabbit! You've nailed my tail down! You've nailed my tail down!'

Brer Rabbit stopped hammering. He winked first one eye and then the other, and rubbed his forehead as if he were mighty puzzled.

'Surely I haven't nailed your tail, Brer Fox!

Surely I haven't! Look close and see, Brer Fox, but be careful you don't fall. For goodness' sake don't say I've nailed your tail, Brer Fox, if I haven't!'

Brer Fox shouted and yelled, and squealed and kicked.

'Lawks-amussy, Brer Rabbit! I tell you, you have nailed my tail down! Un-nail me, Brer Rabbit, un-nail me!'

Brer Rabbit made for the ladder and started down it. He looked up at Brer Fox as if he was mighty sorry, and he said:

'Well, well, well! Just to think I should have been so careless as to nail Brer Fox's tail down! I don't know when I've heard anything that made me feel so mighty bad. If I hadn't seen it with my own eyes I wouldn't have believed it, that I wouldn't.'

Well, Brer Fox yelled, Brer Fox howled, but it wasn't a bit of good. There he was up on the roof with his tail nailed down hard and fast. Brer Rabbit, he kept on talking all the time he was going down the ladder.

'It makes me feel so bad,' he said, 'that I don't know what to do. Every time I think of it I feel an empty place come in my middle.'

By this time Brer Rabbit was down on the

ground, and whilst Brer Fox was yelling, he just kept on talking.

'Yes, there's a mighty empty place in my middle,' he said, 'and if I don't make a mistake, why, here's a tin-pail full of dinner in the corner over there that will just about fit that empty place!'

With that Brer Rabbit ran to the pail, took off the lid, sat down and began to eat. He ate up the greens, he ate up the meat, and he drank the gravy. Then he wiped his mouth on his coat-tail and said:

'I don't know when I've been so sorry about anything as I am about Brer Fox's nice long tail. Surely, surely, I must have been dreaming when I nailed Brer Fox's fine long tail,' said old Brer Rabbit.

And then he skipped out of the garden, Brer Rabbit did, and it wasn't long before he was safely at home, telling his old woman how sorry he was about Brer Fox's lovely long tail.

As for old Brer Fox, he had to sit up on his roof till Brer Wolf came by and un-nailed him. Poor Brer Fox! He might have known Brer Rabbit would trick him somehow.

# Brer Rabbit Saves
# Brer Terrapin

One time Brer Fox was going down the big road and he saw old Brer Terrapin going to his home. Now Brer Fox knew Brer Terrapin was a good friend to Brer Rabbit, and it seemed to him it was a mighty good time to catch him. Brer Fox didn't have any kindly feelings towards people who were friends of Brer Rabbit.

Brer Fox ran back to his own house, which was not far off, and got a bag. Then he ran down the road again, rushed up behind Brer Terrapin, caught him up and threw him into the bag. He slung the bag across his back, then off he went, galloping home.

Brer Terrapin, he shouted, but it wasn't any good. He wriggled and struggled, but that wasn't any good either. Brer Fox just went on going, and there was old Brer Terrapin in the corner of the bag, and the bag tied up hard and fast.

But where was Brer Rabbit whilst all this was going on? Where was that long-eared, hoppetty-skippetty creature, that up-and-down-and-sailing-round Brer Rabbit? He wasn't far off, you may be sure!

Brer Fox went trotting down the big road with the bag on his back – and Brer Rabbit was sitting in the bushes just by the side of the road. He saw Brer Fox trotting by and he saw the bag on his back too.

'Now what's Brer Fox got in that bag?' said Brer Rabbit to himself. 'I don't know what it can be.'

Well, Brer Rabbit sat in the bushes and wondered and wondered, but the more he wondered the less he could think what it was. He watched Brer Fox a-trotting down the road, and still he sat in the bushes and wondered.

'Huh!' said Brer Rabbit at last, 'Brer Fox has no business to be trotting down the road carrying something other people don't know about. I guess I'll go after Brer Fox and find out what's in the bag!'

With that, Brer Rabbit set out. He hadn't got a bag to carry and he went mighty quickly. He took a short cut, and by the time Brer Fox got to his house Brer Rabbit had had time to get into his strawberry-bed and trample down a whole lot of plants. When he had done that, he sat down in some bushes where he could see Brer Fox coming home.

By and by Brer Fox came along with his bag across his back. He unlatched his door, he did, and then he threw Brer Terrapin down in a corner in the bag, and sat down to rest himself, for Brer Terrapin was mighty heavy to carry.

Brer Fox had hardly put a match to his pipe when Brer Rabbit stuck his head in at the door and shouted:

'Brer Fox! Oh, Brer Fox! You'd better take your stick and run out yonder. Coming along just now I heard a fuss going on in your garden, and I looked round and there were a whole lot of folk in your strawberry-bed, just a-trampling the strawberries down! I shouted at them, but they didn't take any notice of a little man like me. Make haste, Brer Fox make haste! Get your stick and run. I'd go with you too, but I've got to get home. You'd better hurry, Brer Fox, if you want to save your strawberries. Run, Brer Fox, run!'

With that Brer Rabbit darted back into the bushes, and Brer Fox dropped his pipe and grabbed his stick and rushed out to his strawberry-bed. And no sooner was he gone than old Brer Rabbit hopped out of the bushes and into the house.

He didn't make a bit of noise. He looked round and there was the bag in the corner. He caught hold of it and felt it to see what was inside. And suddenly something yelled:

'Ow! Go away! Let me alone! Turn me loose! Ow!'

Brer Rabbit jumped back astonished. Then before you could wink an eye he slapped himself on the leg and laughed out loud.

'If I'm not making a mistake, that's nobody's voice but old Brer Terrapin's!' said Brer Rabbit.

'Is that Brer Rabbit?' yelled Brer Terrapin.

'It is,' said Brer Rabbit.

'Then hurry up and get me out,' said Brer Terrapin. 'There's dust in my throat, grit in my eyes, and I can hardly breathe. Get me out, Brer Rabbit.'

'Heyo, Brer Terrapin,' said Brer Rabbit. 'You're a lot smarter than I am – because here you are in a bag and I don't know how in the name of goodness you've tied yourself up in there, that I don't!'

Brer Terrapin tried to explain and Brer Rabbit kept on laughing, but all the same he untied the bag, took Brer Terrapin out and carried him outside the gate. Then, when he had done this, Brer Rabbit ran off to where he knew some wasps had a nest just about as big as a football.

The wasp-nest was in a hollow tree. Brer Rabbit slipped in at the bottom of the tree and there was the nest inside. He slapped his paw over the hole where the wasps went in and out, knocked the nest down into his bag, and there he had it, wasps and all!

Then back he raced to Brer Fox's house and flung the bag down on the floor, tied up fast. Well, the way he slammed that bag down on the floor stirred all those wasps up and put them into a very bad temper! They buzzed fit to make holes in the bag!

Soon Brer Rabbit saw Brer Fox coming down the back-garden, where he had been looking for the folks that had trodden down his strawberries. He had been putting the plants straight and picking off the squashed fruit, and Brer Fox was feeling mighty mad about it too.

By the time Brer Fox got indoors Brer Rabbit was off and away into a bush – and there he sat with old Brer Terrapin, waiting to see what would happen.

Brer Fox went indoors, hitting the ground with his stick, and vowing that he would shake Brer Terrapin to bits, he was in such a bad temper.

He slammed the door and Brer Rabbit and Brer

Terrapin waited. They listened, but at first they couldn't hear anything. By and by they heard the most tremendous noise!

'Seems like a whole crowd of cows running round and round inside Brer Fox's house,' Brer Rabbit said to Brer Terrapin.

'I can hear chairs a-falling,' said Brer Terrapin.

'I can hear the table turning over,' said Brer Rabbit.

'I can hear the crockery smashing,' said Brer Terrapin.

'Huh!' said Brer Rabbit, enjoying himself, 'Brer Fox must be having a fine game with those wasps. What a surprise he got when he opened the bag to get you – and found a wasp's nest instead!'

Just as Brer Rabbit said that, Brer Fox's door flew wide open and out rushed Brer Fox, squalling and howling as if two hundred dogs had got him by the tail!

He ran straight to the river, he did, and plunged in to get rid of the wasps on him. Brer Rabbit and Brer Terrapin sat there in the bushes and laughed and laughed, till by and by Brer Rabbit rolled over and said:

'One more laugh, Brer Terrapin, and you'll have to carry me home!'

'Get on my back then, Brer Rabbit, get on my back,' said Brer Terrapin. 'I'll carry you all right. Shoo! That will teach Brer Fox not to go a-catching an old fellow like me and putting him into a dusty bag!'

Brer Fox came out of the river at last – but to this day he doesn't know how it was that though he put old Brer Terrapin into a bag, it was a nest of wasps that came out! And you may be sure Brer Rabbit never told him!

# Mr Benjamin Ram

Old Mr Benjamin Ram was an odd-looking creature, he surely was. His wrinkly horn and the shaggy hair on his neck made him look mighty fierce, and when he shook his head and snorted it looked as if he were going to paw up all the ground beneath his feet!

Old Brer Fox had been catching and eating Mr Benjamin Ram's children, the little lambs, but he had never got too close to Mr Ram himself.

One time when he was going down the road, talking to Brer Wolf, Brer Fox let out a big sigh and said he was mighty hungry in his middle.

'Why in the name of goodness are you hungry, Brer Fox, when old Mr Benjamin Ram is up in his house there just rolling in fat?' said Brer Wolf, in an astonished voice.

'Huh!' said Brer Fox, 'I know I'm in the habit of eating Mr Ram's children, but I'm sort of scared of the old creature because of his red eye and wrinkly horn.'

Brer Wolf shouted with laughter, and said, 'Good gracious, Brer Fox! I don't know what sort of a fellow you are – why, that old Mr Ram never hurt a fly in all his life, that he hasn't!'

Brer Fox looked very hard at Brer Wolf. Then he said, 'Heyo, Brer Wolf! Many's the time I've seen you hungry, but yet I never heard you talk of making a meal off Mr Benjamin Ram!'

Brer Wolf didn't quite know what to say to this. After a bit he said, 'I should just like to know who in the name of goodness would want to eat a tough old creature like Mr Benjamin Ram! I'd just like to know that, Brer Fox!'

Brer Fox laughed, he did, and then he said to Brer Wolf, 'Ah, yi, Brer Wolf! You ask me what I go hungry for when I could go and eat old Mr Benjamin Ram – but why didn't *you* eat him when *you* were hungry? That's what I want to know!'

Brer Wolf got angry and hit the ground with the end of his stick. 'I've said all I've got to say,' he said. 'That old creature is too tough for me to eat.'

Although he was very hungry, Brer Fox went on laughing. 'Well, Brer Wolf,' he said, 'I'm not going to talk about it any longer – I'm going to do what you say. I'm going to go up to Mr Ram's house and have him for supper – and I wish you'd be so good as to go along and keep me company.'

Well, Brer Wolf didn't like the sound of this at all. 'I'd rather go by myself,' he said.

'Well, you'd better hurry then,' said Brer Fox, 'because it isn't going to take me long to get to Mr Ram's house!'

Brer Wolf was in a fix. He knew quite well that if he backed out of this, Brer Fox would tell Miss Meadows and the girls, and they would laugh at him and tease him. So he marched off towards Mr Benjamin Ram's house.

As he went, a little puff of wind blew up some leaves, and they scared Brer Wolf so much that he jumped as if he had been shot. Brer Fox laughed at him, and this made Brer Wolf so angry that he hurried on in front to Mr Ram's house.

He knocked at the door, he did, and, of course, he expected somebody to come and open it – but instead of that, round the corner of the house came old Mr Benjamin Ram. There he was – red eye, wrinkly horn, and shaggy head. My, what a shock he gave Brer Wolf! Brer Wolf shot down the path, and out of the gate back to Brer Fox as if he'd been fired out of a gun!

Brer Fox laughed and laughed. Brer Wolf looked mighty down in the dumps. 'Have you killed and eaten Mr Benjamin Ram?' asked Brer Fox. 'And have you left any for me?'

'Be quiet,' said Brer Wolf. 'I'm not feeling very well.'

'Well, your legs feel well enough!' said Brer Fox. ' My, how they ran just now!'

'I only ran to see if I could make myself feel better,' said Brer Wolf sulkily.

'Dear, dear!' said Brer Fox. 'When *I'm* feeling poorly, Brer Wolf, I just want to lie down!'

Well, they went on this way, they did, till by and by Brer Fox asked Brer Wolf if he would go with him to catch Mr Benjamin Ram.

'No, Brer Fox,' said Brer Wolf. 'I'm afraid you'll run off and leave me to do the fighting.'

'Indeed I won't,' said Brer Fox. 'And I'll soon show you how to feel safe. I'll get a rope and tie one end to you and one end to me. Then we can neither of us run away! We'll both have to fight!'

Well, Brer Wolf had to be content with that, and they set out to Mr Benjamin Ram's house. Brer Wolf sort of hung back, but he was ashamed to say he was afraid, and on they went until they got right up to Mr Ram's house.

When they got there the old creature was sitting out in the front porch sunning himself. He saw them coming and cleared his throat and shouted:

'Ha, Brer Fox! I see you've got Brer Wolf tied up properly, and you're a-leading him here to me! I'm obliged to you for catching him for me. My larder is getting empty, and I'd like to chop him up and pickle him. Fetch him in, Brer Fox, fetch him in!'

Just about then Mrs Ram looked out of the window and saw the two coming, and she was so scared that she began to bleat at the top of her voice! My! You should have heard her! Her voice even reached the town, it was so loud. It even scared Mr Benjamin Ram himself, but he kept on talking.

'Fetch him in, Brer Fox! Fetch him in! Don't you hear my old woman bleating for him? She hasn't tasted wolf-meat for years. My, won't she be pleased to have some on her table. Fetch him in, Brer Fox, fetch him in!'

Well, when Brer Wolf heard all this he got more scared than ever. First he tried to untie the rope round him, and when he couldn't do it, he turned back and ran for his life, jerking poor Brer Fox off his feet, and dragging him behind him at the other end of the rope as if he were a parcel of bones!

Bumpity-thumpity-bump! Thumpity-bumpity-thump! Brer Fox bumped and thumped over the ground till the rope broke – and then he sat up and saw Brer Wolf disappearing in the wood like a streak of lightning.

And that was the last time Brer Fox tried any tricks with Mr Benjamin Ram. My, what a crowd of fine bruises and bumps he had that day!

# Brer Rabbit Saves His Meat

One time Brer Wolf was coming along home after he had been fishing. He sauntered along the road, with his string of fish across his shoulder, when suddenly he saw old Miss Partridge scrambling round in the bushes. She was trying to take him away from her nest, which was not far off. She hopped out of the bushes and fluttered right along just under Brer Wolf's nose.

Well, Brer Wolf guessed old Miss Partridge was trying to get him away from her nest, so he put down his string of fish and began to hunt about in the bushes for the young birds.

About that time Brer Rabbit happened along. There were the fishes – and there was Brer Rabbit. But when Brer Wolf came out of the bushes, there were no fishes to be seen – and no Brer Rabbit either!

Brer Wolf sat down and scratched his head,

and wondered what could have happened to his fishes. Then he suddenly thought that Brer Rabbit must have been along there. So Brer Wolf set out for Brer Rabbit's house and when he got there he shouted for him.

'Brer Rabbit! Have you taken my fishes?'

'What fishes?' said Brer Rabbit.

'My string of fishes I left away back in the wood,' said Brer Wolf. 'Now, Brer Rabbit, just you tell me the truth. I know you took my fishes.'

Well, they argued up and down. Brer Wolf said Brer Rabbit had his fishes, and Brer Rabbit said he hadn't. And then Brer Rabbit got mad and said:

'Well, if you think I've got those fishes of yours, Brer Wolf, I give you leave to kill my best cow!'

Brer Rabbit didn't for one minute think Brer Wolf would take him at his word – but Brer Wolf did! He went straight-away to the fields, drove up Brer Rabbit's cattle, and killed Brer Rabbit's best cow.

Brer Rabbit felt mighty bad at losing his cow, but he laid his plans, and he told his children that Brer Wolf might kill his cow, but he wasn't going to eat the meat! No, he would see that his own family ate cow-meat before many days were out.

So Brer Rabbit rushed up to the field shouting loudly: 'Brer Wolf! Brer Wolf! Here come the dogs!

Run and hide, quickly! The dogs will get you! I'll look after the cow for you till you come back!'

Brer Wolf got such a fright that he shot off into the bushes like a bullet out of a gun. He was hardly out of sight before Brer Rabbit ran up to the cow, took it away, and put it into the smoke-house for meat. When he had done this he took the cow's tail and stuck the end of it hard into the ground.

Then he yelled out for Brer Wolf.

'Brer Wolf! Brer Wolf! Run here! Your cow's going into the ground! Run quickly!'

When old Brer Wolf got there, which he did in half a minute, he saw Brer Rabbit holding on to the end of the cow-tail, as if he was trying to keep it from going into the ground. Brer Wolf really thought that the cow had run right into the ground and that only her tail was sticking out, and he caught hold of it in a trice. He pulled and pulled to get the cow out – but all that happened was that the tail suddenly shot up from the earth and Brer Wolf sat down very hard.

Then Brer Rabbit winked at his children and said, 'There! The tail's pulled out and the cow's gone!'

But Brer Wolf wasn't one to give up easily. He fetched a spade and a pick-axe and a shovel and he dug and dug for that cow till he couldn't dig any more.

Old Brer Rabbit he sat up in his front porch, smoking his cigar. And every time Brer Wolf stuck his pick-axe in the clay Brer Rabbit giggled to his children and said:

'He diggy, diggy, diggy, but there's no meat there! He diggy, diggy, diggy, but there's no meat there!'

And all the time the cow was lying in the smoke-house and Brer Rabbit and his children were eating fried beef and onions every time they were hungry. Poor Brer Wolf! He had lost both his fishes and his cow!

# Brer Bear Gets a Shock

One time Brer Bear went to look at his honey store and he found that half his honey-jars were empty. Well, he ranted and he roared, he howled and he stamped, and he vowed he'd find the thief if it took him a month of Sundays.

He went stamping out of his house, and who should he meet but old Brer Wolf, come to see if Brer Bear was away from home – for Brer Wolf liked a lick of honey himself, and he was the thief all right!

'Someone's been at my honey, Brer Wolf – someone's been at my honey!' roared Brer Bear. 'Who do you think it can be? I'm just going to squeeze the life out of him!'

Brer Wolf looked alarmed. He didn't want to be squeezed in Brer Bear's big arms! 'Well,' he said, 'I saw that rascal of a Brer Rabbit the other day with honey on his whiskers. Ah, yes, Brer Bear, sure enough you'll find it's Brer Rabbit who's the thief!'

'I thought as much!' yelled Brer Bear in a rage. 'He's always where he shouldn't be. But he's played his tricks once too often!'

He rushed off to find Brer Rabbit, and as he went through the wood, what did he see but old Brer Rabbit sitting on a tree-stump combing his fine whiskers.

'Are you combing the honey out of your whiskers?' shouted Brer Bear, and he rushed at Brer Rabbit.

'Now, now, Brer Bear!' cried Brer Rabbit, in alarm, as Brer Bear knocked him over. 'What's the matter? Can't I comb my whiskers?'

'Not if they've got my honey on them!' roared Brer Bear angrily. 'I'm going to squeeze you, Brer Rabbit – yes, I'm going to squeeze you, and make you say where you've put all my honey!'

Brer Wolf crept up and saw the fight. He rubbed his paws in glee, for he guessed that old Brer Rabbit wouldn't come bobbing up *this* time! Brer Bear got hold of Brer Rabbit and began to hug him so that he couldn't breathe.

'Stop it, Brer Bear, stop it!' panted poor Brer Rabbit. 'I tell you, I don't know anything about your honey.'

'Now you just tell me where you've put my honey and I'll let you go,' said Brer Bear. 'Go on – tell me. If you don't, I'll squeeze you to bits!'

Well, Brer Rabbit could see that Brer Bear meant what he said all right, and he began to think how he could stop him.

'Brer Bear, Brer Bear, how can I tell you where your honey is if you squeeze all my breath out of me!' panted Brer Rabbit.

Brer Bear stopped squeezing quite so hard. 'Will you tell me, Brer Rabbit?' he said.

'Brer Bear, I'm not certain where your honey is, but I think maybe you'll get a nice surprise if you look into that hollow tree that's growing by the pond in the wood,' said Brer Rabbit, trying to get his breath again.

'Are you sure I shall get a surprise if I look there?' asked Brer Bear squeezing Brer Rabbit tightly again.

'Brer Bear, stop hugging me!' begged Brer Rabbit in alarm. 'You're squeezing my chest right through my back! I tell you, you'll surely get a fine surprise if you look inside that tree!'

Brer Bear let Brer Rabbit go. He ambled off to the tree, and Brer Wolf and Brer Rabbit followed him, though poor Brer Rabbit could hardly walk.

Well, Brer Bear, he got to the hollow tree all right. He climbed up to where the hole was, and put in his paw. But it was a very deep hole and he could feel nothing.

'Get down into the hole, Brer Bear, get down into the hole!' squealed Brer Rabbit. So Brer Bear jumped right down into the hole, and pawed about for the honey.

But in that hole lived Cousin Wildcat, his wife, and his family – and when old Brer Bear jumped right down up top of the lot of them, there was a great disturbance!

My goodness! All those wildcats shot out their twenty claws, and clawed at Brer Bear. Cousin Wildcat and his wife buried their sharp teeth into his paws, and before Brer Bear knew what was happening he was in the middle of a fierce fight!

'Ooooph! Grumph! Ow-wow-wow!' growled Brer Bear.

'Yee-ow-yee-ow, yee-ow!' yelled all the wildcats together.

Brer Bear shot out of that hollow tree a whole lot quicker than he went in! My, how quickly he came out! Brer Rabbit had never seen a bear move so quickly!

'You said I'd find my honey there!' roared Brer Bear to Brer Rabbit.

'I didn't!' yelled back cheeky Brer Rabbit. 'I just said you'd get a fine surprise if you looked in that hollow tree. But if you want to find the thief, Brer Bear, just come and look at Brer Wolf here! He's got honey on his nose – and I guess he's been after yours!'

And with that Brer Rabbit turned and ran, and old Brer Wolf, he got such a slap on the nose from angry Brer Bear that he yowled like a hundred wildcats at once!

As for Brer Bear, he wouldn't go near a hollow tree for months, not even when he saw bees coming out of it and knew there was honey there. No – he was much too afraid of getting another fine surprise!

# Brer Rabbit Raises the Dust

Now one time it happened that Brer Fox and Brer Rabbit, Brer Wolf, Brer Bear and the rest were always up at Miss Meadows'. When Miss Meadows had chicken for dinner in would come Brer Fox and Brer Possum, and when she had fried greens in would come Brer Rabbit. If she had new honey it would be Brer Bear that would come popping his head round the door.

'I can't feed everyone,' said Miss Meadows to the girls. 'It's getting to be a real nuisance, having all the creatures pestering round. We shall have to do something to stop them.'

Well, Miss Meadows and the girls, they thought what they could do to stop the animals coming so much. And they decided that the one that could knock the most dust out of a rock, he should be the one that could still come to Miss Meadows' house. The rest must stay away.

So Miss Meadows told everyone that if they would come to her house the next Saturday evening, the whole crowd of them would go down the road to where there was a big flint rock. And each of them could take up the sledge-hammer and see how much dust he could raise out of the rock.

'I shall knock out a cloud of dust!' said Brer Fox.

'You won't be able to see for miles round when I get going with that sledge-hammer!' boasted old Brer Bear.

Well, they all talked mighty biggitty except Brer Rabbit. He crept off to a cool place and there he sat down and puzzled out how he could raise dust out of a rock. He had never seen dust got out of a rock, and he guessed he never would. But he meant to do it somehow.

By and by, whilst he was a-sitting there, up he jumped and cracked his heels together and sang out:

*'Brer Buzzard is clever, and so is Brer Fox,*
*But Brer Rabbit makes them all pull up their socks!'*

And with that he set out for Brer Raccoon's house and borrowed his slippers. When Saturday night came everyone was up at Miss Meadows' house. Miss Meadows and the girls were there; and Brer

Raccoon, Brer Fox, Brer Wolf, Brer Bear, Brer Possum and Brer Terrapin. They were all there.

Brer Rabbit shuffled up late. By the time he got to the house, everyone had gone down the road to the rock. Brer Rabbit was waiting for that – and as soon as he knew no one was at home, he crept round to the ash-bin, and filled Brer Raccoon's slippers full of ashes, and then he put them on his feet and marched off!

Brer Rabbit got to the rock after a while, and as soon as Miss Meadows and the girls saw him they began to giggle and laugh because of the great big old slippers he had on.

Brer Fox laughed too, and thought of something smart to say. 'I guess old Brer Rabbit's got chilblains,' he said. 'He's getting old.'

But Brer Rabbit winked his eye at everybody and said: 'You know, folks, I've been so used to riding on horseback, as these ladies know, that I'm getting sort of tender-footed when I walk.'

Then Brer Fox, he remembered how Brer Rabbit had ridden him one day, and he didn't say another word more. Everybody began to giggle, and it looked as if they would never begin hammering on the rock. Brer Rabbit picked up the sledge-hammer as if he meant to have the first try. But Brer Fox shoved Brer Rabbit out of the way and took the sledge-hammer himself.

Everyone was to have three hits at the rock with the hammer, and the one that raised the most dust out of it was the one who would be allowed to go to Miss Meadows' house as often as he liked. All the others were to keep away.

Well, old Brer Fox, he grabbed the hammer, he did, and he brought it down on the rock – *blim*! No dust came. Then he drew back the hammer and down he came again on the rock – *blam*! Still no dust came. Then he spat on his hands, gave a big swing and down came the hammer – *ker-blap*! And still not a speck of dust flew!

That was Brer Fox's turn finished. Then Brer Possum had a try, but he didn't raise any dust either. After that Brer Raccoon took the hammer, and he tried, but he couldn't make a speck of dust come at all. Then everyone else had a try except Brer Terrapin and Brer Rabbit, but nobody raised any dust at all.

'Now it's your turn, Brer Terrapin,' said Brer Fox.

But Brer Terrapin, he said no. He had watched the mighty blows the others had given for nothing, and he wasn't going to tire himself out too.

'I've got a crick in my neck,' he said. 'I don't

think I'll take my turn. Let Brer Rabbit have his. Looks like we'll none of us be able to raise any dust – so Miss Meadows and the girls won't have the pleasure of anybody's visit!'

Brer Rabbit winked to himself, and grabbed hold of the sledge-hammer. He lifted it up into the air, and as he brought it down on the rock he jumped up and came down at the same time as the hammer – *pow*! And, of course, the ashes flew up out of his slippers and shot all round.

Brer Fox, he started sneezing away because the ashes got up his nose, and Miss Meadows and the girls they began to cough and splutter.

Then Brer Rabbit lifted up the hammer again, jumped high into the air and landed on the rock with his feet and the hammer at the same time – *kerblam*!

'Stand further off, ladies!' he yelled. 'Here comes the dust!'

And sure enough the dust came, for the ashes flew again out of his slippers and everyone sneezed and choked and rubbed their eyes!

Then once more Brer Rabbit jumped up and cracked his heels together and brought the hammer down on the rock – *kerblam*! 'Here comes the dust!' he yelled. And sure enough, the dust came!

Well, after that there wasn't much doubt about who should be the one to visit Miss Meadows and

the girls, and Brer Rabbit went off arm-in-arm with two of the girls, grinning at all the others. They stood there, blowing their noses and glaring at Brer Rabbit; and Brer Fox, he took a sneezing fit and couldn't stop till the next morning.

Brer Raccoon got his slippers back from Brer Rabbit all right, and nobody ever knew what Brer Rabbit had borrowed them for. Cunning old Brer Rabbit! There wasn't much he didn't know!

# Brer Wolf Gets Too Warm

Now after Brer Fox got hit on the nose by Cousin Wildcat it was a mighty long time before he could ramble round and worry old Brer Rabbit. For one thing, Brer Fox had to wear a bandage on his nose, and this didn't make him very beautiful, so he kept at home. But after a while he went out and told every one how Brer Rabbit had tricked him into fighting the fierce wildcat.

Well, Brer Fox told his story so well that all the other creatures agreed that Brer Rabbit was getting worse and worse. Brer Wolf got up and said the time was come when no one should be friends with Brer Rabbit.

'We won't drink out of the same stream as he does, nor walk in the same road, nor live near him, nor go washing in the same washing-hole!' said Brer Wolf.

'We certainly won't!' shouted all the creatures.

'And if we can get hold of that wicked Brer Rabbit, we will. It's time his tricks came to an end.'

Well, Brer Rabbit couldn't help noticing all these things, for when he met some one in the big road they turned off into the wood before he came up to them – and if he shouted 'How-do!' to any one, they didn't answer. It seemed as if Brer Rabbit hadn't any friends at all.

Brer Rabbit guessed he had better make his house a bit stronger. So he worked on his windows and made them fine and strong and put a new bolt on his door. And then, bless us all, if he didn't take it into his head to build a steeple on the top of his house! Yes, a sure-enough steeple, so high that folks going along the big road stopped and said – 'Hey! What kind of town-hall is that?'

Well, folks stopped and asked, but Brer Rabbit hadn't got time to answer. He hammered and he nailed, he knocked and he lammed! Folks went by but he didn't say a word to them. Creatures stood round to watch him, but he didn't look at them. It was work, work, work, from sun-up to sun-down, till that steeple got done.

Then old Brer Rabbit drew a long breath, wiped his forehead, and said: 'Well, if any one can come and catch me now, I'd like to see it!'

With that he went and got something to eat, and he got a long piece of plough-line too, and he told his old woman to put a kettle of water on the fire, and to stand close by.

'And mind this, old woman,' he said, 'whatever I tell you not to do, you do it. Have you got that? What I tell you not to do, is just what you *must* do!'

Then old Brer Rabbit took his rocking-chair up into the big steeple, near the window there, and sat down and looked out.

It wasn't long before every one heard that Brer Rabbit had stopped work, and they came around to see what he meant to do next. But Brer Rabbit, he just sat up there, smoking his cigar, looking out and thinking. Brer Wolf stood up and looked at the steeple, Brer Fox he stood up to look at it too, and so did Brer Bear. All the other creatures did the same. They walked round and nudged one another, and stared and stared. All the time old Brer Rabbit sat up there, smoking his cigar, and looking out and thinking.

By and by old Brer Terrapin came along. Now old Brer Terrapin had been friendly with Brer Rabbit so long that he guessed at once there was soon going to be some fun. He laughed right down

under the roof of his house, Brer Terrapin did, and then he called to Brer Rabbit:

'Heyo, Brer Rabbit! What are you doing away up there?'

'I'm just a-resting myself, Brer Terrapin,' said Brer Rabbit. 'Do come up and see me.'

'Well, between you and me, Brer Rabbit,' said Brer Terrapin, 'I'd find it mighty difficult to climb so high. Suppose you come down here and see me! If you live so high up you might as well grow wings! I'm afraid I can't stretch up and shake hands with you today, Brer Rabbit!'

'Don't worry, Brer Terrapin!' said Brer Rabbit. 'I've a mighty good staircase, and I'll just let it down for you.'

With that Brer Rabbit let down his plough-line. 'Just catch hold of that, Brer Terrapin,' he said, 'and up you'll come, *linkum, sinkum, binkum, boo*!'

Old Brer Terrapin knew quite well that Brer Rabbit was friendly towards him, so he wasn't afraid. But all the same, before he let himself go up on that plough-line he took it into his mouth and pulled on it to make sure it wouldn't break. Then Brer Rabbit shouted out: 'Swing on, Brer Terrapin!' And Brer Terrapin, he took hold and swung on. Brer Rabbit heaved him up, and soon he was sitting up there in the steeple by the side of Brer Rabbit. But my! How funny he looked when Brer Rabbit was hauling him up, with his tail a-wiggling, and his legs all spread out, whirling round and round on the rope and looking mighty scared!

The other creatures saw Brer Terrapin go up safe and sound, and they saw food being passed round and lemonade, and they began to feel that they would like to see the inside of Brer Rabbit's steeple too. Brer Wolf shouted up:

'Heyo there, Brer Rabbit! You're looking mighty comfy up there! How are you?'

Brer Rabbit looked down to see who it was shouting, and when he saw it was Brer Wolf, he winked one eye to himself.

'I'm just so-so, Brer Wolf, but I can eat my food all right. Won't you come up and see me, Brer Wolf?'

'It's a mighty clumsy journey for me to make, Brer Rabbit,' said Brer Wolf, 'but I'll have a try!'

With that Brer Rabbit let down his plough-line, and Brer Wolf caught hold, grinning to himself at the thought of being alone with Brer Rabbit in his steeple. He could make short work of him there!

Brer Rabbit hauled on the rope and Brer Wolf went up. Brer Rabbit hauled and hauled, and when Brer Wolf was almost at the top he heard

Brer Rabbit yell out to his old woman:

'Stir round, old woman, and set the table, for here's old Brer Wolf coming to dinner! But before you set the table fetch the kettle to make the coffee.'

Brer Rabbit hauled and he hauled on the plough-line, and then Brer Wolf heard Brer Rabbit squall out: 'Look out there, with that kettle, old woman! Don't you spill any boiling water on Brer Wolf!'

Well, that was about all that Brer Wolf heard, because the next minute down came some boiling water on him, and Brer Wolf gave a loud squeal and let go the rope! He fell down and bounced on the ground like a rubber ball.

Old Brer Rabbit leaned out of his steeple and said he was sorry his old woman had been so careless. 'You heard me tell her not to scald you, Brer Wolf!' he shouted.

But no matter how much Brer Rabbit said he was sorry, it didn't make the hair come back on Brer Wolf's coat, where the water hit it.

And when the creatures had all gone, Brer Rabbit and Brer Terrapin had a mighty good laughing-spell. Brer Terrapin might have fallen out of the steeple with laughing, but Brer Rabbit caught hold of his tail just in time!

# Brer Bear's Tail

There came a time when Brer Rabbit and Brer Terrapin became very friendly, and went about together trying to trick all the other creatures. There wasn't a day passed but Brer Rabbit called on Brer Terrapin to ask him 'Howdy', or Brer Terrapin called on Brer Rabbit.

One time Brer Rabbit paid a call on Brer Terrapin, but when he got to the house Miss Terrapin told him that Brer Terrapin had gone to visit his uncle, Mr Mud Turtle. So Brer Rabbit set out after Brer Terrapin, and when he got to Mr Mud Turtle's house, he sat with them there and told tales till it was twelve o'clock, and dinner-time. They had crawfish for dinner, and enjoyed themselves very much.

'Now let's all go down to my mill-pond,' said Mr Mud Turtle. 'There's a great big slanting rock there, and it would be fun to slide down it from the top to the bottom – and go into the water – *splash!*'

'That's so,' said Brer Terrapin. 'It's a mighty slippery rock, that. We'll have some fun!'

So they went off to the mill-pond and Mr Mud Turtle took the first turn. He crawled right up to the very top of the big slanting rock, tucked his head and his legs into his shell, let himself go and down he went over the green, slippery rock into the water – *kersplash!*

Then old Brer Terrapin took a turn. He climbed right up to the very top, tucked in his head and his legs, and slid off. Down he sailed into the water – *kersplash!*

Brer Rabbit sat on a rock near by and watched them. He praised them up and begged them to do it again.

'You go on sliding, Mr Mud Turtle,' he said. 'It's a fine thing to see you coming down that rock – *swish – kersplash!* You do it again, Mr Mud Turtle.'

Well, Brer Terrapin and Mr Mud Turtle they went on slipping and sliding and splashing, and Brer Rabbit, he sat by and laughed and clapped for all he was worth. And whilst they were having fun, along came old Brer Bear. He had heard them shouting and laughing and he came to see what they were doing.

'Heyo, folks!' he called. 'What's all this? If my eye doesn't deceive me, here's Brer Rabbit, and Brer Terrapin, and Uncle Tommy Mud Turtle!'

'That's right,' said Brer Rabbit. 'And we're properly enjoying ourselves, Brer Bear!'

'Well, well, well,' said Brer Bear. 'So you're a-slipping and sliding, are you? And what's the matter with you, Brer Rabbit, that you're not joining in?'

Old Brer Rabbit winked hard at Brer Terrapin, and Brer Terrapin gave Mr Mud Turtle a nudge. Here was a chance for playing a trick on old Brer Bear, sure enough!

'My goodness, Brer Bear!' said Brer Rabbit. 'You can't expect a man to slip and slide the whole day, can you? I've had my fun, and now I'm a-sitting here on this rock to let my clothes dry. We're taking

127

turns, and now it's my turn to sit out.'

'Perhaps Brer Bear would like to join in with us,' said Brer Terrapin.

Brer Rabbit began to shout and laugh at this. 'Shoo!' he said. 'Brer Bear's feet are too big and his tail is too long for him to slide down that rock!'

Well, Brer Bear didn't like this. So he spoke up at once.

'My feet may be big and my tail may be long, but I'm not afraid to try slipping and sliding down that rock!'

With that the others made room for him, and old Brer Bear, he climbed up on to the top of the rock, he did, and squatted down. He curled his tail under him and pushed off.

First he went slowly, and he grinned as if he felt mighty good; then he went a bit more quickly, and he grinned as if he felt bad; then he went very quickly, and he grinned as if he felt mighty scared; and then he came to the green and very slippery part, and he shot down to the water like a streak of lightning! He didn't grin any more, poor Brer Bear – he gave a howl that could be heard a mile away, and he hit the water – kerplunkity-plunk – just like a chimney falling!

And when he came up out of the water, what

did Brer Rabbit and Brer Terrapin and Mr Mud Turtle see? They saw that Brer Bear's tail had gone – he hadn't got more than a little dob left, and a mighty strange creature he looked! When he had slid down that rock, his tail had broken off, smick, smack, smoove – and there he was, without a tail!

Brer Bear shot off up the road, howling, and Brer Rabbit shouted out: 'Heyo, Brer Bear! I can lend you some ointment if you want it!'

But Brer Bear didn't even look back! And since that day bears have had no tails to speak of – just little dobs without a wag in them!

# Brer Fox's New House

It happened once that old Brer Fox got himself a fine new house. My, wasn't he proud of it too! He called it Bushy Villa, after his tail, and he got Mrs Bear to make him some blue curtains.

Now Brer Rabbit had wanted the house for himself, and he was in a great rage when he found that Brer Fox had walked in and taken it.

He set off to the house and knocked at the door, blim-blam!

'Who's there?' called Brer Fox.

'Brer Rabbit!' said Brer Rabbit.

'Come right in, Brer Rabbit!' sang out Brer Fox. But Brer Rabbit knew better than that. He just stood out there on the doorstep and shouted.

'Brer Fox! I'd like this house myself. I've come to offer you a good price for it.'

'Then you can think again, Brer Rabbit,' said Brer Fox, pleased to find that he had got something that Brer Rabbit wanted. 'I'm in this house and here I stay! Good morning to you!'

Brer Rabbit was in a fine rage. He set off home, thinking with all his brains – and he had a good many. As he went along, head down and ears up, who should he meet but Brer Terrapin, the same old one-and-sixpence!

'How-do, Brer Rabbit,' yelled out Brer Terrapin. 'Look where you're going!'

'How-do, Brer Terrapin!' said Brer Rabbit, stopping and grinning at his old friend. 'Why, Brer Terrapin, you are just the person I want to see. I've got a plan.'

Brer Terrapin walked along by Brer Rabbit, listening to his plan of getting Brer Fox out of the house.

'You see, Brer Terrapin, if I can frighten him away, he'll sell it to me,' said Brer Rabbit. 'Now what about me sitting up on the roof and hanging things down the chimney when Brer Fox is sitting there reading his paper? Don't you think that would give him a shock?'

'I should just think it would!' said Brer Terrapin. 'And what about me sitting there with him that evening and pretending I can't see anything coming down the chimney? That would be funnier still.'

So it was arranged that Brer Terrapin should drop in at Brer Fox's house the next evening, and that Brer Rabbit should sit up on the roof with a fishing-line and drop things down on the end of the string.

'I'll tie my old tin teapot on first,' giggled Brer Rabbit. 'Then I'll tie an old boot. And then I'll tie Brer Fox's own hat. I'll slip into the hall and get it, once you are sitting talking to him, Brer Terrapin. That will give him a shock all right!'

Well, the next evening Brer Terrapin ambled along to Brer Fox's, and knocked at the door, blim, blam! Brer Fox was pleased to see him and asked him in.

'I've got a good fire, Brer Terrapin,' he said. 'Come along in and warm your toes.'

As soon as they were safely in the parlour, Brer Rabbit crept into the hall and took Brer Fox's best hat. Then, with his old tin teapot under his arm, and a dirty old boot and his fishing-line in his pocket, he climbed quietly up to the roof. He sat beside the chimney and cocked his ear up to hear what Brer Terrapin was saying to Brer Fox.

'You know, Brer Fox,' Brer Terrapin was saying, 'this house feels kind of funny to me. I guess I wouldn't like to live in it myself!'

'Pooh!' said Brer Fox; 'you don't know what you are talking about, Brer Terrapin. This house is just an ordinary, comfortable place, with nothing odd about it at all.'

'There'll be something odd mighty soon!' said Brer Rabbit to himself, and he tied the tin teapot on to the end of his line. He dropped the line carefully down the chimney, and the teapot rattled against the bricks all the way down, clitter-clatter, clitter-clatter!

Brer Fox heard the noise and looked surprised. Brer Terrapin sucked at his old pipe and pretended to hear nothing at all. Down the chimney came the tin teapot and swung over the flames, just near Brer Fox's nose.

Brer Fox stared as if he couldn't believe his eyes. A teapot! Down the chimney! Hanging there as if by magic! Now what could be the meaning of that?

He spoke to Brer Terrapin in a low voice. 'Brer Terrapin! What do you suppose that tin teapot is doing in my chimney?'

Brer Terrapin turned and stared at Brer Fox as if he were greatly surprised. 'Tin teapot!' he said. 'What are you talking about, Brer Fox? Tin teapot, indeed! You'll be telling me it's dancing a jig next!'

Brer Rabbit, up on the roof, grinned when he

heard that. He at once jerked his line and the teapot jumped up and down for all the world as if it were dancing a jig. Brer Fox clutched his whiskers and groaned.

'It *is* dancing a jig!' he said. 'Brer Terrapin, do just look! Surely you can see a tin teapot dancing about in the chimney?'

Brer Terrapin turned towards the chimney and shut his eyes. 'No,' he said truthfully, 'I can't see any teapot there, Brer Fox. Are you playing a joke on me?'

The teapot disappeared, and Brer Fox heaved a sigh. 'Well, it's gone now,' he said. 'What a peculiar thing! A teapot in my chimney, and you don't see it, Brer Terrapin!'

'Don't you tell that kind of story to an old chap like me,' said Brer Terrapin, settling himself more comfortably in his chair. 'It's no good you expecting me to believe tales of teapots, Brer Fox, nor of anything else either!'

Slither-slither-slosh! Down the chimney came the old boot, tied tightly to the end of the string! Brer Fox leapt up from his chair in fright and stared at it.

'There's a boot now!' he cried. 'Can't you see it, Brer Terrapin?'

'No, that I can't,' said Brer Terrapin, looking at the chimney with his eyes shut again. 'I can't see a thing. Do sit down, Brer Fox, and don't keep jumping and shouting. You make me quite uncomfortable.'

'Well, I'm not used to teapots and boots jigging in my chimney-place,' said Brer Fox fiercely. 'You said there was something funny about this house, Brer Terrapin, and so there is. I don't like it.'

'Sit down, Brer Fox, sit down,' begged Brer Terrapin, sucking at his pipe. 'How can a man enjoy his pipe when you keep shouting about teapots and boots I can't see? Don't be silly.'

The boot disappeared. Brer Fox stared at the chimney-place for a while and then sat down on the edge of his seat, watching the chimney. No sooner had he sat down than the boot slithered down again, and poor Brer Fox shot out of his seat, fell over Brer Terrapin, and sat down heavily on the floor.

Brer Terrapin wanted to laugh but he dared not. 'Goodness gracious, Brer Fox, what are you doing now?' he said. 'Something else come down the chimney? Well, well, well, I don't know what you wanted to buy this house for! I heard that Brer Rabbit wanted it, and I'm sure I don't know why

135

you didn't let him have it.'

'I don't know why either,' groaned Brer Fox. 'I'd sell it to him now, I know that!'

Brer Rabbit grinned in delight. He tied the fine new hat on to the end of his line, and let that down the chimney too. Swish-swish-swish it came, sweeping all the soot on to the brim as it went, so that Brer Fox's fine hat looked very sorry for itself when at last it appeared in the fireplace.

Brer Fox stared in horror. 'Look, Brer Terrapin, look!' he said. 'There's my new hat! Oh my, oh my, it's my new hat! I can't bear it! I can't bear it!'

Brer Rabbit leant right over the chimney and nearly burst himself with laughing. But he didn't know what was going to happen next! Brer Fox was so wild at seeing his beautiful new hat dancing in the chimney covered with soot that he suddenly made a dart at it and caught hold of it! He pulled hard – and Brer Rabbit overbalanced and fell right into the chimney himself! Down he went, slither-swish, and landed in the hearth. He gave a great yell when he sat on the flames, and shot off like a bullet out of a gun!

Even Brer Terrapin got a shock that time, and he ran out of the house faster than any terrapin ran before. Brer Fox was scared too, for he wondered what was coming down the chimney *this* time! But when he saw it was Brer Rabbit, he was after him like lightning.

And Brer Rabbit lost a few hairs out of his tail

that night, he was so nearly caught. He didn't get Brer Fox's house after all, and how he shook his fist when Brer Fox met him and called after him, 'Hie! Sweep! Would you like to come and do my chimneys for me?'

Aha, Brer Rabbit, you didn't win that time!

# Brer Fox and Mr Jack Sparrow

One day, after he had been tricked by old Brer Terrapin, Brer Rabbit was sitting down in the woods trying to puzzle out how he might get even with Brer Terrapin. He felt mighty lonesome and he felt mighty mad, Brer Rabbit did.

There he sat, all by himself, and thought and thought, and by and by he jumped up and shouted:

'Well, I'll eat my tail if I can't outdo old Brer Fox – and Brer Terrapin – and the whole lot of them! I'll show Miss Meadows and the girls that I'm the best of the lot! I'll make Brer Fox come a-crawling round me, oh yes, I will!'

There was a little Jack Sparrow up in the tree, and he heard what Brer Rabbit said.

'I'm going to tell Brer Fox what you said,' sang out the Jack Sparrow. 'I'm going to tell Brer Fox what you said! Chick-a-biddy-wind-a-blowing-acorns-falling! I'm going to tell Brer Fox!'

Well, when Brer Rabbit heard that Jack Sparrow was going to tell tales of him, he was mighty mad and mighty wild. He just didn't want Brer Fox or anybody to know what he had been planning. He sat and thought for a moment.

'The one that sees Brer Fox first will be the one he listens to!' said Brer Rabbit with a grin. 'I'm off home and on the way I'll call on Brer Fox and tell him just a few things!'

He hadn't gone far when who should come round the corner but old Brer Fox himself.

'Heyo, Brer Fox!' said Brer Rabbit. 'Now then, just you tell me what all this fuss is between you and me?'

'What fuss?' said Brer Fox in surprise.

'Oh, I hear tell you're going to send me packing, and grab my family and burn my house down!' said Brer Rabbit, looking mighty fierce.

Then Brer Fox got mad and shouted, 'Who's been telling you all those make-ups?'

'Oh, I'm not telling you that,' said Brer Rabbit.

'You just go right on and tell me who said that!' said Brer Fox. 'Go on, now, Brer Rabbit – you tell me! Someone's been making trouble between you and me, sure enough, and I didn't know a thing about it!'

'Well, I didn't mean to tell you,' said Brer Rabbit, 'but it was that meddling Jack Sparrow I heard saying all this. And, Brer Fox, when I heard him say you were going to send me off and grab my family, and burn my house down, I just lost my temper, so I did, and I got so mad that I stamped around and knocked down a few trees!'

Brer Fox gaped to hear this and got a bit further away from Brer Rabbit.

'I think I'll be going home,' he said. And off he went.

But bless us all, he hadn't gone far before Jack Sparrow flipped down on a bush by the side of the road and shouted out:

'Brer Fox! Oh, Brer Fox! Brer Fox!'

Brer Fox cantered on as if he didn't hear Jack Sparrow. Then Jack Sparrow began to yell again:

'Brer Fox! Oh, Brer Fox! Hold on, Brer Fox! I've got some news for you. Wait, Brer Fox! I'll tell you something that will astonish you!'

Of course, Jack Sparrow didn't know that Brer Fox had seen Brer Rabbit first, and he didn't guess all that Brer Rabbit had told Brer Fox about him. But Brer Fox knew all right, and he went on his way, pretending that he didn't either see or hear Jack Sparrow. He meant to play a little trick on him!

By and by Brer Fox lay down by the roadside, and kind of stretched himself, and yawned as if he meant to take a nap. The tattling Jack Sparrow flew along and kept on calling Brer Fox, but Brer Fox didn't answer a word. He was pretending he was deaf.

Then the little Jack Sparrow flew down to the ground and fluttered about in the grass. Brer Fox looked up and saw him there, and when the little tale-teller saw him looking, he shouted and shouted:

'I've got something to tell you, Brer Fox! I've got something to tell you!'

'Get on my tail, little Jack Sparrow,' said Brer Fox, 'because I'm deaf in one ear and I can't hear out of the other. Get on my tail!'

Then the little bird hopped up on Brer Fox's tail.

'Get on my back, little Jack Sparrow,' said Brer Fox, 'because I'm deaf in one ear and I can't hear out of the other!'

Then the little bird hopped on to his back.

'Hop on my head, little Jack Sparrow,' said Brer Fox, 'because I'm deaf in both ears.'

Up hopped the little bird.

'Hop on my tooth, little Jack Sparrow,' said Brer Fox, 'because I'm deaf in one ear and I can't hear out of the other.'

The little taming bird hopped on to Brer Fox's tooth – and then – and then – Brer Fox opened his mouth wide – and when he shut it again the tattling Jack Sparrow was gone!

And when Brer Rabbit came along there the next day and found a few little feathers, he shook his wicked head and said: 'All tale-tellers come to a bad end! I could have told Jack Sparrow that – only he didn't ask me!'

# Brer Rabbit and the Butter

It happened once that the creatures made a lot of very fine butter, and they agreed to put it into a cool shed, and share it between them.

But Brer Rabbit wasn't to have any at all, because he was such a rascal. Brer Fox winked all round and said, 'That will teach old Brer Rabbit to stop tricking us! When he doesn't get his butter, he'll be sorry!'

Now Brer Rabbit was as angry as a dozen wildcats when he heard that he wasn't to share in the butter. He sat in his house and he scratched first one ear and then the other, trying to think of some way he could get that butter.

Well, he guessed if he went along that way at night he'd get that butter all right! So each night Brer Rabbit slid between the trees and came to the shed where the butter was kept. He opened the door, went to the butter-pail and scooped out a nice pat of butter. Then off he went as quietly as he had come.

Now when the creatures found their butter going every night, they knew there was a thief somewhere. And they guessed it was their old friend, Brer Rabbit!

'We'll set a trap for him!' said Brer Fox, grinning. 'That's what we'll do. We'll spread the shed-floor with black soot, and old Brer Rabbit won't see it in the dark! It will get on to his shoes, and in the morning we'll see a sooty track leading back to his house – then we'll all know who the thief is!'

Well, every one thought that was a fine idea, and Brer Wolf, he swept his chimney, put the soot into a sack and took it along to the butter-shed. He spread the floor with the soot and went away.

Now that night along came Brer Rabbit as usual for his pat of butter. It was dark and he couldn't see the soot – but he could smell it all right! Oh yes, Brer Rabbit knew the smell of fresh soot, and he stood there in the shed and sniffed hard.

'Soot on the floor!' said Brer Rabbit, and he grinned to himself. 'Put there to catch me! Ha, they think they'll see my sooty footsteps leading to my house – and they'll come and say I steal the butter. No, no, Brer Fox, you can't trick me so easily as that!'

Brer Rabbit took his pat of butter and skipped out on his sooty feet. He walked as heavily as he could to a tree. Then he took off his sooty shoes and pressed them hard against the tree-trunk so that it looked for all the world as if some one had been walking up there!

Then Brer Rabbit skipped home in his bare feet, carrying the shoes, as happy as a jay-bird!

The next morning the creatures were excited to see the sooty footmarks. They all followed them till they came to the tree, and they were *most* astonished to see the footprints going up the trunk!

'Strange!' said Brer Fox, looking hard at them.

'The thief must live up in this tree,' said Brer Wolf, peering up. 'But only Cousin Wildcat lives in trees.'

'Well, one of us must go up and see who lives here,' said Brer Bear. 'Brer Turkey-Buzzard, you fly up and see what you can find.'

So Brer Turkey-Buzzard flew up, but though he spent hours looking into every hole and along every branch, he simply could *not* find the thief!

Well, the next night Brer Rabbit skipped along for his butter again, and walked hard on the soot. When he left the shed he walked along to the bank of the river. Then he took off his shoes and ran along home in his bare feet once more.

The next day all the animals found the sooty footprints once again, and followed them in glee. This time they would surely find the thief!

'The footmarks stop just here!' said Brer Fox in astonishment, and he pointed to the bank of the river. 'Maybe Brer Terrapin, or his Uncle Mud-Turtle, is the thief!'

'Indeed we're not!' said Brer Terrapin, who had come along with the others. 'Last night we were at a party at Mr Benjamin Ram's, as he'll tell you. We didn't go near the butter-shed!'

'Well, it's a strange thing,' said Brer Wolf,

puzzled. 'First those footsteps lead us to a tree – and now they lead us to a river!'

The next night Brer Rabbit fetched his butter and danced off in his sooty shoes. He skipped along till he came to the middle of a field, then he took off his shoes and ran home.

And when the creatures found the footmarks stopping in the middle of the field, they looked at one another in amazement.

'Well, the thief must have wings!' said Brer Fox. 'He couldn't just disappear like that! I wonder if it's Brer Turkey-Buzzard.'

'No, it isn't,' said Brer Turkey-Buzzard indignantly. 'I was away at my uncle's all last night, as he will tell you.'

Now just then along came old Brer Rabbit, and he saw all the animals looking puzzled and talking to one another. So he skipped up and said how-do to them.

'What's puzzling you?' he asked. 'You tell me, and I'll help you!'

So they told him about the missing butter, and how they couldn't make out who the thief was because one time he walked up a tree, and another time he went into the river, and the third time he just disappeared in the middle of a field!

'You let *me* keep your butter for you in *my* shed and it'll be all right!' said Brer Rabbit. 'I guess no thief will dare to come around tricking me! You let me take care of the butter!'

'Well, we'll pay you a pat of butter each day if you'll keep the thief away,' said Brer Fox. 'But if you don't, you won't get any butter, Brer Rabbit!'

'You trust me to keep the thief away!' grinned old Brer Rabbit. 'I won't need any soot to catch him either! The thief's afraid of me! I'm fierce, I am, and no one will take your butter!'

So the butter was moved to Brer Rabbit's shed, and the creatures gave him a large piece of it every day for keeping it safe. No thief came near it, of course, so the creatures were very pleased.

'Oh, Brer Rabbit's a mighty fierce fellow!' they said to each other. 'No thief dares to get our butter now!'

And they wondered why old Brer Rabbit grinned when he heard them. He's a rascal, isn't he?

# Brer Rabbit Gets Brer Bear

One time when Brer Rabbit was going loping home from a party up at Miss Meadows', who should he come across but old Brer Bear! Of course, after the wicked way that Brer Rabbit had tricked Brer Bear in Brer Fox's pea-patch, there weren't very good feelings between the two of them.

But Brer Rabbit, he was as cheeky as ever, and he shouted out: 'Heyo, Brer Bear! How are you getting along? I haven't seen you for a week of Sundays! How is everybody down at your house?'

Well, Brer Bear, he meant to grab Brer Rabbit this time, so he answered mighty politely.

'Fine, thank you, Brer Rabbit, fine. And how's yourself?'

'Oh, I've got a thorn in my paw,' said Brer Rabbit, 'but my old woman will take that out for me as soon as I get home.'

'Let me see it,' said Brer Bear – and as soon

as Brer Rabbit stretched out his paw, Brer Bear grabbed it and held on to it as if he couldn't let go.

'You come along home with me and I'll get the thorn out for you, Brer Rabbit,' said Brer Bear, talking in a friendly voice, but snapping his jaws all the same.

Brer Rabbit didn't like the look of things at all. But he didn't give his feelings away, he just went on walking beside old Brer Bear, who was holding his paw hard enough to squash it to bits.

'I've been busy this last month, Brer Bear,' said Brer Rabbit, talking just as friendly as Brer Bear. 'I've been cleaning up a big bit of new ground I've got.'

'Well, you'll like a bit of a rest now, I expect,' said Brer Bear, with a nasty sort of grin.

'And do you know what I found in my new ground, Brer Bear?' said Brer Rabbit. 'I came across one of these old, old bee-trees. It was a tree that was hollow from the bottom to the top, and the bees had found it and put their nest there, and the honey was just oozing out of it!'

'Is that so?' said Brer Bear, in a disbelieving sort of manner.

'That surely is so,' said Brer Rabbit, 'and if you don't mind just coming along with me, Brer Bear, you'll get enough honey to last you and your family till the middle of next month!'

'Well, I believe I'll go along,' said Brer Bear, who thought maybe there might be a speck of truth in Brer Rabbit's tale – and if there wasn't, well, Brer Rabbit would be sorry!

And with that they set out for Brer Rabbit's new patch of ground, which wasn't very far. They got there after a while, and old Brer Bear, he put his nose up into the air and said he could smell the honey all right!

They got to a big hollow tree, and sure enough, there were bees coming in and out, humming mighty loud.

'Yes, that honey smells good,' said Brer Bear, and his mouth began to water.

Brer Rabbit bent his head down to a hole at the bottom of the tree.

'I can see the honeycomb,' he said. 'My, this is a mighty fine bee-tree, Brer Bear.'

'I can hear the bees a-zooming,' said Brer Bear, who was longing to get at the honey and yet didn't want to let go Brer Rabbit's paw.

'Well, what about it?' said Brer Rabbit. 'Will you do the climbing, Brer Bear, and I'll do the rushing round? You climb up to the hole at the top there, and I'll take this pine-pole and push the honey up where you can get it.'

Well, that sounded pretty good to old Brer Bear, so he climbed up the tree and jammed his head in at the hole. Sure enough Brer Rabbit grabbed the pine-pole and put it in the little hole at the bottom – but he didn't push the honeycomb up to Brer Bear! No, he just stirred up those bees till they were mad enough to sting for a year! And they all swarmed up the tree to get out of the hole there.

But old Brer Bear's head was jammed in there, waiting for the honey, and those bees, they couldn't get out at all. So they just swarmed on to Brer Bear's head and stung him hard.

And before he could get his head out it was all

swollen up, and he couldn't take it out at all! So there he swung, growling and grunting, his head bigger than a dinner-pot, whilst Brer Rabbit danced round and sang:

*'Trees stand high and honey's mighty good,*
*Watch those bees a-stinging in the wood!'*

Then Brer Bear growled more than ever and tried to jerk out his head, but it wasn't a bit of good. He had to wait till the swelling went down before he could take his head away – and by that time Brer Rabbit was gone!

# Brer Rabbit and the Alligator

One time Brer Rabbit went down to the river to catch some fish for breakfast. He saw something long and brown lying in the mud, and he thought it was a big log. He was pleased, and he ran up to it.

'Here's a fine big log to fish from. I'll stand on it to catch the fish.'

So Brer Rabbit jumped on to the log. He got ready his line. He fixed his hook. As he was doing this the log moved.

Brer Rabbit was mighty scared and he squealed out, 'Oh, my goodness!' He looked down – and his eyes nearly dropped out of his head when he saw that what he had thought was a log was really a big alligator.

Mr Alligator swam away with Brer Rabbit on his back. He flicked his tail round and knocked Brer Rabbit between his two front paws. He grinned

very wide indeed, and sniffed at Brer Rabbit with
his nose.

'I'll take you to my home,' said Mr Alligator. 'I've
got seven eggs there, and when they hatch into
baby alligators they shall have you for their dinner.'

Mr Alligator swam towards the hole in the
bank where he lived. He crawled into the hole and
carried Brer Rabbit in with him. Brer Rabbit was
mighty scared.

'I've a good mind to eat you myself,' said Mr
Alligator, looking at Brer Rabbit, who was plump
and not at all bony. 'Yes, so I have, Brer Rabbit.'

'Please, Mr Alligator, leave me here to look after
your eggs for you,' said Brer Rabbit. 'I'm a good
nurse, I am. I can look after your eggs whilst you
go a-swimming down the river, and you'll know
they're safe. You let me nurse your eggs.'

Mr Alligator flicked his big tail and said, 'I'll try
you for one day. If you mind my eggs well, I'll not
eat you.'

Then the old alligator went away and left Brer Rabbit to mind his eggs. He had got to get something for his breakfast. Brer Rabbit sat down beside the eggs. He couldn't get out of the hole, and he was so scared that he shivered like a jelly.

Brer Rabbit waited and waited for Mr Alligator to come back. By and by he got hungry. He waited and he waited. He minded the eggs and turned them over with his paw. Soon he felt so hungry that he could hardly hold up his head. He sucked his paw. He waited and he waited. The alligator didn't come. He had gone a long way down the river. Brer Rabbit sucked his other paw and waited and waited. Still the alligator didn't come.

Then Brer Rabbit stood up. 'Huh!' said he, 'I'm not going to starve myself when there's plenty of food under my nose.'

He snatched up one of the seven alligator eggs, made a hole in it, and sucked it. It was a big egg and it made a good meal. Brer Rabbit threw the egg-shell right to the back of the hole. He rubbed his middle and grinned.

'Hoo! I feel better now. I don't know what I'm going to tell the old alligator when he comes back, but I don't care. I feel good and I'm not going to worry about any old alligator. I'll think of something when he comes.'

Brer Rabbit lay down. He curled himself up on the eggs. He shut his eyes and slept soundly. By and by, when night was almost come, Mr Alligator came back. He shouted loudly to Brer Rabbit:

'Hey, Brer Rabbit! How can you mind my eggs when you've gone to sleep?'

Brer Rabbit sat up at once. 'My eyes have gone to sleep, but my ears are wide awake,' he said.

Mr Alligator flicked his tail and said, 'Where are my eggs?'

Brer Rabbit felt a bit scared. Suppose Mr Alligator counted his eggs?

'They're all here, Mr Alligator,' he said. 'Wait – let me count them – one, two, three, four, five, six, seven. Yes, they're all here, Mr Alligator.'

Mr Alligator was pleased. He opened his mouth wide and grinned. 'You've minded them well, Brer Rabbit,' he said. 'Bring each one out for me to see. I want to count them.'

Brer Rabbit felt mighty scared at this. He carried one egg out to Mr Alligator, who sniffed it. Brer Rabbit took it back and brought out the second. Then he took that back and brought out the third – then the fourth – then the fifth – and then the sixth, which was the last one.

After that Brer Rabbit stopped, and didn't know what to do. Mr Alligator yelled out, 'Fetch me the seventh one.'

Well, Brer Rabbit, he just picked up the first one again and hurried out with that. Mr Alligator, he didn't know it was the same egg he had seen the first time, and he just sniffed at it and told Brer Rabbit to take it back.

'You've minded them well,' he said to Brer Rabbit. 'You can mind them again tomorrow.'

So the next day Mr Alligator went off again and left Brer Rabbit minding his eggs. And Brer Rabbit felt so mighty hungry that he ate another one. That night when Mr Alligator came home, Brer Rabbit took him out the five eggs and then took the first two out again, to make seven – and Mr Alligator, he didn't know anything was wrong at all.

Well, every day Brer Rabbit ate an egg belonging to Mr Alligator, and each night he carried the same eggs out so that Mr Alligator would think there were seven. And at last there was only one egg left.

'I'll have to carry it out seven times,' grinned Brer Rabbit to himself, when he heard Mr Alligator coming home.

'Where are my eggs, Brer Rabbit?' called Mr Alligator.

'They're all here, Mr Alligator,' Brer Rabbit shouted out from the hole in the bank.

'I met Brer Fox today, Brer Rabbit,' said Mr Alligator, 'and he told me you are mighty fond of eggs. So this time I think I'll mark each egg as you bring it, and then I'll know for certain you haven't been eating *my* eggs, Brer Rabbit. Ha, you may be a clever man, Brer Rabbit, but Mr Alligator is just as smart as you. And I tell you this, if so much as one of my eggs is missing I'll have you for my supper tonight, sure as I've got a tail.'

Brer Rabbit shook in his shoes. He felt more scared than he had ever been in his life. But he put on a bold face and shouted back to Mr Alligator:

'That's right, Mr Alligator! You mark your eggs and then you'll know. And don't you listen to any tales from Brer Fox – he's a scamp and I'd just like to tell him so.'

'Bring out the first egg and let me mark it,' shouted Mr Alligator.

So Brer Rabbit brought out the first and only egg. Mr Alligator rubbed some mud on it to mark it. He gave it back to Brer Rabbit. 'Now bring out the next,' he said.

Brer Rabbit ran back to the hole. He rubbed off the mud on the egg, made it quite clean, and took it out again to Mr Alligator. 'Number two egg,' he said.

Mr Alligator took it and made a mark on it with mud again. He didn't know it was the same egg, because Brer Rabbit had rubbed it clean. 'Bring out the third egg,' he said.

So Brer Rabbit ran back again, rubbed the egg clean, and took it out for the third time to Mr Alligator. 'Number three egg,' he said.

Well, that rascal of a Brer Rabbit brought the same old egg out seven times to Mr Alligator, and each time Mr Alligator marked it with mud and Brer Rabbit rubbed it off in the hole. And when Mr Alligator had marked the egg seven times, and thought it was the seventh egg, he was very pleased.

'Yes, Brer Rabbit, you've minded them well,' he said. 'There are my seven eggs all perfect. I won't eat you for supper.'

'Mr Alligator,' said Brer Rabbit, popping his head out of the hole, 'I can hear Brer Fox a-barking away in the woods yonder. Will you give me leave to go and tell him what I think of him? He's no business to be telling you stories about me, when I'm doing my duty and minding your eggs so well.'

'Yes, you go and tell him, Brer Rabbit,' said Mr

Alligator. 'You go and tell him. But mind you're back before daybreak to nurse my eggs again. I'll go in and look after them whilst you're gone.'

Brer Rabbit thanked Mr Alligator kindly and hopped out of the hole. He jumped on to Mr Alligator's back and ran lightly across it to the bank. He stood there and watched Mr Alligator go in to his hole to mind his eggs. And then he didn't wait any more, because he heard a loud bellow and a great scrambling round in the hole, and knew Mr Alligator had found he had only one egg left.

My, you couldn't see Brer Rabbit for dust then. He tore off at top speed, and he didn't go down to the river again till he heard that Mr Alligator had gone away for good. He didn't think Mr Alligator would ask him to mind his eggs for him again.

# Brer Rabbit and Brer Bear

One summer Brer Fox said to himself that he'd better hurry up and plant his pea-patch. So he got his spade, dug up his ground and planted out his peas.

Old Brer Rabbit came by when he was planting them, and when he thought of juicy ripe peas he winked his eye at his children and sang:

*'Ti-yi! Tungalees!*
*I'll eat his peas, I'll pick his peas!*
*I'll get each pod and give it a squeeze,*
*Ti-yi! What juicy peas!'*

Sure enough when the peas began to ripen, Brer Fox found that someone had been down in the pea-patch, eating his peas, and he felt mighty mad. He guessed he knew who the someone was, but old Brer Rabbit was so smart that Brer Fox

163

really didn't know how to catch him.

By and by, one day Brer Fox took a walk all round his pea-patch and it wasn't long before he found a hole in the fence that had been rubbed quite smooth with somebody passing in and out.

'Look at that!' said Brer Fox to himself. 'Right there is where the thief comes in and out. This is where I'll set a trap!'

He saw a young hickory-tree growing near by. He took a piece of string and tied one end to the top of the tree. He pulled the string and the tree bent half over. Then Brer Fox made a loop-knot at the other end of the string and fixed it neatly round the hole in the fence, keeping it in place with a stick. As soon as anyone crept in through the hole, the string would tighten round him, and the hickory tree would jerk up straight, taking the robber with it, swinging on the end of the string. My, that would be a fine scare for old Brer Rabbit, next time he came lolloping in through the hole!

Next morning, when old Brer Rabbit came slipping along and crept through the hole, the loop-knot caught him tightly, the hickory flew up straight, and there was Brer Rabbit swinging between the earth and the sky!

There he swung, afraid of falling, and yet afraid

of not falling – for he didn't know what old Brer Fox would say when he came along and found him there!

While he was making up a tale to tell to Brer Fox when he came, he heard a lumbering noise down the road, and presently along came Brer Bear. Brer Rabbit hailed him.

'Heyo, Brer Bear!'

Brer Bear looked about in surprise, and by and

by he saw Brer Rabbit swinging from the tree.

'Heyo, Brer Rabbit!' he shouted. 'How are you this morning?'

'Much obliged to you, I'm just middling, Brer Bear,' said Brer Rabbit.

'What are you doing up there?' asked Brer Bear in surprise.

'Huh, I'm making a shilling a minute up here,' said Brer Rabbit.

'How's that?' asked Brer Bear, still more surprised.

'I'm up here frightening the crows out of Brer Fox's pea-patch,' said Brer Rabbit. 'Brer Fox pays me well for it.'

'That's a fine job,' said Brer Bear.

'Well, you come and have a turn at it,' said Brer Rabbit, in a generous sort of voice. 'You've a large family of children to work for, Brer Bear, and you'd make a fine scarecrow. I don't mind letting you have my job for a little while, just to do you a kindness.'

'I'll take it, then,' said Brer Bear, pleased. 'How do I get up there, Brer Rabbit?'

'Bend down the tree,' said Brer Rabbit. 'And undo the string. It's quite easy.'

Well, it wasn't long before Brer Rabbit was safely

on the ground and old Brer Bear was swinging high up in Brer Rabbit's place. Then Brer Rabbit, he set out for Brer Fox's house, shouting:

'Brer Fox! Oh, Brer Fox! Come out here, Brer Fox, and I'll show you the man who's been stealing your peas!'

Brer Fox grabbed his walking-stick, and went running down to his pea-patch. When he got there, sure enough there was old Brer Bear swinging in the trap!

'Oh, yes! You're caught!' said Brer Fox, and before Brer Bear could explain, Brer Rabbit jumped up and down shouting:

'Yes, there's the robber, Brer Fox! Whip him well, and don't you listen to any cheek from him!'

So, every time poor Brer Bear tried to explain how he came to be there, Brer Fox hit him a whack with his walking-stick, and made him squeal so that he couldn't say a word.

Whilst all this was going on, Brer Rabbit slipped off and got deep down into a mud-hole, for he knew Brer Bear would be after him as soon as he was free. He just left his big eyes sticking out of the mud-hole, for all the world like a frog peeping out.

By and by old Brer Bear came galloping down the road, looking everywhere for Brer Rabbit.

When he got to the mud- hole he saw Brer Rabbit's eyes sticking out.

'Howdy, Brer Frog!' he said. 'Have you seen Brer Rabbit anywhere?'

'He's just gone by,' said Brer Rabbit, and Old Man Bear shot off down the road like a runaway horse, trying to catch up with Brer Rabbit.

And soon Brer Rabbit came out of the mud-hole, dried himself in the sun, brushed off the mud and went ambling home, whistling a little tune he knew:

*'Ti-yi! Tungalees!*
*I ate those peas, I picked those peas!*
*I got each pod and gave it a squeeze,*
*Ti-yi! What juicy peas!'*

Oh, wicked Brer Rabbit!

# Brer Rabbit Catches Mice

Now once it happened that Brer Fox stored away some fine carrots and juicy turnips in his little old shed. He was mighty pleased with them, for he had grown them himself, and meant to have them in his soup that winter.

And of course old Brer Rabbit smelt them out, and made up his mind to share those carrots and turnips – though he didn't mean to ask Brer Fox's permission!

So, each night, he crept to the door of the shed and opened it quietly. In he went, and nibbled a carrot here, and a turnip there.

Well, Brer Fox was angry to find his stores nibbled like that. He stared round his shed each morning and wondered who the thief was. He saw Brer Rabbit passing by in the distance and he called to him.

THE BRER RABBIT STORY COLLECTION

'Heyo, Brer Rabbit! Do you know anything about nibbled carrots?'

'Nibbled carrots!' said wicked Brer Rabbit, pretending to be surprised. 'You don't mean to say you've got carrots in that shed that have been nibbled, Brer Fox?'

'That's just what I do mean to say,' said Brer Fox, looking at Brer Rabbit in a very straight way.

'It must be that you've got mice there,' said Brer Rabbit. 'I'd put a few mouse-traps down, Brer Fox, that's what I'd do!'

And with that old Brer Rabbit went off whistling, telling himself he must remember to look out for a mouse-trap when he went a-nibbling that night!

But Brer Fox didn't put any traps down. No, he kept awake himself, and when he heard the door of his shed creaking he jumped out of his chair and crept out into the garden. He went to his shed, and flashed his lantern inside.

Brer Rabbit had heard him coming – but he couldn't get out of the door in time. So what did he do but turn his back to the wall of the shed, and stick his bobtail out through a hole in the wood. And there he was a-sitting when Brer Fox popped his head in at the door!

'Oh, Brer Rabbit! So I've just caught you, have I!' said Brer Fox.

'What do you mean, caught me?' asked Brer Rabbit, in a most astonished voice. 'Here I've come to spend the whole night in your shed, to catch the mice that nibble your carrots – and you say you've caught me! That's not a nice way to repay a good deed, Brer Fox, and I'm really surprised at you.'

Brer Fox looked astonished. 'How are you catching mice for me?' he said.

'Why,' said Brer Rabbit, 'can't you see what I'm doing? I'm sitting here patiently with my tail out of a mouse-hole – and I'm waiting for a mouse to come along and nibble it – and then I'll pull in my tail like a shot and drag the mouse in at the hole for you!'

'I've never heard of that way of catching mice before,' said Brer Fox, looking even more astonished. 'Have you caught any yet?'

'Sh!' said Brer Rabbit. 'I think I can feel one a-nibbling!'

Brer Fox shushed. But after a time Brer Rabbit sighed and shook his head.

'No,' he said. 'That one ran away. It's a pity my

THE BRER RABBIT STORY COLLECTION

tail is so short, Brer Fox. Now, if I had a fine long one like yours, I'd catch twenty mice a night!'

'Would you really?' said Brer Fox, most interested. 'Well, what about me poking my tail out through a hole and seeing if I can catch some?'

'Oh, I wouldn't bother to do that,' said Brer Rabbit. 'You wouldn't have the patience to sit still long enough for a mouse to come.'

'Indeed I would,' said Brer Fox. 'I'm as patient as you are, any day.'

Well, in the end Brer Fox found a good big mouse-hole and stuck his tail out of it so that it twitched on the ground outside the shed. And there he sat, whilst Brer Rabbit sat near him, his bobtail out too.

'Ha! I can feel one a-nibbling!' said Brer Rabbit suddenly. 'Catch hold of my tail tightly, Mouse! Catch hold of it, I say!'

Brer Rabbit suddenly jerked his tail in and turned round to look at it as if he expected to see a mouse hanging on to the hairs. But there was nothing there, of course.

'Dear, dear!' said Brer Rabbit, sounding most disappointed. 'What a pity! I made sure there was one that time. Keep still, Brer Fox, and see if he comes to your tail. And if you feel him a-nibbling, just call out, "Catch hold of my tail, there, catch hold of my tail"'

Now, just about daybreak, as Brer Rabbit very well knew, Brer Bear came along that way. And that was what Brer Rabbit was planning for. He listened and he listened for Brer Bear's footsteps, and pretty soon he heard them – clump-clump-clump.

He began to talk to Brer Fox so that he wouldn't hear them. 'I can feel a mouse a-nibbling and a-gnawing!' he said. 'Catch hold of my tail, there, catch hold of my tail! You shout too, Brer Fox, in case there's one at your tail too.'

So Brer Fox shouted out, 'Catch hold of my tail, there, catch hold of my tail!'

And just at that moment Brer Bear passed the shed, and saw Brer Fox's tail hanging out of the hole, and he heard him shouting, 'Catch hold of my tail, there!'

'Funny thing!' said Brer Bear, sniffing at Brer Fox's tail, and touching it with his paw. 'It looks like Brer Fox's tail. But what is it doing here? And why should I catch hold of it?'

When Brer Fox felt Brer Bear sniffing at his tail, he got very excited, because he really thought it was a mouse at last.

'Catch hold of my tail, there!' he shouted. 'Catch hold of my tail!'

Brer Bear caught hold of his tail and held it tight. Brer Fox suddenly looked most astonished. This couldn't be a mouse!

'Something's got my tail!' he said to Brer Rabbit in a scared voice. Brer Rabbit ran to the door when he heard that welcome news, for he knew that Brer Fox couldn't get away to go after him then. He shot out of the door.

'I'll go and see what it is that's got your tail!' he shouted – and he took a look at Brer Bear and winked.

'Hold on for a bit, Brer Bear!' he said. 'Hold on for a bit!' And with that he scampered away through the wood, lippitty-clippitty, and he didn't stop to laugh till he was safe at home with his door locked!

As for Brer Fox, there he had to stay in the shed till Brer Bear let go his tail. And what a quarrel there was then, to be sure, with Brer Fox calling Brer Bear names, and Brer Bear shouting at Brer Fox. They don't really know to this day that old Brer Rabbit played a mighty clever trick on them!

# Brer Terrapin Shows His Strength

One night Miss Meadows and the girls gave a candy-party, and so many people came that they had to put the sugar for the candy into the big wash-pot, and make a big fire to boil it in the yard.

Brer Bear helped Miss Meadows to bring in the wood, Brer Fox made up the fire, Brer Wolf kept the dogs off, Brer Rabbit greased the bottom of the plates to keep the candy from sticking, and Brer Terrapin, he climbed up on a chair and said he'd see that the candy didn't boil over.

All the animals were there, and they were being mighty polite to one another, too, because Miss Meadows had put her foot down and said that if they came to her place they were to be friends with one another, or she'd know the reason why!

Well then, whilst they were all sitting out there in the yard, with the candy boiling and

176

blubbering, they began to talk mighty biggitty.

'I'm the swiftest runner here!' said Brer Rabbit, greasing the plates. Brer Terrapin said nothing. He just rocked to and fro in his chair and watched the candy boiling.

'I'm the smartest here!' said Brer Fox, at once, throwing some wood on the fire. Brer Terrapin said nothing. He just went on rocking away.

'I'm the savagest!' said Brer Wolf, snarling at the dogs sniffing around. Brer Terrapin rocked and rocked in his chair.

'I'm the strongest!' said Brer Bear, carrying a great log up to the fire. Brer Terrapin rocked himself and rocked, and by and by he winked at the candy and said:

'Well, well, it looks as if an old shellyback like me isn't anyone at all in this crowd, yet here I am, and I'm the same man that showed Brer Rabbit he wasn't the swiftest runner – didn't I beat him in a race? And I'm the same man that can show Brer Bear he isn't the strongest!'

All the others stared at Brer Terrapin and laughed and shouted at him, for they knew that Brer Bear had the strength of ten. Miss Meadows came up just then, to stir the candy, and she asked them what they were laughing at.

'Old Man Terrapin says he's stronger than Brer Bear,' they told her.

'How are you going to show you are stronger than Brer Bear?' asked Miss Meadows.

'Give me a good strong rope,' said Brer Terrapin, 'and let me get into a puddle of water, and then let Brer Bear see if he can pull me out! I tell you, he won't be able to budge me an inch!'

Then they all laughed again, and Brer Bear said: 'We haven't got a rope.'

'No,' said Brer Terrapin, 'and you haven't got the strength either, Brer Bear!' And then he rocked himself in his chair and watched the candy bubbling.

After a while Miss Meadows said she would lend them some rope, and whilst the candy was cooling on the plates, they could all go to the pond and see if Brer Terrapin was as strong as he made out. Brer Terrapin wasn't very big, and it sounded mighty funny to hear him boasting that he could out-pull Brer Bear.

Well, Miss Meadows gave them the rope and they all set out for the pond. When Brer Terrapin found the place he wanted, he took one end of the rope and gave the other end to Brer Bear.

'Now then, ladies and gentlemen,' said Brer

Terrapin, 'you all go with Brer Bear up to those trees yonder and I'll stay here, and when you hear me shout, then is the time for Brer Bear to pull! You take care of your end of the rope,' he said, 'and I'll take care of mine!'

Then they all went up to the trees and left Brer Terrapin by the pond. When they were a good distance away Brer Terrapin dived down into the water and tied his end of the rope hard and fast to an old tree-stump down at the bottom of the pond. Then he swam up to the surface and gave a yell.

'Pull away, Brer Bear!' he shouted. 'Pull away! I'm a-waiting to be pulled out of the water, I am! Pull away!'

Brer Bear wrapped the rope round his paw, winked at everybody and gave a big jerk at the rope. But Brer Terrapin didn't budge out of the water. He just sat there. Then Brer Bear put both paws to the rope and gave a bigger pull, but all the same, Brer Terrapin, didn't budge!

Then Brer Bear turned himself round and put the rope over his shoulders, and tried to walk off with Brer Terrapin but Brer Terrapin, he didn't move an inch out of the pond.

Then Brer Wolf took hold of the rope too and helped Brer Bear to pull, but it didn't make any difference at all. Brer Terrapin just sat in the pond and nobody could pull him out! Then everyone took hold of the rope and began to pull at the same time, panting and puffing like steam-engines going up a hill!

'Heyo there!' yelled Brer Terrapin. 'Pull a bit harder, can't you? I don't think you're trying!'

Well, when they heard that, they dropped the rope and looked at one another in surprise. They just couldn't understand Brer Terrapin being so hard to pull out of the water.

As soon as Brer Terrapin saw the rope going slack, and knew they weren't pulling any more, he dived deep into the pond and undid his end of the rope from the tree-stump at the bottom. By the time everyone got up to the pond, Brer Terrapin was sitting in the edge of the water as natural as could be, holding the rope in his hands.

'Heyo, folks!' he said. 'That last pull of yours was a mighty stiff one, and it would have got me out if it had been a bit stronger. You're mighty strong, Brer Bear, and you pull like a yoke of cart-horses, but I guess I can out-pull you any time!'

Well, Brer Bear didn't want to hear any more of this, so he said he expected the candy was ready for eating and they all set out to see. And when they got to the yard, sure enough the candy was ready. All the animals set to work to eat it, but this time there wasn't any biggitty talk!

As for Old Man Terrapin, he sat himself up in his chair again and rocked away merrily, eating the biggest pieces of candy he could see. And nobody, not even Brer Bear, dared to say he was greedy!

# Brer Wolf is Still in Trouble

One time Brer Rabbit got Brer Wolf out of a mighty bad fix. It happened after Brer Wolf had had some of his hair scalded off him when Brer Rabbit's old woman spilt the kettle over him. Brer Wolf had to go away by himself to let his hair grow again, and he was gone so long that Brer Rabbit wondered what had happened to him.

'Well, I expect I can come down safely out of my steeple now,' said Brer Rabbit, 'and say how-do-you-do to folks.'

So down he came, smartened himself up and then he set out for a walk to see who he could meet. He went to the cross-roads and chose a road to go down. Then off he galloped, enjoying stretching out his legs after being so long up in his steeple!

Well, he went on and on and he didn't meet anybody at all. Then he thought he heard something

182

and he stopped to listen – and he heard somebody yelling.

'Oh my, oh my! Won't somebody come and help me?'

Brer Rabbit heard this and he listened hard. It wasn't long before he heard the somebody yelling out again. 'Oh my, oh my! Please, won't somebody come and help me?'

Brer Rabbit, he put up his big ears and shouted back, 'Who are you, anyhow, and what in the name of goodness is the matter?'

'Oh, please, somebody, do run here quickly!'

Brer Rabbit got ready to run, and yelled out, 'Whereabouts are you, and how did you get there?'

'Oh, do please come quickly and help a poor miserable creature. I'm down here in the ditch under a big rock!'

Well, Brer Rabbit didn't quite know if it was a trick somebody was playing him, so he crept down into the ditch very quietly and looked in – and whoever do you suppose he saw there?

It was old Brer Wolf, that Brer Rabbit had scalded a week back. He was lying down in the ditch, and bless gracious, on top of him was a great big rock! It was so big that it looked as if it was squashing him flat – but he had strength enough, to yell and shout – and he yelled in such a miserable way that Brer Rabbit felt really sorry for him.

Brer Rabbit held his coat-tails up out of the way and slid down to the bottom of the ditch to see if he could help Brer Wolf.

When Brer Wolf saw him coming he spoke mighty politely to him.

'Oh, Brer Rabbit, kind sir, would you please help me in the removing of this rock?' he said.

'I expect I can help you all right,' said Brer Rabbit.

'Well, Brer Rabbit, kind sir, just you hurry and do it!' groaned Brer Wolf.

So Brer Rabbit caught hold of the rock and pulled hard, and it wasn't long before he had it on the move, and pretty soon that rock rolled into the ditch-bottom and Brer Wolf was free!

Well, Brer Wolf stretched himself a bit to find out how many of his legs were broken – and it turned out that he wasn't hurt very much. Well, when he found this, Brer Wolf grinned and thought he could pounce on Brer Rabbit easily enough, and pay him out for all the tricks he had played on him. And no sooner did he think that than he grabbed Brer Rabbit by the back of the neck and the middle of the back!

Brer Rabbit kicked and squealed, but it wasn't

any use, because the more he kicked the tighter Brer
Wolf held him – and he squeezed him so hard that
Brer Rabbit was afraid he was going to be choked.

'Well now, Brer Wolf!' said poor Brer Rabbit. 'Is
this the way you thank folks for saving your life?'

Brer Wolf gave a big grin and said, 'I'll thank
you kindly first, Brer Rabbit, and then I'll have you
for dinner!'

'If you talk like that, Brer Wolf,' said Brer
Rabbit, 'I'll never do you another good turn as
long as I live!'

Brer Wolf grinned some more and said, 'That
you won't, Brer Rabbit, that you won't! You won't
do me another good turn till you make me a
good dinner!'

Well, Brer Rabbit thought hard for a moment
and then he spoke solemnly to Brer Wolf. 'Where I
come from Brer Wolf, it's against the law for folks
to kill any one that's done them a good turn, and I
expect it's the law around here, too.'

'I'm not so mighty sure about that,' said Brer
Wolf.

'Well,' said Brer Rabbit, 'what about us going to
old Brer Terrapin, who's a mighty clever man, and
see what he says about it?'

'I don't mind doing that,' said Brer Wolf, 'so long

as I take you there in my mouth, Brer Rabbit!'

With that they set out for old Brer Terrapin's house, and when they got there Brer Wolf told his side of the story and Brer Rabbit told his. Old Brer Terrapin put on his spectacles, cleared his throat, and said:

'This seems all mixed up to me. I can't make head nor tail of it. Before I take any sides in the matter you'll just have to take me to see the place where Brer Wolf was when Brer Rabbit found him.'

Well, they took Brer Terrapin to the ditch and they showed him the place where Brer Wolf had lain under the big rock. Old Brer Terrapin he walked round, he did, and poked at the place with the end of his stick.

By and by he shook his head and said:

'I do hate to put you folks to such trouble, but I'm afraid I'll have to see just how Brer Wolf was caught, and just how the rock was on top of him. I guess you'll both think I'm a troublesome chap, but I'll just have to get this right before I take sides.'

Then Brer Wolf lay down where he was when Brer Rabbit found him, and the others rolled the rock on top of him so that Brer Terrapin could see everything just so. They rolled the rock on top of him, and there he was. Brer Terrapin walked all round and round and looked at him. Then he sat down, he did, and frowned as if he were thinking mighty hard and mighty deep.

By and by Brer Wolf began to grumble.

'Ooh, Brer Terrapin, this rock's getting mighty heavy!'

Brer Terrapin went on frowning and thinking. Brer Wolf began to wriggle under the rock and shouted, 'Ooh, Brer Terrapin, this rock's squashing the breath out of me!'

Then Brer Terrapin sat up straight on his back legs, and spoke in a solemn voice.

'Brer Rabbit, listen to me. *You* were in the wrong, not Brer Wolf. You hadn't any business to go worrying around Brer Wolf when he wasn't bothering you. He was minding his own business and you should have been minding yours.'

Brer Rabbit looked quite ashamed of himself. Brer Terrapin went on talking.

'When you were going along this road this morning, Brer Rabbit, you must surely have been going somewhere. If you *were* going somewhere, you'd better be going right now. Brer Wolf wasn't going anywhere this morning, and he isn't going anywhere now either! You found him under that rock, and under that rock you must leave him!'

And bless gracious, if those two creatures, Brer Rabbit and Brer Terrapin, didn't rush off and leave old Brer Wolf under that rock. Well, it served him right, didn't it?

# Brer Fox Gets into Trouble

One time Brer Rabbit stole so many greens out of a garden that Mr Man set a trap for him. And Brer Rabbit was so greedy that he walked right into the trap – spang! – before he knew it was there.

Well, it wasn't long before Mr Man came around, and when he saw Brer Rabbit in the trap he smacked his hands together in joy and shouted: 'You're a nice fellow, you are! You've been gobbling up my greens and now you're trying to run off with my trap! You're a mighty nice chap, that's what you are! But now that I've got you I'll just about settle a few things with you, Brer Rabbit, so I will!'

And with that Mr Man went off to the bushes to find a handful of sticks to whip Brer Rabbit. Old Brer Rabbit said nothing, but he felt mighty lonesome and he sat there looking as if every minute was going to be the next.

Well, whilst Mr Man was off looking for switches,

who should come sauntering along but Brer Fox? When he saw Brer Rabbit tied up in the trap, he laughed and he danced all around him.

But Brer Rabbit burst out laughing himself, and he laughed fit to kill himself.

'What's the joke?' asked Brer Fox, in surprise.

'The joke is that Miss Meadows and the girls are having a party,' said Brer Rabbit, 'and they wanted me to go and I wouldn't. They said I must come, and I said no, and they said yes, and then by and by they tied me up here whilst they went off shopping for the party. They said I'd be here when they came back then, and they'd take me along to the party when they'd done their shopping.'

'Well, it seems mighty funny to me that you don't want to go to a party,' said Brer Fox.

'Ah, but you don't know my troubles,' said Brer Rabbit, with a deep groan. 'My children are ill and I want to go and buy some pills for them, and how can I, all tied up like this? You wouldn't feel like a party any more than I do, Brer Fox, if your children were ill and you wanted to go and buy pills for them and you couldn't.'

'Well, I'll go and buy some pills for them,' said Brer Fox.

'That's kind of you, Brer Fox,' said Brer Rabbit.

'You always were a good friend to me. But it would be kinder still if you'd just take my place here, and go down to the party with Miss Meadows and the girls instead of me, and let me go off shopping for my children.'

'Well, I don't mind doing that,' said Brer Fox. 'I always did like pranking up at Miss Meadows'.'

'Well, you undo me, then,' said Brer Rabbit, 'and I'll do you up in my place, Brer Fox.' So Brer Fox undid Brer Rabbit and Brer Rabbit tied him up tightly in his place.

'Now I'm off to get some pills for my poor children,' said Brer Rabbit. 'You make my excuses nicely to Miss Meadows and the girls, Brer Fox.'

Well, Brer Rabbit was hardly out of sight before up came Mr Man with a handful of sticks from the bushes, all tied up into a switch to whip Brer Rabbit. And when he saw Brer Fox in the trap, he stopped and stared in surprise.

'Heyo!' said Mr Man. 'You've changed your colour, and you've got bigger, and you've grown a fine tail out at the back there! What kind of a creature are you, anyway!'

Brer Fox lay still and Mr Man went on talking.

'It's a mighty big piece of luck for me,' he said. 'I catch the chap that nibbles my greens and at the same time I catch the fellow that steals my geese!'

And with that he began to hit poor Brer Fox with his hickory switch till it sounded like somebody beating a dusty carpet! Brer Fox, he jumped and he squealed and he howled, but Mr Man hit out at him as if he were fighting a wasps' nest.

Well, by and by the hickory switch got worn out and Mr Man set off to get some more. No sooner was he out of hearing than Brer Rabbit came along.

He had been hiding in the bushes listening to the slaps and squeals.

'Heyo, Brer Fox,' he said. 'Has Miss Meadows come along yet to fetch you?'

'You wait till I fetch *you*!' said Brer Fox, in such a tearing rage that he pawed up the ground in big chunks.

'Well, it's mighty funny Miss Meadows hasn't been along yet,' said Brer Rabbit. 'I've been right down to the doctor's, and Miss Meadows ought to have been here by now. Well, Brer Fox, I hope you won't have to wait long. I must get along home.'

Brer Rabbit turned as if he were about to go, and Brer Fox stopped tearing up the ground and began to speak politely.

'I'll thank you to turn me loose, Brer Rabbit,' he said. 'I'd be grateful to you if you would let me free. You've tied me up so tightly that it makes my head swim, and I don't think I'll be able to go to Miss Meadows' party if I feel so giddy. You turn me loose, Brer Rabbit, and I'll thank you.'

Brer Rabbit sat down and yawned. He began to scratch his ear as if he were thinking hard about something.

'Well, Brer Fox, you surely look pretty bad,' he

said. 'You look as if somebody's been combing your fur up the wrong way.'

Brer Fox didn't say a word. But Brer Rabbit kept on talking.

'Brer Fox, there isn't any bad feeling between us, is there? Because, if you are feeling mad about anything, I'm going along home. I'm not staying here if you feel mad.'

Brer Fox gritted his teeth, but he said: 'Bless us all, Brer Rabbit, why should I be mad with you? No, there's no bad feeling between us. You untie me, Brer Rabbit, and you'll soon see I'm a good friend of yours.'

So Brer Rabbit untied Brer Fox just as he heard Mr Man a-whistling for his dogs – and Brer Fox shot off one way, and Brer Rabbit shot off the other.

But Brer Rabbit took mighty good care to keep out of Brer Fox's way for a long time after that!

# Brer Rabbit is Nearly Caught

Once Brer Rabbit and Brer Terrapin sat talking and drinking lemonade in Brer Rabbit's kitchen. They were great friends, and my, how they laughed when they thought of all the times they had tricked Brer Fox!

But just as they were laughing, Brer Terrapin suddenly stopped, with his mouth wide open, staring hard at something.

'What's the matter, Brer Terrapin?' said Brer Rabbit, in surprise. 'Have you got a bone stuck in your throat? Don't look like that!'

'Brer Rabbit, I saw Brer Fox and Brer Wolf pass by your window!' said Brer Terrapin, in a very scared voice. 'I believe they're come to call on you. I don't like it, Brer Rabbit, I don't like it!'

'Quick!' said Brer Rabbit, as he heard a great banging at his front door. 'Hide! Get under that saucepan, Brer Terrapin! And I'll get under this bucket!'

So in a twink the two were well hidden. There stood the pail and the saucepan upside down by the sink with the brushes and brooms – and Brer Terrapin and Brer Rabbit were trembling underneath!

'Blam-blam-blam!' Brer Fox knocked on the door again – and then, as there was no answer, he opened the door and looked round.

'Come on in, Brer Wolf,' he said. 'There's no one home. Brer Rabbit must have just gone out with some one. Look, they've been having lemonade, and they've left some in the jug! Let's finish it!'

'Right!' said Brer Wolf, pleased, for he was thirsty. 'Then we'll hide under the bed and wait for Brer Rabbit to come back. My, he'll be properly caught this time! He won't find that any of his tricks will help him now.'

Brer Rabbit was boiling with rage under his bucket. To think that Brer Wolf and Brer Fox were drinking his lemonade! And goodness knew how long they would stay under the bed waiting for him!

'Glop-glop-glop!' Brer Wolf finished the lemonade, and then scrambled under the bed. He left his tail hanging out. Brer Fox got under the bed too. It was a tight squeeze, and he left *his* tail out as well!

'Hope he won't be long!' said Brer Wolf, who felt uncomfortable under the small bed.

'Sh!' said Brer Fox. 'If you talk maybe he'll hear you, and then he'll be scared away.'

The two of them lay still. Brer Rabbit and Brer Terrapin hardly dared to breathe. Brer Wolf suddenly sneezed and nearly blew the bed up into the air. Brer Fox was angry.

'Brer Wolf, can't you be quiet even for one moment?' he said.

'Don't talk to me like that, Brer Fox,' said Brer Wolf, in a huff. 'I couldn't help sneezing. Be quiet yourself!'

Whilst they were talking, Brer Rabbit and Brer Terrapin moved a little nearer the bed – but Brer Terrapin's saucepan made a little scraping noise. Brer Fox heard it.

'What was that?' he said. 'Was that you making a noise again? Do be quiet, Brer Wolf – clanking like that!'

'Clanking! Who's clanking?' said Brer Wolf, annoyed. 'What do you think I am? A wheel-barrow?'

Brer Rabbit and Brer Terrapin moved a little nearer. Brer Rabbit's bucket made a clanking noise on the stone floor. Brer Wolf heard it.

He turned to Brer Fox. 'Ha!' he said. '*You* made a noise then – I heard you! Be quiet!'

'I didn't make any noise,' said Brer Fox. ' Sh! Is that someone coming?'

But it was only the wind blowing the curtains. Brer Rabbit and Brer Terrapin moved a little nearer, and the noise made Brer Wolf and Brer Fox jump.

'This house is full of noises,' said Brer Fox. 'I'd hate to live here!'

Now Brer Rabbit was so near Brer Wolf's tail that he could reach out a paw from under his bucket and pinch the long tail! Pinch!

'Ooo-ow!' cried Brer Wolf, in a rage. 'What did you do that for, Brer Fox?'

'What did I do what for?' said Brer Fox, in astonishment, thinking that Brer Wolf must be mad. 'I didn't do a thing!'

'You pinched my tail!' shouted Brer Wolf. 'And now you've done it again!'

'I didn't!' said Brer Fox – and just then Brer Terrapin reached out a front paw and dug his claws into Brer Fox's bushy tail. 'Ooooh! You've pinched *my* tail! Brer Wolf, don't behave so stupidly. Brer Rabbit will hear us!'

Brer Rabbit pinched Brer Wolf's tail again and Brer Terrapin dug his claws into Brer Fox's. The two creatures slapped at one another, and then began to fight under the bed. They tried to stand up – and over went the bed on top of Brer Terrapin's saucepan and Brer Rabbit's bucket!

They were scared, for they could not see what had happened. They tried to back away to the sink again under their bucket and saucepan, but they were covered with bedclothes, and couldn't see where they were going.

But Brer Wolf and Brer Fox saw the lumps under the bedclothes moving, and they stared in astonishment. 'Look!' said Brer Wolf. 'The bed's coming alive! Let's go!'

'It's something under the clothes!' said Brer Fox. He jerked off the blankets, and there he saw the bucket and the saucepan – and Brer Terrapin, trying to get away, put out all his feet, which showed under the saucepan's edge!

'Ow! It's a saucepan with feet!' squealed Brer Fox, in fright. 'And look at that bucket! It's walking! It's alive too!'

Brer Wolf and Brer Fox gave one scared look at the jiggling saucepan and bucket and fled out of the door as fast as they could go.

Brer Terrapin tipped over his saucepan, and Brer Rabbit threw off his bucket. Then they both sat and laughed till Brer Terrapin nearly cracked his shell and Brer Rabbit nearly cracked his sides!

'I guess old Brer Wolf and old Brer Fox won't come *this* way again in a hurry,' said Brer Rabbit, as he and Brer Terrapin put the bed into its place again. 'My, you must have looked odd with your feet sticking out under the saucepan, Brer Terrapin! It's a mercy we got under so quickly – we'd have been somebody's dinner by now, if we hadn't!'

# Brer Fox and Miss Goose

Miss Goose used to take in washing for everybody, and she made money at it, and got sleek and fat. She used to take the dirty linen down to the brook and bang it clean with her battling-stick, till it came white as snow.

Well, one day Brer Fox and Brer Rabbit were sitting talking to one another in the cotton-patch not far off the brook. As they chattered away, they heard a noise – *blim, blim, blim*!

'What's all that noise?' said Brer Fox.

'That's old Miss Goose, down at the brook, battling the clothes with her battling-stick,' said Brer Rabbit.

Well, when Brer Fox heard that old Miss Goose was down at the brook dabbling in soap-suds and washing clothes, he took a peep at her. And when he saw how fat and sleek she was he licked his lips.

'One of these days I'll go and pay a visit to old

Miss Goose and ask her how she's feeling!' said
Brer Fox.

As soon as Brer Rabbit heard Brer Fox say that,
he guessed there was something up. Brer Rabbit
winked to himself, and thought he'd have some fun
whilst he could. Soon Brer Fox said he must be
going, so they said good-bye and went off.

Brer Fox set out for his home, but Brer Rabbit
he slipped round and called on Miss Goose. She
was down at the brook, washing and boiling and
battling clothes.

Brer Rabbit marched up to her.

'Howdy, Miss Goose,' he said.

'Howdy, Brer Rabbit,' said Miss Goose. 'I'd
shake hands with you, but I'm all soapy.'

'Don't worry about that,' said Brer Rabbit.

Well, after Brer Rabbit had talked to Miss
Goose for some time she told him she wasn't
feeling very well.

'I'm getting stiff and I'm getting clumsy,' she
said, 'and, more than that, I'm getting blind. Just
before you happened to come along, Brer Rabbit, I
dropped my spectacles into the washing-tub here,
and if you'd come along then, Brer Rabbit, I might
have thought you were that nasty sly Brer Fox, and
I would have picked up my tub and emptied all the

THE BRER RABBIT STORY COLLECTION

boiling suds over you! Yes, and you would have been properly scalded. It's a good thing for you I found my spectacles,' said old Miss Goose.

'Well, now that you mention Brer Fox's name, I've got something to tell you about him,' said Brer Rabbit. 'He's a-coming to call on you, Miss Goose. He's coming, for sure – and when he comes, it will be in the night, Miss Goose!'

Miss Goose wiped her hands on her apron, and put her spectacles up on her forehead, and looked as scared as could be.

'Lawks-a-mussy!' said poor Miss Goose. 'Supposing he comes, Brer Rabbit! What shall I do? There's nobody in the house but me!'

Then Brer Rabbit sort of winked at Miss Goose and said: 'Miss Goose, the time has come when you must roost up high at night. If you don't roost up high, Sis Goose, Brer Fox will get you.'

'What shall I do, what shall I do!' said poor Miss Goose.

'Now you just listen to me,' said Brer Rabbit. 'You go home tonight with your washing. Tie up a big bundle of clothes and put them into your bed. But don't you get into bed, Sis Goose – no, you fly up high on a rafter in the ceiling and roost there. And when Brer Fox comes, you let him grab the bundle of clothes on the bed and run off with them! You'll be safe, Sis Goose, so don't you worry any more!'

Well, Miss Goose said she was much obliged to Brer Rabbit, and she picked up all her things, and waddled off home, looking mighty scared. When she got home she did just as Brer Rabbit had told her to. She tied up a big bundle of white clothes and set them right in the middle of her bed. Then she sent a messenger to Mr Dog and asked him if he'd mind coming round that night as she was feeling a bit scared.

So Mr Dog, he came round and sat up with Miss Goose, and when she flew up to the rafter to roost he went out and lay down under the house.

Just before day, whilst it was still dark, Brer Fox came creeping along. He pushed on the door and it opened easily. He peeped in and he saw something big and white lying in the middle of the bed. He rushed in, grabbed the big white bundle, which he thought was Miss Goose, and off he ran!

Just then Mr Dog rushed out from under the house, and if Brer Fox hadn't dropped the bundle of clothes he would have been caught.

Well, from that night the tale went round that Brer Fox had been up to Miss Goose's, stealing her clothes, and for a long time nobody asked Brer Fox out, and nobody said howdy to him when they met him.

Brer Fox thought that Brer Rabbit had told Mr Dog to hide under Miss Goose's house, and bad feelings began between Brer Fox and Mr Dog from that day. They hate one another even now, and as soon as Mr Dog smells Brer Fox, and Brer Fox smells Mr Dog, there's a great upset and they go scampering over half the country before they've finished with one another!

# Brer Rabbit and Cousin Wildcat

Now Cousin Wildcat had not forgotten how Brer Rabbit had tried to set Brer Fox on him, and he lay in wait for him. And as Brer Rabbit was going along down the road, lickety-clickety, clickety-lickety, he suddenly felt something drop down on him! When Brer Rabbit pulled himself together he found that it was Mr Wildcat hugging him from behind and whispering in his ear!

Old Mr Wildcat had been lying stretched out on a tree branch that overhung the road, and when he had heard Brer Rabbit lickety-clicketing down the road he grinned to himself, and got ready to drop right down on him. And there he was, hugging and squeezing Brer Rabbit for all he was worth.

Brer Rabbit kicked and squalled. By and by he got his breath and said, 'Oh! Oh, my goodness gracious me! What's happened now?'

Cousin Wildcat, he rubbed his wet nose on Brer

Rabbit's ear, and made a cold chill run up his back. By and by he said, 'Oh, Brer Rabbit, don't I just love you! You've been tricking all my cousins and my family, and it isn't so mighty long since you set Brer Fox on me so that I nearly tore him in two! Oh, Brer Rabbit, don't I just love you!'

Then Cousin Wildcat laughed and struck his teeth together close to Brer Rabbit's ear. Brer Rabbit spoke up.

'Goodness, Cousin Wildcat, the only reason I sent Brer Fox up to you that day was because I thought maybe you'd like to have him for your supper. Dear me, Cousin Wildcat, if you're going to be upset with me because of a thing like that, I'm not going to be friends with you any more!'

Mr Wildcat wiped his nose on Brer Rabbit's ear, and looked as if he were thinking hard. Brer Rabbit went on talking.

'Now just you tell me, Mr Wildcat – have I ever bothered you? Just you tell me that!'

'No, Brer Rabbit, I can't say that you have bothered me,' said Cousin Wildcat.

'No, you can't,' said Brer Rabbit. 'And more than that, Cousin Wildcat, I've done my level best to help you. And though you've jumped down on me like this and scared me dreadfully, I'm willing to do you another good turn to show you what a good friend I can be to you. I can hear some wild turkeys yelping out yonder, and if you'll let me off this time, I'll go out and call them up, and you can lie down as if you were dead, and they'll all come round you and stretch their necks out over you to see you, and you can jump up and get the whole lot of them before they can get out of the way!'

Mr Wildcat listened and thought hard. If there

was one kind of meat he liked better than another, it was turkey meat!

'Are you joking, Brer Rabbit?' he asked.

'Well, if I was off home walking by myself I might be joking,' said Brer Rabbit, 'but how in the name of goodness can I joke when you're on top of me hugging me so tightly, Cousin Wildcat?'

'Well, if you mean what you say, you can get up and call those turkeys here,' said Cousin Wildcat, and he got off Brer Rabbit's back.

Wasn't Brer Rabbit pleased to get rid of him? He went into the bushes and began to yelp like a wild turkey, and he knew mighty well how to do that. Cousin Wildcat lay down on the ground for all the world as if he were dead.

Well, it didn't take Brer Rabbit long to get some turkeys along, for he was a good yelper, and all the turkeys came up to see who it was yelping. There they all came, with Brer Gibley Gobbler leading them. Brer Rabbit ran to meet them, and he winked at them, and whispered about old Mr Wildcat, and how he was only pretending to be dead.

Well, by the time the turkeys got up to Mr Wildcat, there was a great chattering and disputing going on among them. One turkey said Mr Wildcat was dead. Another said he wasn't. Another said it looked as if he was. Another said it looked as if he wasn't. They stretched out their necks and lifted their feet high as if they were going to lean over Mr Wildcat, but not one of them got too close to him!

Cousin Wildcat lay there and he didn't move. The wind ruffled up his fur, but he didn't move; the sun shone down hotly on him, but he didn't move. The turkeys gobbled and yelped round him, but they didn't go any nearer. They shouted and quarrelled about Mr Wildcat, they stretched out their necks and lifted up their feet – but not a turkey went really near to Mr Wildcat.

Well, they went on like this, enjoying the joke, till by and by Mr Wildcat got tired of waiting and he jumped up, he did, and made a dash at the nearest turkey. But the turkey was ready, and when Mr Wildcat ran at him he just rose up into the air, and Mr Wildcat ran under him!

Then Mr Wildcat ran at the next turkey, and that one flew up too. And it went on like this till poor Mr Wildcat was so stiff in the joints and so out of breath that he just had to lie down on the ground and rest. And whilst he did this, Brer Gibley Gobbler and all his family flew on their way, laughing and yelping loudly.

When he got back his breath Cousin Wildcat

looked round for Brer Rabbit. But he was nowhere to be seen. Cousin Wildcat shouted for him.

'Brer Rabbit! Hey, Brer Rabbit! Come along here. I want to talk to you.'

But Brer Rabbit didn't come. So Cousin Wildcat got up and hunted round for him and he wasn't anywhere to be seen. Whilst all the gobbling and yelping had been going on Brer Rabbit had bowed his good-byes to every one and then run off as if a hundred dogs were after him! He wasn't staying till the end!

And the next day old Brer Gibley Gobbler sent him a fine turkey wing to make a fan out of, and Brer Rabbit sent it to Miss Meadows and the girls. My, what a fuss they made of Brer Rabbit for sending them such a beautiful present! He just sat there like a king and grinned away at everybody!

# Brer Bear and
# Brer Bull-Frog

Brer Bear was very angry because he hadn't caught Brer Rabbit after the trick he had played him in Brer Fox's pea-patch. He sat and thought how Brer Bull-Frog had told him where to find Brer Rabbit, and he was in a rage with Brer Bull-Frog because he had told him wrong.

He didn't know that what he had thought was Brer Bull-Frog was really Brer Rabbit sitting in a mud-hole, with only his big eyes sticking out, so that he looked like a frog! No – he thought it was Brer Bull-Frog all right, did Brer Bear.

'I'll pay old Brer Bull-Frog out if it takes me a year to do it!' said Brer Bear to himself. But he didn't have to wait a year, nor even a month, because hardly a week afterwards when Brer Bear was going home after hunting for honey in a bee-tree, who should he see but Brer Bull-Frog sitting out on the edge of a mud-puddle, fast asleep!

Brer Bear dropped his axe, he did, and crept up. He reached out with his paw, and scooped old Brer Bull-Frog up just so! He scooped him in and there he was!

When Brer Bear had got his claws well over Brer Bull-Frog, he sat down and talked to him.

'Howdy, Brer Bull-Frog, howdy! And how are your family? I hope they are well, Brer Bull-Frog, because this day you've got some business with me that will last you a mighty long time!'

Well, Brer Bull-Frog was so surprised and scared that he didn't know what to say. He didn't know what Brer Bear had against him, and he didn't say a word. But old Brer Bear kept on talking.

'You're the man that sent me the wrong way after Brer Rabbit the other day! Oh yes, you are! You tricked me properly, Brer Bull-Frog. You had your fun, and now I'm going to have mine!'

Then Brer Bull-Frog began to get scared, he did, and he said: 'What have I been doing, Brer Bear? How have I been tricking you?'

Then Brer Bear laughed till he shook, but he went on talking.

'Oh no, Brer Bull-Frog! You're not the man that stuck your head up out of the water and told me Brer Rabbit had just gone by! Oh no! You aren't the man! Sure you aren't! I guess you'll say that about that time you were at home with your family where you always are. Well, I don't know where you were, but I know where you are *now*, Brer Bull-Frog, and I'm a-going to punish you for tricking me about Brer Rabbit the other day. You won't trick any more folks along this road!'

Well, of course, poor Brer Bull-Frog didn't at all know what Brer Bear meant, for it hadn't been he who had tricked Brer Bear at all – but Brer Bull-Frog knew something would have to be done, and that mighty soon, because Brer Bear was looking more and more angry and was snapping his jaws together in a way Brer Bull-Frog didn't like at all.

Then Brer Bull-Frog began to shout and squeal. 'Oh, pray, Brer Bear! Let me off this time and I won't ever trick you again. Oh, mercy, Brer Bear! Do let me off this time, and I'll show you a tree in the woods where the bees have a nest full of honey! It's the fattest bee-tree you ever saw! Oh, pray, Brer Bear, let me off!'

But old Brer Bear went on snapping his jaws and looking fiercer than ever. Brer Bull-Frog croaked in fright and squealed: 'Oh, pray, Brer Bear! I won't ever trick you again! Oh, mercy, Brer Bear! Let me off this time!'

But old Brer Bear wouldn't listen to him. He meant to get rid of Brer Bull-Frog, and he sat and thought how he was going to do it.

'I can't drown you,' he said, 'because you live in the water. I can't burn you because I haven't got a fire. Now what shall I do with you, Brer Bull-Frog?'

Then Brer Bull-Frog stopped his crying and boo-hooing and said: 'If you've made up your mind to kill me, Brer Bear, carry me to that big flat rock out there on the edge of the mill-pond, where I can see my family, and, after I've seen them, you can take your axe and hit me.'

This seemed quite a fair and sensible thing to Brer Bear, and he agreed. He picked up old Brer Bull-Frog by one of his behind legs, slung his axe on his shoulder, and off he went to the big flat rock on the edge of the mill-pond.

When he got there he put Brer Bull-Frog down on the rock, and Brer Bull-Frog sat up and looked round as if he were saying good-bye to his folks. Then Brer Bear took a long breath and picked up his axe. He spat on his hands, lifted up his axe, and brought it down on the rock – *pow!*

Aha! That was just what old Brer Bull-Frog was waiting for! He knew Brer would have to lift up his axe before he could hit him – and between the time that Brer Bear raised the axe and brought it down again old Brer Bull-Frog leapt up and dived down into the mill-pond – *kerblinkityblunk!*

Well, Brer Bear nearly split the rock in half and almost fell into the water himself, he hit so hard! When he looked down, he couldn't see Brer Bull-Frog anywhere at all – but very soon he heard a little song being sung, way out on the pond.

It was sung by old Brer Bull-Frog, who had swum up to the top of the water, a good way from Brer Bear, and he was singing loudly:

*'Ingle-go-jang, my joy, my joy,*
*Ingle-go jang, my joy!*
*I'm right at home, my joy, my joy,*
*Ingle-go-jang, my joy!'*

But it didn't bring any joy to Brer Bear! He threw his axe at Brer Bull-Frog, who at once dived down out of danger. And old Brer Bear went home, grunting and groaning, declaring that Brer Rabbit and Brer Bull-Frog between them had lost him the best axe he ever had. Poor old Brer Bear!

# Brer Rabbit and the Greens

Once upon a time Brer Fox and Brer Bear went to get some greens for dinner. Brer Fox put his into a bag and Brer Bear put his into a basket.

And just as they walked around the field to go home, who should they see sitting fast asleep, leaning against a cabbage, but old Brer Rabbit!

'Look!' said Brer Fox, putting down his bag and creeping up to Brer Rabbit. 'We've got him this time, as sure as ninepence!'

Brer Rabbit snored just a little. He was very tired, for he had been fishing all night long and had caught nothing at all. His whiskers fluttered as he breathed, and Brer Fox grinned to himself. This was easy! To think of all the times cunning old Brer Rabbit had tricked him – and now he was here for the taking!

Brer Fox caught hold of Brer Rabbit by the scruff

of the neck, and there he dangled in the air, a very frightened creature.

'What's this? What's this?' squealed Brer Rabbit.

'Nothing much,' said Brer Fox, stuffing Brer Rabbit into his big coat-pocket and holding him there. 'I've caught you at last, that's all, Brer Rabbit. You shouldn't go sleeping out in the sun like that for every one to see you!'

'Brer Fox, your pocket is too warm,' said Brer Rabbit, scrambling round. 'Let me out for a breath of air.'

'You're going to stay there,' said Brer Fox. He picked up his bag of greens, and together he and Brer Bear went homewards, grinning at each other to think how easily old Brer Rabbit had been caught at last.

'Brer Fox, Brer Fox, I'm smothering!' cried Brer Rabbit. 'Let me get my head out of your pocket, do! Just my head, so that I can breathe.'

'It's no good your talking and talking and asking and asking,' said Brer Fox. 'I've listened to you too much, Brer Rabbit, and this time I'm not paying any attention to what you say. You're going home in my pocket, and my, but I'll have a good dinner today!'

Brer Rabbit didn't say any more. He just sat and thought hard.

Soon Brer Fox came to his house and asked Brer Bear in to have a drink of his honey-syrup, a thing Brer Bear was very fond of. The two put down their bag and basket of greens and Brer Fox banged the door.

Suddenly Brer Rabbit jumped right out of Brer Fox's pocket and ran scurrying round the room.

'Run, run!' said Brer Fox, laughing. 'The windows are shut, Brer Rabbit, and the door is shut too, and Brer Bear is standing in front in case you think of opening it! Run, Brer Rabbit, and hide yourself somewhere. I'll find you, there's no doubt about that!'

Brer Rabbit didn't say a word. He ran under the bed and found a mat there. He hid beneath it. Brer Fox peeped under the bed and laughed.

'Ho, Brer Rabbit, aren't you clever enough to find a better place than that?' he cried. 'I can see you, hiding behind that mat of mine! I can see you.'

Brer Rabbit never said a word. He stayed under the mat until he heard Brer Fox pouring out the honey-syrup, and then he wriggled out from the mat and went quietly to where Brer Fox's big slippers stood at the other side of the bed.

Brer Rabbit took the slippers to the mat and humped them underneath so that it looked for all the world as if Brer Rabbit was still hiding under the mat himself!

Brer Rabbit grinned a little grin. He crept quietly to where Brer Bear had put down his basket of greens, and when neither Brer Fox nor Brer Bear was looking his way, he squirmed into the basket between two big cabbages. And there he lay as still as one of the greens themselves!

Soon Brer Bear said he must be going. He picked up his basket of greens and put them on his shoulder.

'Well, see you tomorrow, Brer Fox,' he said. 'Thanks for the honey. Now, where's that rascal of a Brer Rabbit? Don't let him slip out when I open the door, or you'll lose your dinner!'

Brer Fox looked under the bed and saw the humped-up mat. 'It's all right!' he said. ' Brer Rabbit is still hiding under the bed! I can see where his back hunches up my mat!'

Brer Rabbit knew it was Brer Fox's own slippers hunching up the mat, and he grinned to himself in Brer Bear's basket of greens.

'Well, good-bye,' said Brer Bear, opening the door. He went out and shut it. 'Huh!' he said to himself. 'Old Brer Fox has got Brer Rabbit at last. No doubt about that at all!'

He walked on home. Presently Brer Rabbit gave a deep groan in the basket. Brer Bear stopped, very startled. He looked all round. Nobody was about at all.

Brer Rabbit groaned again. 'Ooohahooohah!'

'Gracious goodness!' said Brer Bear, alarmed. 'Whatever's that? Who's there? Is anybody ill? Shall I fetch a doctor?'

'Oooohah!' groaned Brer Rabbit in the cabbages, thoroughly enjoying himself now.

'It sounds as if it's in my basket!' said Brer Bear, terrified. 'Can it be the cabbages talking?'

'Ooooh-ah-OOOOOOOH!' said Brer Rabbit, with a louder, deeper groan than ever. 'Put me dow-oo-ow-oo-wn!'

'It *is* those cabbages!' squealed poor Brer Bear, and he put his basket down with a bump. Brer Rabbit made two holes in a cabbage leaf and stuck his big eyes through them. Just as Brer Bear opened the lid he saw the eyes looking at him, and he gave a squeal and fled down the road.

'My cabbages have eyes!' he cried. 'My cabbages are looking at me!'

Brer Rabbit hopped out of the greens and laughed till he cried. Then he ate half a cabbage, put the basket on his back, and went off home, whistling.

On his way he passed Brer Fox's house, and saw Brer Fox looking gloomily out of the window.

'Heyo, Brer Fox!' called Brer Rabbit. 'Did you find me under the mat all right? I hope you enjoyed your dinner!'

And with that he galloped off with the greens, lippitty-clippitty – just in time too, for Brer Fox jumped clean through the window and nearly caught him by the tail!

# Brer Rabbit Gets a House

One time a whole lot of the animals made up their minds they would go shares in building a house. There was old Brer Bear and Brer Fox and Brer Wolf and Brer Raccoon and Brer Possum – everyone right down to old Brer Mink. There was a whole crowd of them, and they set to work to build a house in less than no time.

Brer Rabbit was there too, of course, but he said it made his head swim to climb up the scaffold and build like the others, and he said too that he always got sun-stroke if he worked in the sun – but he got a measure, and he stuck a pencil behind his ear, and he went round measuring and marking, measuring and marking. He always looked so busy that all the other creatures said to one another that Brer Rabbit was doing a mighty lot of work.

And folk going along the road said that Brer Rabbit was doing more work than anyone. But really Brer Rabbit wasn't doing anything much, and he might just as well have been lying by himself in the shade, fast asleep!

The other creatures really built the house, and my, it was a fine house too! It would have been a fine house in these days, let alone those days. It had an upstairs and a downstairs, and chimneys all round, and a room for each of the creatures that had helped to build it.

Well, Brer Rabbit picked out one of the upstairs rooms for himself. Then he went and got himself a gun and put it up in his room. After that he got himself a brass cannon, and he dragged it up to his room one day when not one of the others was about. And after that he got himself a tub full of dirty, soapy water, and this he took upstairs to his room too, when nobody else was looking!

Well, when they had all got the house fixed up nicely, and were sitting in the parlour after their supper, Brer Rabbit yawned and stretched himself as if he were tired.

'Well, folks,' he said, 'I believe I'll say good night to you and go up to my room.'

'Good night, then, Brer Rabbit,' said all of them. Brer Rabbit went out of the door and up the stairs. All the others were chatting and laughing away as happy as you please, delighted with their new house.

Well, no sooner was Brer Rabbit up in his room than he opened his door again and stuck his head out of it.

'When a big man like me wants to sit down, where shall he sit?' sang out Brer Rabbit.

Then all the other creatures laughed and shouted back: 'If a big man like you can't sit in a chair he'd better sit down on the floor!'

'Watch out down there, then!' yelled old Brer Rabbit, 'because I'm a-going to sit down!'

With that, BANG! He let off his gun! Well, this sort of astonished everyone, and they looked round at one another in alarm, thinking that Brer Rabbit was a mighty heavy sitter-down.

'What in the name of goodness was that?' said Brer Possum.

They listened and they listened, but they didn't hear anything more, and before long they had forgotten about it and were chattering gaily about all kinds of things.

By and by Brer Rabbit flung his door open upstairs again, and stuck his head out.

'Hie!' he sang out. 'When a big man like me wants to sneeze, where's he going to sneeze?'

Then all the other creatures they laughed like anything and shouted back:

'If a big man like you wants to sneeze he can sneeze where he pleases!'

'Watch out down there, then!' yelled Brer Rabbit. 'Because I'm going to sneeze right here!'

And with that, Brer Rabbit let off his cannon – *bulderum-m-m-m-m*! It made such a bang that all the windows shook and rattled, and the house shivered as if it was going to fall down, and old Brer Bear, he fell out of the rocking-chair – *kerblump!*

When the creatures got over their fright a bit and settled down again, they looked at one another.

'Brer Rabbit's got a mighty bad cold,' said Brer Possum, in a scared sort of voice. 'I believe I'll just step out for a while, till he's got rid of it.'

'I'll come with you, Brer Possum,' said Brer Mink, getting up. 'If Brer Rabbit sneezes again like that I'm not a-going to get any sleep in the house tonight, that's sure!'

So off the two went, arm-in-arm, and didn't turn up again that night. The other creatures watched them go, but they said they were going to stay, no matter how bad a cold Brer Rabbit had. And after a while they began to talk and laugh just as usual. About then Brer Rabbit opened his door again, and stuck out his head.

'When a big man like me wants to wash his hands, whereabouts is he to throw the dirty water?'

The other creatures glared at Brer Rabbit, and yelled back angrily:

'Big man or little man, throw your water where you please!'

Then Brer Rabbit yelled out: 'Watch out down there, then – here comes my water!'

And with that he tipped up the tub of dirty water, and it went slish-sloshing down the stairs! And when the other creatures heard it coming they jumped up like mad and rushed to the doors and the windows! Some of them went out at the back door, and some of them went out at the front. Brer Bear fell out of the window, and Brer Fox tried to climb up the chimney-place. Some went one way and some went another – but they all went sailing out!

As for Brer Rabbit, he stood at the top of the stairs, grinning – and then he just shut up the house and fastened all the windows. Then he went to bed, he did, and pulled the covers up to his ears, and slept as if he was at peace with all the world.

'If those other creatures get scared and run away from their own house, what business is it of mine?'

said Brer Rabbit. 'I'm not scared of anything!'
And he never spoke a truer word!

# Mr Lion and Brer Rabbit Go Hunting

Now the more Mr Lion thought about how Brer Rabbit tricked every one, the cleverer he thought Brer Rabbit was. And it came into his head that if he could make a friend of old Brer Rabbit maybe he'd get on a lot better. So he set off and found Brer Rabbit's house.

'Brer Rabbit, will you come hunting with me?' shouted Mr Lion, banging at the door.

'No, Mr Lion. I'm afraid you'd do all the hunting and I'd do all the running!' shouted back Brer Rabbit.

'Brer Rabbit, you're mighty clever, and I couldn't catch you if I tried,' said Mr Lion. 'I give you my word I want to be your friend. Come on, now, and go hunting with me.'

Well, when Brer Rabbit heard Mr Lion say he'd give him his word, he knew Mr Lion was speaking the truth, for no one had ever known old Mr Lion to break a promise. So Brer Rabbit hopped out of his house and joined Mr Lion. They each had a gun, and off they went across the countryside to hunt for food.

When they saw plovers in the air Mr Lion raised his gun and shot, bang-bang! But he always missed. Brer Rabbit, he raised his gun and shot, and he always hit what he was shooting at. But no sooner did the bird he shot fall down than Mr Lion would cry:

'It's mine! It's mine! I killed it!'

Well, Mr Lion was such a big fellow that Brer Rabbit was afraid of quarrelling with him, but he made up his mind to get even with him. They went on and they went on. Mr Lion kept missing his shots and Brer Rabbit kept hitting everything, and Mr Lion, he always said the kill was his.

They hunted all day long, and when night came they were such a long way from home that they had to camp out. So they found a stream, and when they came to it they cleared a space, built a fire on the bank, and cooked their supper.

After supper they sat up and told tales, and Brer Rabbit, he said what a mighty good hunter Mr Lion was, and Mr Lion, he leant back on his elbow and felt mighty biggitty. Then, when Brer Rabbit saw

Mr Lion getting sleepy, he said: 'I'm a monstrous heavy snorer, Mr Lion, when I fall asleep, and I hope and trust I shan't disturb you this night.'

Mr Lion threw back his mane out of his eyes and said: 'I'm a monstrous heavy snorer myself, Brer Rabbit, and I'll feel mighty glad if I don't rouse you up in the night too.'

'Well, Mr Lion,' said Brer Rabbit, 'I wish you'd be so good as to show me how you snore just *before* you get to sleep.'

Mr Lion drew in his breath mighty hard and showed Brer Rabbit, 'Grr-grr, grr-grr!'

'Thank you, Mr Lion,' said Brer Rabbit, 'and now I wish you'd be so good as to show me how you snore when you're really *sound* asleep.'

Well, Mr Lion, he sucked in his breath and

made a snoring noise – 'Orr-phm, grrrr-rr! Orr-phm, grrr-rrr!' and it sounded just as if a house was falling down each time!

Brer Rabbit looked astonished. He rolled his eyes round and said: 'I always heard tell you were a mighty big man, Mr Lion, and you surely are!'

Mr Lion looked pleased. Pretty soon he shut his eyes and began to nod. Then he lay down and stretched himself out, and it wasn't long before he had begun to snore like he snored when he wasn't quite asleep – 'Grr-grr, grr-grr!'

Brer Rabbit, he lay there. He didn't say a word. He just kept his eye on the bag where Mr Lion had put all the birds that Brer Rabbit had shot that day. He lay there with one ear up and both eyes open. By and by Mr Lion began to snore like he did when he was sound asleep.

'Orr-phm, grrr-rr! Orr-phm, grrr-rr!' he went. When old Brer Rabbit heard this, he got up and sprinkled himself all over with cold ashes from the fire, and then he picked up a whole lot of hot coals and flung them on Mr Lion. Mr Lion, he jumped up, he did, and asked who did that, and Brer Rabbit, he lay there on the ground and kicked at his ears with his hind foot and shouted, 'Ow! Ow! Ow!'

Mr Lion saw the ashes all over Brer Rabbit and he thought some one had been along and flung the fire over both of them to burn them. He didn't know what to think. He looked all round but he didn't see any one. He dropped his head and listened but he didn't hear anything either. Then he lay down again and dropped off to sleep. After a while he began to snore as he had snored before – 'Orr-phm, grrr-rr! Orrphm, grrr-rr!'

Then Brer Rabbit jumped up again and sprinkled some more cold ashes on himself and flung some burning coal on Mr Lion. Mr Lion jumped up at once and yelled:

'There it is again!'

Brer Rabbit was lying on the ground, kicking and squalling.

'Hey, Mr Lion, you ought to be ashamed of yourself, trying to burn me up like this!'

'Brer Rabbit, I never did anything of the sort!' said Mr Lion. Brer Rabbit looked very doubtful. Soon he put his nose into the air and sniffed.

'Phewee! I smell old rags a-burning!' he said.

Mr Lion looked angry. 'It isn't old rags, Brer Rabbit. It's my hair a-scorching!'

Well, they both looked all round, they did, but they didn't see any one at all. Brer Rabbit vowed he was going to keep awake and do some watching next time, because he said he meant to catch whoever it was playing pranks on them. With that Mr Lion lay down again and it wasn't long before he dropped off to sleep.

Well, then, the very same thing happened again. The cold ashes fell on Brer Rabbit and the hot coals fell on Mr Lion! But by the time Mr Lion jumped up Brer Rabbit was on his feet, shouting and pointing: 'I saw him, Mr Lion! I saw him! He's gone across the stream! I saw him!'

With that Mr Lion let out a bellow and jumped right across the stream. He tore off, hoping to catch whoever it was that had thrown the hot coals on him, but he couldn't see any one at all, though he ran for miles.

And no sooner was he over the stream than old Brer Rabbit, he took up the bag of birds and shot off home lippitty-clippitty, as fast as he could! My, how he laughed to himself as he went, thinking what Mr Lion would say when he got back to the camp-fire and found nobody there!

And what *did* Mr Lion say? Well, when he found Brer Rabbit gone and the bag of birds gone, he just pawed up the ground and bellowed loud enough to be heard for ten miles round. All the creatures

that heard him shivered in their shoes – except old
Brer Rabbit, and it would take a lot more than that
to make *him* shiver, wouldn't it!

# Brer Fox Catches Mr Horse

Once Brer Rabbit got Brer Fox into worse trouble than ever before. It was after Brer Fox had nearly got caught by Mr Dog, and was lying in his house, snapping his jaws whenever he thought of Brer Rabbit, and wondering how he could trick him and pay him back for all the things he had done to Brer Fox.

Brer Rabbit got to hear that Brer Fox was planning how to trick him, and he thought it would be a good thing if he could get the better of Brer Fox first. Then old Brer Fox would lie low for a bit and leave Brer Rabbit alone.

Well, one day, when Brer Rabbit was going along the road, he saw a great big horse lying stretched out flat on its side in a field. Brer Rabbit crept up as near as he dared to see if the horse was alive or dead.

The horse lay quite still. Brer Rabbit crept up

nearer and nearer, and by and by he saw the horse switch its tail, and then Brer Rabbit knew it was alive.

With that Brer Rabbit loped off down the road, and almost the first one he met was Brer Fox. Brer Rabbit shouted to him:

'Brer Fox! Oh, Brer Fox! Come here! I've got some good news for you! Come here, Brer Fox!'

Well, Brer Fox stopped, and when he saw that it was Brer Rabbit calling him he came galloping back, because it seemed as good a time as any to grab Brer Rabbit and take him home for dinner. But before he got too near, Brer Rabbit shouted again:

'Come on, Brer Fox! I've found a place where you can get fresh meat to last you till Christmas!'

'Whereabouts?' said Brer Fox.

'Just there in the field,' said Brer Rabbit.

'What sort of meat is it?' said Brer Fox.

'It's a whole horse lying down flat on the ground,' said Brer Rabbit. 'We can easily catch him and tie him.'

'Well, come on then,' said Brer Fox, and off they went.

When they got to the field, there was the horse, sure enough, stretched out in the sun, fast asleep. Brer Fox and Brer Rabbit looked at him and began to squabble about the best way to tie him up so that he couldn't get loose. One said one thing and the other said another thing.

Then at last Brer Rabbit said: 'The best plan I know, Brer Fox, is for you to get down in the grass and let me tie you to the horse's tail, and then, when he tries to get up, you can hold him down easily. If I were as big and strong a man as you, Brer Fox, I'd let you tie *me* to the horse's tail, and I'd hold him down myself. But I'm sure *you* could hold him down all right, Brer Fox. But if you're afraid, we'll drop the idea and think of some other plan.'

Well, Brer Fox didn't quite like the idea of being tied to the horse's tail, and yet he didn't want Brer Rabbit to think he was scared. He always liked to talk biggitty in front of Brer Rabbit. So at last he said he would be tied to the horse's tail.

Well, Brer Rabbit made Brer Fox kneel down in the grass and he tied him up tightly to the horse's tail. Then after Brer Fox was tied up hard and fast, Brer Rabbit stepped back, crossed his arms and grinned till his mouth reached his ears.

'If ever there was a horse caught, then we've caught this one!' he said. 'It rather looks as if we've put a bridle on the wrong end, but I expect Brer

Fox has got the strength to hold the horse all right!'

Then Brer Rabbit cut a long switch from the hedge and trimmed it up, and when it was ready, he stepped up and hit the horse a rap – *pow*! The horse woke up very suddenly, and was so surprised that he leapt right up in the air and landed on his four feet. When he did that, of course, there was old Brer Fox dangling in the air, hanging from the horse's tail!

Brer Rabbit darted out of the way, and shouted loudly.

'Hold him down, Brer Fox! Hold him down! I'll stand out here and see fair play! Hold him down, Brer Fox! Hold him down!'

Of course, when the horse felt Brer Fox hanging behind him on his tail he thought something strange was the matter, and he began to jump round and rear up and down, and poor Brer Fox was shaken about like a rag in the wind!

All the time Brer Rabbit jumped around and shouted and yelled. 'Hold him down, Brer Fox! Hold him down! You've got him now, for sure! Get a tighter grip and hold him down!'

The horse was really scared, and couldn't think what it was that bumped against him at the back. So he jumped up in the air and humped up his back, and reared and bucked, and snorted and stamped. But still Brer Fox hung on, and still Brer Rabbit skipped around, yelling and shouting.

'Hold him down, Brer Fox! You've got him where he can't get you! Hold him down, Brer Fox!'

By and by, when Brer Fox got his breath, he yelled back at Brer Rabbit.

'How in the name of goodness can I hold this horse down unless I get my claws in the ground? Stop jumping about there, Brer Rabbit, and come and give me a hand.'

But old Brer Rabbit, he stood back a little further and shouted still more loudly.

'Hold him down, Brer Fox! Hold him down! You've got him now, for sure! Hold him down!'

By and by the horse began to kick out with his hind legs, and he kicked poor old Brer Fox so hard that he squealed. And then he kicked Brer Fox again so hard that he kicked him loose and sent him whirling over and over in the air and then down on the ground – *kerblap*!

And still wicked Brer Rabbit kept jumping round and shouting at the top of his voice!

'Hold him down, Brer Fox! Hold him down!'

But Brer Fox didn't want any more to do with the horse. He crawled away home – and on the way it sort of came to him that once again Brer Rabbit had played a trick on him. And he snapped his jaws and looked round – but old Brer Rabbit, he had gone home, laughing and rolling on the ground every time he thought of Brer Fox hanging on to the horse's tail!

# Brer Rabbit and the Pears

One day, when Brer Rabbit trotted through the wood, he happened to see a little pear tree that was hung with large pears. He stopped and had a look at it.

'Those pears will be ripe next week,' he said to himself. 'And I'll be the one to pick them! My, won't they be juicy and sweet!'

So, the next week, he trotted by that way again and, sure enough, the pears were as ripe as could be. But somebody was up the tree picking them!

It was Brer Bear. Brer Bear liked a nice juicy apple or pear, and he had had his eye on that tree for a long time. And there he was, up in the tree, picking away as fast as he could, putting the ripe yellow pears into his basket, and now and then popping one whole into his big mouth.

Now Brer Rabbit wasn't in Brer Bear's good books at all just then, for he had taken some honey

BRER RABBIT AND THE PEARS

from a bee-tree that Brer Bear had specially wanted for himself. So it was quite a shock to Brer Rabbit to see Brer Bear there. He guessed Brer Bear wouldn't give him any of those pears just now.

Brer Rabbit looked at the little pear tree. He didn't like to climb up it in case Brer Bear pushed him down. No, that wouldn't do at all. But how in the world was he going to get any pears for himself?

Brer Rabbit sat and thought. Brer Bear hadn't seen him yet. Brer Rabbit crept off and went to Brer Terrapin's house under the water. He called down to him.

'Heyo, Brer Terrapin! Are you in this morning?'

'Oh yes, I'm in all right,' said Brer Terrapin, and he swam up to the top of the water. 'How are you feeling, Brer Rabbit?'

'Mighty hungry, Brer Terrapin,' said Brer Rabbit. 'Mighty hungry. And I've got a plan to get some fine juicy pears, if you'll come along and help me.'

Well, Brer Terrapin liked pears too, so he clambered out of the water, shook his feet, and they set off together. Brer Rabbit told Brer Terrapin his plan, and Brer Terrapin laughed till he nearly cracked his shell.

By and by they came up to the pear tree. Brer Bear was still up there, picking the pears. Brer

Rabbit and Brer Terrapin sat down under the tree for all the world as if they didn't know any one was there at all.

'Well, Brer Terrapin,' said Brer Rabbit in a loud voice, 'how's yourself?'

'Not too good, Brer Rabbit, not too good,' said Brer Terrapin. 'You know, ever since that tiresome Brer Bear tried to pull my tail out, I've had the trimble-trembles.'

'Oh, he's a bad fellow, Brer Bear is,' said Brer Rabbit. 'I'm no friend of his and he's no friend of mine.'

Now Brer Bear, sitting up in the tree, was most astonished and annoyed to hear all this. He sat there quietly, listening with both his ears.

'He's mean and he's selfish,' said Brer Terrapin loudly. 'That's what he is. And I wish he could hear me say so.'

Brer Rabbit stopped himself giggling. 'He's greedy too,' he said. 'Do you know, if he finds a bee-tree, he never even offers me a sip of the honey there?'

Now this was a real story, for Brer Bear had often given Brer Rabbit a share of his honey. Brer Bear, he sat up in the tree boiling with rage, longing to get at Brer Rabbit and give him a good slap.

'He's a slow chap,' said Brer Terrapin. 'My, you call me slow, Brer Rabbit – but if I ran a race with Brer Bear I'd be at the winning-post before he was half-way there!'

'And he hasn't as many brains as a caterpillar,' said Brer Rabbit, enjoying himself. 'My, Brer Terrapin, what would Brer Bear say if he heard us talking like this about him?'

'What would he *do*?' giggled Brer Terrapin.

'I guess he'd throw something at us,' said Brer Rabbit. 'Yes, I guess that's what he'd do. Throw something at us, hard, and hit us. Ho ho! it's a good thing he isn't here, and hasn't got anything to throw!'

Well, this was too much altogether for Brer Bear. He gave a fierce growl, picked a large pear and threw it down the tree.

'I *am* here!' he grunted loudly. 'And I *have* got something to throw! Take that – and that!'

Brer Rabbit and Brer Terrapin jumped up as if they were too astonished for anything. Brer Rabbit saw the pear coming and neatly caught it. The other one smashed on Brer Terrapin's shell. Brer Terrapin put out his head and began to lick it off with great delight.

'Goodness! It's Brer Bear up the tree!' said Brer

Rabbit, pretending to be most upset and surprised. 'He's heard all we said! Brer Bear, Brer Bear, now just stop throwing things at us. You'll hurt us!'

'That's just what I mean to do, you nasty tale-telling creatures!' roared Brer Bear, feeling angrier and angrier. He took a pear from his basket and threw it straight at Brer Rabbit. 'Take that! Huh, I'll teach you to sit under a tree and talk like that about me! I'm throwing *this* pear for your story-telling – and *this* for your meanness – and *this* for your unkindness!'

Thud, plop, plop! Down came the pears! Some of them Brer Rabbit caught, others smashed on the ground and Brer Terrapin gobbled them up. One rolled away and Brer Rabbit picked it up.

'Stop, Brer Bear, stop! You'll hurt us!' cried Brer Rabbit, knowing quite well that Brer Bear would go on all the more if he were begged to stop. And so Brer Bear did. He was in such a rage that he threw down every pear in his basket, and picked every pear off the tree. Down they came, plop, plop, plop, and Brer Rabbit picked them up in glee.

At last there were no more pears left to throw. Brer Rabbit looked up and winked at Brer Bear.

'Well, you won't be wanting your basket now, will you?' he said. 'So what about throwing that down too, Brer Bear? It would be mighty useful for me to carry these pears home!'

And then Brer Bear knew that it was all a trick to get his pears, and he growled in rage. He began to climb down the tree, grunting and growling, and Brer Rabbit knew it was about time to go.

'Come on, Brer Terrapin,' he said. 'We've been here long enough. We'll go home.'

So off they went, the two of them – Brer Rabbit with his pockets crammed full of ripe pears, and Brer Terrapin with his shell dripping with pear juice. My, how they giggled when they thought of Brer Bear throwing down his pears! Wicked Brer Rabbit – whatever will he do next?

# Brer Rabbit up the Chimney

One day, not long after Sis Cow had tried to catch him, Brer Rabbit thought he would drop in and see Miss Meadows and the girls, so he got out his looking-glass and made himself smart. Then he set out.

As he went cantering along the road who should he see but old Brer Terrapin – the same old sixpence! Brer Rabbit stopped and rapped on the roof of Brer Terrapin's house. Brer Terrapin always carried his house with him, rain or shine.

'Are you in, Brer Terrapin?' asked Brer Rabbit.

'Yes, I'm at home,' said Brer Terrapin.

'Howdy then, Brer Terrapin,' said Brer Rabbit.

'Howdy, Brer Rabbit,' said Brer Terrapin.

'Where are you going, Brer Terrapin?' said Brer Rabbit.

'Nowhere, Brer Rabbit,' said Brer Terrapin. 'Just ambling along.'

'I'm on my way to see Miss Meadows and the girls,' said Brer Rabbit. 'Why don't you come along with me, Brer Terrapin?'

'I don't mind if I do,' said Brer Terrapin. So they set out together. By and by they got to Miss Meadows' house and in they went.

When they got in, Brer Terrapin was so low on the ground that he couldn't see anyone. He wasn't high enough on a chair so Brer Rabbit picked him up and put him on the mantelpiece. Brer Terrapin sat back there, he did, just as proud as a peacock.

Of course they all began to talk of Brer Fox, and Miss Meadows and the girls laughed loudly when they remembered how Brer Rabbit had ridden Brer Fox and stuck the spurs in him. They made lots of fun and giggled and joked. Brer Rabbit sat in his chair, smoking his cigar. Then he cleared his throat and said:

'I'd have ridden Brer Fox over this morning, ladies, but I rode him so hard yesterday that he went lame in one of his front legs, and I expect I'll have to get rid of him.'

'Well,' said Brer Terrapin, 'if you are going to sell him, Brer Rabbit, sell him somewhere out of this district, because he's been here too long already. Why, I met Brer Fox along the road only yesterday, and what do you think he said to me?'

'Tell us, Brer Terrapin,' begged the girls.

'He shouted out, "Heyo, Smelly Shellyback!"' said Brer Terrapin.

'Oh my! Fancy that!' said Miss Meadows. 'Brer Fox called Brer Terrapin a Smelly Shelly. How *could* he talk that way to a nice fellow like Brer Terrapin?'

But goodness gracious! Whilst all this was going on, Brer Fox was standing at the back door with one ear at the keyhole, listening! Listeners don't hear any good of themselves, and Brer Fox didn't either!

By and by Brer Fox stuck his head in at the door and shouted, 'Good evening, folks, I wish you mighty well!'

And with that he made a dash at Brer Rabbit. Miss Meadows and the girls began to shout and squeal, and Brer Terrapin began to scramble round on the mantelpiece, and suddenly off he fell, and blip! He hit Brer Fox right on the back of his head!

This kind of stunned Brer Fox and he fell down on the floor. When he sat up again all he saw was a saucepan of greens overturned in the fireplace and a broken chair. Brer Rabbit was gone, Brer Terrapin was gone, and Miss Meadows and the girls were gone!

Brer Rabbit had shot up the chimney – and had knocked over the pot of greens in the fireplace. Brer Terrapin had crept under the bed and got behind the clothes-chest, and Miss Meadows and the girls had all run out into the yard.

Brer Fox felt the back of his head, where Brer

Terrapin had dropped on him, and looked all round. But he couldn't see any sign of Brer Rabbit.

Soon the smoke and the ashes flying up the chimney got into Brer Rabbit's nose, and he sneezed – *huckychow*!

'Aha!' said Brer Fox, 'you're up there, are you? Well, I'm going to smoke you out, if it takes me a month. You're mine this time, Brer Rabbit.'

Brer Rabbit didn't say a word.

'Aren't you coming down?' said Brer Fox. Brer Rabbit still said nothing.

Then Brer Fox went out to fetch some wood to put on the fire, and when he came back he heard Brer Rabbit laughing.

'What are you laughing at, Brer Rabbit?' said Brer Fox.

'Can't tell you, Brer Fox,' said Brer Rabbit.

'You'd *better* tell me,' said Brer Fox. 'I'm just a-going to slam some wood on the fire, and you'll be roasted up there.'

'Well, I'll tell you, Brer Fox,' said Brer Rabbit. 'I'm laughing because somebody's gone and hidden a box of money up here in the chimney, and it's right under my nose!'

'I don't believe you!' said Brer Fox

'Look up and see,' said Brer Rabbit. So Brer Fox

254

poked his head up the chimney to see, and Brer Rabbit kicked out with his feet and sent a whole heap of soot down into Brer Fox's eyes! Brer Fox rushed out to the yard to bathe his eyes, and Brer Rabbit came down from the chimney and said good-bye to the ladies.

'How did you send Brer Fox off?' said Miss Meadows, in surprise. 'He came rushing out as if the dogs were after him!'

'Oh, I just told Brer Fox that if he didn't go along home and stop playing his pranks on folks, I'd take him out and whip him,' said Brer Rabbit, twirling his whiskers.

And off he went, whistling as gaily as a blackbird!

# Brer Fox's Fish-Trap

One year there was a very dry summer, and the rivers and ponds got dried up so that there was hardly any drinking-water to be found. Even the big river got low, and as for the streams, some of them disappeared altogether.

The animals all had to go to the big river to drink. They met there, and the biggest ones drank first, and they drank so much that there was hardly any left for the little ones.

Brer Rabbit didn't mind very much. He always knew how to look after himself, and if any one was going to get water it was old Brer Rabbit. The other creatures saw his footprints by the riverside and they waited for him, but they never caught him.

Brer Fox wasn't so lucky. He always seemed to go for a drink when Mr Lion and Brer Bull and the big creatures were there, and they crowded him out and chased him away. So poor Brer Fox, he was always thirsty and he didn't know what to do about it.

'I'll go along to Brer Rabbit's house and see how he manages to get a drink,' said Brer Fox to himself, and off he set.

Brer Rabbit was at home. He was sitting outside his front door singing a little song:

*'Oh, Mr Rabbit, your eye's mighty big!*
*Yes, sir, yes! It's made for me to see!*
*Oh, Mr Rabbit, your tail's mighty short,*
*Yes, sir, yes! But it just fits me!'*

'Howdy, Brer Rabbit?' said Brer Fox.

'Howdy, Brer Fox?' said Brer Rabbit. 'What are you wanting this morning? You look mighty down in the mouth.'

'Brer Rabbit, I can't seem to get anything to drink,' said Brer Fox. 'When I go to the big river Mr Lion roars at me, and Brer Bull crowds me out, and the rest of them chase me away. Now, you're a smart fellow, Brer Rabbit – can't you tell me how to get a drink when I want one?'

Well, Brer Rabbit, he sat and thought hard for a few minutes, then he grinned. 'Oh yes, Brer Fox,'

he said, 'I can tell you what to do. You've come to
the right man for help, you have.'

'What shall I do then, Brer Rabbit?' asked
Brer Fox.

'You go home and rub some treacle over
yourself,' said Brer Rabbit. 'Then go out into the
woods and roll over and over in some leaves. They
will stick to the treacle, and you'll be covered from
head to foot with them.'

'What shall I do after that?' asked Brer Fox, in
astonishment.

'Well, you go down to the river and hide in a
bush,' said Brer Rabbit. 'And when the creatures
all come to get a drink, you jump out at them, Brer
Fox – and you'll scare them all into the middle of
next week!'

'Huh!' said Brer Fox. 'That sounds mighty good
to me, Brer Rabbit. I always said you were a smart
fellow!'

'I haven't finished yet,' said Brer Rabbit, who
was really enjoying himself. 'After you've scared
every one away, go and wallow in the water and
drink all you like – and pretty soon, Brer Fox, the
fishes will all come swimming up to get a bite of
treacle, and you'll be able to catch as many as you
want to. And, if you're a nice fellow, Brer Fox, I'll

take it kindly of you if you'll bring me one of the fish for myself.'

'I'll do that, Brer Rabbit,' promised Brer Fox. 'Yes, I'll surely do that.'

With that off he ran home. He went to his cupboard and took down a jar of treacle. He smeared it all over himself from head to foot – and a mighty sticky mess he looked when he had finished! Then he went out into the woods and rolled over and over in the leaves and rubbish there till he looked as odd as could be!

When Brer Fox was ready he went down to the river and hid himself. By and by all the creatures came along to drink the water, and whilst they were a-pushing and a-scuffling and a-snuffling, Brer Fox, he jumped out of the bushes at them, and switched himself round and round, squealing loudly.

Well, all the creatures looked at this odd thing and they didn't know what to make of it at all! Brer Wolf saw him first and he was so startled that he jumped right over Brer Bear's head to get away! Brer Bear shot backwards, yelling, 'Who's that? Who's that?'

Then every one saw the queer-looking creature and rushed away like apples rolling downhill, and before Brer Fox had time to do a few more squeals he had the river to himself!

The creatures didn't go very far. They soon stopped and looked round. Then they began to creep back a little nearer, trying to make out what this fearsome-looking thing was that had given them such a fright. When they got near enough to see, there was Brer Fox walking up and down, up and down, switching his tail about and squealing whenever he thought about it.

The animals didn't know what to think at all. They watched, and Brer Fox marched up and down. Still they watched and still he marched up and down. It went on like this till Brer Fox thought it was about time he made himself into a fish-trap and wallowed in the water as Brer Rabbit had said. Then the fishes would come up to him for a bite of treacle and he'd get an armful of them.

So Brer Fox marched into the water and lay down in it. He rolled over and over and wallowed in it, watching for the fishes to come. But they didn't come and they didn't come.

Brer Fox didn't know what Brer Rabbit knew! Brer Rabbit knew that as soon as Brer Fox went into the water the river would wash away the leaves and the dirt and the treacle – and there would be Brer Fox, plain for any one to see!

Well, the water washed away the treacle, and off went the leaves and the dirt downstream, and there was Brer Fox, just himself and nobody strange at all!

The animals were all watching Brer Fox rolling in the water – and bless gracious, how they stared when they saw the leaves floating off him and saw that he was just Brer Fox. Then they knew he had played a trick on them and they were mighty wild.

'Brer Wolf! Brer Wolf!' yelled Brer Bear. 'You head him off down there, and I'll head him off up here. We'll catch Brer Fox sure as a fly's got wings!'

Brer Fox, rolling in the water, still watching for the fish that didn't come, heard Brer Bear's voice, and looked up to see what the fuss was about. When he saw Brer Bear coming one way and Brer Wolf coming another, he jumped out of the river in a mighty hurry. He took a look down at himself and saw that the treacle and leaves had gone – and then off he went as if a hive of bees were on his tail.

He wasn't any too soon. As it was, Brer Bear got the tip-end of his tail – another moment and he'd have caught him!

Brer Fox went home through the woods, wet and angry. As he passed Brer Rabbit's house he saw him out in the porch, rocking himself in a rocking-chair and singing his song:

*'Oh, Mr Rabbit, your ears are mighty long!*
*Yes, sir, yes! My ears are made to last!*

*Oh, Mr Rabbit, your teeth are mighty sharp!*
*Yes, sir, yes! They cut down the grass!'*

Brer Fox was going by without a word, but Brer Rabbit saw him. 'Heyo, Brer Fox!' he shouted. 'Have you brought me a fish from your fish-trap?'

But Brer Fox, he didn't answer a word. He gave Brer Rabbit one look, and if looks could have killed – well, Brer Rabbit would have dropped down dead, there isn't a doubt of that!

# Brer Fox tries Another Fish-Trap

Now although Brer Fox was very angry with Brer Rabbit for tricking him into making himself a fish-trap, he couldn't help thinking it certainly would be a mighty fine idea to make a real fish-trap. So he set to work to make one.

Brer Rabbit saw him working away at the trap and he walked over to see him.

'What are you making, Brer Fox?' he said.

'A fish-trap,' said Brer Fox, rather proud of himself. 'Why don't you make one too, Brer Rabbit? Fish is a change from fresh meat and salad.'

'Thank you very much, Brer Fox,' said Brer Rabbit politely, 'but I'm not wanting fish for dinner just now, and anyway I'm too busy to make fish-traps.'

Well, Brer Fox, he finished his fish-trap at last, and then he went in his boat up and down the river hunting for a good place to put it. He hunted and he hunted and at last he found the right place. He put his trap there and set it.

Then he rubbed his hands in delight and thought of all the fish he would catch. He didn't know that Brer Rabbit was sitting on the bank under a bush, watching him fix that trap. No – if Brer Fox had known that, he wouldn't have felt quite so happy.

Brer Rabbit watched Brer Fox carry stones and rocks to put on his trap to hold it in place. He grinned to see Brer Fox getting hotter and hotter.

Brer Fox felt very tired after all his hard work. He went home, washed his face and hands, and sat down to rest. After he had taken a good long rest he went down to the river to see if he had caught any fish in his trap. He was rather afraid of water-snakes when he put his hand in the trap, but all the same he felt all round the trap to see if he could feel any fish – and there were none there at all.

So back home he went once more. 'I guess I must wait a few days before I go and look again,' said Brer Fox. 'I'll go down to my trap at the end of the week.' So towards the week-end he went down to his trap, felt all round it, and was mighty disappointed to find no fish there.

It went on like this till Brer Fox was quite tired of running to and from his fish-trap and never finding a thing there. And one day, when he was looking around his trap, he saw foot-prints that told him some one had been along there.

'Yes, some one's been robbing my fish-trap,' said Brer Fox. 'And if I don't make any mistake I sort of know who that someone is!'

He got into his boat, paddled it to an overhanging bush nearby and slid under it with his boat so that he was quite hidden. He watched all the morning. Nobody came. He watched all dinner-time and after, and nobody came. Towards the evening, just as Brer Fox was making ready to come out from under the bush and slip off home, he heard a noise by the fish-trap. He peeped out – and there was old Brer Rabbit in a boat, poling it along to the trap.

Brer Rabbit wasn't using a paddle to get his boat along, as Brer Fox did – no, he was standing up in his boat and using a long pole to push it along, just as we do when we are punting. Old Brer Rabbit, he stood in the back part of the boat, pushed his pole to the bottom of the river, gave it a shove, and sent his boat along at a good speed.

Brer Fox felt mighty mad when he saw this, and he watched and waited. 'I'll just wait till Brer Rabbit comes by me and then I'll go after him in my boat and catch him!' said Brer Fox. 'I guess I can paddle my boat quicker than he can pole his!'

Brer Rabbit poled right up to the fish-trap, bent down and put his paw into it. He pulled out a great big fish – then he reached in and pulled out another fish, then he pulled out a third, and it went on like this till he had got his boat almost full of fish from Brer Fox's fish-trap!

Just about then Brer Fox paddled his boat out from under his bush and came towards Brer Rabbit.

'Ah-yi, Brer Rabbit!' yelled Brer Fox. 'You're the man that's been robbing my fish-trap all this time! I've got you this time! Oh, you needn't try to run! I've got you this time for sure!'

Brer Rabbit jumped round and saw Brer Fox. He flung the last fish into his boat, grabbed for his pole and started off, with Brer Fox just behind him. Now Brer Fox could paddle much faster than Brer Rabbit could pole, and Brer Rabbit knew this – but did he care? Not a bit of it! Old Brer Rabbit had a trick up his sleeve all right. He had more fun in getting away from Brer Fox that time than ever he had before in all his life!

How old Brer Bull-Frog laughed to see what happened! He was a-sitting there on the bank and he saw it all. Brer Rabbit had to stand at the back of his boat to pole it – and as soon as Brer Fox's

boat touched his, Brer Rabbit took his pole and pushed hard at Brer Fox's boat. And the harder he pushed, the farther forward he sent himself and the farther backward went Brer Fox! Oh, it looked mighty easy to old Brer Bull-Frog sitting on the bank there, and all Brer Fox could do was to shake his fist and grit his teeth – but he couldn't get in front of Brer Rabbit's boat, no matter how he tried.

And when Brer Fox stopped to smack Brer Bull-Frog on the nose for laughing so much, Brer Rabbit slipped ahead, landed on the bank, took up the fish, and raced for home. Oh no, Brer Fox, you can't catch old Brer Rabbit!

# Brer Rabbit Runs a Race

One day, when Brer Rabbit was going lippitty clippitty down the road, he met old Brer Terrapin, and after they had said how-do-you-do, Brer Rabbit told Brer Terrapin how grateful he was to him for falling off the mantel-piece on top of Brer Fox's head.

Then Brer Terrapin said: 'Brer Fox ran mighty fast that day, but if *I'd* been after him, instead of you, Brer Rabbit, I'd have caught him.'

'I could have caught him easily enough myself, only I didn't like to leave the ladies,' said Brer Rabbit.

'I could have caught him before you did,' said Brer Terrapin.

'You're an old slow-coach that doesn't start till other people have got there!' said Brer Rabbit.

'You mind what you're saying, Brer Rabbit,' said Brer Terrapin. 'I'm swifter than you, I am.'

'I can outrun you any day, Brer Terrapin,' said Brer Rabbit.

'I can be there and back before you've even started,' said old Brer Terrapin.

'I tell you you don't know what you're talking about!' said Brer Rabbit.

'Well, in my chimney at home I've got a silver shilling hidden,' said Brer Terrapin. 'We'll have a race, Brer Rabbit, and if you win, then I will give you my silver shilling.'

'And in my chimney *I've* got a silver shilling!' said Brer Rabbit. 'And you shall have it if you can beat me in a race.

'Huh, Brer Terrapin, I could leave you far behind, I could sow barley as I went along and it would be ripe before you got to the winning-post!'

Well, old Brer Turkey Buzzard said he would hold their shillings and arrange the race for them. Before long, everything was ready. The race was to be four miles, and the ground was measured off. At the end of every mile a post was stuck up.

'Brer Rabbit, you are to run down the high road, and Brer Terrapin, you are to run through the woods,' said Brer Turkey Buzzard.

'Brer Terrapin is silly to run through the woods instead of down the high road,' said Brer Fox. 'He could get along more quickly on the road.'

But Brer Terrapin stuck out that he would go through the woods. He had a mighty good reason for it too.

Miss Meadows and the girls and all the neighbours made up their minds to see the race, and Brer Rabbit practised for it every day, skipping over the ground as gaily as a grass-hopper!

Old Brer Terrapin lay low in the marsh. He had a wife and three children, had old Brer Terrapin, and they were all so alike that you couldn't tell one from the other. It was just impossible to know which was Brer Terrapin, which was his wife and which were his children.

Well, on the day of the race, Brer Terrapin, his old woman and his three children all got up before sunrise and went to the racing-place. Brer Terrapin's old woman took up her stand near by the first post, she did, and the children went one to each of the other four mile-posts, and old Brer Terrapin he took up his stand near the winning-post. So there was a terrapin by every mile-post.

By and by along came everybody to see the race. Judge Turkey Buzzard came, and Miss Meadows and the girls, and all the other creatures, and last of all Brer Rabbit with ribbons tied round his neck and on his ears. My, he did look smart!

Everybody went to the winning-post to see who was going to win, Brer Rabbit or Brer Terrapin. When the time came to start the race, old Brer Turkey Buzzard pulled out his watch and shouted out:

'Are you ready?'

Brer Rabbit yelled 'Yes!' and old Mrs Terrapin shouted 'Yes!' from the woods. Brer Rabbit started out on the race and Mrs Terrapin set off quietly for home. She hadn't got to do any more than shout 'Yes!' to Brer Turkey Buzzard.

Judge Turkey Buzzard spread his wings and rose into the air. He skimmed along to see that the race was run fairly.

When Brer Rabbit got to the first mile-post one of the Terrapin children crawled out of the woods and made for the mile-post too. Judge Turkey Buzzard thought he was the same terrapin that had shouted 'Yes!' to him at the other mile-post.

As Brer Rabbit reached the mile-post he yelled out: 'Where are you, Brer Terrapin?'

'Here I come a-panting!' said the terrapin.

Brer Rabbit was surprised to find the terrapin so near him, and he set out faster than ever, and the terrapin made for home. He had no more to do in the race. But when Brer Rabbit reached the next mile-post, another terrapin crawled out of the woods near by. He was the second of the terrapin children, but he looked exactly like Old Man Terrapin himself.

'Where are you, Brer Terrapin?' shouted Brer Rabbit, as he got near the second mile-post.

'Here I come a-puffing!' said the terrapin.

Brer Rabbit set out again, faster than before, and came to the next mile-post – and there was the terrapin again. Brer Rabbit felt mighty surprised to think old Brer Terrapin could run so fast. He didn't know of the terrapin's little trick.

Then there was only one more mile to run. Brer Rabbit was getting out of breath.

By and by Old Man Terrapin, who was sitting in the woods not far from the winning-post, looked down the road, and saw old Brer Turkey Buzzard sailing along in the air, and he knew it was time for him to show up. So he scrambled out of the woods, rolled across the ditch and shuffled through the crowd of folks to the winning-post, and crawled behind it.

By and by along came Brer Rabbit. He looked round and didn't see Brer Terrapin. So he shouted out, 'I've won the race, folks, I've won the race!'

Then Miss Meadows and the girls and everybody else began to laugh fit to kill themselves, and old Brer Terrapin, he raised himself up from behind the winning-post and said: 'Just give me time to get my breath! I was here before you, Brer Rabbit, and I guess I've won the race and the money too!'

Then Brer Turkey Buzzard tied the purse of money round Brer Terrapin's neck, and, with everyone laughing and clapping, he ambled off home.

As for Brer Rabbit, he knew he had been tricked – but he just couldn't guess how, no matter how he kept on thinking!

# Brer Rabbit Tricks Mr Man

One day Brer Rabbit was going along the big road when he met Mr Man driving along with a wagon full of greens. Mr Man was taking them to market, and he meant to get a good price for them too!

Well, Brer Rabbit saw those greens, and he made up his mind that Mr Man had too many, and he, Brer Rabbit, hadn't enough.

'There's something wrong somewhere,' said Brer Rabbit. 'If there wasn't, I'd have a wagon full of greens too! Now, why haven't I got one?'

When Mr Man drove up, Brer Rabbit shouted to him:

'Mr Man, please, sir, give me a lift!'

Mr Man stopped his horse and said: 'Heyo, Brer Rabbit! How's this? You are going one way and I'm going the other. What good is a lift going to do you when I'm going the wrong way?'

Brer Rabbit scratched the back of his neck with

his hind foot and shouted out: 'Mr Man, you can't know me very well if you don't know I'll take a lift no matter which way I'm going!'

Well, after some time Mr Man said Brer Rabbit could get up and have a lift.

'You come and sit here with me,' said Mr Man. 'I'd like to talk to you to pass away the time.'

'Oh no, Mr Man,' said Brer Rabbit. 'I'd be scared of falling off if I sat in front with you. I'd rather sit right flat down in the bottom of the wagon.'

So he climbed into the back of the wagon and crouched down there at the bottom as if he were afraid to move.

By and by, whilst they were going down a steep hill and Mr Man had to keep an eye on his horse, Brer Rabbit took hold of two big cabbages and flung them out on to the road. Just as they hit the ground with a thud, Brer Rabbit shouted out 'OW!' at the top of his voice, to hide the noise.

Mr Man looked round in surprise. 'What's the matter?' he said.

'Oh, nothing at all, Mr Man,' said Brer Rabbit, 'except that the wagon went over a stone and gave such a jolt that I nearly fell out.'

Well, they went on a little farther, and Brer Rabbit took hold of two more cabbages. When Mr

Man had his eye on the horses Brer Rabbit threw the cabbages out – thud – on the road. Just as they hit the ground Brer Rabbit shouted out, 'BLAM!' at the top of his voice.

This drowned the noise of the cabbages falling and made Mr Man jump. 'Whatever's the matter now?' he said.

'Nothing at all, Mr Man,' said Brer Rabbit, 'except that I saw a big bird flying along and I pretended I had a gun and shot at him, blam!'

Mr Man turned back to his horse again. Brer Rabbit waited until they came to a mighty slippery place and Mr Man had to guide his horse carefully. Then he took up four cabbages and threw them out – thud! But just as they struck the ground Brer Rabbit gave such a loud yell that Mr Man almost fell off his seat. 'BLAM-BLAM!'

'Bless gracious, Brer Rabbit, whatever are you doing now?' yelled Mr Man. 'I nearly drove into a tree, you startled me so!'

'Sorry, Mr Man,' said Brer Rabbit. 'I saw Cousin Wildcat making a face at me through the trees, and I just pretended I had a great big gun and shot at him, blam-blam!'

Well, Brer Rabbit kept on like this, making loud noises whenever he threw out the cabbages, till at

last the wagon was quite empty. Mr Man didn't
notice this until he had got a good way to market,
and then he looked round to say something to old
Brer Rabbit – and saw that his wagon was empty!

Mr Man stopped his horse and stared at
the empty wagon in the greatest astonishment.

'Where's my greens?' he yelled. 'Where are my nice cabbages? Oh, you long-eared rascal! Where are my lovely cabbages? You give me those cabbages, Brer Rabbit, or you'll be sorry for yourself.'

Brer Rabbit sat at the back of the wagon and listened as if he were mighty astonished. 'Now, now, Mr Man,' he said, 'just keep quiet. If folks come along this way they'll think you are acting mighty odd.'

'You give me my cabbages, you long-eared scamp!' roared Mr Man. 'Look at all the way I've come to market to sell them – and now I'm nearly there and they've all gone!'

'Well, Mr Man, I haven't got your cabbages,' said Brer Rabbit. 'That I haven't. Could I hide a hundred cabbages in my coat, do you think? No, that I couldn't. And I couldn't eat them all, either. No, Mr Man, your cabbages have just disappeared, and it's no use asking me where they've gone, for I don't know where their friends are.'

'You give me my cabbages,' shouted Mr Man, and he threw the reins on the horse's back and stood up to get hold of Brer Rabbit.

Well, Brer Rabbit began to get a bit scared and guessed it was time to go. So he dropped off the back of the wagon as nimbly as you please.

'The sun's getting low, Mr Man, and I'd better be going. The sooner I go the better, because if you go on like this you'll soon be accusing me of taking all those cabbages, and you can see I haven't got a single one of them. Thank you for the lift, Mr Man, and I wish you mighty well.'

He trotted off down the road, carrying an old sack over his shoulder that he had found at the bottom of the wagon. And it wasn't long before that sack was full of cabbages – yes, as full as could be! Brer Rabbit picked up every one of them – and the only thing that surprises me is that he didn't get the horse and wagon as well! Oh, he's a sly fellow and a wicked one is Brer Rabbit!

# CONTENTS

# Brer Rabbit's a Rascal!

Now, once when Brer Rabbit was hard at work scraping the stones off his bit of ground, he heard a cry for help. Off he went, rake in hand, to see what the matter was.

It was the little girl belonging to the farmer. She had been fishing in the river and had slipped and fallen in. 'Save me,' she cried, and went swirling past Brer Rabbit, her skirt spreading out on the water.

Well, old Brer Rabbit he ran beside her, jabbing with his rake. And at last he got hold of the little girl's belt and hauled her to the bank. There she sat, sobbing and crying, her arms round Brer Rabbit's neck.

'You come home to your Ma,' said Brer Rabbit. 'You're wet. She'll dry you and give you a good hot drink.'

So off they went together, the little girl clinging to Brer Rabbit as if she would never let him go.

And my word, when the farmer heard how he had saved his little girl there wasn't anything he wouldn't have done for old Brer Rabbit.

'There's a sack of carrots over there,' he said. 'Take it. And there's a sack of potatoes, too. You're welcome to it. And while you're about it, help yourself to a sack of turnips. You're a born rascal, Brer Rabbit, but you're good-hearted, so you are! Now off you go while I still think good things of you!'

Now, when Brer Rabbit was wheeling home his three sacks, whistling a merry song and feeling on top of the world, who should come along but Brer Fox, Brer Bear and Brer Wolf. How they stared when they saw Brer Rabbit with so much food!

'Carrots! Turnips! Potatoes! Sacks of them!' said Brer Fox. 'Hey, Brer Rabbit, give us some. And don't tell us you've come by them honestly, because we shan't believe you!'

Brer Rabbit was most annoyed. 'You go and ask the farmer!' he said. 'He gave me them with kind words, so he did!'

'Now you're telling stories,' said Brer Wolf. 'You give us some of those carrots and turnips and potatoes, Brer Rabbit – or we'll come along one night and help ourselves!'

'I *might* have given you some,' said Brer Rabbit, wheeling his barrow away with his head in the air. 'I *might* have given you some if you knew how to behave!'

Brer Bear, Brer Fox and Brer Wolf stared after Brer Rabbit. Brer Fox scratched his head. 'Well, however he got those sacks he's going to share them with us, whether he wants to or not! Shall we go along to his place tonight and see where he's put the sacks?'

'Yes,' said the other two, and Brer Fox grinned

at them. 'Meet me here. We'll slip along in the shadows – and my, won't Brer Rabbit be angry in the morning!'

Now, old Brer Rabbit had a kind of feeling that Brer Fox, Brer Wolf and Brer Bear might be along that night. He wheeled his sacks to his shed and he emptied all the carrots, potatoes and turnips out on the ground. He picked out the bad ones and set them aside. Then he took a big broom and swept all the roots along the ground to his cellar.

Bumpity-bumpity-bump – they rolled down into his cellar and he shut and locked the door. Then he went back to the shed again. He took the sacks to the pile of stones he had scraped off his ground and he filled them almost to the top with the stones. But right at the very top he didn't put the stones – he put a layer of bad carrots, a layer of poor potatoes, and in the third sack a layer of rotten turnips. Oh, Brer Rabbit, you're a wily one!

He dragged the sacks back to his shed and set them up against the walls. Then he went indoors, leaving the shed door unlocked.

'And if this isn't a nice easy way of getting rid of all those stones, well, I'll never know a better one!' said old Brer Rabbit.

Now, that night along crept Brer Fox, Brer Bear and Brer Wolf. There was a little moon so they kept well in the shadows. They came to the shed and tried the door. It wasn't locked – that was fine!

They slipped inside. Brer Bear pointed to the three sacks in glee. He looked in the top of one. He could see dimly in the moonlight – and he saw potatoes!

'Here are the potatoes,' he said. 'I'll take this sack. You follow with the others, Brer Wolf and Brer Fox.'

They staggered out with the sacks. 'My sack is mighty heavy!' said Brer Fox, groaning. 'I never thought turnips could be such a dreadful weight.'

'These carrots are heavy, too,' panted Brer Wolf.

'My, they must be good solid ones!'

Brer Rabbit saw the three of them through his window, staggering up the lane in the shadows. He grinned to himself. 'Nice of them to carry those tiresome stones away!' he said. 'I must thank them when I see them!'

Well, by the time Brer Fox, Brer Wolf and Brer Bear had reached their homes they couldn't walk a step farther! They sank down on the ground, panting. Brer Bear thought he would make some potato soup and he shook the sack hard – and out came six poor potatoes – and about twenty big stones!

Then Brer Bear knew he had been tricked and he rushed to tell Brer Fox and Brer Wolf. But they had already found out, and dear me, the names they called old Brer Rabbit would have made his whiskers curl if he had heard them!

Brer Rabbit went out of his way to meet the three the next day. He raised his hat politely and gave his very best bow.

'My best thanks, gentlemen, for so kindly removing all those stones for me,' he said. 'I shall have another sackful tomorrow if one of you would like to call for it.'

And then, my goodness me, he had to run for his life – but he didn't mind that because Brer Rabbit could always run faster than anyone else. As for Brer Bear, Brer Wolf and Brer Fox, they had to carry all the stones out of their gardens and empty them into the ditch. They were so stiff afterwards that they couldn't walk properly for days!

Ah, Brer Rabbit, it's hard to get the better of you, you rascal!

# You Can't Trick Brer Rabbit!

It happened once that Brer Fox thought of a good way to catch Brer Rabbit for his dinner. He waited until he saw Brer Rabbit coming along down the lane, and then he set up a mighty groaning and limped along as if one of his legs were badly hurt.

'Ooh my, ooh my!' he groaned, pretending that he didn't see Brer Rabbit. 'I'm sure I shan't get home! My leg's broken, that's certain!'

He suddenly fell down on the ground, and

lay there making a great hullabaloo. Brer Rabbit stopped a little way behind him in surprise.

'What's got you, Brer Fox?' he asked.

'I've just broken my leg,' said Brer Fox. 'You come and help me home, Brer Rabbit, there's a good fellow. Give me your arm, for I can't walk alone. You mustn't leave me here like this, for I'd die. I can't walk another step!'

But Brer Rabbit wasn't easily tricked. 'You wait there, Brer Fox,' he said. 'I'll get help for you.'

'But I'll die before you bring help,' said Brer Fox, making a great moaning noise again. 'You come along and help me now, Brer Rabbit.'

'I'll go and get you something to eat, first,' said Brer Rabbit. 'That will get your strength up so's you'll be able to walk with me.'

'That's kind of you, Brer Rabbit,' said Brer Fox. So off went Brer Rabbit. Nearby was Brer Bear's house, and Brer Rabbit knew he had been baking a meat-pie that day. He saw that Brer Bear had put it on the window-sill to cool. He snatched it up and ran off to Brer Fox with it.

'Here you are, Brer Fox,' he said. 'You eat that up and you'll feel better. I'll be back in two shakes of a duck's tail to help you home.'

Brer Fox took the pie greedily and began to gobble it up. Brer Rabbit rushed back to Brer Bear's house and banged on the door, crying, 'Heyo, Brer Bear! Have you lost a fine meat-pie? There's old Brer Fox a-sitting down the lane, and he's gobbling up a pie as fast as he can!'

Brer Bear went to the window-sill to see if his pie were there, and when he saw it was gone, he shouted in a fearful rage.

'Stars and moon! It's gone. I'll bite Brer Fox's head off for that!'

Off he ran out into the lane, grunting and growling most fearsomely. 'Oy, oy, yi, yi, where's Brer Fox? I'll bite his head off! I'll gobble his tail!

I'll cook his whiskers! Where's my meat-pie?'

As soon as Brer Fox heard this awful noise and saw Brer Bear pounding down the lane he turned pale with fright. He threw the pie into the hedge and leapt to his feet.

'You mind your broken leg, Brer Fox!' yelled Brer Rabbit, laughing fit to kill himself. 'You mind that broken leg!'

But Brer Fox didn't wait to think of his leg. No, it had mended itself all in a hurry, and you couldn't see him for dust! As for old Brer Rabbit, he took the pie out of the hedge and sat down to enjoy it. It's a pity to waste anything, isn't it?

# A Happy New Year!

Did you ever hear the tale of how Brer Fox and Brer Wolf planned to break into Brer Rabbit's house one night and steal all the little fat youngsters there?

'We'll make him tear his whiskers and dance with fury!' grinned Brer Fox. 'Ho, ho! What will he say when he finds all his young ones gone one morning? He'll think twice before he plays a joke on *us* again!'

'We'd better choose a very dark night when there is no moon at all,' said Brer Wolf. 'In two weeks from now, shall we say? Very well, Brer Fox. Meet me outside Brer Rabbit's gate in the middle of the night – and we'll have a fine time!'

So on the night planned Brer Fox and Brer Wolf met silently outside Brer Rabbit's gate. It was about ten minutes to midnight – and to Brer Fox's enormous surprise there was a bright light in Brer

Rabbit's parlour! There was also a great noise of shouting, laughing and dancing.

'Strange!' said Brer Fox, puzzled. 'He must be having a party. I say, Brer Wolf, let's hide under a bush in the garden, and jump on the guests as they come out! Brer Hare and his family are sure to be there, and all Brer Rabbit's cousins. We shall have a fine feast!'

So into the garden they crept and squatted under a bush.

Now Brer Rabbit certainly *was* having a party! You see, it was New Year's Eve, and he meant to see in the New Year with all his friends. They were very happy indeed, and most excited.

'Let's welcome the New Year in at midnight with as much noise as we can,' said Brer Rabbit. 'That would be fun! Here, Brer Terrapin, you can have a couple of saucepans to bang if you like – and you, Brer Turkey-Buzzard, can borrow my frying pans.'

'I'll have the dinner-bell,' said Brer Frog, leaping down from the curtain at last. 'And *I'll* take the pail from under the sink and bang it with the rolling-pin,' said Brer Bear, happily. 'And *I'll* have the old tin tray,' said Brer Hare. 'Oh, yes, and the shovel, too – my, I'll make a fine din!'

Well, just at midnight, when the clock was striking twelve, Brer Rabbit threw open his front door, and all his guests streamed out to welcome in the New Year, carrying with them the saucepans, frying-pans, dinner-bell, pail and tray. Brer Fox and Brer Wolf, who were waiting patiently under their bush, leapt out at once, thinking that their chance had come – but, stars and moon, what was all this? Crash, clang, ding, clonk, smash, bang, crash, ding, clonk ... all the guests began to bang together their saucepans, pans and pails, and Brer Fox and Brer Wolf stopped still in horror and alarm! They were terrified out of their lives!

Brer Rabbit saw them in the light that came from his parlour, and in a trice he knew they were up to something. 'Come on, boys!' he shouted to his guests. 'Wish them a Happy New Year!'

Then, to Brer Fox's and Brer Wolf's terror, everyone tore after them, banging, clanking, dinging, crashing for all they were worth, and shouting at the tops of their voices, 'A Happy New Year, a Happy New Year!'

'*That's* a good beginning to the year, anyway,' said Brer Rabbit, in delight, as he watched Brer Fox and Brer Wolf streak away like lightning. 'Come along in again, friends. Happy New Year, everybody!'

Brer Fox and Brer Wolf stopped still in horror and alarm!

# Brer Rabbit's New Year Gift

Now it happened once that Brer Fox took to hiding round corners and under bushes and behind fences waiting to spring out at Brer Rabbit whenever he passed, and Brer Rabbit got quite jumpy and upset.

'Now look here, Brer Fox,' said Brer Rabbit, 'this isn't friendly of you. One of these days you'll scare me out of my skin, and you'll be sorry.'

Brer Fox grinned. 'It's just what I'm hoping to do,' he said. 'Once I make you really jump out of your skin, Brer Rabbit, you'll be all ready for the cooking pot.'

Well, that didn't please Brer Rabbit at all. He thought for a mighty long time, and then he brightened up. '*I'll* soon stop Brer Fox's tricks!' he said to himself, and off he went to the town. He bought a large watch with a very loud tick. He wrapped it up and sent it through the post with a label inside that said, 'To Brer Fox, from an Unknown Friend.'

Well, when Brer Fox opened the parcel and found the watch inside, and the message, he was mighty pleased. He put the watch into his waistcoat pocket, and went out to show it to everyone, Brer Rabbit as well.

'My!' said Brer Rabbit, pretending to be most surprised. 'That's a beautiful watch, Brer Fox. Just you leave it about, and I'll come and get it. I'd dearly like it myself!'

'Huh!' said Brer Fox. 'I shan't leave it about, don't you worry, Brer Rabbit. I shall always wear

307

it and there won't be any chance of you finding it.'

Well, that was just what Brer Rabbit wanted, of course! He grinned to himself and did a little dance as soon as Brer Fox was round the corner. Now he would be able to hear Brer Fox whenever he was anywhere near!

'If he hides behind the fence I shall hear tick-a-tock, tick-a-tock as soon as I come along!' thought Brer Rabbit. 'And I'll jump on him, so I will! And if he hides under a bush I'll hear tick-a-tock, tick-a-tock long before I get up to him – and I'll creep round the bush and get hold of his tail! And if he's hiding round a corner, I'll hear tick-a-tock, tick-a-tock, and I'll go round the other way and yell in his ear! My, I'll have a fine time now old Brer Fox has got that watch!'

Well, for some time Brer Fox was so pleased with his watch and went about showing it to so many people that he quite forgot about lying in wait for Brer Rabbit. And when Brer Rabbit met him one morning he said, 'Heyo, Brer Fox! I'm glad my skin's safe now! That watch of yours has made you forget your silly tricks.'

Now that made Brer Fox think. 'Ha!' he said to himself, 'maybe it was Brer Rabbit sent me this watch. Maybe it's he who is the Unknown Friend – and he thinks the new watch will make me forget to scare him. Ah, Brer Rabbit, you're sly – but I'm slyer! I'll soon teach you that I'm up to all my tricks, and, tails and whiskers, I'll give you such a scare before the week is out that your hair will stand on end and your bobtail will curl with fright!'

Brer Rabbit watched Brer Fox's face and he guessed his thoughts. He scampered off, lippitty, clippetty, laughing as he went.

Brer Rabbit was too smart to be caught by Brer Fox!

# Brer Bear's Eggs

Once it happened that Brer Bear kept chickens and stored up the eggs in pickle so that he could use them in the winter-time. Brer Rabbit got to hear of this, and he licked his lips. He trotted round to old Brer Bear's, sat down, and gossiped with him. Soon he led Brer Bear to talk of his eggs, and Brer Rabbit said, 'And how many eggs have you put away, Brer Bear?'

'I don't know,' said Brer Bear. 'I can't count more than five.'

'Oh, that's bad,' said Brer Rabbit. '*I'll* count them for you, if you like. Show me where the eggs are.'

So Brer Bear showed him. They were locked up in a shed. Brer Rabbit counted them over and there were forty.

'Suppose somebody steals some,' said Brer Rabbit, 'how are you going to know?'

'I *shan't* know!' said Brer Bear, sorrowfully.

310

'Well, look here,' said Brer Rabbit. 'If you like, I'll come along and count them for you every day, Brer Bear. Then you'll know if the number is all right.'

'Thank you, Brer Rabbit,' said Brer Bear, gratefully. So each morning Brer Rabbit scampered along to Brer Bear's lippitty, clippetty – but instead of counting them, the wicked creature took an egg for himself every day!

Well, after thirty-nine days there was only one egg left. Brer Rabbit arrived that morning to find Brer Fox sitting with Brer Bear. When Brer Fox heard that Brer Rabbit was counting Brer Bear's eggs for him each morning, he threw back his head and laughed uncontrollably.

'Ho! Brer Bear, you don't suppose you've got your forty eggs there *now*, do you?' he said. 'Brer Rabbit doesn't do these good deeds for nothing. Not he!'

Brer Bear was worried – but he didn't like to think such things of Brer Rabbit. As for Brer Rabbit, he looked very hurt, and spoke humbly to Brer Bear.

'Oh, Brer Bear,' he said. 'I hope you won't listen to Brer Fox. Let me go into the shed, and I will bring out your eggs and show you there are forty.'

'Very well,' said Brer Bear. So into the shed hopped Brer Rabbit, took up the one egg there, marked a figure 1 on it, and went out to show it to Brer Bear and Brer Fox. Then back he went, licked the figure 1 off, and wrote the figure 2 on the egg. He ran out and showed it to Brer Bear.

'Number 2 egg!' he said. Then back he went, licked off the 2 and wrote 3 instead. And so the wicked rascal went on until he had reached number 40 – but all the time he only showed the same one egg, and neither Brer Bear nor Brer Fox knew it. Brer Bear was pleased to think he had his 40 eggs safe, and he said so. 'Brer Rabbit, you can have that last egg for your trouble!' he said. So Brer Rabbit put the egg into his pocket, said goodbye, and ran off, grinning.

But Brer Fox saw that grin – and he went and looked in the shed to see the other eggs – and found none there! Then he knew the trick that Brer Rabbit had played, and he told Brer Bear he'd go along to Brer Rabbit's house and see if he could find the eggs for him. But Brer Rabbit saw him coming, broke all his eggs into a jug of milk and drank them up!

Six of the eggs were bad – and Brer Rabbit lay

in bed for three days, groaning, for he had a dreadful pain.

'When bad habits and bad eggs go together, there's sure to be a bad pain!' said Brer Fox. 'Serves you right, Brer Rabbit!'

# Bobs Meets Brer Rabbit

Once upon a time Bobs the dog buried a very large bone in the farmer's field of carrots. He thought it would be safe there – but it wasn't! For one night who should come along that way, digging up carrots, but old Brer Rabbit – and, of course, he found Bobs' bone.

'My!' said Brer Rabbit, 'here's a bone to make soup. I'll have carrot-and-bone soup tonight, so I will!' He tucked the bone in his pocket, and set off down the lane. But he hadn't gone far before he met Bobs ambling along – and Bobs smelt the bone at once!

'Fine smell of bone about,' he said to Brer Rabbit. 'Can *you* smell it, Brer Rabbit?'

'*Bone!*' said Brer Rabbit, pretending to be surprised. '*Bone*, Bobs! Don't be silly. You can smell the bone in your leg, that's what you can smell!'

But Bobs knew better. He looked at Brer Rabbit

and saw his bulging pockets. So he was mighty polite and chatted away to Brer Rabbit as if he had known him for years.

'You come along to my kennel and see what a fine big house I've got!' said Bobs. 'I may have some biscuits there.'

So Brer Rabbit trotted beside Bobs, and the two of them went lippitty-clippetty to Old Thatch. Bobs led Brer Rabbit to his big kennel. Brer Rabbit, sniffing for biscuits, hopped in and Bobs banged the door and bolted it! Aha, Brer Rabbit, you're caught now!

'Let me out, Bobs,' said Brer Rabbit. 'I'll escape if you don't, and I shan't be friends with you any more!'

'You can't escape from there!' said Bobs, with a grin so wide that his whiskers nearly fell off. 'I'm going to tell Sandy about you!'

But he didn't go to tell Sandy. No, Bobs had a better plan than that! He slipped off to the gardener's shed, where he remembered seeing the gardener's old cap and old red scarf hanging! He put the cap on his head, and twisted the scarf round his neck. Then he woofed to himself in glee! Old Brer Rabbit was going to be properly tricked! He ran back to the kennel, but when he got near he began to whistle as if he were just someone passing by. Brer Rabbit looked out of the window of the kennel and saw him – but he didn't know it was Bobs, of course!

'Heyo, friend!' said Brer Rabbit. 'Aren't you mighty cold out there tonight?"

'Very cold!' said Bobs, in a funny deep voice. 'You are lucky to have a warm house to sleep in, I can tell you!'

'Well, I do feel so sorry for you, that I will lend you my house to sleep in this cold night,' said Brer Rabbit, pretending to be very kind. 'You just open the door, friend, and you can sleep here with me.'

317

'I want something to eat first,' said Bobs, 'I'm so very hungry!'

'Well, take this bone and these carrots,' said Brer Rabbit, pushing them through the window. 'And now just open the door, and you can come in and snooze on the straw.'

Bobs took the bone and the carrots and grinned. He unbolted the door of the kennel – and Brer Rabbit shot out. 'Tell Bobs I've escaped after all!' he shouted.

'Oh, he knows that all right!' called Bobs, in his own voice. 'Thanks for leaving me the bone and the carrots, Brer Rabbit! I won't ask you to stay and share them!'

# Pull his Ears, Brer Fox!

Now once it happened that Brer Fox went fishing, and caught a mighty lot of fish. He strung them on a line and carried them proudly through the wood, showing them to everyone he met. Brer Rabbit heard him boasting about them, and he ran to Brer Donkey, who was grazing in a nearby field.

'Come with me,' he said to Brer Donkey. 'You like a bit of fish, don't you? Well, here's a chance to get some!'

Brer Donkey squeezed through the hedge and went to a big bush of bramble with Brer Rabbit.

'Now you sit yourself down there,' said Brer Rabbit to Brer Donkey. 'And just stick your ears up straight as soon as I get in beside you. Don't you show anything except your ears, Brer Donkey, and don't you show those till I get in beside you – and go on showing them till you see it's time to stop.'

'Just as you say, Brer Rabbit,' said Brer Donkey,

and he settled himself down at the bottom of the bramble bush.

Now along came Brer Fox, swinging his string of fish, and humming a little song. Out stepped Brer Rabbit and bid him 'How do you do?'

'That's a mighty fine string of fish you've got,' said Brer Rabbit, staring hard at it.

'Yes,' said Brer Fox. 'Would you like to hear how I caught them all?'

'I would,' said Brer Rabbit. 'But I'm not sitting beside you, Brer Fox. Oh, no! You're not going to have rabbit-pie for dinner!'

'And you're not going to have fish for dinner,' said Brer Fox, looking mighty cautious. 'You just sit down in front of me, Brer Rabbit, where I can see you – and I'm going to hang my fish *behind* me, over this branch.'

'That suits me all right,' said Brer Rabbit, and he skipped into the bramble bush beside Brer Donkey.

'Stick your ears up so that I can see you,' said Brer Fox, and at the same moment old Brer Donkey stuck up his hairy ears and twitched them about. Brer Fox took a glance at them, and reckoned they were Brer Rabbit's ears all right. And he began the long, long tale of how he caught his fish. Brer Donkey twitched his ears all the time as if he were listening hard – but old Brer Rabbit, he crept out of the bramble bush, dashed down a hole nearby and came up just behind Brer Fox. And it wasn't long before that string of fish slipped from the branch where it hung – and disappeared down the burrow too.

Then Brer Rabbit popped up into the bramble bush again, giggling like a green woodpecker. 'Heyo, Brer Fox, watch your fish!' he called. Brer Fox turned round – and saw that his fish were gone! And in the same moment old Brer Donkey set down his ears, and Brer Rabbit set his up – and out he walked, ears and all, in front of Brer Fox.

'I suppose you'll say I took your fish, Brer Fox?' he said, with a grin.

'Well, you didn't,' said Brer Fox. 'I saw your ears a-listening to me all the time. Ah, wait till I catch that thief!'

But when he passed by Brer Rabbit's house that night, and smelt the smell of frying fish, and saw Brer Donkey and Brer Rabbit having a good tuck-in, Brer Fox was mighty puzzled. But he wasn't puzzled any more when Brer Donkey stuck his head out of the window, twitched his hairy ears, and cried, 'That was a mighty fine tale of yours about the fish, Brer Fox, a mighty fine tale.'

# Brer Rabbit Gets Caught

Did you ever hear how Brer Rabbit got caught by Brer Fox, and was marched off over the fields? Well, it happened that Brer Rabbit was busy scrabbling for carrots, and didn't hear Brer Fox creeping up – and suddenly there was a pounce and a shout, and there was Brer Rabbit properly caught by the fur at the back of his neck!

'Ooh-ow!' said Brer Rabbit in a fright.

'Aha!' said Brer Fox. 'I've really got you this time, Brer Rabbit – yes, there's no doubt about it at all. And you're going home with me. Come along!'

So they went along and they went along, Brer Rabbit racking his brains for some way of escape. At last he began to puff and pant in a most alarming manner.

'What's the matter, Brer Rabbit?' said Brer Fox, surprised.

'Oh, Brer Fox, please, sir, you go so fast!' said Brer Rabbit. 'You've such long legs, I can't keep up with you. I'll be nothing but skin and bone by the time I get to your house if you hurry me along like this.'

Well, Brer Fox much preferred Brer Rabbit to be plump, and not skin and bone, so he went more slowly. But Brer Rabbit still panted as if he had been running a mile.

'Oh, Brer Fox, please, sir, could we have a rest for a minute?' begged Brer Rabbit in a humble voice. 'Just a little small rest. Look, there's a nice little hillock of grass I could sit on for a moment. And there's a nice hard stone for you.'

'Huh!' said Brer Fox, in disgust. '*I'll* take the grassy hillock and *you* can have the hard stone, Brer Rabbit. You can have a very little small rest.'

So Brer Rabbit sat on the stone, and Brer Fox sat on the hillock of grass – which, as Brer Rabbit knew very well indeed, was nothing but an ant-hill. Yes, a fine big ant-hill where red stinging ants lived, and mighty angry they were to have their precious city sat upon so hard!

'It's good of you to give me a rest, Brer Fox,' said

Brer Rabbit. 'But don't you take your hand away from the back of my neck, or I might escape. You hold me tight.'

'You don't need to tell me that,' said Brer Fox, scornfully. Brer Rabbit watched a dozen ants run up Brer Fox's fur – then a dozen more, and then a hundred! Brer Fox put up his back leg and scratched himself because the ants tickled. Then they began to bite him, and he put up both hind legs and rubbed hard. Then they bit him everywhere, for they were angry with him for sitting on their town. Brer Fox gave a great yell and leapt up into the air.

'I'm sitting on an ant-hill!' he howled. 'Ooh! They're all over me! They're biting and stinging me!'

Well, those ants gave poor Brer Fox such a bad time that he hadn't any paw left to hold Brer Rabbit – he wanted all four of his paws to deal with the angry ants! And soon he was leaping high into the air and then rolling on the ground scratching and yelling for all he was worth.

Well, you may be sure Brer Rabbit didn't stay to watch him! No – he was off down the nearest rabbit-hole with a flash of his white bobtail. But he was mighty careful after that not to scrabble for carrots when Brer Fox was anywhere about!

# Brer Wolf's Dinner Party

Once Brer Wolf thought he would give a dinner party. So he asked Brer Rabbit, Brer Hare and Brer Turkey Buzzard to come, and also Brer Fox and Brer Bear.

Brer Hare was delighted. He didn't often go to parties. Brer Turkey Buzzard had been to one, and had never forgotten it because he had eaten so many ices. He longed to go to another. Only Brer Rabbit didn't seem too glad about the party.

It wasn't like Brer Wolf to give a party. He was a mean old thing who wouldn't even waste his breath to blow a hot pudding. Brer Rabbit puzzled his brains about it – and then he began to hang about Brer Wolf's house to see what things were being sent for the party.

But no matter how much Brer Rabbit watched, he couldn't see a thing arriving at Brer Wolf's!

Well, maybe he was going to cook the dinner all himself then.

So Brer Rabbit hid under a bush and watched Brer Wolf's chimney to see if a great amount of smoke came out of it, which would show he was having a mighty big cooking-fire. But no, only a wisp of smoke showed – Brer Wolf couldn't even be boiling an egg!

Brer Rabbit didn't like the look of things at all. On the day of the party he met Brer Hare and Brer Turkey Buzzard, both dressed up in their best, and they went towards Brer Wolf's house. 'Wait here a moment,' said Brer Rabbit at the gate. He tiptoed towards the house and looked in at the window. He saw the table laid all ready – but it was set with three plates only, and three knives and forks. A great pot of boiling water hung over the fire, and an empty dish was warming by the flames.

Three plates – and six guests! Brer Rabbit knew what *that* meant all right! He poked his head in at the window and saw Brer Wolf, Brer Fox and Brer Bear all hiding behind the door.

'Heyo!' said Brer Rabbit, cheerfully. 'What are you all doing there, hiding like that?'

'We're – er – we're just playing a game of hide-and-seek till you come,' said Brer Wolf, hurriedly.

'And why are there only three plates on the table?' asked Brer Rabbit, grinning.

'Well – somehow I'm not hungry, and nor are Brer Fox and Brer Bear,' said Brer Wolf. 'So we've just laid for you and the others, you see.'

'And what are we to eat?' asked Brer Rabbit, looking all round the kitchen.

'It's a s-s-surprise,' stammered Brer Wolf.

'And *I've* got a surprise for *you*, too,' said Brer Rabbit, with his most cheerful grin. 'I and my friends aren't hungry either, so we won't visit you today, thank you very much. Hope you'll feel hungry this evening – I rather think you will!'

And with that Brer Rabbit skipped off with Brer Hare and Brer Turkey Buzzard – and that was the last of Brer Wolf's party!

333

# Brer Rabbit and Brer Turkey Buzzard

I happened once that Brer Fox chased after Brer Rabbit and got so close to him that all Brer Rabbit could do was to run into a hollow tree. The hole was too small for Brer Fox to get in after him, so Brer Fox lay down to get his breath.

While he was lying there, Brer Turkey Buzzard came flapping along and thought Brer Fox was dead.

'Brer Fox is dead, and I'm so sorry!' he said.

'No, I'm not dead,' said Brer Fox. 'I've got old man Rabbit penned up in this tree. You sit and keep guard, Brer Turkey Buzzard, and I'll go and get my axe to chop down the tree.'

Well, Brer Fox loped off and Brer Buzzard stood by the tree-hole. By and by, when all was still, Brer Rabbit began to scramble about inside the tree, and shouted out, 'Brer Fox! Brer Fox!'

Nobody said anything. Brer Fox was gone. Then Brer Rabbit shouted like mad and said, 'You needn't talk if you don't want to, Brer Fox! I wish mighty bad that Brer Buzzard was here!'

Then Brer Buzzard tried to talk like Brer Fox. 'What do you want with Brer Buzzard?' he said.

'Oh, nothing much, except that there's the very fattest grey squirrel in here that ever I did see!' said Brer Rabbit. 'If Brer Buzzard was here, I'd drive him out of a little hole at the back of this tree and he could catch him easily.'

'Drive him out, then,' said Brer Buzzard, 'and I'll see that Brer Buzzard gets him!'

And with that Brer Buzzard slipped round to the other side of the tree.

Then Brer Rabbit shot out of the other hole

and set out for home! As for old Brer Buzzard, he reckoned he would stay and watch Brer Fox chop down the tree all for nothing! So he waited. And presently along came Brer Fox with his axe.

'How's Brer Rabbit getting on?' said Brer Fox. 'Oh, he's in there, he's in there!' said Brer Buzzard. 'He's very still, though. Perhaps he's taking a nap!'

'Well, I'm just in time to wake him up!' said Brer Fox, and he began to chop the tree. And every time he brought his axe down – pow! – on the tree old Brer Buzzard did a little dance and shouted out, 'Oh, he's in there, Brer Fox, sure! He's in there!'

Well, Brer Fox lammed away at that hollow tree, and when he had got it half cut through he suddenly caught sight of Brer Buzzard laughing at him behind his back! Then he knew something was up, and he went and peeped inside the hole of the tree.

'Look here, Brer Buzzard!' he called. 'Come and see if this isn't Brer Rabbit's foot hanging down here!'

Then Brer Buzzard hopped up and stuck his head in the hole – and Brer Fox grabbed hold of him, and there he was, caught.

'So you've tricked me, have you?' said Brer Fox. 'Well, I left you here to watch Brer Rabbit – and I come back and find him gone! I'm going to settle you right now, Brer Buzzard!' said Brer Fox.

With that he took hold of Brer Buzzard by the tail, meaning to dash him on the ground – but it was just about the time of year that Brer Buzzard moulted – so all his tail feathers came out in Brer Fox's hand, and Brer Buzzard sailed away into the air like a balloon. And as he went he shouted, 'You've given me a good start, Brer Fox!' And Brer Fox – he sat and watched him fly out of sight!

# Brer Rabbit's Fence

Brer Rabbit's fence was in a very bad way. It wanted painting, there was no doubt about that! Brer Rabbit went to have a look at it and groaned.

'I've tooth-ache in one arm and ear-ache in the other!' he said. 'How can I paint all that long fence!'

However, it had to be done, so he got a can of paint and began. Slish-slosh, slish-slosh went his brush, to and fro. Presently along came Brer Bear.

'That's a fine sloshy job you're doing,' he said to Brer Rabbit. 'Could I have a turn, do you think?'

'Certainly, Brer Bear!' said Brer Rabbit, and he gave Brer Bear the brush at once. Slish-slosh, slish-slosh, went Brer Bear very happily. He *was* enjoying himself!

Soon along came Brer Turkey Buzzard, jerking his big head to and fro as he walked. He stood and watched Brer Bear with envy. What a lovely job!

'Brer Rabbit's letting *me* have a turn,' said Brer Bear. 'Isn't it kind of him?'

'Can *I* have a turn, too?' said Brer Turkey Buzzard.

'Certainly, Brer Turkey Buzzard,' said Brer

Rabbit, kindly. 'Just let Brer Bear finish this bit of fence.'

So after a bit Brer Turkey Buzzard took up the brush and began to paint, too. Brer Hare came along and watched, and Brer Fox and Brer Wolf came up arm-in-arm.

'Here, Brer Turkey Buzzard, you're doing that wrong!' said Brer Wolf, and he snatched the brush away. '*This* is how you do it.'

Slish-slosh went the brush, and Brer Turkey Buzzard got a big dab of paint in the eye. He let out a squawk, but Brer Wolf took no notice.

'Brer Rabbit, it's *my* turn after Brer Wolf,' said Brer Fox, showing all his sharp teeth. Brer Rabbit pretended to look frightened. He nodded his head.

'Y-y-y-yes, Brer F-f-f-fox,' he said. 'You shall have the next turn – a nice *long* turn, if you like!'

So Brer Fox had a turn next – and a good long turn it was, too! By the time he had finished, the fence was completely painted. Not a bare place was left. It shone as bright as new, and Brer Rabbit was mighty pleased. He had been sitting in an armchair by the window, watching. Dear me, how nice it was to see other people doing his work!

Brer Fox dipped the brush into the can for the last time, and sloshed it down a big post to give it a good coat. 'There!' he said. 'No one else can have a turn. There's no paint left!'

Everyone stood admiring the fence. Presently Brer Possum strolled up, and how he did gape to see the fence all finished, for it hadn't even been begun when he had passed by that morning.

'Heyo, Brer Rabbit!' he called, seeing Brer Rabbit at the window. 'That's pretty quick work! How did you get your fence done so quickly? You must be tired out!'

'Oh no, Brer Possum,' called back Brer Rabbit at once. 'I'm not a bit tired. I just told my friends to come along here and do the work for me, and they did. Brer Fox did the most. He was afraid I might *bite* him if he didn't work hard!'

And with that Brer Rabbit slammed down his window and laughed till he cried to see everyone's face! As for Brer Fox, he couldn't bear even the *smell* of paint after that!

# Brer Rabbit Joins the Party

Brer Bear was going to give a party to Brer Fox and Brer Wolf. Brer Rabbit wasn't asked, and he was in a rage about it because he knew Brer Bear was cooking chicken and fish, so it would be a mighty fine feast.

When Brer Bear was cooking for the party Brer Rabbit turned up and asked if he could help him.

'If you like,' said Brer Bear, 'but you can't come to the party, Brer Rabbit, so don't you think so. Brer Wolf and Brer Fox said they wouldn't come if I asked you too.'

Brer Rabbit didn't say anything for a minute, and then he suddenly sniffed at the fish Brer Bear was cooking. 'What's the matter?' asked Brer Bear.

'Smells bad to me,' said Brer Rabbit. 'Of course, it's your own business, Brer Bear, but *I* wouldn't give bad fish to any guests of mine.'

'It smells good enough to me,' said Brer Bear sniffing at it.

'Well, you give it to Brer Fox and Brer Wolf, then,' said Brer Rabbit. 'But if I hear of them being mighty ill I'll know who it was poisoned them, Brer Bear.'

Brer Bear looked alarmed. 'Stars and moon!' he said anxiously. 'I wouldn't like to poison them. Maybe I'll eat the fish myself and give the chicken to Brer Fox and Brer Wolf.'

'Yes, you do that,' said Brer Rabbit. 'And see here, Brer Bear, I'll stay and see to the washing-up for you, if you like. I don't want any of the dinner, but I don't mind giving a hand to an old friend when he's got a party.'

So Brer Rabbit stayed, and when Brer Fox and Brer Wolf came to the feast he sat down as good as gold in a corner. Brer Bear gave his friends the chicken and began to eat the fish himself. Brer Rabbit watched him with a very worried look on his face. Brer Bear couldn't help wondering if the fish was bad.

'You're not looking very well, Brer Bear,' said Brer Rabbit, all of a sudden. 'You look pale and miserable.'

Brer Bear felt more and more worried. How dreadful if he were poisoned by the fish Brer Rabbit said was bad! He felt quite upset and pushed his plate away.

'You're not well, Brer Bear,' said Brer Rabbit. 'You're poisoned by that fish! Poor Brer Bear! You go to the doctor at once, Brer Bear. Brer Fox and Brer Wolf will hold you up if your legs give way.'

Brer Bear was terribly frightened. He really did feel as if his legs were giving way. Brer Fox and Brer Wolf got up and held him. Then, groaning and moaning, Brer Bear went off to the doctor, dragged along by Brer Fox and Brer Wolf, who were nearly as frightened as he was.

'I'll look after your dinner for you!' called Brer Rabbit as they went. He grinned to himself, and you should have seen how well he looked after that dinner! First of all he ate up the fish, which was as good as any he had ever had, and then he gobbled up the chicken from Brer Wolf's plate and Brer Fox's dish. Then he washed up and left everything clean. Soon he heard Brer Bear and the others coming back. Brer Bear looked as wild as could be, so Brer Rabbit didn't stay to ask how he was. He just called out 'Your dinner's quite all right!' and ran off lippitty, clippitty through the woods, laughing as loudly as a green woodpecker!

# Brer Rabbit and the Teapot

Now once when Brer Rabbit was giving a big tea-party to all his friends and relations, and was busy pouring out cups of tea from an enormous brown teapot, Brer Fox and Brer Bear strolled in.

Well, of course, all the guests fled out of the back door and out of the windows as if a big wind had suddenly blown them away. All except poor

Brer Rabbit, and he hadn't time to leap through a window. He only just had time to put the enormous teapot down, jump into it himself, and put on the lid. There he shivered in the teapot, although the tea was hot round his legs!

Brer Fox and Brer Bear leaned against the table, waiting for the guests to come back. 'Then we'll pounce on a few,' said Brer Fox, 'and join the tea-party!'

That made Brer Rabbit as mad as could be! He

wriggled a paw down the teapot spout and jabbed Brer Fox hard in the back.

Brer Fox was surprised. He rubbed his back and glared at Brer Bear. 'Stop poking me!' he said.

Then Brer Bear looked surprised. 'I didn't poke you,' he said. Just then Brer Rabbit jiggled the lid up and down and made it say 'Jiggle, jiggle, jiggle.'

'Don't jiggle the table,' said Brer Fox.

'I'm not,' said Brer Bear. 'It's you!'

Brer Rabbit slipped his paw down the spout again and gave Brer Fox another hard jab. Brer Fox nearly fell on his nose. He shook his fist in Brer

Bear's face. 'If you jab me again, I'll fight you!' he said. 'I didn't bring you here to treat me like this!'

'Jiggle, jiggle, jiggle,' said the teapot lid. Then Brer Rabbit poked Brer Bear in his most ticklish spot, and Brer Bear gave a yell and slapped Brer Fox in the face. 'Stop tickling me!' he cried.

Then what a fight there was! How the fur flew over Brer Rabbit's kitchen! How the chairs went over with a crash! Brer Rabbit trembled in the teapot, for he was afraid that the table would be knocked over and the teapot would fall and break. But it didn't.

Brer Fox and Brer Bear stopped for a minute's rest. Brer Rabbit longed to see what was happening. He lifted up the teapot lid very cautiously on his long ears and peeped out. And at that very moment Brer Fox saw him!

'Oooooh!' he shouted in fright. 'That teapot's got ears! And now it's got eyes! Ooooh, Brer Bear, save me!'

Brer Rabbit giggled so much that he nearly upset the teapot, He stuck his paw out of the spout and waved it to and fro. That made Brer Bear shiver and shake so much that he could hardly stand. Brer Rabbit lifted the lid up and down on his ears, and then jiggled it again. Then he gave a little hop inside the teapot, and the teapot hopped up in the air and down, too! That was too much for Brer Bear and Brer Fox. They fled out of the kitchen as fast as ever they could, shouting 'It's after us, it's after us!'

And then old Brer Rabbit climbed out of the big teapot, wiped himself with a tea-cloth, and sat down and laughed till he cried. Oh, Brer Rabbit, how *do* you think of all your pranks and tricks?

# Bobs Meets Brer Rabbit Again

One fine morning, when Bobs the dog was ambling down the lane, whom should he meet all alive-o but Brer Rabbit. He stopped and stared, and then in a trice he captured him!

'So *you're* the rabbit that eats the cabbages in our garden!' he barked. 'Well, you won't eat any more.'

'You've made a mistake!' said Brer Rabbit. 'That's my brother that eats the cabbages!'

'I don't believe you!' said Bobs, with a growl.

'You're the one! You just come along and I'll lock you up in my kennel. Then Sandy and I will ask the mistress to cook you for our dinner.'

Poor Brer Rabbit began to shiver and shake. 'I tell you, Bobs, you're making a mistake!' he said again. 'My brother is exactly like me. You wouldn't like to cook an innocent bunny for your dinner, would you?'

'I shouldn't mind a bit, if he was as fat as you,' said Bobs. 'I don't believe your tale of a brother, Brer Rabbit! But if we *do* happen to meet a rabbit *exactly* like you, with the *same* number of whiskers and everything, well, I *might* let you go!'

He marched Brer Rabbit up the lane and into the gates of Old Thatch. Soon they came to the little bridge over the stream. When they were in the middle of the bridge Brer Rabbit stopped short and pointed into the water.

'There's my brother!' he said. 'Look! Isn't he exactly like me?'

Bobs looked into the water. Sure enough, looking back at him was a bunny just exactly like Brer Rabbit! Bobs counted the whiskers on Brer Rabbit's cheeks, and then he counted those on the rabbit in the water. There were just the same number! As he was counting them the rabbit in the water made a rude face, and Bobs growled angrily.

'Hie, Sandy!' he called. 'Come and hold this rabbit while I get the one in the water! Then I'll just see which one it is that steals our cabbages!'

Sandy came running up and took hold of Brer

Rabbit. Splash! Bobs jumped into the stream after the rabbit he had seen in there looking up at him. He growled and spluttered, barked and wuffed – but, dear me, it was very strange, he *couldn't* seem to find that rabbit!

Brer Rabbit looked at Sandy. He was a very

little dog. 'My!' said Brer Rabbit, 'just look at that
bone there!'

He pointed downwards to the planks and
Sandy bent down to sniff. Brer Rabbit gave him
a sharp push, and splash – into the stream went
Sandy, right on top of Bobs. Bobs thought he was
the rabbit and grabbed hold of him with his teeth.
'Shake him, Bobs! Shake him!' yelled Brer Rabbit.
'You've got my brother!' So Bobs shook poor
Sandy till all his teeth rattled! Then he suddenly
saw who it was!

'Goodbye, goodbye, I'll tell my brother I've had
such a pleasant morning with you!' giggled Brer

Rabbit. 'At least I would if I had a brother – but I haven't!'

And off scampered that wicked rabbit in a mighty hurry!

# Brer Rabbit's New Shoes

Now once it happened that Brer Rabbit bought himself a pair of new shoes. They were mighty smart ones – black, with red laces – and Brer Rabbit was as pleased with them as a dog with two tails.

He showed them off to all the animals and they got very tired of seeing his new shoes.

'If you got some new manners it would be better,' grumbled Brer Fox.

'New shoes are wasted on you,' said Brer Wolf. 'You should spend your money on a new face. I'm tired of seeing that old one of yours.'

These rude remarks didn't upset old Brer Rabbit at all. He just went on wearing his new shoes, showing them off, and being as grand as could be till Brer Fox and Brer Wolf longed to get hold of him and spank him.

'Let's lie in wait for him,' said Brer Fox. 'I'm just about tired of seeing those new shoes of his. Let's lie in wait for him, pounce on him, take his new shoes, and throw them into the very middle of the pond!'

'That's a fine idea!' said Brer Wolf, pleased. 'Brer Rabbit goes to market tomorrow. Let's hide somewhere in the bushes when he comes back. Then we'll jump out on him and give him the fright of his life – and he'll have to say good-bye to his new shoes.'

So when Brer Rabbit came whistling back from market next day, Brer Fox and Brer Wolf waited for him. Brer Rabbit had on his new shoes, of course – but he wasn't quite so pleased with them as everybody thought. They hurt him!

'They're just a bit too small,' thought Brer Rabbit sadly. 'I should have got a size larger. Now what a pity that is! I can't afford to buy another pair. And I think I'd rather have had a yellow pair with green laces. But still, it's too late now. I must just go on wearing them, and letting them hurt me.'

He was thinking all this when he got to the top of the hill that looked down on the wood where he lived. And flying above the wood he saw Old Turkey Buzzard, looking down on the trees as if he saw something interesting there.

Brer Rabbit called to him. 'Heyo, Brer Buzzard,

what's up down there in the wood? Looks like you're watching something.'

'So I am, Brer Rabbit, so I am,' said Brer Buzzard, sailing over to Brer Rabbit on his big wings. 'I can see those two rogues, Brer Fox and Brer Wolf – and it looks to me as if they're lying in wait for somebody. So it does.'

'Is that so?' said Brer Rabbit, thinking mighty quickly. 'Well, there's only one person coming along this way today, and that's me. So it doesn't need much puzzling to know who's the man they're waiting for! Brer Turkey Buzzard, I'm a-going to hide myself in this bush, and it will take Brer Fox and Brer Wolf a month of Sundays to find me!'

With that Brer Rabbit skipped into the bush nearby, stuck his feet well out at the bottom, and waited to see what Brer Turkey Buzzard would say.

'Your feet show, with your new shoes on,' said Brer Turkey Buzzard at once.

'Can't help that,' said Brer Rabbit, grinning a bit to himself. 'Now don't you tell where I am, Brer Turkey Buzzard.'

Brer Turkey Buzzard sailed off into the air. Soon he came to where Brer Fox and

Brer Wolf were hiding, and he called to them.

'If you want that scamp of a Brer Rabbit, I can tell you where he is. He's hiding himself in a bush at the top of the hill, and you can see where he is because his big feet stick out at the bottom – and he's got those new shoes on.'

'Thanks, Brer Turkey Buzzard, you're a friend,' said Brer Fox, with a grin. 'Brer Rabbit won't have those new shoes on long!'

Brer Fox and Brer Wolf made their way to the top of the hill – and it wasn't long before they saw a bush that made them nudge one another and grin. Sticking out at the bottom were Brer Rabbit's grand new shoes!

'There he is, a-hiding in that bush!' whispered Brer Fox.

But Brer Fox was wrong. Brer Rabbit wasn't in that bush at all! As soon as Brer Turkey Buzzard had sailed off to Brer Fox and Brer Wolf, Brer Rabbit had slipped out of the bush and had taken off his shoes. Then he had stuck his shoes at the bottom of the bush so that it looked exactly as if he were in the bush himself, with his feet sticking out at the bottom.

Then old Brer Rabbit skipped to another bush and squeezed himself right into the middle of it. He waited and he waited – and he didn't have to wait long before up crept Brer Fox and Brer Wolf.

Brer Rabbit put his paw over his mouth to stop himself from laughing out loud when he saw the two nudging one another and pointing to the bush where his shoes were. Brer Fox went to one side of the bush and Brer Wolf went to the other.

'Heyo, Brer Rabbit! 'said Brer Fox, speaking to the bush.

There was no answer.

'Now, Brer Rabbit, we know you're in that bush, because your great big feet are sticking out at the bottom,' said Brer Fox. 'You're so mighty proud of those new shoes of yours that you can't even hide them when you want to! Come on out, and we'll give you a spanking!'

No answer from the bush at all. Brer Rabbit giggled to himself. Brer Fox got angry.

'Now look here, Brer Rabbit, you're a sensible man, aren't you? Well, you don't want us to have to pull you out, do you? You just come out yourself. That bush is prickly and we're not going to tear our clothes to bits, I can tell you!'

Brer Fox got no answer at all. Then Brer Wolf spoke up.

'Brer Rabbit! You're not dumb, are you? If you

don't speak up and come out, we'll beat the bush down! Then you'll be sorry!'

Brer Rabbit didn't say a word, but he nearly cracked his sides with trying not to laugh.

'Brer Fox, come on! We'll beat that bush with sticks till we make old Brer Rabbit come jumping out in a hurry,' said Brer Wolf in a rage. 'He thinks we won't try to drag him out because of the thorns. Well – we'll beat him out! Get a stick and we'll begin.'

Now it was a hot day, and beating a bush is hot work. So Brer Fox and Brer Wolf took off their coats and laid them down on the grass. Then they cut themselves big sticks and set to work. My, how they beat that bush!

Smack, slap, bang, smack! Blip, blap, smack!

They made such a noise that they didn't hear Brer Rabbit squeeze out of the bush he was in and go to their coats. They didn't see him pick up their coats and stuff them down a rabbit-hole. They didn't see anything at all except the bush they were beating.

After a bit their arms ached badly and they stopped beating the bush. They stared at one another, panting.

'He must be black and blue by now,' said Brer Fox. 'Brer Rabbit, come along out! We know you're still there because your feet are sticking out!'

Then Brer Wolf looked round for his coat. He meant to get out his handkerchief and mop his face. But his coat wasn't there. He stared round in surprise.

'What have you done with my coat, Brer Fox?' he asked.

'Nothing,' said Brer Fox, looking round too. 'Where's my coat?'

'They've both gone,' said Brer Wolf, puzzled. 'Who's taken them?'

'Well, if Brer Rabbit wasn't in this bush I'd think he'd played one of his tricks!' said Brer Fox in a temper. 'That's what I think, Brer Wolf!'

Brer Wolf stared at the bush they had been beating. An idea came into his head. He suddenly bent down and snatched at the shoes sticking out at the bottom. They came away in his hand!

'Look there!' he cried. 'No feet in them! Brer Rabbit stuck them there to make us think he was in the bush! He's taken our coats, that's what he's done!'

'Well, we'll take his shoes,' yelled Brer Fox, and he picked them up. He threw them high into the air and they landed in a tree. The little Jack Sparrows flew away in a fright.

'Brer Rabbit won't wear *those* shoes again!' said Brer Fox. He'll have to wear his old ones – and serve him right too!'

But he didn't! He came out next day in a marvellous pair of new yellow shoes with green laces, and he paraded up and down, showing them off till everyone was wild with him.

'I didn't like the others,' he said. 'They were too small. So I got Brer Fox to throw them away in the trees and I bought myself a better pair.'

'How did you get the money?' asked Brer

Terrapin, in surprise. Brer Fox and Brer Wolf listened in a rage.

'Well, you see, Brer Fox and Brer Wolf are just the kindest friends to me,' said Brer Rabbit, with a grin. 'They gave me their coats – and I exchanged them for this pair of shoes. My, you should see how fast I can run in them!'

And he did too – far too fast for Brer Fox and Brer Wolf to catch him!

# Brer Wolf and Brer Fox

Once day Brer Wolf and Brer Fox began to quarrel with one another. It all happened because Brer Rabbit met them, yelled out 'Howdy!' and disappeared into a briar-bush before either Brer Wolf or Brer Fox could get him.

'There goes the man that's tricked you more often than you can count!' said Brer Wolf to Brer Fox.

'And he hasn't tricked you, I suppose!' said Brer Fox, in a disagreeable sort of voice. 'Oh, no, I suppose he hasn't tricked you, Brer Wolf! What a short memory you've got. Now just let me remind you of a few things – do you remember when Brer Rabbit ...'

'I don't remember anything,' said Brer Wolf. 'I don't think of Brer Rabbit more than I can help. But I do remember how he frightened you when he was all covered with leaves, shouting out that

367

he was the Wull-of-the-Wust! Ho, you looked scared enough then, Brer Fox!'

'Well,' began Brer Fox, in a rage, 'and weren't you with me, then? Didn't your whiskers shake as if they were leaves in the wind? Didn't your ears shiver and your tail drop? Lands' sakes, Brer Wolf, you were a lot more scared than I was!'

'Indeed I wasn't,' said Brer Wolf, and he began to snap his jaws. Brer Fox snapped his too, and before they had taken two steps they were at one another! Brer Fox lammed out at Brer Wolf and sent him flying. Brer Wolf shot to his feet and snapped his big teeth at Brer Fox. Then Brer Fox sailed in again and hit Brer Wolf on the nose.

Well, Brer Wolf was the bigger of the two, so it wasn't long before Brer Fox knew he'd better be going! So he watched his chance, and slipped away under Brer Wolf's paws and ran into the wood.

Brer Wolf shot after him, and he ran so fast that he was on Brer Fox's tail all the time. And Brer Fox knew that the only way to save his skin was to hide in a hole somewhere, so the first hollow tree he came to he dived inside!

Brer Wolf made a grab at him, but he was just in time to be too late! Brer Fox was in that hole and in that hole he stayed. It was too small for Brer Wolf to get inside, so Brer Wolf sat outside and thought what he was going to do to get Brer Fox out. And Brer Fox lay in the hole and wondered what Brer Wolf was going to do!

'Well,' said Brer Wolf, at last, 'seems I can't get Brer Fox out – but I can make him stay in! Oh, yes, I can make him stay in all right! He'll wish he'd never gone inside that tree before long. I'm a-going to get some big chunky stones, and they'll be set in the hole of the tree, and old Brer Fox won't come out again. Oh, no, he won't!'

So Brer Wolf hunted round a bit and got together a big pile of earth, rocks and sticks, and he filled up the hole with them. He knew Brer Fox wouldn't be able to get out, and he chuckled to himself as he lammed the rocks and the sticks into the hole.

Whilst all this was going on Brer Turkey Buzzard flew above, going about his business. He happened to look down and what did he see but old Brer Wolf a-piling up rocks and sticks in the hole of the hollow tree. Brer Turkey Buzzard was quite astonished.

'I'll just sort of flop down and look into this,' he said to himself, 'because if Brer Wolf is hiding his dinner there expecting to find it when he comes back, then he's gone and put it in the wrong place!'

With that old Brer Turkey Buzzard flopped down and sailed round nearer. Then he flopped down a bit more and sat on the top of the hollow tree. Brer Wolf got a glimpse of Brer Buzzard's shadow but he took no notice. He just went on putting the chunks of wood in the hole.

Presently Brer Turkey Buzzard began to talk to him.

'What are you doing there, Brer Wolf?'

'No business of yours, Brer Buzzard,' said Brer Wolf.

'Brer Wolf, if you ever want to buy a little politeness, you come along to me and I'll sell you some,' said Brer Buzzard.

'You sell it to Brer Rabbit, Brer Buzzard, or keep it for yourself,' said Brer Wolf. 'You could both do with some!'

'I never did like you, Brer Wolf,' said Brer Buzzard.

'You be careful what you say to me, Brer Buzzard,' said Brer Wolf, snapping his jaws. 'If you aren't careful I'll put you in this hollow tree with Brer Fox!'

'Hoo!' said Brer Buzzard, flapping his big wings, 'you don't mean to tell me you've got Brer Fox in that tree, Brer Wolf! You're just telling me that because you don't want me to go looking for your dinner there, or your gold, that you're hiding!'

Brer Wolf didn't say another word. He kept on piling up the hole till it was properly stopped up, and then he brushed the dust off his clothes and set out for home. Old Brer Turkey Buzzard, he sat up at the top of the tree and listened and listened, and untangled his tail-feathers, but he couldn't hear a thing inside the tree. Brer Fox lay low and kept

quiet, so there wasn't anything for Brer Buzzard to hear.

After a while Brer Buzzard sailed round in the air again, and this time he sang, and this is the song he sang:

'*Boo, boo, boo, my filler-me-loo,*
*There's a man out here with news for you!*'

Now when one of the creatures sang this, anyone that heard it would answer at once. But Brer Fox, he didn't answer a word. He just lay low and kept quiet. Brer Buzzard flopped down to the tree again, and put his head on one side and listened with both his ears. But he couldn't hear a thing.

'This is mighty funny,' he thought to himself. 'If Brer Fox was inside, he'd answer me all right. But he doesn't answer, so maybe he isn't there – and if he isn't there, then nobody else is – and it must be Brer Wolf's dinner there, or maybe his gold! Well, I'll wait a while and then I'll sail around again and sing.'

So he sat on the tree and waited. Then after a time he sailed into the air and sang his song.

*'Boo, boo, boo, my filler-me-loo,*
*There's a man out here with news for you!'*

He flopped down on the tree and listened hard. But not a sound did he hear. Brer Fox, he lay low inside the tree.

'This is where I get right down and find Brer Wolf's dinner!' said old Brer Turkey Buzzard to himself. So down he sailed to the ground and cocked his head at the pile of stones and sticks round about the hole.

He took one chunk out and listened. Not a sound came from the hole. He took another chunk out and listened. No, not a sound from the hole. Brer Fox lay as low as he could, listening to Brer Buzzard uncovering the hole.

Brer Buzzard went on taking away the wood and the earth and the stones. Soon Brer Fox could see daylight – and when he saw fat old Brer Buzzard there his mouth began to water too! Brer Buzzard worked on, taking chunks and sticks away, singing a little song in between whiles, and keeping a sharp look-out for Brer Wolf in case he came back.

When the hole was almost uncovered Brer Buzzard sniffed to see if he could smell the dinner he thought might be inside the hole. But he couldn't smell dinner – and yet he could smell something! It couldn't be gold – gold didn't smell. Then what could it be?

'Tails and feathers, Brer Wolf was telling me the truth – it's Brer Fox in there!' Brer Buzzard screeched suddenly. And he rose up into the air just as Brer Fox shot out of the hole and made a grab at him. Brer Fox caught three of his tail-feathers, but that was all. Brer Buzzard sailed away high in the air, and Brer Fox sat outside that hole, holding the feathers in his hand and looking as disappointed as three wet Saturdays!

'Is that the way to treat a friend!' screeched Brer

Buzzard in a rage. 'Didn't I set you free? I'm off to tell Brer Wolf you're out of the hole!'

Brer Fox didn't wait to hear any more. He raced through the wood, lippitty, clippitty, and didn't stop till he was safe indoors with all the windows and doors bolted!

# Brer Rabbit and Mr Man

It happened one day that Brer Rabbit met Brer Fox, and they asked each other, 'Howdy?'

'Howdy, Brer Fox?' said Brer Rabbit. 'I hope you're feeling well.'

'Howdy, Brer Rabbit?' said Brer Fox. 'Thank you kindly, but I'm feeling poorly.'

'Is that so?' said Brer Rabbit. 'Then we'd better go along together, Brer Fox, for I'm feeling mighty poorly too.'

'I'm so hungry I could eat grass,' said Brer Fox.

'I'm mighty hungry too,' said Brer Rabbit. 'But I want something more than grass. Look, Brer Fox, who's this a-coming down the road?'

'It's Mr Man,' said Brer Fox. 'And what's that he's got over his shoulder, Brer Rabbit?'

'It's a great big hunk of beef!' said Brer Rabbit.

'I'd like mighty well to get a taste of that beef,' said Brer Fox.

Well, Mr Man came along, and Brer Fox and Brer Rabbit looked and looked at him and the meat. They winked at one another.

'I've just got to get that meat!' said Brer Rabbit.

'It looks mighty far off to me,' said Brer Fox.

'Now just you listen to me, Brer Fox,' said Brer Rabbit. 'You follow along behind me a good way off, and watch what I do. I've got a mighty fine plan!'

And with that Brer Rabbit set off and soon caught up with Mr Man.

'Howdy, Mr Man?' said Brer Rabbit.

'Howdy, Brer Rabbit?' said Mr Man. 'Fine day, this.'

'It is that,' said Brer Rabbit. And then they went on together, chatting away like old friends.

Brer Rabbit kept on sniffing the air – sniff-sniff-sniff.

'Have you got a bad cold?' asked Mr Man.

'No, Mr Man,' said Brer Rabbit. 'I haven't got a cold – I'm only smelling something – and it doesn't smell to me like ripe peaches either! No, that it doesn't!'

'Well, I can't smell anything wrong,' said Mr Man. Pretty soon Brer Rabbit began to hold his nose and pretend to feel sick. After a while he shouted out to Mr Man.

'Gracious goodness, Mr Man! It's that meat of yours that is smelling so bad! Wherever did you pick up that meat?'

This made Mr Man feel sort of ashamed of himself, to be carrying bad meat home. He thought it was mighty strange that he couldn't smell it was bad – and no wonder either, for that meat was as fresh as a new-laid egg! There was nothing bad about it at all – it was just Brer Rabbit's wicked trick.

Brer Rabbit went to the other side of the road, and held his nose for all he was worth. Mr Man looked sorry, and before they had gone much farther he put the meat down on the side of the road.

'What shall I do about it?' he said. 'It can't be very bad – but if it smells like you say I'll have to do something about it before I take it home.'

'Well,' said Brer Rabbit, looking wise, 'I did once hear tell that if you take and drag a piece of meat through the dust it will make it fresh and good again. I've never tried it myself, mind you, but those that have done it tell me it comes all right again. And, anyway, it can't do any harm to the meat, because you can always wash the dust off!'

'I haven't got any string to pull it along in the dust,' said Mr Man.

Brer Rabbit laughed loudly, but he still held his nose.

'If you'd lived in the woods as long as I have, you wouldn't be without strings!' he said.

And with that Brer Rabbit hopped into the bushes, and soon came back with a long string of bamboo vines tied together to make a good strong rope.

'That's a mighty long string,' said Mr Man.

'To be sure it is!' said Brer Rabbit. 'But if you have a short string, you're going to smell that meat, Mr Man, and you don't want to do that. It's a dreadful smell, sure enough!'

Then Mr Man tied his piece of meat on to the end of the bamboo rope.

Brer Rabbit broke a branch off an elder bush and said he would stay behind with the meat and brush the flies off it, as Mr Man pulled it along. So Mr Man, he went on in front and dragged the meat, and Brer Rabbit stayed behind, he did, to take care of it!

And he did take care of it, too! He got a rock,

undid the meat, and tied the rock on to the string instead! Mr Man went on in front, pulling the rope without looking back – and when Brer Fox came on behind, there, sure enough, was the hunk of meat lying by itself in the road – and on ahead was Brer Rabbit pretending to brush flies off the large rock! Mr Man he went on in front, dragging and pulling.

After a while Mr Man looked back to see what Brer Rabbit was doing, and to ask him if the meat was smelling better – but where was old Brer Rabbit?

He had run back to join Brer Fox – and he was just in time, too, because in another minute Brer Fox would have gobbled up all that meat, and that would have been the end of it!

And that's the way Brer Rabbit got Mr Man's meat. Ah – but wait a minute: who's going to eat it – Brer Fox, or Brer Rabbit?

# How Brer Rabbit Got the Meat

Well, after Brer Rabbit got the meat from Mr Man, and rushed back to Brer Fox – *terbuckity-buckity, buck-buck-buckity* – they carried the meat a good way off in the woods, and laid it down on a clean piece of ground.

'We'd better taste it,' said Brer Fox.

'That's so,' said Brer Rabbit.

So Brer Fox gnawed off a big hunk, shut both eyes and chewed and chewed and tasted and tasted, and chewed and tasted. Brer Rabbit watched him, and then he started on the meat too.

Brer Fox smacked his lips, looked closely at the meat, and said: 'Brer Rabbit, it's lamb!'

'No, Brer Fox, surely not!'

'Brer Rabbit, it's lamb!'

'Brer Fox, to be sure not!'

Then Brer Rabbit gnawed off a chunk, shut both eyes, and chewed and tasted and tasted and

382

chewed. Then he smacked his lips and said: 'Brer Fox, it's pork!'

'Brer Rabbit, it's not!'

'Brer Fox, I vow it's pork!'

'Brer Rabbit, it just can't be!'

'Brer Fox, it surely is!'

Well, they tasted and they argued and they argued and they tasted. After a while Brer Rabbit said he wanted some water, because pork always made him thirsty, and he rushed off into the bushes. He came back wiping his mouth and clearing his throat as if he had just been drinking – but he hadn't really.

Well, as soon as Brer Fox saw Brer Rabbit wiping his mouth, he felt thirsty, and he spoke to Brer Rabbit.

'Brer Rabbit, where did you find the water?'

'Across the road, and down the hill, and up the big gully,' said Brer Rabbit, at once.

Well, Brer Fox, he loped off, he did, and after he had gone Brer Rabbit waved his paw to him in a cheeky manner, and grinned all across his face. Brer Fox crossed the road, rushed down the hill – but he couldn't find any gully. He kept on till he found a gully at last – but there wasn't any water there!

Whilst Brer Fox was gone, Brer Rabbit dug a hole in the ground and hid the meat there. After he had hidden it well he went to a tree and cut a long hickory stick. Then he sat down and waited for Brer Fox to come back.

Very soon he heard him. Then Brer Rabbit got into a clump of bushes, and took the hickory stick with him. There was a young tree near by, and Brer Rabbit began to hit it with his hickory stick as hard as ever he could. And every time he hit the tree Brer Rabbit squealed out as if Mr Man had got him and was beating him hard!

*Pow-pow-pow!*
'Oh, mercy, Mr Man!'
*Pow-wow!*
'Oh, please, Mr Man!'
*Chippy-row, pow!*
'Oh, Mr Man, let me go! Brer Fox took your meat!'
*Pow-pow-pow!*
Well, when Brer Fox heard all this noise going

on – *pow-pow-pow*, as if Brer Rabbit was being well whipped – and then Brer Rabbit squealing, he stopped in a hurry and listened hard.

And every time Brer Fox heard that hickory stick coming down *pow*, he grinned to himself.

'Ah-yi, Brer Rabbit! You tricked me about that water, didn't you! And now Mr Man's got you! Ah-yi!'

Well, after some time, the noise stopped, and Brer Fox listened to see what was going to happen next; and he heard a noise as if Brer Rabbit was being dragged off by Mr Man – but it was really old Brer Rabbit dragging a big branch through the bushes, and grinning from ear to ear! Brer Fox listened to this, and he felt mighty pleased.

'Ho! Mr Man's dragging Brer Rabbit off by his hind legs! Ah-yi! You tricked me about that water, Brer Rabbit! Now you're getting punished for it! Ah-yi!'

By and by Brer Rabbit came tearing through the woods as if he'd escaped from Mr Man. He was shouting at the top of his voice.

'Run, Brer Fox, run! Mr Man says he's going to take the meat up the road to where his son is – and then he's coming back after *you*, Brer Fox! He's cut a new hickory stick to beat you. Run, Brer Fox, run!'

Brer Fox flicked up his heels and ran as if the dogs were after him – and old Brer Rabbit, he sat down by the hole where he had hidden his meat, and he dug it up and ate it in peace. And when he thought of Brer Fox running away from it, he just laughed and danced and kicked up his feet like mad. There never was such a rascal as old Brer Rabbit.

# Brer Fox Has a Surprise

Once upon a time Brer Rabbit wanted to play a trick on Brer Fox. He took Brer Terrapin into his secret, and the two of them made a plan, with many grins and giggles.

Brer Rabbit fetched a sack, and propped the mouth open with a stick. Inside he put a fish he had caught the day before. It smelt rather strong, but that was how he wanted it to smell.

'Now we'll get into the hedge and wait for Cousin Wildcat to come along,' he said.

So the two of them crept into the hedge and lay low. Presently along came Cousin Wildcat, hissing between his teeth, and kicking the dead leaves with his feet.

When he came near the sack he smelt the fish. He stopped at once and sniffed.

'I smell fish!' he said. 'Good fish – a day old!'

Brer Rabbit nudged Brer Terrapin and the

two of them tried their hardest not to laugh.

Cousin Wildcat sniffed again. Then he saw the sack with its neck propped open, and he was rather astonished. He went nearer to see what it was – and the smell of the fish came strongly from out of the sack.

'The fish is in there!' said Cousin Wildcat, and looked around to see who the sack belonged to. But he could see nobody.

'Funny!' he said. 'Very funny! I suppose somebody is fishing somewhere and they are putting their fish into this sack. But why leave the sack alone? Somebody might take the fish. In fact, I think I had better take it myself in case someone comes along and gets it.'

So in the sack went Cousin Wildcat after that fish. And as soon as he was well in the sack Brer Rabbit ran out of the hedge, pulled the string that ran round the neck of the sack, and there was Cousin Wildcat nicely caught inside!

My, how he wriggled and struggled! How he yowled and bit and scratched at that sack! But he couldn't get out, for the sack was well and truly tied at the neck by old Brer Rabbit!

'We'll let him struggle till he's tired out,' whispered Brer Rabbit. 'Then you can go and fetch

Brer Fox and say exactly what we've planned for you to say.'

So they let poor Cousin Wildcat wriggle and fight and struggle inside the sack till he was too tired to do it any more. When he was lying still, Brer Rabbit winked at Brer Terrapin and Brer Terrapin began to lumber away to Brer Fox's house, which was quite nearby.

When he got there he saw Brer Fox in the garden, digging. 'Heyo, Brer Fox!' cried Brer Terrapin. 'Will you come and help me, please?'

'What's the matter?' asked Brer Fox.

'I've found some-body tied up in a sack in the woods,' said Brer Terrapin. 'And it might be Brer Rabbit, you know. Could you come and undo the sack? My great clawed feet won't undo knots.'

'Oh, I'll certainly come along,' said Brer Fox at once, feeling sure that it must be Brer Rabbit in the sack, for he knew that Brer Terrapin was Brer Rabbit's friend. 'I'll certainly come along. It will be a great pleasure, Brer Terrapin.'

Brer Fox meant to carry Brer Rabbit home in that sack! That certainly *would* be a great pleasure! Aha, he would have that scamp of a rabbit in his power for once!

Brer Terrapin grinned to himself. He took Brer Fox to the woods and they came to the sack. Cousin Wildcat was lying quiet. Brer Rabbit was well hidden in the hedge.

'There's the sack,' said Brer Terrapin. 'It may not be Brer Rabbit in it, Brer Fox, so look out when you undo the string.'

'I think I'll undo the sack when I get home,' said Brer Fox, and he jerked the sack up to his shoulder. That stirred up Cousin Wildcat and he began to yowl like a railway engine letting off steam.

'Never heard Brer Rabbit make *that* noise before,' said Brer Fox to Brer Terrapin. 'He must be mighty frightened ! Ow!'

Brer Fox yelled out 'Ow!' because Cousin Wildcat had just dug a very sharp claw into his shoulder. He dug another one in, and Brer Fox grew angry.

'You wait till I get you out of this sack, Brer Rabbit!' he shouted. 'I'll empty you into a pan of water on my stove and you'll cook there for my dinner!'

Cousin Wildcat went quite mad in the sack. He wriggled and fought till Brer Fox could hardly hold the sack on his shoulder, and at last he let it drag

 along the ground. This bumped Cousin Wildcat dreadfully, and he grew even madder.

Brer Terrapin went along with Brer Fox,

and Brer Rabbit skipped behind the hedge, watching. Brer Fox went into his house and put a big pan of water on to the stove. Then he pulled open the string round the neck of the sack – and out fell Cousin Wildcat into the water!

Well, all cats, wild or tame, hate water, and Cousin Wildcat hated it more than most. He leapt out of that pan as soon as he was in it – and he flew at poor Brer Fox like a Spitfire! My, how he spat and hissed and bit and scratched! Brer Fox shut his eyes and fought for all he was worth – and at last Cousin Wildcat jumped out of the window and disappeared into the woods with a yowl! Brer Fox quite thought it had been Brer Rabbit all the time, and he sat down in a chair and got his breath back, feeling very puzzled indeed to think of Brer

Rabbit's suddenly sharp claws.

Brer Rabbit peeped in at the door, grinning all over his face. 'Like another fight with me, Brer Fox?' he asked, and he put up his two small fists. 'Come along! It was good of you to let me out of the sack – but you couldn't expect me to like the pan of water! Come along – let's have another fight!'

But Brer Fox had had such a shock that he wasn't going to fight with anybody in the world, not even with old Brer Terrapin who was laughing fit to crack his shell. He got up and banged his door.

'Tell me when you want a fight, Brer Fox, and I'll come and give you one!' shouted Brer Rabbit,

as he went off with Brer Terrapin. But he didn't
hear a word from Brer Fox for many a long day.

# Brer Rabbit and the Flower Pot

Once Miss Bear said to Brer Bear, 'Brer Bear, I want to cook some onions for dinner. You go and get some out of the shed.'

Brer Bear's onions were stored in his shed, big and round and shiny. Brer Bear went to get some.

He got eight large onions and went back to Miss Bear. 'Now you just sit out there in the garden and peel them for me,' she said. 'They make my eyes water, but maybe yours won't.'

So Brer Bear sat on the garden seat in the sun, and began to peel the onions. And who should come by at that very moment but old Brer Rabbit. He sniffed the smell of onions at once. My, it was good!

'Heyo, Brer Bear!' said Brer Rabbit, peeping over the fence. 'Those are fine onions you've got. You might spare me a little one for my supper tonight.'

'Brer Rabbit, I'm sparing you nothing, unless

you'd like the peel,' said Brer Bear. 'And don't you think you can steal any, because you can't. I'm sitting here by my onions till they're finished – and if you think you can get even the smallest one, well, you're welcome to try. But you'll get my hand at the back of your neck too!'

'Brer Bear, keep your smelly old onions,' said Brer Rabbit in a huff. 'I'm off to get a lift to the market, and I'll buy better onions there than any of yours!'

Off he went, and Brer Bear grinned to himself. 'He won't find better onions than these, and he knows it!' he said. 'He'll have to spend all day looking round the market for onions as big as these!'

But Brer Rabbit hadn't gone to market. No – he was just the other side of the hedge, watching to see if Brer Bear would leave his onions for a minute. Hadn't Brer Bear said he could have one if he could get one? All right – Brer Rabbit guessed he *would* get one.

But Brer Bear didn't leave his onions at all until he wanted to blow his nose. And then he didn't go indoors to get his hanky. He went to the kitchen window and yelled.

'Miss Bear – hey, Miss Bear! Pass me out my red hanky!'

While his back was turned for that second, Brer Rabbit hopped in at the gate, went to a big red flower pot that stood upside down nearby, and popped himself under it. The pot covered him up completely. Brer Bear got his red hanky and went back to his seat to peel his onions.

Pretty soon Brer Rabbit moved a little nearer to Brer Bear, but nothing could be seen except that the flower pot slid along a little way. Brer Bear didn't notice it.

Brer Rabbit slid a little nearer and then a little nearer still. Still Brer Bear didn't notice. He went on peeling the onions, wiping the tears from his eyes every now and again.

At last Brer Rabbit was so near the onions that he could smell them. He waited until he heard old

Brer Bear sneeze – and then, quick as lightning, Brer Rabbit put a paw out from under the pot, took hold of an onion, pulled it back under the pot, and stayed quite still.

'A-TISH-OO!' said Brer Bear and sneezed into his hanky. Then he reached down to the ground for the last onion.

But it wasn't there! Brer Bear looked all round him, quite surprised. The onion had been there the minute before. Well, then, it should be there now. But it wasn't.

'Most peculiar,' said Brer Bear, and he felt about in the bits of brown that had come from the outside of the onions. But the onion wasn't there either.

Then Brer Bear noticed something that made him feel rather peculiar. A large flower pot nearby moved off a little. Brer Bear stared at it. It kept quite still.

'My eyes must be going wrong,' thought Brer Bear, mopping them. 'Flower pots don't walk.'

But that one did. Even as Brer Bear looked at it again, it moved a little further off, and then stayed still once more.

'Well, now, I never saw a flower pot that walked before!' said Brer Bear, puzzled. 'No, that I never did. Things are coming to a strange pass if flower pots begin to walk.'

Now just then Brer Fox came walking by and he called over the fence. 'Heyo, Brer Bear! How's yourself?'

'Brer Fox, I'm feeling mighty odd,' said Brer Bear. 'I'm seeing flower pots that walk.'

'What did you say?' said Brer Fox, thinking he must have heard wrong. Brer Bear told him again. Brer Fox came in at the gate. He looked round at the flower pots in the garden. There were three or four there, as well as the one that Brer Rabbit was hiding under.

'Well, they all seem to be staying quite still,' said Brer Fox. 'Your eyes must be wrong.'

'Yes, I think they must be,' said poor Brer Bear. 'Maybe I ought to wear glasses. See – that's the one that keeps moving, Brer Fox. That one there.'

He pointed – and Brer Fox stared as if his eyes would drop out of his head. Certainly that flower pot was moving! It was moving towards the gate.

'Stars and moon!' said Brer Fox, feeling a bit scared. 'That's an odd thing. Does it just walk like that, Brer Bear – it doesn't do anything else, does it? Because if it does, I'm going. I don't like things like that.'

Well, when old Brer Rabbit heard what Brer Fox said, he grinned to himself. All right – if Brer Fox was going to be scared, Brer Rabbit would scare him properly! So old Brer Rabbit began to jig up and down inside the pot, and he made it dance like mad.

Brer Fox clutched hold of Brer Bear in fright, and the two of them shivered and shook.

'It's dancing now!' said Brer Bear in a shaking voice.

And then that pot began to sing! Of course, it was just old Brer Rabbit singing away in a funny deep voice under the pot, but it sounded mighty strange, all the same.

*There isn't a pot in the world like me,*
*I'm just as mad as a pot can be,*
*Hi-tiddle-hi, and ho-tiddle-ho,*
*I'll dance on my heel and I'll dance on my toe!'*

Then the pot went quite mad, and rushed round in circles, jiggled and jerked, and made terrible screeching noises till Brer Bear and Brer Fox almost fell over in fright.

Miss Bear came out to see what the matter was. 'Lawks!' she cried, 'look at that! Oh my, oh my, what's going to happen next?'

Well, what happened next, happened all in a hurry. The pot danced to the gate and went through it. It disappeared behind the hedge – and as soon as it was out of sight Brer Rabbit popped out from under it, scurried into the hedge with his onion, and laughed fit to kill himself.

After a bit Brer Bear, Miss Bear, and Brer Fox tiptoed to the gate and looked down the lane. And there they saw the pot, tipped on its side, quite still. They stared at one another. More and more peculiar!

Then a bit of brown onion-peel flew into the roadway by their feet, and a cheeky voice cried out:

*'Hi-tiddle-hi! and ho-tiddle-ho,*
*I'll dance on my heel and I'll dance on my toe!'*

And down the road, as quick as could be, danced old Brer Rabbit, first on his heels, and then on his toes, munching away at the onion as he went. Brer Bear gave a bellow and went after him – but Brer Rabbit was mighty quick and went down a hole before Brer Bear could so much as touch his tail!

'He got that onion after all!' said Brer Bear. 'My, he's a scamp if ever there was one. Now I wonder how he got it?'

But none of the three could guess. As for the flower pot, Brer Bear threw a stone at it and broke it.

'I'm not going to have you dancing and singing at me any more!' he said. And didn't old Brer Rabbit laugh when he heard that!

# Brer Fox is Much Too Smart

One day Brer Fox remembered how Brer Rabbit had tricked him by lying down in front of him pretending to be dead. And Brer Fox thought it was a mighty good idea.

'Seems like I might trick Mr Man if I did the same,' said Brer Fox to himself. 'Suppose I did that when Mr Man was going along to the market with his chickens and ducks and other goods. Maybe Mr Man would leave his goods and go back and collect the dead fox he thought he'd seen – and I could make off with a nice meal!'

So Brer Fox kept watching for a chance to play

the same kind of game. By and by he heard Mr Man coming down the high road in a one-horse wagon, carrying some chickens, some eggs, and some butter to market.

Brer Fox heard him coming, he did, and what did he do but go and lie down in the road in front of the wagon! Mr Man, he drove along, clucking to the horse and humming to himself, and when they had almost got up to Brer Fox the horse shied. Mr Man was surprised.

'Wo there!' he cried. And the horse woed. Then Mr Man looked down to see why his horse had shied, and he saw Brer Fox lying out there on the ground just as if he was dead.

'Heyo!' he shouted. 'There's the chap that's been stealing my chickens! Somebody's shot him with a gun – and I wish it had been two guns, so I do!'

With that Mr Man drove on and left Brer Fox lying there. Then Brer Fox got up and ran round through the woods and lay down in front of Mr Man again. Mr Man came driving along and he saw Brer Fox and said: 'Heyo! Here's the chap that has been killing my pigs! Somebody's killed *him*, and I wish they'd done it a long time ago!'

Then Mr Man, he drove on, and the wagon-wheel came mighty near to running over Brer Fox's nose. But all the same Brer Fox leapt up and ran round ahead of Mr Man and lay down in the road once more. And when Mr Man drove up again, there he was all stretched out, big enough to fill a two-bushel basket, looking as dead as could be.

Mr Man drove up and stopped. He looked down on Brer Fox in surprise, because he thought this was the third dead fox he had seen that morning. Then he looked all round to see if he could spy what it was that was killing so many foxes! But he didn't see anything and he didn't hear anything either.

Then he sat and thought, and by and by he said to himself he'd better get down and have a look at the fox, and see if there was some curious kind of illness that was killing off all the foxes in the wood.

So he got

down from the wagon and pulled at Brer Fox's ear. It was quite warm and soft. He felt Brer Fox's neck. It was as warm as his ear. Then he poked Brer Fox in the ribs. No bones seemed to be broken. Then he felt Brer Fox's legs, but they were all as sound as could be. Then he turned Brer Fox over and there didn't seem to be a thing the matter with him at all.

When Mr Man saw this, he was astonished.

'Heyo, there! What does this mean?' he said to himself. 'This chicken-stealer looks as if he's dead, but he hasn't got any broken bones, and he isn't cut or bruised! He feels warm and alive. Something's wrong here, for sure!'

Mr Man scratched his head and looked down at Brer Fox. He thought of the other two dead foxes he had seen that day, and he thought of all the chickens, eggs and butter in his cart.

'This pig-stealer *might* be dead, and then again he mightn't!' said Mr Man. 'Before I go back and get those other foxes, I'll just make sure.'

He caught up his whip. 'To make sure he's not alive I'll just give him a whack with my whip-handle,' said Mr Man. And with that Mr Man lifted up his whip and hit Brer Fox a clip behind the ears – *pow!* – and the blow came so quick and so hard that Brer Fox really thought he had been killed!

But before Mr Man could lift up the whip again and give him another clip, Brer Fox scrambled to his feet, and ran for his life through the woods!

He was alive all right – and that's all Brer Fox got for playing Mr Smarty and copying old Brer Rabbit!

# Good for You, Brer Rabbit

Once Brer Fox and Brer Wolf found a key in the road. They picked it up and looked at it – and then they winked at one another.

'Ho! This is Brer Rabbit's front door key! Now, isn't that a bit of luck!'

'We'll be able to unlock his door and hide in his kitchen,' said Brer Wolf.

'And pounce out at him when he comes in!' said Brer Fox.

'We'll do it this very day!' said Brer Wolf.

So the two of them went right off to Brer Rabbit's house, and unlocked his door. They knew he had gone to market, because it was Thursday, and he always went on that day.

They shut the door again, and looked round the kitchen 'Where shall we hide?' said Brer Fox.

'I'll go into that cupboard, where the brooms and brushes are kept,' said Brer Wolf. And in he went, squeezing his big body between broom-handles and mops.

'I'm going into this cupboard under the dresser,' said Brer Fox. 'There are a whole lot of pans and dishes here, but I think I can manage to squeeze inside.'

The two of them lay in their cupboards as quiet as mice, waiting and waiting for Brer Rabbit to come home from market. They got rather stiff, but they didn't dare to move in case Brer Rabbit happened to come in just at that moment.

Pretty soon along came Brer Rabbit, all hung about with his marketing. He had cabbages and butter, a tin of pepper and a tin of salt, a jar of honey, a pot of jam, six new-laid eggs, and a lot of other things besides. He set them down to get his key out of his pocket.

Brer Fox and Brer Wolf heard him coming. 'Now don't you make a sound, Brer Fox!' hissed

Brer Wolf from the broom cupboard.

'Well, don't you either!' whispered Brer Fox.

Brer Rabbit couldn't find his key in his pocket. He hunted first in this one and then in that one. 'Surely I haven't lost it!' he groaned. 'I did hear something drop on my way to market. Oh my, I do hope I haven't lost it.'

Well, of course, he *had* lost it, so he didn't find it in his pockets. In despair he tried the handle of his door – and it opened! Brer Rabbit stared at it in surprise.

'Well, didn't I lock the door behind me this morning when I left?' he said to himself. 'I always do. This is mighty funny.'

He took a look round – and there in the dust outside the front gate he saw the footmarks of Brer Fox and Brer Wolf, as plain as could be!

'Oho!' said Brer Rabbit to himself, scratching his ears and thinking hard. 'Oho! And aha! This is where old Brer Rabbit does a bit of thinking!'

He rubbed his nose, and felt certain that Brer Fox and Brer Wolf had picked up his key, and come along and used it on his door! That's why the door wasn't locked now. They were hiding inside – and hoped that he would come and skip indoors as usual. Then what a commotion there would be!

411

'This won't do,' said Brer Rabbit. 'This just won't do! I've got to get them out of there somehow – and I can't go in myself, because if I do they'll get me!'

He sat down on his parcels and packets – and a tin rolled out from them. It was the tin of pepper. Brer Rabbit picked it up and grinned. Pepper! That was just the thing!

Brer Fox and Brer Wolf were peeping out of the key-holes in the cupboards, watching and waiting for Brer Rabbit to come in. They were shivering with excitement, for Brer Rabbit looked as fat as butter that day.

Brer Rabbit took the tin of pepper and went to the open door. He cautiously put his paw round and shook the tin with all his might. Shake, shake, shake! Shake, shake, shake, shake! My goodness, you should have seen the pepper fly out of that tin! It flew up to the ceiling. It flew down to the floor. It flew to the other side of the room and back again. It went in at the cracks and key-holes of the cupboards – and it found its way to the eyes and noses of Brer Fox and Brer Wolf!

Brer Wolf felt a sneeze coming. It came nearer and nearer to his nose. He tried his hardest to stop it. He put his paws to his mouth and nose and stopped breathing, hoping that the sneeze wouldn't come.

And when it came it was a MONSTER sneeze. 'A-TISH-ISH-OOO!'

Two brooms fell down and a mop fell sideways, knocking Brer Wolf on the nose. Brer Fox called out angrily, in a loud whisper:

'Brer Wolf! Must you make a noise like that just when Brer Rabbit is around?'

And then the pepper got into Brer Fox's nose and eyes, too. He screwed up his face. He tried to squash the sneeze into his throat and not let it come. But it did come.

'Woosh, WOOSH!' sneezed Brer Fox, and then he coughed as if he had whooping-cough, for the pepper was as strong as could be. He just couldn't stop. He coughed a saucepan down on top of him. He coughed two dishes from the shelf above and they flattened both his ears. Then he sneezed again so loudly that a saucepan fell right on his head like a hat.

'Brer Fox! What do you think you're doing?' said Brer Wolf in a rage. 'You tell *me* not to make a noise – but you sound like a thunderstorm and an earthquake all in one!'

Brer Rabbit giggled to himself. Then he spoke in a loud voice, as if he were very puzzled.

'Dear me! What's all that noise in my kitchen, I wonder? I don't like it. No, indeed I don't. It sounds as if robbers and thieves are there, stealing

my brooms and my saucepans. I'm going to get Mr Dog, and ask him to sniff around and hunt out those robbers. An, Mr Dog has big, sharp teeth and a dreadful bite – *he'll* soon sniff them out!'

Then Brer Rabbit made a pattering noise with his feet as if he were running down the path to fetch Mr Dog. He crouched down behind a bush and waited.

Now, when Brer Fox and Brer Wolf heard Brer Rabbit talking about Mr Dog they shivered and shook, for if there was one person they were really afraid of, it was sharp Mr Dog. He had chased them many a time. Brer Wolf spoke from the broom cupboard.

'Brer Fox! Isn't it time we went? I don't mind waiting about for Brer Rabbit – but I'm not waiting for Mr Dog!'

'Nor am I!' said Brer Fox, with a mighty sneeze, and he got out of the pan cupboard. 'Goodness me, we must both have got terrible colds, the way we're sneezing and coughing. We'd better go home and get into bed with hot-water bottles. I never knew a cold come on so suddenly!'

Brer Rabbit gave a bark like a dog. Brer Wolf and Brer Fox jumped, and made for the door as fast as they could. They got there at the same moment, and stuck.

'Let me out first!' panted Brer Fox, and he hit Brer Wolf with his fist. Brer Wolf gave him a punch back, and Brer Rabbit almost killed himself with laughing to see them.

Then down the path they went at top speed, Brer Fox still with a saucepan on his head that slipped down over his eyes so that he couldn't see where he was going.

'Yap-yap-yap!' barked Brer Rabbit, and the two of them went faster than ever. Everyone thought they must be running a race.

And after that Brer Rabbit had a new lock put on his door. He didn't want any more unexpected visitors!

# Mr Benjamin Ram
## and his Fiddle

Mr Benjamin Ram was a handy man with the fiddle. He lived all by himself out in the middle of the wood, and he was such a fine fellow to have at a dance that all the other creatures liked him very much. When there was any party on they always sent for old man Ram and his fiddle.

And as soon as Mr Benjamin Ram began to play tunes on his fiddle, why, everyone in the room was up and dancing, shaking their feet and tapping their toes for all they were worth – even old Brer Wolf had to dance when he heard Benjamin Ram's fiddle going.

After the party the other creatures always filled up a bag of peas for old man Ram, and he carried it home with him. He didn't ask anything more than that, for he was a kindly fellow, and liked nothing better than to tune up his fiddle and get people to shake their toes.

One time, just about Christmas, Miss Meadows and the girls thought they would give a party, and they sent word to Mr Benjamin Ram to come and bring his fiddle. So, when the day came, Mr Benjamin Ram set out. But the wind blew cold, and the clouds spread so thickly across the sky that it was almost as dark as night.

'No matter!' said Mr Benjamin Ram. He had his walking-stick with him, and his fiddle tied up in a bag. He knew the way very well, but seeing that it looked so like rain old man Ram thought he would take a short cut instead of keeping to the high road.

Well, that's just where Benjamin Ram went wrong, because in an hour or two he had lost his way! He went this way, and he went that way, and he went the other way, but all the same he was lost.

Some folks might have sat right down and shouted and yelled to see if they couldn't wake up their friends, but old man Ram didn't. He hadn't got a wrinkle on his horn for nothing.

He just stuck his chin in the wind, he did, and he marched right on. He kept on and on, and it wasn't long before he began to feel mighty lonesome.

He kept walking on till the night came, and still he went on, till by and by he came to a little hill. He stopped to look round, and not far off he saw a light shining. When he saw this, old Benjamin Ram clattered his hoofs together for joy, and set off to the house where the light was.

When he got there, he knocked.

'Who's that?' said a voice.

'I'm Mr Benjamin Ram, and I've lost my way, and I've come to ask you if you can take me in for the night,' said old man Ram.

'Walk right in!' called the voice. So with that he opened the door and walked in, and made a bow. But he had no sooner made his bow and looked round than he began to shiver and shake, because sitting right there in front of the fire was old Brer Bear, grinning and showing all his white teeth. And if Mr Benjamin Ram hadn't been so old and stiff he would have shot out of the door and away, but before he had time even to think about such a thing old Brer Bear jumped up, shut the door and fastened it with a great big chain.

Old Mr Ram knew he was caught then, but he put a bold face on and made another low bow.

'I hope Brer Bear and Mrs Bear and the family are well,' he said. 'I've just dropped in to warm myself and to ask the way to Miss Meadows'. Perhaps

Brer Bear would be good enough to set me on my way again?'

'To be sure,' said Brer Bear, with a grin. 'Just put your walking-stick over in the corner, and set your bag on the floor, and make yourself at home. We haven't got much in the house, but what we have you shall share – for we'll take good care of you, Mr Benjamin Ram!'

Brer Bear threw another log on the fire and slipped out to the kitchen, where he whispered to Mrs Bear. 'Old woman, old woman! Here's fresh meat come to supper!'

Poor Mr Benjamin Ram heard the whisper and he shook in his shoes. He knew he couldn't get away, and whilst he was sitting there it crossed his mind that he might as well play one last tune on his fiddle. With that he untied his bag and took out the fiddle. He began to tune it – *plink, plank, plunk, plink! Plunk, plank, plink, plunk!*

Now, when old Mrs Bear heard the strange and curious noise of the fiddle being tuned up she couldn't think what in the world it was! Of course, Mr Benjamin Ram didn't know how astonished Mrs Bear was, and he kept on tuning up, pulling the fiddle strings tighter and sounding them with his hoof – *plank, plink, plunk, plank!* Then old Mrs

Bear, she took hold of Brer Bear's arm and said:

'Hey, old man! What's that noise?'

Then both of them pricked up their ears and listened, and just then Mr Benjamin Ram put the end of the fiddle under his chin, and began to play an old, gay tune. Well, Brer Bear and Mrs Bear, they listened and listened, out there in the kitchen, and the harder they listened the more scared they got, because old Benjamin Ram, he just played like a madman, sort of wild and fierce, and the notes squealed and shrieked on his fiddle like hens squawking in the rain.

Then Brer Bear and Mrs Bear couldn't stand it any longer and they took to their heels and fled to the swamp at the back of the house as if a hive of bees was after them!

Well, old man Ram went on and on fiddling, and at last he stopped. He didn't see Brer Bear anywhere, and he didn't hear Mrs Bear. He looked in the kitchen. No bear there. He looked in the cupboard. No bear there. He looked in the back porch. No bear there either.

'Hoo!' said Mr Benjamin Ram in surprise. 'No bear here and I guess there won't be tonight if I can help it!' And with that he shut all the doors and locked them, and he hunted round and found some peas and bread in the loft. He ate them for his supper, and then he lay down by the fire and slept like a log all night through.

Next morning he awoke very early, and he set out from Brer Bear's house, and found the way to Miss Meadows'. Folks were still dancing there, and when they saw him coming in at the door they all ran to him. One took his hat, and one took his stick, and the other took his fiddle.

'Gracious goodness, Mr Ram!' they cried. 'Where in the world have you been? We're so glad you've come. Stir round, folks, and get Mr Ram a cup of hot coffee!'

'Well, folks,' said Mr Benjamin Ram, as he put his fiddle under his chin once more, 'this is the second time I've played my fiddle in a few hours – and the first time the folks shook their toes all right! They shook them so well that I never saw them again! Now then – shake your feet and let's see you dance – *plink, plonk, plank, plunk!'*

# Brer Rabbit's Astonishing Prank

Brer Rabbit was always one for thinking out new tricks. He didn't copy anyone else, and nobody knew what he was going to do next. He was the funniest creature of the whole lot. Some folks called him lucky, and when he got in a fix he nearly always came out on top.

One time Brer Rabbit thought he'd pay a call on old Brer Bear – but he was mighty careful to make sure that Brer Bear and his family were out, before he went! He sat down by the side of the road and he watched them go by – old Brer Bear, old Mrs Bear and the twin children, Kubs and Klibs.

Old Brer Bear and old Mrs Bear they went on ahead and Kubs and Klibs came shuffling and scrambling along behind. When Brer Rabbit saw this, he thought that now was the time to go and pay a visit at Brer Bear's house. So off he went.

It wasn't long before he was in Brer Bear's

house, sniffing here and prying there. He looked in the cupboards and he pried in the drawers. Whilst he was going around peeping here, there and everywhere, he began to feel about on the shelves, and a bucket of honey that Brer Bear had put up there fell down and spilt all over Brer Rabbit. A little more and he would have been drowned in honey! From head to heels Brer Rabbit was covered in honey; he wasn't just splashed with it, he was covered with it. He had to sit still whilst the honey dripped out of his eyes before he could see anything.

Well, after a little, he looked round and said to himself: 'Heyo, there! What am I going to do now? If I go out into the sunshine the bumble bees and the flies will swarm up and take me – and if I stay here, Brer Bear will come back and catch me. I don't know what I'm a-going to do!'

By and by an idea came to Brer Rabbit, and he slipped out of Brer Bear's house and into the woods. And when he got there, what did he do but roll himself over and over in the leaves and the dust to try and rub the honey off himself. He rolled around, and the leaves all stuck to him! The more he rolled the more the leaves stuck to him, till after a while Brer Rabbit was the most curious-looking creature you ever saw! And if Miss Meadows and the girls had seen him then and there, they certainly wouldn't have asked him to call at their house any more. Indeed and they wouldn't!

426

Well, Brer Rabbit jumped around, he did, and tried to shake the leaves off himself. But the leaves, they weren't going to be shaken off. Brer Rabbit shook and shivered, but the leaves all stuck to him. The capers he cut out there in the woods all by himself were most astonishing! But not a leaf could he shake off.

Brer Rabbit saw that this wasn't going to be any good, so he thought he'd better be going home, and off he went. But you never saw such a strange sight in your life as Brer Rabbit looked, stuck all over with leaves, from whiskers and ears to toes! He walked along, he did, and at every step he took, the leaves went swishy-swushy, splishy-splushy, and from the fuss he made and the way he looked you would have thought him the savagest creature that had lived on the earth since old man Noah turned the animals out of the Ark! And if you had met him you wouldn't have been with him long! You'd have run away as fast as could be.

Well, the first person Brer Rabbit met was old Sis Cow, and no sooner did she lay eyes on him than she threw up her tail and raced away as if a pack of dogs was after her! This made Brer Rabbit laugh, because he knew that if a sensible old creature like Sis Cow ran away like mad in the broad daylight, there must be something mighty curious-looking about the leaves stuck all over him.

The next person Brer Rabbit met was a girl carrying a basket of corn and a basket of piglets, and when she saw Brer Rabbit coming prancing and dancing along, she flung down her baskets and fairly flew down the road! And the piglets, they set off through the wood, and such a noise as they made with their running and their snorting and their squealing has never been heard before or since!

It went on like this whenever Brer Rabbit met anybody – they just turned and ran for their lives!

Of course, this made Brer Rabbit feel mighty biggitty, and he thought it would be a good joke to drop round and see old Brer Fox. And whilst he stood there thinking about this, along came Brer Bear and all his family. Brer Rabbit grinned to himself, and started off across the road towards Brer Bear.

Old Brer Bear stopped and looked at him, and Brer Rabbit went nearer and nearer. Old Mrs Bear stood it as long as she could and then she threw down her sunshade and climbed up a tree! Brer Bear looked as if he was not going to run away, but when Brer Rabbit jumped straight up into the air and gave himself a shake that set the leaves going swishy-swushy, splishy-splushy, well, old Brer Bear gave a grunt and tore down a whole fence, trying to get away from Brer Rabbit. And Kubs and Klibs, they took their hats in their hands and they went skaddling through the bushes like a pack of horses!

Well, Brer Rabbit paraded on down the road, and by and by he came across Brer Fox and Brer Wolf, who were busy fixing up a plan to catch Brer Rabbit, and they didn't see Brer Rabbit till they were right up to him! And goodness! When they saw him they gave him all the room he wanted!

Brer Wolf, he tried to show off, he did, because he wanted to look biggitty in front of Brer Fox, and he stopped and asked Brer Rabbit who he was. Well, old Brer Rabbit, he jumped up and down in the middle of the road, till all the leaves on him went swishy-swushy, splishy-splushy, and he shouted out:

'Oh, I'm the Wull-of-the-Wust! I'm the Wull-of-the-Wust, and you're the man I'm after!'

Then Brer Rabbit made as if he were going to jump at Brer Fox and Brer Wolf, and the way those two creatures ran for their lives was a sight to see!

Brer Rabbit got home at last and gave himself a good wash. And a long time after that, it happened that Brer Rabbit came up behind Brer Fox and Brer Wolf, and he hid behind a tree-stump and yelled out:

'I'm the Wull-of-the-Wust, and you're the men I'm after!'

Brer Fox and Brer Wolf shot off in a great fright, but before they had gone very far Brer Rabbit ran from behind the stump and waved to them – and he laughed fit to kill himself when he saw the surprised faces of Brer Fox and Brer Wolf.

Brer Rabbit told Miss Meadows about it, and the next time Brer Fox called, the girls began to giggle and laugh. And then they asked Brer Fox to be careful, in case the Wull-of-the-Wust dropped in. But Brer Fox looked mighty glum, he did, and just vowed to himself he would get even with Brer Rabbit, if it took him a month of Sundays to do it!

# Brer Fox Tricks Brer Terrapin

Brer Fox had been tricked so many times by Brer Rabbit that he just longed to trick somebody himself, to show he could be clever when he wanted to.

So he looked round to see which of the other creatures he could trick, and one day, when he was going along the road, he met old Brer Terrapin. Well, Brer Fox thought it would be very easy to trick Brer Terrapin because he was so slow and Brer Fox thought it would be fine to play a joke on him.

So he marched up to Brer Terrapin,

mighty biggitty, and called to him:

'How do you find yourself this morning, Brer Terrapin?'

'Slow, Brer Fox, mighty slow,' said Brer Terrapin. 'Day in and day out I'm mighty slow, and it looks as if I'm getting slower. I'm slow and poorly, Brer Fox. How do you feel yourself?'

'Oh, I'm up-and-doing, same as I always am,' said Brer Fox. 'What makes your eyes so red, Brer Terrapin?'

'It's all the trouble I see,' said Brer Terrapin. 'I see trouble, Brer Fox, and you see none. Trouble comes to me, and piles up on trouble!'

'Good gracious, Brer Terrapin, you don't know what trouble is,' said Brer Fox. 'If you want to see some sure-enough trouble, you should come along with me. I'm the man that can show you trouble!'

'Well, then,' said Brer Terrapin, 'if you're the man that can show me trouble, then I'm the man that wants to have a look at it!

'Well, have you seen the Old Scarecrow?' asked Brer Fox.

'No, but I've heard tell of him,' said Brer Terrapin.

'Well, the Old Scarecrow is the kind of trouble I'm telling you about,' said Brer Fox. 'If you want to see trouble, you just come along with me and I'll take you up to the broom-sage field, and we'll wait there a while and it won't be any time before we catch sight of the Old Scarecrow. Then you'll know what trouble is all right, Brer Terrapin.'

Now Brer Terrapin couldn't help feeling there was something wrong somewhere, but he was too flat-footed to have any scuffle with Brer Fox, and he said to himself he'd better go along with him and just trust to luck. So they went along and came to the fence round the broom-sage field.

'You help me over the fence and maybe I'll see the Old Scarecrow somewhere about,' said Brer Terrapin.

Well, as soon as Brer Terrapin was in the field across the fence, looking out for the scarecrow that wasn't there, Brer Fox set out to make some trouble for poor Brer Terrapin. He rushed off to Miss Meadows' house and asked her for a piece of burning wood to light his pipe.

He took the chunk of wood, ran back to the field and set the dry grass there on fire – and it wasn't long before it looked as if the whole field would blaze up!

Now, when old Brer Terrapin had gone across the fence and had begun to wade through the grass the very first person he met there was Brer Rabbit, lying asleep on the shady side of a tussock of grass. Brer Rabbit always slept with one eye open, and he was awake as soon as he heard Brer Terrapin scuffling and scrambling along. They shook hands with one another and said 'Howdy?'

As they were talking they saw the field getting afire, and Brer Terrapin was scared stiff.

'Don't you worry now, Brer Terrapin,' said Brer Rabbit. 'This is the trouble that Brer Fox sent you to look for! Well, it's a blessing you met me, Brer Terrapin, because if you hadn't you'd have been roasted to death!'

This made Brer Terrapin more scared than ever, and he said he wanted to get out of the field. But Brer Rabbit said he'd take care of him, and he took

Brer Terrapin to the middle of the field, where there was a big hollow tree-stump. Brer Rabbit lifted Brer Terrapin on to this stump, and Brer Terrapin slipped down into the hole. Brer Rabbit crept in after him, and when the fire came a-snipping and a-snapping round they sat as safe in the stump as a bird in its nest!

When the fire was over Brer Terrapin looked round, and he saw Brer Fox running up and down outside the fence as if he were looking for something inside the field.

Then Brer Rabbit, he stuck his head up out of the hole and saw Brer Fox too, and he began to shout in a squeaky voice like Brer Terrapin's: 'Brer Fox! Oh, Brer Fox! Come over here to this tree-stump. I've got Brer Rabbit caught in here!'

And when Brer Fox heard that he jumped over the fence and landed down on the half-burnt grass. It hurt him so much and stung his feet so hard that he squealed and rolled over. And the more he rolled, the more he burnt himself, and Brer Rabbit and Brer Terrapin they shouted and laughed till they couldn't laugh any more.

When Brer Fox got out of the field at last and went limping down the road, old Brer Terrapin yelled after him:

'Oh, there's trouble here, for sure, Brer Fox, and you found it, didn't you? Oh, you found it all right, Brer Fox, so you did!'

# Brer Rabbit's Shilling

Now once it happened that the snow fell very thickly, and Brer Rabbit's house was white from roof to door. Brer Rabbit looked out of the window and sighed.

'I'll have to get out my broom and do a bit of sweeping,' he said. 'My arms aren't so strong as they used to be. I don't reckon I want to sweep too long – but who is there who would do it for me?'

He sat and thought for a while, and then he pulled his whiskers and smiled.

'Maybe I'll get someone to do my sweeping after all!' he said. 'We'll see!'

He put on his hat and coat and scarf and sat by his window, watching for the creatures to go by on their way to market. As soon as he saw somebody ambling along in the distance, he skipped out into his front garden. But he didn't take his broom. No – he put his hands in his pockets, hunched up his shoulders, and went up and down his garden path, shuffling with his feet in the snow, as if he were looking for something.

Presently along came Brer Fox. He looked over the wall and greeted Brer Rabbit.

'Heyo, Brer Rabbit! You look as if you've lost something!'

'Do I?' said Brer Rabbit. 'Well, maybe you're right and maybe you're wrong.'

'Shall I come in and help you look for it?' said Brer Fox, obligingly. He felt certain that Brer Rabbit wouldn't be out in his garden on such a cold morning, if what he had lost wasn't worth hunting for. 'Maybe you've lost a shilling?'

'Maybe I have and maybe I haven't!' said Brer Rabbit. 'That's neither here nor there. I'm thinking of getting a broom and sweeping this snow away. Then if I've lost anything, maybe I'll find it. But my arms are tired this morning, so I thought I'd just have a look first, before sweeping.'

'Oh, are your arms tired?' said Brer Fox. 'Well, see here, Brer Rabbit, I'll do a bit of sweeping for you. My arms are as strong as anything. You get me a broom and I'll be pleased to do a bit of sweeping.'

Brer Rabbit grinned to himself. He knew that Brer Fox only meant to do the sweeping because he hoped to find what was lost! He went to his shed and fetched out a mighty big broom.

'Here you are,' he said to Brer Fox. 'I'd think it mighty kind of you if you'd do a bit of sweeping, mighty kind!'

'Don't mention it,' said Brer Fox, politely. He took the broom and began to sweep, keeping a sharp eye open for any money that might be buried beneath the snow.

Pretty soon along came Brer Bear, and he looked in astonishment at the sight of Brer Fox sweeping up Brer Rabbit's snow, for it was well known that the two were enemies.

'What are you doing that for?' he asked Brer Bear.

'Oh, Brer Rabbit's lost a shilling in the snow,' grinned Brer Fox. 'And maybe I'll find it. If I do, Brer Rabbit won't see it again!'

'Hooo! A silver shilling!' said Brer Bear, surprised. 'Well – in that case I think I'll run along and get my broom too. I could do with a silver shilling, so I could.'

And to Brer Fox's disgust Brer Bear went along home, found a broom, and came back with it. Soon he was sweeping hard, listening for the tinkle of a shilling. Brer Rabbit looked out of his window and grinned away to himself when he saw the two of them so hard at work. They had already swept halfway down his path to the gate.

Not long after this, Brer Possum came along, and how he stared to see Brer Fox and Brer Bear sweeping so busily in Brer Rabbit's garden!

'What's all this?' he asked. 'Is Brer Rabbit ill or something? What are you sweeping his path for? Not out of the kindness of your hearts, I guess!'

'You be quiet,' said Brer Fox, with a grin. 'We're hunting for a shilling that Brer Rabbit dropped in the snow. He thinks we're sweeping to save his poor tired arms – but we're not!'

'Well, I guess I'll join in,' said Brer Possum, at once. A shilling meant a lot of money to old Brer Possum. My, what couldn't he buy at the market for a shilling!

He saw Brer Rabbit at the window and he shouted to him: 'Heyo, Brer Rabbit! Sorry to hear your arms are bad. I don't mind giving a hand with your snow if you've got a broom to lend me!'

Brer Rabbit opened the window and threw out another broom. 'Thanks, Brer Possum,' he said. 'I didn't know I'd got such good friends.'

So in half a minute Brer Possum was also sweeping hard – swish, swish, swish, went the three brooms, and Brer Rabbit sat at his window and hugged himself, watching the workers panting and puffing in his garden. Now, when his path was swept quite clean, right to his gate, Brer Rabbit threw open his window.

'You *are* good friends!' he said. 'Don't you stop to do any more. I'm much obliged to you. Shut the gate after you, please!'

'Well! Hark at that!' said Brer Fox, indignantly. 'Doesn't offer us a cup of tea even! To think of all the hard work we've done for nothing – and we haven't even found the shilling!'

Brer Fox went to the window, and Brer Rabbit

hurriedly shut it down. Brer Fox looked in. He saw
Brer Rabbit put his hands into his pockets – he saw
him give a delighted grin. He saw him pull out a
bright shining shilling and hold it up to look at it.

'It was in my pocket after all!' shouted Brer
Rabbit through the window. 'Think of that now!
It was in my pocket all the time! Well, well, well!'

Brer Fox glared at him. 'I don't believe you ever
did drop it in the snow,' he said.

'Well, of course I didn't,' said Brer Rabbit, in a
surprised voice. 'Whatever made you think that?
Dear, dear – you surely haven't been sweeping my

snow just to find a shilling you thought I'd dropped, have you? And I thought you were all doing it out of kindness, so I did!'

Brer Fox was so angry that he threw Brer Rabbit's broom up on to his roof. He stalked out of the gate, and Brer Bear and Brer Possum went with him.

'If I wasn't tired out, I'd sweep all the snow back again on to his path!' grumbled Brer Bear. 'That creature's sharper than a knife!'

Brer Rabbit laughed loudly when he saw the three marching out of his front gate, down a nicely-swept path. 'Thanks!' he called out. 'Come again tomorrow if the snow falls to-night!'

He had to get a ladder and fetch his best broom down from the roof. But he didn't mind that, not he! He'd got his path swept for nothing, clever old Brer Rabbit!

# Brer Bear Goes to the Well

One day it happened that Brer Rabbit met old Brer Bear ambling along, and he skipped up to him.

'Good-day, Brer Bear,' said Brer Rabbit. 'How's yourself?'

'Oh, up and down, up and down,' said Brer Bear. 'So you're not caught yet, Brer Rabbit? My, it just beats me how you manage to skip about as you do, the biggest scamp in the woods, and never get caught.'

Well, Brer Bear, *you'll* never catch me!' said Brer Rabbit. 'I'm too smart for you. You're slow in your feet and slow in your mind too. I'm quick in my feet and quick in my mind! No one's any match for me, not even Brer Fox!'

Now it doesn't do to boast, not even if you are as clever as Brer Rabbit. Something horrid always happens to boasters – and no sooner were the words out of Brer Rabbit's mouth, than Brer Fox popped out from behind a tree and caught him by the back of the neck!

'*I'm* pretty quick on my feet this morning, Brer Rabbit,' grinned Brer Fox. 'Oh yes – I heard you coming along boasting so loudly that you didn't see me hiding behind that tree. You didn't see Brer Bear wink at me. So we are too slow for you, are we? Well, this time you're wrong. You're going home with me – and you're going to be cooked for my dinner!'

'Let me have a share,' begged Brer Bear. 'You can't eat all of him. He's pretty fat.'

'Well, you come along too, then,' said Brer Fox, swinging Brer Rabbit to and fro in a way that made him very angry indeed. They went along to Brer Fox's house, and Brer Fox shut all the windows tight and locked the door. Then he dumped Brer Rabbit into a cupboard and shut the door.

Now no sooner did Brer Rabbit get into that cupboard than he began to scurry round and round it, making all kinds of excited squeals and squeaks. Brer Fox and Brer Bear were astonished.

'Now what's the matter, Brer Rabbit?' said Brer Fox at last.

'There's an enormous fat mouse in here,' panted

Brer Rabbit. 'My, he *is* fat. I thought maybe I could catch him and eat him.'

'Don't you do anything of the sort,' said Brer Fox fiercely. 'Any mouse in my cupboard is *mine*. I'll open the door and you shoo him out.'

So Brer Fox opened the door, but no mouse came out. 'He's gone into that box,' said Brer Rabbit.

Brer Fox took up the box – and at the same moment Brer Rabbit shot out of that cupboard into the kitchen. He looked around for a hiding-place, and saw Brer Fox's big old boiling-saucepan set ready at the side of the fireplace. He slipped the lid to one side and jumped in. Then he slipped the lid on and lay in that saucepan as quiet as could be.

Well, Brer Fox and Brer Bear were so busy looking for that mouse that at first they didn't bother about where Brer Rabbit had gone. 'He can't get away,' said Brer Fox. 'The windows are fastened, and the door is locked.'

Well, they didn't find that mouse, of course, because there never had been one there. It was just a trick of old Brer Rabbit's to get out of the cupboard.

'A silly trick!' said Brer Fox. 'He may get out of the cupboard – but he can't get out of my kitchen! My word, when I find him I'll give him such a spanking that he won't know whether he is standing on his head or his heels!'

Brer Fox began to look for Brer Rabbit. He couldn't find him. 'Well, he's here somewhere,' he said to Brer Bear, 'and when I find him I'll pop him into my saucepan and boil him for our dinner. I hope he's trembling when he hears that!'

Brer Rabbit lay low in the saucepan

and didn't say a word. Brer Fox was angry. He turned to Brer Bear who was standing doing nothing to help.

'Don't stand there doing nothing!' he said. 'Go to the well and fill the saucepan with water. Then it will be ready to boil Brer Rabbit in when I find him. And go out of the door quickly in case Brer Rabbit makes a run for it.'

Brer Bear picked up the saucepan – with Brer Rabbit in it, of course – and went to the door. He opened it quickly, got through it as fast as he could, and shut it behind him.

'I'll have found Brer Rabbit by the time you get back!' Brer Fox shouted after him, and began to hunt everywhere again. But it wasn't much good looking in the kitchen for Brer Rabbit – he was going to the well in the saucepan. He felt very pleased with himself.

He began to jiggle the lid up and down. 'Jiggle-jiggle-jing!' went the lid. 'Jiggle-jiggle-jing!'

Brer Bear looked down, surprised. He wasn't used to saucepans behaving like that. He took hold of the lid and set it on very firmly indeed. But old Brer Rabbit pushed it loose again, and 'Jiggle-jiggle-jing!' it went, 'jiggle-jiggle-jing!'

Brer Bear set the saucepan down on the ground

and put the lid on as hard as he could. And as he pushed it on, Brer Rabbit pushed it off. So it felt to Brer Bear as if the lid was being very obstinate, and he began to shout angrily at the saucepan.

'How dare you behave like that? You keep your lid on properly!'

'Shan't!' shouted Brer Rabbit in a voice as like a saucepan as he could manage.

Brer Bear nearly fell over with surprise when the saucepan answered him back. He sat down and stared at it.

'Don't you dare to be cheeky to a smart fellow like *me!*' he said to the saucepan.

'Smart fellow, did you say?' said Brer Rabbit, still pretending to be the saucepan. 'Well, do you think it's smart to let old Brer Fox order you off to the well, so that he can find Brer Rabbit and gobble him up before you come back? That's what he's doing, for sure!'

'Well, stars and moon, I never thought of that!' said stupid old Brer Bear, getting up. 'I'll just go right back and see if I catch him eating up Brer Rabbit!'

He ambled back to Brer Fox's house and opened the door. Brer Fox was looking puzzled. He had hunted everywhere for Brer Rabbit, and hadn't found him. He stared at Brer Bear.

'You're back quickly,' he said. 'Where's the saucepan?'

'That *saucepan* told me something strange,' said Brer Bear. 'It told me you had ordered me off to the well for water so that you could gobble up Brer Rabbit by yourself.'

'The saucepan told you!' said Brer Fox, in astonishment. 'Are you mad, Brer Bear? Saucepans don't talk.'

'Yours does,' said Brer Bear. 'I heard it. It's a mighty cheeky saucepan, too. If it were mine I wouldn't have it in my house.'

'Brer Bear, I tell you saucepans don't talk,' said Brer Fox. Then a thought flashed into his mind, and he stared at Brer Bear in dismay. 'Brer Bear! That wasn't the saucepan. It was Brer Rabbit! He hid in the saucepan! You took him out in it! And he cheeked you, and sent you back here so that he could escape. Quick – where did you leave the saucepan? Maybe he couldn't get the lid off and is still there!'

So the two of them rushed out to the saucepan – but as you can guess, it was quite empty! Brer Rabbit was gone.

'You're just as stupid as ever!' shouted Brer Fox to Brer Bear.

'Well, you're not very smart yourself, to tell me to go out to the well with the saucepan – and Brer Rabbit inside it all the time!' said Brer Bear.

A voice floated down to them from far up the hill. This is what it sang:

*'Slow in your feet*
*And slow in your mind,*
*Always too late, always behind!*
*But I'm quick in my mind,*
*And quick in my feet,*
*Oh, Brer Rabbit finds you all easy to beat!'*

'Well, you can guess who *that* is, Brer Bear,' said Brer Fox, with a nasty look. And Brer Bear *could* guess – quite easily!

# Brer Rabbit Goes to the Party

It happened one time that Brer Fox gave a party, and asked Brer Bear, Brer Wolf, Brer Raccoon and some others. But he didn't ask Brer Rabbit. All the same, when Brer Rabbit heard about it, he made up his mind to go! Well, those that had been invited went to Brer Fox's, and Brer Fox asked them in and got them chairs, and they sat there, laughing and talking. Then by and by Brer Fox put out some food and drink, and told them to help themselves.

Well, whilst they were eating and drinking, what do you suppose Brer Rabbit was doing? Oh, he was sailing round as usual, fixing up his tricks! He had been looking for a big drum he had, and when he found it he fixed it on to the front of him and made his way down the road to Brer Fox's.

As he went he beat the drum till it sounded like a mixture of hail and thunder. My, what a noise it made! It went like this:

'Diddybum, diddybum, diddybum-bum-bum – diddybum!'

Well, all the creatures were eating and drinking and laughing, and they didn't hear any noise, but all the same here came Brer Rabbit:

'Diddybum, diddybum, diddybum-bum-bum – diddybum!'

By and by, Brer Raccoon, who always had sharp ears, asked Brer Fox what that noise was, and by that time all the animals stopped to listen. And along came Brer Rabbit, beating that drum like thunder and hail!

'Diddybum, diddybum, diddybum-bum-bum – diddybum!'

The creatures kept on listening to this loud and curious noise, and Brer Rabbit got nearer and nearer. Soon Brer Raccoon reached under his chair for his hat.

'Well, Brer Fox,' said he, all of a shiver and shake, 'I expect I'd better be going. I told my old woman I wouldn't be a minute, and here I've been two or three hours!'

With that Brer Raccoon skipped out – but he hadn't got much farther than the back gate before all the others joined him, running along as if they were in a race, and old Brer Fox leading them, looking as scared as could be! My, he didn't know what that noise was, and he didn't mean to wait and see, either!

Off the animals went, tumbling over one another, and scrambling about in alarm till they got to the woods.

Old Brer Rabbit came on down the road – diddybum, diddybum, diddybum-bum-bum – diddybum – and goodness gracious, when he came to Brer Fox's house there was nobody there! Brer

Rabbit rapped on the open door and shouted: 'Is there anyone at home?' And then he answered himself. 'No, Brer Rabbit, the folks are all out!'

Then Brer Rabbit began to laugh, he did, fit to kill himself, and then he kicked Brer Fox's door wide open and marched in. He yelled, 'Heyo, Brer Fox!' But there was nobody there, as he very well knew. So Brer Rabbit walked in and took a chair and made himself at home, even putting his feet up on the sofa!

He hadn't sat there long before he saw the good things on the table! So up he got and he was soon tucking into the food and drink as if he hadn't had a meal for a twelvemonth!

All this time the other creatures were hiding in the bushes listening for the diddybum, and getting ready to rush off at the least sound. But they didn't hear anything more, so Brer Fox said he was going back to the house, and who was going with him?

They all started out, they did, and they crept towards Brer Fox's house, but they were mighty slow and careful, and if a leaf had fallen off a bush, well, you wouldn't have seen any of the creatures for dust! They heard no noise, and they kept on creeping till they got to the house.

When they got there the first thing they saw

was old Brer Rabbit standing by the table, stuffing himself full of good things. Brer Fox just stood by the door, staring at Brer Rabbit, and he snapped his jaws together and shouted loudly.

'Ah yi, Brer Rabbit! Many a time you escaped, but this time I've got you!'

Well, everyone shot in and got hold of old Brer Rabbit, and there he was properly caught. Brer Bear put on his spectacles and looked round at the company and said that any man caught stealing his neighbour's goods must be drowned.

'That's right enough,' said Brer Fox at once. 'Sure, that's right enough, Brer Bear. Brer Rabbit will have to be drowned.'

Then Brer Rabbit pretended to be scared, and he squealed and cried and shouted and begged them, in the name of goodness, not to fling him into the pond because they all knew he couldn't swim.

'But if you've made up your minds to throw me in, then for pity's sake give me a walking-stick to hold on to whilst I'm a-drowning,' said Brer Rabbit.

Old Brer Bear looked sternly at Brer Rabbit. 'Seeing it's the last thing you'll have, you can have a stick,' he said. So Brer Fox gave him one. And then they put Brer Rabbit into a wheelbarrow and wheeled him along to the pond and threw him into the water.

Well, Brer Rabbit landed on his feet, as light as a cat, and picked his way out of the pond with the help of the walking-stick! The water was so shallow that it hardly came over Brer Rabbit's shoes, and when he got out on the other side, he waved his stick to Brer Fox and grinned.

'So long, Brer Fox!' he called. 'So long! Thanks for the nice party!'

# Brer Fox and Brer Terrapin

Once Brer Terrapin found some big quill-feathers that had belonged to Brer Turkey Buzzard. They were lying on the ground, and Brer Terrapin picked them up. When he found that they were hollow, he blew down them.

A merry whistling noise came from them, and Brer Terrapin was delighted. He went down the road, whistling and singing loudly. And this was the song he sang:

*Brer Terrapin's clever, Brer Terrapin's strong,*
*He can run a swift race, he can sing a loud song,*
*Tirallee, tirallee, tirallee, too,*
*Brer Terrapin's smarter than you, than you!*

Well, Brer Terrapin sang this song to Brer Fox when he met him, and Brer Fox didn't like it. He sang and whistled it to Brer Bear, and Brer Bear

459

shouted at him. He whistled and sang it to Brer Rabbit, but Brer Rabbit just didn't take any notice at all.

Soon all the animals got angry when they heard Brer Terrapin coming along with his quill-pipes, whistling how clever and smart he was. They looked for some quill-feathers for themselves, but they couldn't find any.

Brer Fox asked Brer Turkey Buzzard if he would lend him some quills, but Brer Buzzard said no, he needed all he had got. Brer Fox said couldn't he spare a few, and Brer Buzzard said, well, Brer Fox could come and have a look to see if any of his quills were good enough. But when Brer Fox got near and was looking at his feathers, Brer Turkey Buzzard flapped his wings hard in Brer Fox's face and nearly blew his whiskers off! Then away he sailed into the air, squawking with laughter.

Well, Brer Fox saw that he wouldn't be able to get any quills out of Brer Buzzard. He wanted them so badly that he went to find Brer Terrapin.

'Will you sell those quill-pipes?' said Brer Fox.

But Brer Terrapin, he held on to those quills tightly, and said no, they weren't for sale.

'Well, will you lend them for a week, then?' asked Brer Fox. 'I'd like to play tunes on them to my children.'

Brer Terrapin shook his head. He knew very well he wouldn't get them back once he had lent them to old Brer Fox. And as soon as Brer Fox had turned away to go, Brer

461

Terrapin began to whistle his song.

'Brer Terrapin's clever, Brer Terrapin's strong!' But when he saw Brer Fox turning back, he took the quills out of his mouth and hid them away carefully in his shell. He knew old Brer Fox well enough!

Now Brer Fox worried and worried about those quills, and made up his mind to get them somehow. So one day he set out to find Brer Terrapin again, and when he had come across him, he began to talk to him very politely.

'How are you feeling today, Brer Terrapin?' he asked.

'Not too bad, and not too good, Brer Fox,' said Brer Terrapin, putting his head inside his shell for safety.

'And how are all your family, Brer Terrapin?' said Brer Fox, coming a bit nearer.

'So-so, so-so,' said Brer Terrapin, putting his little tail inside his shell.

'Brer Terrapin, could you let me have a look at those buzzard quills of yours?' said Brer Fox, not coming any nearer at all. 'You see, I have goose feathers at home, and if I could see your quills closely, maybe I could make my goose feathers into quill-pipes like yours. You know how badly I've wanted your quills, Brer Terrapin. Well, just show me them and maybe I can make some like them."

Well, Brer Terrapin thought about this, with his head and his tail tucked safely away in his shell. He was a kind fellow, and he liked to do what people asked, if he could. And he didn't see why Brer Fox shouldn't see his quill-pipes, if he wanted to make some like them. So by and by he held out the quills for Brer Fox to see.

Brer Fox bent down close – and then, quick as lightning, he jerked the quills out of Brer Terrapin's hand, picked them up, and dashed off as quick as could be! Brer Terrapin shouted after him as loud as he could yell, but he knew it was no good. He didn't even bother to go after Brer Fox, because he knew he couldn't catch him. So he just sat there, looking as if he'd lost all the friends he had in the world. Poor Brer Terrapin!

Well, Brer Fox was pleased to have got the quill-pipes, and he marched around, feeling mighty biggitty, singing and whistling. And every time he met old Brer Terrapin he played on the pipes and sang this song:

*Brer Fox is clever, Brer Fox is strong,*
*He can run a swift race, he can sing a loud song.*

*Poor old Brer Terrapin, what will he do?*
*Brer Fox is smarter than you, than you!*

And Brer Fox, he danced round and round old Brer Terrapin till Brer Terrapin had to shut his eyes, he felt so giddy! But he didn't say a word, though he felt so bad.

At last, one day when old Brer Terrapin was sitting on a log sunning himself, Brer Fox came up again, playing the same old song. But Brer Terrapin he stayed still. Brer Fox came a little nearer and played more loudly, but Brer Terrapin, he kept his eyes shut and stayed quiet.

Brer Fox came nearer still and climbed up on the log beside Brer Terrapin. Brer Terrapin said nothing. Brer Fox pushed himself nearer to him on the log and played the song again. And still Brer Terrapin said nothing.

'Heyo!' said Brer Fox, at last, rather out of breath with all his whistling. 'Brer Terrapin's mighty sleepy this morning!'

Brer Terrapin kept his eyes shut and stayed as still as the log. Brer Fox got nearer and nearer to him, trying to see if he was really asleep – till suddenly Brer Terrapin opened both his eyes *and* his mouth, and made a grab at Brer Fox. But he missed him! Brer Fox laughed fit to kill himself, and marched off, playing the same old tune.

Next morning Brer Terrapin sat and thought for a while – and then he went to a mud-hole and wallowed in it, rolling over and over, smearing himself with mud till he looked exactly like a clod of earth. Then he crawled out of the mud-hole and lay down under a log on which he knew Brer Fox sat every morning when he brushed out his fur.

Well, Brer Terrapin lay there, he did, and after

a bit, along came Brer Fox. He sat down on the log and began to swing himself forwards and backwards. Brer Terrapin took a look at him and crept a little nearer. Brer Fox didn't see him. He thought Brer Terrapin was just a lump of dirt.

At last Brer Terrapin had crept just underneath Brer Fox's foot – and he opened his mouth and made a grab at him – and caught him by the foot!

Well, once Brer Terrapin caught hold of anything, nothing but thunder and lightning would make him leave go! He just sat there and held on to Brer Fox's foot, and Brer Fox, he jumped and jerked about, but Brer Terrapin wouldn't let him go.

'Brer Terrapin, please let me go!' yelled Brer Fox.

Then Brer Terrapin talked away down in his throat, because his mouth was over Brer Fox's foot.

'Give me my quills!'

'Leave go, and I'll go and fetch them,' said Brer Fox.

'Give me my quills!'

'Do pray let me go and get them!'

'Give me my quills!'

That was all that Brer Fox could get out of Brer Terrapin! At last Brer Fox's foot hurt him so much that he had to do something about it, and he shouted out to his old woman to bring him the quills. But she was busy about the house and didn't hear him. So he called Toby, his son.

'Toby! Oh, Toby!'

'What do you want, Daddy?' shouted Toby.

'Fetch Brer Terrapin's quills.'

'What's that you say, Daddy? Fetch you some pills?'

'No, you turnip-head! Fetch Brer Terrapin's quills!'

'What's that you say, Daddy? Put something on the sills?'

'No, you snail-head! Fetch Brer Terrapin's quills!'

'What's that you say, Daddy? Something to spill?'

After a bit old Mrs Fox heard the shouting

467

and she listened and found out that Brer Fox was yelling for the quills. So she fetched them and took them out to Brer Terrapin. And he let go his hold of Brer Fox's foot and took them. But for a long while after that old Brer Fox walked mighty strangely – hoppitty-fetchity, hoppitty-fetchity, hoppitty-fetchity! And he didn't go near Brer Terrapin for a month of Sundays!

# Brer Rabbit Tricks Brer Fox

Now although Brer Rabbit was supposed to be the only creature allowed to call on Miss Meadows and the girls, Brer Fox often used to pop in and see them, too. And he was so polite and said such smart things that Miss Meadows and the girls, they let him come as often as he liked.

Well, that didn't please Brer Rabbit, who liked to be the only one around. And soon Brer Rabbit began to think how he might put a stop to Brer Fox's visits.

As he was sitting down by the side of the road, thinking this, and thinking that, fixing up his tricks, he heard a clatter up the long green lane, and along came old Brer Fox – *too-bookity-bookity-bookity-book!* He was galloping along like a pony in the field, and he was all smartened up, too, looking as slick and as shiny as if he'd just come out of a shop window!

'Where are you a-going, Brer Fox?' asked Brer Rabbit.

'I'm a-going to take dinner at Miss Meadows', said Brer Fox, grinning at Brer Rabbit.

'That's a pity, Brer Fox,' said Brer Rabbit. 'I'd got some mighty good news for you!'

'What's that?' said Brer Fox.

'Well,' said Brer Rabbit, scratching his ear with his hind foot, 'I was taking a walk the day before yesterday when I suddenly saw the biggest and the fattest bunch of grapes that ever I laid eyes on! They were so fat and so big that the juice was just dropping out of them. The bees and the wasps were swarming there after the sweetness, and little old Jack Sparrow and his family were all there, dipping their beaks into the juice!'

Well, when Brer Fox heard this his mouth began to water, and he looked most kindly at Brer Rabbit. He sidled up to him and said:

'Come on, Brer Rabbit! Let's both go and get those grapes before they are all gone!'

Old Brer Rabbit laughed and shook his head. 'I'm hungry myself,' he said, 'but I don't like grapes. I'm just a-rushing round to find a bit of parsley to keep the breath in my body! And if you go alone, Brer Fox, and get those grapes, what will Miss Meadows and the girls do?

471

They are expecting you to dinner, you said.'

'Oh, well, I can drop round and see them after I've had the grapes,' said Brer Fox.

'Well, all right, then,' said Brer Rabbit. 'I'll just tell you how to find them. You know that place where you went blackberrying for Miss Meadows?'

'Yes,' said Brer Fox, listening carefully.

'Well, the grapes aren't there,' said Brer Rabbit. 'You get to the blackberry patch, and you follow the stream there till you come to a few nut-trees – but the grapes aren't there. Then you go to the left and cross the hill till you come to a big oak-tree – but the grapes aren't there. You go down the hill till you come to another stream, and by that stream there's a dogwood tree leaning over, and by the dogwood tree is a grape-vine, and on that vine you'll find

472

the grapes. They're so ripe that they look as if they've all melted together, and I expect you'll find them covered with bees and wasps, but you can take that fine bushy tail of yours and brush all the insects away!'

'I'm much obliged to you,' said Brer Fox, and he set off at a gallop. When he was out of sight Brer Rabbit took a blade of grass and tickled himself in the ear with it, and then he shouted and laughed and laughed and shouted till he had to lie down in the grass and get his breath back again.

After some time he jumped up and set off after Brer Fox. Brer Fox didn't look behind at all, he was so eager to find those grapes. On and on he went till he came to the dogwood tree, and near by was the grape-vine.

And sure enough, when old Brer Fox looked up at the vine, he saw what he thought was the biggest bunch of grapes he had ever seen in his life – all covered with wasps.

'Heyo!' said Brer Fox, in delight. 'There's a fine bunch of grapes! And my gracious, haven't the wasps found them too! Well, I'll wipe them off with my tail.'

So he balanced himself on a branch near by, and swung his big bushy tail at the bunch of grapes to brush off the wasps. But goodness gracious, no sooner had he done that than he let out a squall that Miss Meadows heard two miles away!

Old Brer Rabbit had tricked Brer Fox properly! That bunch of grapes, so fine and big, was not grapes at all, but a great big wasps' nest built in the vine! Brer Fox knocked it down with his tail, and the nest dropped right on top of him! And the wasps, they swarmed out in a rage and set to work to sting poor Brer Fox till he squealed out in fright.

Brer Fox ran, and kicked, and scratched, and bit, and scrambled, and shouted and howled, but it wasn't a bit of good. Those wasps just wouldn't leave him alone! At one time it looked as if Brer Fox was going to run towards the place where Brer Rabbit was hiding, and as soon as Brer Rabbit saw that, he was up and away! He didn't want any wasps after him! He went sailing through the woods and he didn't stop till he came to Miss Meadows' house.

'Heyo, Brer Rabbit,' said Miss Meadows. 'Where's Brer Fox?'

'He's gone grape-hunting,' said Brer Rabbit. 'I just now saw him.'

'Well, to think of that!' said Miss Meadows crossly. 'He said he was coming to dinner. I've done with Brer Fox. He said he'd come to dinner, and he goes off grape-hunting. Here's his dinner been ready for a long time, and we've all been waiting for Brer Fox. I shan't ask him again. You'd better stay instead, Brer Rabbit.'

At first Brer Rabbit said he wouldn't stay, but by and by he took a chair and sat down. He had only just begun his dinner when he saw old Brer Fox going by outside.

'There goes Brer Fox,' he said to Miss Meadows and the girls. 'My, isn't he fat! Looks like he's been gobbling all the grapes on the hills!'

Poor Brer Fox! He didn't want anyone to see him at all, because the wasps had stung him hard, and his head was swelled up, and his legs too.

Brer Rabbit put his head out of the door and shouted to him.

'Heyo, Brer Fox! Did you find those grapes all right?'

But Brer Fox, he didn't answer a word!

# Brer Rabbit and the Moon

There were times when all the creatures became friendly together and shared everything.

One time, when they were friends like this, Brer Rabbit saw that he was getting fat and lazy. This always happened when he didn't do any tricks, and the more peace there was, the worse Brer Rabbit felt. And by and by he got very restless.

When the sun shone he'd go and lie in the grass and kick at the gnats, and nibble at the mullein-stalks and wallow in the sand. But this didn't make him any thinner. One night, after supper, whilst he was running round a bit to try and get thinner, he came up with old Brer Terrapin, and after they had shaken hands and sat down on the side of the road, they began to talk about old times.

'You know, Brer Terrapin,' said Brer Rabbit, at last, 'I just feel I've simply got to have some fun.'

'Well, Brer Rabbit,' said Brer Terrapin, 'then I'm

the man for you to have your fun with. What are we going to do?'

'We'll play a trick on Brer Fox, Brer Wolf and Brer Bear,' said Brer Rabbit. 'We'll all meet down by the mill-pond tomorrow night and have a fishing-party. I'll do the talking, Brer Terrapin, and you can sit back and say "yes" to all I say.'

Brer Terrapin laughed. 'If I'm not there tomorrow night you'll know a grasshopper has run off with me!' he said.

Well, Brer Rabbit set out for home, and on the

way he told all the others about the fishing-party and they were pleased and promised to be at the mill-pond the next night. Miss Meadows and the girls got to hear of the party and they said they'd come along too.

Sure enough, when the time came, they were all there. Brer Bear fetched a hook and line, Brer Fox fetched a dip-net, and Brer Terrapin fetched a box of bait.

Miss Meadows and the girls they stood by the edge of the pond and squealed every time Brer Terrapin shook the box of bait at them. Brer Bear said he was going to fish for mud-cats. Brer Wolf said he was going to get horny-heads. Brer Fox said he'd catch some perch for the ladies. Brer Terrapin said he wanted to catch minnows and Brer Rabbit winked at Brer Terrapin and said he was after a few silly-billies!

Well, they all got ready, and Brer Rabbit marched up to the pond as if he were going to throw his hook into the water – but just as he was about to fling it in he stopped and stared hard at the water as if he saw something peculiar there. The other creatures all stopped and watched him. Brer Rabbit dropped his rod and stood there scratching his head, looking down into the water.

Miss Meadows and the girls felt a bit uncomfortable when they saw Brer Rabbit staring hard like this. 'Heyo, Brer Rabbit,' they called, 'what in the name of goodness is the matter with the water?'

Well, Brer Rabbit went on scratching his head and looking into the water, and by and by he took a long breath and said: 'Folks, we might just as well pack up and go home, because there won't be any fishing for us!'

With that old Brer Terrapin scrambled to the edge of the water and looked in. He shook his head, and said: 'To be sure – to be sure! Tut-tut-tut! That's so, Brer Rabbit, that's surely so!' And then he crawled back again as if he were thinking hard.

'Don't be scared, folks,' said Brer Rabbit. 'There isn't much the matter except that the moon has dropped into the water! If you don't believe me you can look for yourself.'

Well, Brer Fox looked into the pond, and said, 'Well, well, well – sure enough, there's the moon!'

Brer Wolf looked in. 'Mighty bad, mighty bad!' he said.

Brer Bear looked in and gave a grunt. 'Who'd have thought it, who'd have thought it?' he said.

Miss Meadows and the girls looked in too and said, 'Isn't it too bad!'

Then Brer Rabbit looked in again and said: 'Well, folks, it's no good shaking your heads and sighing about it. Unless we get the moon out of the pond there'll be no fish for us to catch tonight! And if you ask Brer Terrapin, he'll tell you the same.'

'But how can we get the moon out of the pond?' asked everyone.

'Better leave that to Brer Rabbit,' said Brer Terrapin.

Brer Rabbit shut his eyes and looked as if he were thinking deeply. Then by and by he spoke. 'The quickest way out of this difficulty is to send to old Mr Mud Turtle and borrow his drag-net, and drag the moon up from there.'

'Well, I'm very glad to hear you say that,' said Brer Terrapin, 'because old Mr Mud Turtle is my uncle, and he'll do anything for me.'

So Brer Rabbit went for the drag-net, and whilst he was gone old Brer Terrapin began to talk. 'You know, folks,' he said, 'I've heard that those who find the moon in the water and fetch it out find a full pot of money there too! Yes, I've heard that tale time and again!'

This made Brer Fox, Brer Wolf and Brer Bear feel mighty good.

'Seeing that Brer Rabbit has been good enough to go to fetch the drag-net, we'll do the dragging,' they said. When Brer Rabbit got back, he saw what was up, and he pretended he was going in after the moon, but the other creatures stopped him.

'You're a dry-foot man,' they said to Brer Rabbit. 'You don't like the water. We'll do the dragging for the moon.'

So Brer Fox, he took hold of one end of the net, Brer Wolf took hold of the other end, and Brer Bear he waded along behind to lift the net up.

They made one haul with the net and lifted it up. No moon! They made another haul – no moon! They dragged the net again – no moon! Then by and by they waded farther out from the bank. Water ran into Brer Fox's ears, and he shook his head. Water ran into Brer Wolf's ears, and he shook his head too. Water ran into Brer Bear's ears, and he had to shake his head as well. And whilst they were all busy shaking their ears, they waded out to a very deep part where the bottom of the pond dropped right away!

Brer Fox stepped off the bottom and went right under! Brer Wolf ducked himself and went under too, and Brer Bear he plunged in and disappeared as well! And goodness gracious, they all kicked and spluttered and splashed as if they wanted to throw all the water out of the mill-pond.

When they came out Miss Meadows and the girls were laughing and giggling, and well they might, for Brer Fox, Brer Wolf and Brer Bear looked mighty odd. Brer Rabbit took a look at them, and squealed with laughter too.

'Well, folks,' he said at last, 'I expect we'd all better go home and get into dry clothes. Better luck next time! I hear that the moon will take a bait of silly-billies, and it seems as if she found her bait all right tonight!'

And with that Brer Rabbit and Brer Terrapin went off to have supper with Miss Meadows and the girls, and Brer Fox, Brer Wolf and Brer Bear went off dripping – and what they said about Brer Rabbit that night would have made his ears drop off, if he could have heard!

# Brer Rabbit Scares his Friends

In the days when Brer Rabbit lived, the creatures had their ups and downs just as we do. They had their bad times and they had their good times. Some years their crops were good, and some years they were bad. Brer Rabbit was like the rest of the creatures – sometimes he had plenty of money, sometimes he had none. And when he had it he spent it.

One season Brer Rabbit did mighty well with his melons, and he said if they fetched all the money he hoped they would, he'd be able to go into town and buy a great many things.

'You do that, Mr Rabbit, you do that,' said his old woman. 'You buy us all something. You get seven tin cups for the children to drink from, and seven tin plates for them to eat from, and a coffee-pot big enough for all of us.'

'That's just what I'll do,' said Brer Rabbit.

486

'I'll set out for the town next Wednesday, old woman, and I'll come back with all the things you want!'

Well, Mrs Rabbit was mighty pleased to hear this, and she slapped on her bonnet and ran up to Mrs Mink's house to tell her all about it.

'You know, Mrs Mink, Mr Rabbit is going to go to town on Wednesday, and buy all the children something! What do you think of that?' said Mrs Rabbit.

Well, Mrs Mink was surprised to hear this, and when Brer Mink came home that night she told him about it.

'Brer Rabbit is going to town on Wednesday and is going to buy something for all his children,' she said. 'Why can't you buy something for *your* children, Mr Mink, that's what I want to know!'

And then they began to quarrel, and Mr Mink was so cross that he went out and slammed the door behind him.

Well, Mrs Mink, she told Mrs Fox how Brer Rabbit was going to go shopping and Mrs Fox, she went for Brer Fox when he came home that night, and asked him why he couldn't go shopping like Brer Rabbit and bring presents home for his children!

Then Mrs Fox told Mrs Wolf and Mrs Wolf told Mrs Bear, and it wasn't long before everyone around knew that Brer Rabbit was going shopping on Wednesday and was going to bring something home for his children. And all the other creatures' children asked their daddies why they wouldn't buy them something.

Well, Brer Fox, Brer Wolf and Brer Bear felt mighty wild with Brer Rabbit for stirring up all their wives and children about his shopping.

'We'll fix up a plan to catch Brer Rabbit on his way back from town on Wednesday,' said Brer Fox.

'And we'll take away everything he's bought!' grinned Brer Wolf.

'And I'd just like to see his old woman's face when she sees Brer Rabbit coming home from town without a thing after all!' said Brer Bear.

When Wednesday came, Brer Rabbit had an early breakfast and set out for the town. He had plenty of money in his pocket, and he went and looked at all the shops there were. He bought himself some cigars and a red pocket handkerchief, and he bought his old woman a large coffee-pot, and he got his children seven tin cups and seven tin plates. When the sun was just going down he started out for home.

He walked along, he did, feeling mighty biggitty, but by and by he sat down under a blackjack tree, for he felt a bit tired. He fanned himself with one of the tin plates and yawned loudly.

Well, whilst he was doing this, a little tree-creeper bird ran up and down the tree behind him, making a mighty fuss. After a while Brer Rabbit got cross, and shooed him away with the tin plate. That made the little tree-creeper madder than ever, and it flew on to a branch just by Brer Rabbit's head, and sang a little song.

*Pilly-wee, pilly-wee,*
  *I can see what you can't see!*
*I see, pilly-wee,*
  *I see what you can't see!*

Well, he kept on like this, he did, till Brer Rabbit began to look round to see what it could be that the tree-creeper could see. And suddenly he saw marks in the sand, where someone had been sitting a little while back. And Brer Rabbit looked at these marks closely, and saw what the little tree-creeper meant!

Brer Rabbit scratched his head and spoke softly to himself.

'Ah-yi! ' he said. 'Here's where Brer Fox has been sitting, and there's the mark of his nice bushy tail! And here's where Brer Wolf has been sitting, and there's the mark of his fine long tail! And here's where Brer Bear's been squatting down, and there's the mark that shows he hasn't got a tail! They've all been here – and I guess they're hiding down in the hollow yonder waiting for me!'

With that Brer Rabbit put all his goods into the bushes, and crept round and about to see what he could see. And sure enough, when he crept near to the little hollow down the hill, he saw them all a-waiting for him. But they didn't see him! Brer Fox was on one side of the path, and Brer Wolf was on the other side, and Brer Bear, he was curled up, having a nap!

Well, Brer Rabbit took a peep at them, he did, and he smacked his lips and pulled his whiskers for joy. He held his hands across his mouth and laughed fit to burst himself – but he didn't make a sound!

Then off went Brer Rabbit to the bushes where he had left his goods, and when he got there he danced around, and slapped his legs and did all kinds of weird things. He meant to play a fine trick on the others!

Then he got to work. He took the coffee-pot, turned it upside down, and stuck it on his head!

Then he ran a string through the handles of the tin cups and slung them across his shoulder. Then he divided the tin plates up, and took some in one hand and some in the other. When he was quite ready he crept to the top of the hill, took a running start, and flew down the hill like a hurricane – *rickety, rackety, slambang!*

Well, bless us all, the creatures had never in their lives heard a noise like that, and they hadn't seen anyone looking like Brer Rabbit, either, with the coffee-pot on his head, the cups rattling on the string, and the plates waving and shining in the air, and banging whenever Brer Rabbit clapped them together! *Rickety, rackety, slambang!*

Now old Brer Bear was taking a nap in the hollow, and the noise scared him so much that he rushed off and ran right over Brer Fox. He rushed out on to the path, but when he saw Brer Rabbit flying down towards him, looking mighty odd, he rushed off again, and fell over Brer Wolf. What with all the scrambling and scuffling, Brer Rabbit came right up to them before they could get away!

And how he shouted! Goodness gracious, you should have heard him!

'Give me room! Turn me loose! I'm old man Spewter-Splutter, with long claws and scales down

my back! I'm snaggle-toothed and double-jointed!
Give me room!'

And then he'd give a yell, and bang the tin plates
together and rattle all the cups – *rickety, rackety,
slambang!* And when Brer Fox, Brer Bear and Brer
Wolf saw what was coming on them, they just took

to their heels and ran for their lives!

Brer Bear ran straight into a tree-stump and split
it into bits – and do you know, when Brer Rabbit
and his children went along that way the next

morning, they got enough firewood from that split stump to last them all the winter!

Ah, Brer Rabbit's a sly one, he is! There's no tricking him, that's certain!

# Brer Fox is a Snowman

Now once Brer Fox thought of a very good trick to play on Brer Rabbit. He called on Brer Wolf and told him about it.

'Listen,' he said. 'What about you and me going along to Brer Rabbit's garden when he's out this morning and building a fine big snowman?'

'Well, there doesn't seem much sense in that,' said Brer Wolf.

'Wait and let me tell you,' said Brer Fox. 'You see, we'll build the snowman – and then he'll see it when he comes home, and he'll laugh. And tonight I'll go along and knock it down, and stand there myself instead, with a white sheet round me. Then, when he comes out, he won't know it's me, and I can jump out on him nicely!'

'All right,' said Brer Wolf. 'We'll do that. We'll go right along now.'

So off they both went. Brer Rabbit was out

shopping, so Brer Wolf and Brer Fox had plenty of time to get to work. Snow was thick on the ground, and they soon built a fine big snowman in Brer Rabbit's garden.

'Make it as like me as you can,' said Brer Fox. 'Not too fat because I'm rather thin now.'

Well, they finished it by the time Brer Rabbit came home, and how he laughed when he saw it. 'It's a mighty good snowman, isn't it?' he said to Brer Raccoon, who was walking along with him. 'I wonder who made it?'

Brer Terrapin was ambling along slowly in the

snow and he called out to Brer Rabbit. 'I know who made it. Brer Wolf and Brer Fox did!'

Brer Rabbit stared at the snowman and grew very thoughtful. 'Now why did Brer Wolf and Brer Fox trouble themselves to come and build a snowman in my garden?' he said. 'Now, I just do wonder why?'

The more he thought about it, the more he wondered. He felt quite uncomfortable about it. 'I think somehow I'll send a note along to Mr Dog, and ask him to keep me company tonight,' he thought. 'Mr Dog's so sensible and wise. I shall feel safe with him. I can't help feeling there is something tricky about that snowman, for all he's made of soft white snow.'

So he sent a note along and asked Mr Dog to come along that night and have supper with him. And Mr Dog arrived in good time, with his tail brushed, and a very smart new collar on.

Now, as the two of them were having supper, Old Brer Fox crept up outside, and knocked down the big snowman. He had a big white sheet wrapped around himself. He had cut two holes for eyes so that he could look through them. He stood himself up in the same place where the snowman had been and he waited.

There was a light in Brer Rabbit's house, so Brer Fox knew Brer Rabbit was there. He stood out there in the cold moonlight and wondered how to get old Brer Rabbit out in the garden so that he could pounce on him.

'I'll sing a song,' thought Brer Fox. 'He will think it's a poor old beggar-man singing for money. He'll either come out to give him money, or he'll come out to chase him away.'

So Brer Fox lifted up his voice and sang.

*'I'm out in the moo-oo-oonlight,*
*A beggar-man worn and old,*
*I'm shivering down to my shoo-oe-soles*
*Because I'm so terribly cold.*
*Ooooooh! Ooooooh! Ooooooh!'*

Brer Rabbit and Mr Dog were most surprised to hear this song. They pricked up their ears and listened.

'Funny,' said Brer Rabbit. 'Beggar-men don't usually come around singing at this time of night.'

'It sounds a bit like Brer Fox's voice,' said Mr Dog, listening.

'It does,' said Brer Rabbit. 'He's been looking out for me lately. He doesn't like me, Mr Dog.'

'I know,' said Mr Dog, grinning. 'I'm not surprised. You've played some mighty good tricks on him, Brer Rabbit.'

'Will you come out and see if the old beggar-man is Mr Fox?' asked Brer Rabbit.

Mr Dog had had a mighty good supper, and he was feeling grateful to Brer Rabbit. He nodded his big head. 'Yes, I'll come along,' he said.

So the two went to the door and opened it. When Brer Fox saw that Mr Dog was there too he was startled. He didn't like Mr Dog at all. Mr Dog could run fast and always chased Brer Fox when he could. So Brer Fox stopped his singing and stood as still as could be, hoping that Brer Rabbit and Mr Dog would think he was just a snowman and nothing else.

'He's stopped singing,' said Brer Rabbit, looking all round in the moonlight. 'I can't see anyone at all. He must have gone.'

'There's only the old snowman standing there alone,' said Mr Dog.' Well – he can't sing – so whoever it was must have gone.'

'We'd better go into the warm again then,' said Brer Rabbit. But before he could step inside, Mr Dog caught him by the arm.

'I can smell Brer Fox,' he said.

'Can you really?' said Brer Rabbit, half frightened. 'Well, where can he be? Is he hiding somewhere? If he is, he's waiting around for me! I guess it must have been him after all, singing that beggar-man song.'

'I'll sniff around a bit and see if I can find him,' said Mr Dog, and he ran out into the garden.

Well, Brer Fox was so frightened that he began to shiver with fear. He didn't dare to run away because he was all wrapped up in the sheet, and Mr Dog would easily be able to catch him. So he just stood out there in the moonlight and shook from ears to toes.

Mr Dog sniffed around the garden. He was puzzled. He could quite well smell Brer Fox – but yet he couldn't see him anywhere. It was most extraordinary.

'Heyo, Brer Rabbit,' he called, 'it's a funny thing but there's Brer Fox's smell around here, without Brer Fox. How do you make that out?'

Brer Rabbit couldn't make it out at all. He couldn't make out something else either. He had caught sight of the snowman shivering and shaking like a jelly, and he was most astonished.

'Mr Dog,' he called, 'I think my eyes are going wrong. Seems to me as if the old snowman over there is shaking like a jelly. Do you think he's scared of you? Are snowmen scared of dogs?'

'I'll bark at him and see!' said Mr Dog and he ran right up to the snowman and barked in his loudest voice. Well, Brer Fox couldn't stand that! He gave a dreadful yell, and tore off down the garden as fast as he could go, with the white sheet all wrapped round him!

'The snowman's running away!' shouted Brer Rabbit, beside himself with delight. 'The snowman's running away!'

Well, of course, Mr Dog ran after him – and it

wasn't long before he caught him either. He bit through the sheet and got hold of Brer Fox's leg.

'Let me go,' yelled Brer Fox. 'Let me go! Ow, let me go! I'm a poor old snowman, I am! Let me go!'

Mr Dog gave him the worst shaking he had ever had in his life, and then let him go. The sheet was in holes, and Brer Fox's head came through one of the biggest holes as he ran. Brer Rabbit saw it and began to laugh.

'Ho, ho, ho! You came to catch me, Brer Fox – and you got caught yourself! Ho, ho, ho! Run, Mr Dog, run – catch him again and bite him!'

But Mr Dog was laughing too much to run any more. The two of them watched poor Brer Fox running between the trees, stumbling over the white sheet.

'He won't build snowmen in my garden any

more,' said Brer Rabbit, wiping the tears off his whiskers. 'No, that he won't!'

And Brer Fox never did! It took him a day and a half to mend his bitten sheet, and he was in such a bad temper that even Brer Wolf didn't dare to go near him for three weeks!

# Mr Lion Hunts for Mr Man

Mr Lion set himself up to be the head of all the other creatures, and he went around the neighbourhood ramping and roaring because he felt so biggitty! Everywhere he went he heard talk of Mr Man, and the wonderful things he did.

'He's not so big as you, maybe, Mr Lion,' said Brer Rabbit, 'but he's a whole lot cleverer!'

'He's not so strong as you, maybe, Mr Lion,' said Brer Bear, 'but he's much more cunning.'

'His voice is not so loud as yours, and his feet are not so silent, but he's twice as smart as you are, Mr Lion,' said Brer Fox.

Well, Mr Lion didn't want to hear about Mr Man. He wanted folks to listen to all the grand things that he, Mr Lion, had done. But every time he began to talk biggitty someone stopped him and told him about Mr Man.

Well, things went on like this till by and by Mr

Lion shook his big mane, he did, and let out a mighty loud roar.

'I'm going to hunt round and round, high and low to see if I can find Mr Man,' he said, 'and when I find him I'll give him the sort of whacking he's never had yet! My, won't I make Mr Man scared of Mr Lion!'

'You'd better let Mr Man alone,' said everyone. But Mr Lion shook his mane and set off to hunt him down.

By and by, as he was going along, with his tongue hanging out because he was so hot, he came up with Brer Steer, who was grazing along the side of the road. They bowed to one another, and then Mr Lion asked Brer Steer some questions.

'Is there anybody round in these parts called Mr Man?' he said.

'To be sure there is,' said Brer Steer. 'Anyone can tell you that. I know him very well.'

'Well, then, he's the very chap I'm after!' said Mr Lion.

'What do you want with Mr Man?' asked Brer Steer.

'Oh, I've just come along to give him a good whacking,' said Mr Lion. 'I'm going to show him who's king here!'

'Well, if that's what you've come for,' said Brer Steer, 'you'd better just turn yourself around, and point your nose towards home, because you'll only run yourself into pain and trouble, Mr Lion.'

'I tell you, I'm going to whack that Mr Man,' said Mr Lion. 'I've come for that, and that's what I'm a-going to do!'

Brer Steer drew a long breath and stared at Mr Lion 'You see me here, standing in front of your eyes, Mr Lion – and you see how big I am, and what long, strong horns I've got? Well, big as my

hoofs are, and sharp though my horns be, Mr Man
came out here and caught me, and put me under
a yoke, and hitched me up to a cart, and made me
haul his wood. He drives me anywhere he wants
to. Yes, that he does. Better let Mr Man alone, Mr
Lion. If you play about with him watch out that
he doesn't hitch you up to a cart and have you
prancing around carrying all his loads!'

Mr Lion let out a roar and set out down the
road. It wasn't long before he came across Brer
Horse, nibbling at the grass. Mr Lion spoke to
him. 'Is there anybody round these parts called Mr
Man?' he asked.

'Sure there is,' said Brer Horse. 'I know him
mighty well, and I've been knowing him a long
time, too. What do you want with Mr Man?'

'I'm a-hunting him up so as to give him a mighty
good whacking,' said Mr Lion, switching his tail
about.

Brer Horse looked at Mr Lion as if he were very
sorry for him. By and by he said:

'I think you'd better let Mr Man alone. You see
how big I am, and what great strength I've got,
and how tough my hoofs are? Well, this Mr Man,
he can take me and hitch me up to his cart, and
make me drag him all around, and after that he can

fasten me to the plough and make me break up all his new ground. You'd better go along home, Mr Lion. If you don't, you'll have Mr Man making you break up his new ground for him!'

In spite of all this Mr Lion shook his mane and said he was going to whack Mr Man anyhow. He went on down the road and by and by he came up with Mr Jack Sparrow. Mr Jack Sparrow flew round Mr Lion, and chirruped and fluttered about in surprise and admiration.

'Heyo, there!' he said. 'Who would have expected to see Mr Lion down in these parts? Where are you going, Mr Lion?'

'I'm a-going to find Mr Man,' said Mr Lion. 'Do you know him?'

'Oh, yes,' said Mr Jack Sparrow, 'I know him mighty well.'

'Where is he?' asked Mr Lion.

'He's across there in his new ground,' said Mr Jack Sparrow. 'What do you want with him, Mr Lion?'

'I'm a-going to give Mr Man a whacking,' said Mr Lion, shaking his mane.

'You'd better let Mr Man alone,' said Mr Jack Sparrow. 'You see how little I am, and you know how high I can fly? Well, in spite of that, Mr Man can fetch me down when he wants to! You'd better tuck your tail behind you and set out for home, Mr Lion, in case Mr Man fetches *you* down too!'

But Mr Lion vowed he was going after Mr Man, and go he would, and go he did. He hadn't ever seen Mr Man, and he didn't know what he looked like, but he went on towards the new ground. And sure enough, there was Mr Man, cutting up logs to make himself a new fence. He was splitting a tree-trunk in two, and as he split it, he was putting in wedges of wood to keep the split open.

He was splitting away when by and by Mr Man heard a rustling out in the bushes, and he looked up and there was Mr Lion.

'Howdy,' said Mr Lion. 'Do you know Mr Man?'

'I know him as well as I know my own brother!' said Mr Man.

'I want to see this Mr Man,' said Mr Lion, switching his tail.

'Well,' said Mr Man, with a grin, 'I'll fetch him for you, if you like. But see here, Mr Lion, you'd better just hold this tree-trunk open for me whilst I'm gone. I've got it nicely split down the middle, and I don't want the crack to close up again. Stick your paw in the crack and hold it open for me whilst I go and fetch Mr Man.'

So Mr Lion, he marched up and slapped his paw into the crack – and then Mr Man knocked out the wedges that kept it open, and the crack closed up, and there Mr Lion was, caught by the paw so that he couldn't get away!

Mr Man stood by and laughed. 'If you'd been a steer or a horse, you would have run away!' he said. 'And if you'd been a smart little Jack Sparrow you'd have flown off, but here you are, and you put your paw in and caught yourself!'

And with that Mr Man went to the bushes and cut a big stick, and he whacked Mr Lion with it till he begged for mercy. And down to this day you can't get any lion to help Mr Man when he's splitting logs!

# Brer Bear's Red Carrots

Once Brer Bear had a whole field of fat red carrots. They grew there in hundreds, with their feathery green tops nodding in the breeze. Brer Rabbit thought they looked marvellous.

Now Brer Rabbit had just turned over a new leaf that week, and he felt it would be wrong to go and help himself to Brer Bear's carrots. 'I must give people a chance to be kind,' he said to himself. 'I'll go and tell Brer Bear that I've turned over a new leaf and that I just can't let myself dig up any of his carrots without asking – and maybe he'll give me a whole lot.'

So off he went to Brer Bear. Brer Bear was sitting in his front porch, basking in the sun. He wasn't very pleased to see Brer Rabbit, because he kept remembering the tricks that Brer Rabbit had played on him.

'Good morning, Brer Bear,' said Brer Rabbit politely. 'It's a nice day, isn't it?'

'None the nicer for seeing *you*!' growled Brer Bear.

'Oh, Brer Bear! That's not a kind way to talk,' said Brer Rabbit, shocked. 'Why, I came to tell you that I'd turned over a new leaf!'

'About time too,' said Brer Bear.

'You've a fine field of carrots,' said Brer Rabbit. Brer Bear looked up at once.

'Oho! So it's my carrots you've come about,' he said. 'I didn't quite believe that new-leaf idea of yours, Brer Rabbit.'

'Well, that's just where you are wrong,' said Brer Rabbit, trying to keep his temper. 'I came to tell you that if I hadn't turned over a new leaf I'd have gone and dug up your carrots without asking you, to make myself some soup. But as I've made up my mind to be better in future, I came to ask you if I might have a few carrots. You can spare a few, surely?'

'Not to you, Brer Rabbit, not to you,' said Brer Bear. 'And what's more, you can't make me give you any, no matter how many new leaves you turn over! No – once a scamp, always a scamp, is what I say. And I'm not giving any carrots to you at all.'

Brer Rabbit stamped away in a rage. What was the use of turning over a new leaf if he couldn't get what he wanted? No use at all! All right – he would show Brer Bear that he would *have* to give him some carrots. Yes, he'd show him!

That night Brer Rabbit took his spade and went to Brer Bear's field. He dug up a whole sackful of fine red carrots. My, they were fat and juicy! But Brer Rabbit didn't eat a single one. No – he wasn't going to do that till Brer Bear had given him some.

He hid the sack of carrots under a bush and went home. Next morning he was up bright and early and went to the bush. He dragged the sack out and took it away down the lane not far from Brer Bear's house. It was very heavy indeed. Brer Rabbit puffed and panted as he dragged it along.

He waited until he saw Brer Bear coming down

the lane for his morning walk. Then he set to work to drag the sack again, puffing as if he were a train going uphill! He pretended not to see Brer Bear, and Brer Bear was mighty astonished to see Brer Rabbit dragging such a heavy sack down the lane.

'Heyo, Brer Rabbit,' he said. 'You seem to be too weak to take that sack along.'

'Oh, Brer Bear, I've done such a foolish thing!' panted Brer Rabbit. 'I've got such a lot of carrots to put in my store that I can't take them home! I shall have to leave them all here in the lane! Oh, why didn't you give me just a few when I asked you yesterday! Now all these will go to waste, for I'll have to leave them under a bush. I can't possibly drag the sack any farther.'

Brer Bear didn't think for a moment that they could be *his* carrots. He opened the neck of the sack and looked inside. Yes, there were fine fat carrots there all right. He supposed that Brer Rabbit must have gone to market and bought them.

'You can't waste carrots, Brer Rabbit,' said Brer Bear. 'It would be wrong.'

'I know that,' said Brer Rabbit. 'But what am I to do?'

'I'll have them myself, if you'd like to take a few jars of honey in exchange for them,' said Brer Bear, thinking that if he took the sackful it would save him the trouble of digging his own carrots that day.

'Oh, Brer Bear! How *kind* of you!' said Brer Rabbit, rubbing his whiskers in delight. 'I thought yesterday that you were rude and unkind, Brer

Bear. But today you are quite different. You are good and kind and generous. I like you.'

Brer Bear couldn't help feeling rather pleased at this. He went into his house and brought out three jars of honey. Brer Rabbit smelt them in delight.

'*Three* jars, Brer Bear! It's more than generous of you! How mistaken I was in you! I did so long for a few of your nice carrots yesterday, but this honey is almost better than carrots – though how I *do* long for carrot soup!'

'Well – you can have a few carrots out of this sackful if you like,' said Brer Bear, still feeling very generous. 'Here you are – one, two, three, four, five, six, seven, eight! Nice fat ones too!'

'Brer Bear, you're a mighty good friend!' said Brer Rabbit, stuffing the carrots into his big pockets and picking up the honey. 'I meant to make you give me a few of your carrots – but I didn't hope that you would give me your honey too! Good-day – and thank you!'

Brer Rabbit skipped off as merry as a grasshopper in June. Brer Bear stared after him, scratching his head. Now what did Brer Rabbit mean by saying that he would make Brer Bear give him some of his own carrots?

And then Brer Bear suddenly had a dreadful thought and he hurried off to his field as fast as his clumsy legs would take him. There he saw where Brer Rabbit had dug up a whole sackful of carrots!

And how poor Brer Bear stamped and raged!

'I've given him eight of my best carrots – and three pots of my best honey! Oh, the rascal – oh, the scamp! Turning over a leaf indeed! I'd like to turn *him* over and give him a good spanking. And one of these days I will!'

But he hasn't yet! Brer Rabbit is much too clever to go near Brer Bear for a very long time.

# Brer Turkey Buzzard in Trouble

Now it happened that Brer Turkey Buzzard once thought it would be fun to fly after Brer Rabbit and say rude things. Brer Rabbit had often tricked old Brer Buzzard, and Brer Buzzard was mighty tired of it.

So every time that Brer Rabbit went out for a walk, there was Brer Turkey Buzzard sitting on a nearby tree, waiting to squawk rude things at him.

'Heyo, Brer Rabbit, heyo, old stick-in-the-mud!' Brer Buzzard screeched. 'Where's your tail? Is that all you've got for a tail! My, I'd be ashamed if that was all I'd got for a tail!'

And then Brer Buzzard would stalk around on his branch and show off his fine tail.

Another time Brer Buzzard shouted out rude things about Brer Rabbit's whiskers.

'Heyo, Brer Rabbit! How are your whiskers this

morning? Is that all the whiskers you can grow?
They're mighty poor!'

Brer Rabbit was angry. 'Well, where are your
whiskers, I'd like to know?' he yelled to Brer
Buzzard.

'I sold them to a rag-and-bone man and he must
have sold them to you!' squawked Brer Buzzard
very rudely.

Brer Rabbit felt so angry that he made a rush at
Brer Turkey Buzzard – but Brer Buzzard just sailed
into the air, squawking with laughter.

Then Brer Rabbit tried pretending not to hear
when Brer Buzzard called after him – but that
wasn't much good, because Brer Buzzard only
became ruder and ruder, and soon there was quite
a crowd of creatures following Brer Rabbit just to
laugh at the bad things Brer Buzzard said!

Well, pretty soon Brer Rabbit began to think
hard about all this. He wasn't used to being treated
in such a way – and the worst of it was he couldn't
get hold of Brer Buzzard, because he just rose into
the air as soon as Brer Rabbit got near him!

At last Brer Rabbit thought of an idea. He shut
himself up in his house for two days and gave out
that he had a bad cold. Then, on the third day,
he went out with his head all wrapped up in a

THE BRER RABBIT STORY COLLECTION

shawl and a thick coat round his shoulders. He sniffed as he went, and sneezed into a big yellow handkerchief.

Brer Turkey Buzzard was waiting for him as usual. He had had time to think of a few more quite new rude things. He opened his beak as Brer Rabbit came out.

'Heyo, Brer Rabbit!' he squawked. 'Why don't you buy a little honey to make you sweet? You look mighty sour to-day!'

Brer Rabbit took no notice. Brer Turkey Buzzard shouted even more loudly. Brer Rabbit looked round as if he heard something.

'Did you speak to me, Brer Buzzard?' he asked politely. 'My cold must have made me deaf.'

He sat down by the roadside. Brer Turkey Buzzard flew down to a nearby tree and shouted again.

'I'm sure you must be saying something very interesting,' said Brer Rabbit, putting his paw behind one ear as if to hear better. 'But I'm hard of hearing today. Is it anything important you have to say?'

'Why don't you wash behind your ears?' cried Brer Buzzard rudely.

'Why don't I lend you my shears?' said Brer

Rabbit, looking rather surprised. 'What do you want my shears for? To cut off your tail?'

'I said, 'Why don't you wash behind your *ears*?' shouted Brer Buzzard, hopping to the ground.

'Really, Brer Buzzard, you must think me very rude,' said Brer Rabbit, unwrapping the shawl from his head. 'I'm deaf both sides, it seems. Could you speak a little louder.'

Brer Buzzard hopped nearer and squawked even more loudly.

Brer Rabbit shook his head politely and put a paw behind *both* ears. 'You'll have to shout right into my ears, I'm afraid,' he said. 'I can't seem to hear a thing.'

Brer Turkey Buzzard hopped right up and leaned over Brer Rabbit's big ears.

'Why don't you wash behind...' he began to shout – but that's as far as he got. As quick as lightning Brer Rabbit flung the shawl over Brer Buzzard's head and held him tight!

Brer Buzzard kicked out with his feet and struck with his wings – but he couldn't see because his head was in the shawl. He began to squawk loudly.

'Now, now,' said Brer Rabbit, shaking him. 'That's not the way to talk. In fact, Brer Buzzard, it strikes me that you don't know how to talk politely at all! I think I'd better teach you. Now what was it you said about my tail the other day? Something rude, I know.'

Brer Buzzard said nothing. He was afraid of repeating anything now.

'Yes – I remember. You said you'd be ashamed if you had a tail like mine! Well, well, Brer Buzzard, I'm sure you won't mind giving me a few of your tail-feathers to make myself a tail as grand as yours!'

And what did old Brer Rabbit do but whip a big handful of feathers out of Brer Turkey Buzzard's tail! Brer Buzzard gave a loud squawk. Brer Rabbit unwrapped the shawl and let him go.

'Thanks for the new tail,' said Brer Rabbit, and he began to tie the tail-feathers neatly on to his own bobtail. 'I shall tell everyone how kind you've been to me, Brer Buzzard! Do keep near to me so that every one can see you've given me your tail!'

Brer Buzzard took a look at his own poor tail and gave a squawk of dismay. He flew off in shame to hide himself – but old Brer Rabbit, he paraded about with a long tail of fine buzzard-feathers for weeks after that!

And Brer Turkey Buzzard was mighty polite to him when he met him again. He knew it wasn't any good trying to get the better of Brer Rabbit!

# Brer Rabbit's Apple Tree

Now once Brer Bear and Brer Fox put their heads together and made up their minds to catch Brer Rabbit the very next time they saw him.

'That tiresome creature is always up to tricks,' complained Brer Bear.

'But this time we'll have him, and he won't escape!' grinned Brer Fox. 'He'll be going along through his orchard this evening. We'll wait there and catch him!'

'Where shall I meet you?' asked Brer Bear.

'Under the tree in the middle of the orchard,' said Brer Fox. 'Good-bye till then!'

So that evening, a little while before Brer Rabbit was due to stroll through his orchard, Brer Fox turned up. He went to the middle tree, and sat down with his back to the trunk.

It was an apple tree and the apples were ripe. The evening was windy, and as the breeze blew, an apple became too heavy for its stalk and fell off.

Thud! It fell right on to Brer Fox's head and gave him a terrible shock. He blinked his eyes and looked round. Who was throwing things at him? He would soon show them what happened to people who hit him like that!

Another apple fell, thud! This time it hit him on his long nose, and Brer Fox leapt up in pain. He looked wildly round, but not a soul could he see. Then a third apple fell and knocked his left ear quite flat. Brer Fox gave a howl of rage and ran round and round the tree to see who was throwing apples at him. He never once thought that he was sitting under an apple tree!

'Ho! So somebody is hiding, and having a nice little game with me!' thought Brer Fox. 'Well, I'll hide too – and when I see who it is I'll pounce out on them and bite their ears off!'

So he hid behind a bush and waited. But nobody came. Then, after a while, Brer Bear shuffled up to meet old Brer Fox. He sat down under the apple tree, lifted up his head and yawned widely.

And at that very moment a big apple fell off the tree, right into his mouth, and almost choked him! Brer Bear coughed and choked, and the apple shot out of his mouth again. Brer Bear sat up in anger.

'Now who's flinging apples at me!' he grunted.
'Why, I might have choked to death! Just wait till I
see who it is.'

Bump! A large apple fell on to his forehead and
another on his shoulder. Brer Bear jumped up in
a rage. He stood there, watching and waiting to
see who it was that was throwing apples so hard
at him.

Now old Brer Rabbit left his house just about
that time, and he made his way through the orchard.
He kept his eyes and ears wide open, as he always
did, and before long he saw some footprints in a
muddy patch.

'Ha!' said Brer Rabbit, stopping and scratching his chin. 'Those are Brer Fox's footmarks. Now what is he waiting about here for? I'll go carefully.'

So he went very carefully and quietly, and before long he spied old Brer Fox hiding behind the bush, watching out to see who had thrown apples at him. Brer Fox didn't see Brer Rabbit. Brer Rabbit tiptoed away, and presently he spied Brer Bear standing under the apple tree, looking as angry as a hen left out in the rain.

'Now what's the matter with *him!*' wondered Brer Rabbit. And then he guessed! A large apple suddenly fell from the tree and hit Brer Bear on his blunt snout. He gave a yell and rubbed his nose.

'Wait till I see the person that's throwing things at me!' growled Brer Bear, looking all around. Brer Rabbit grinned a little to himself, and then he walked boldly up to Brer Bear.

'Is someone throwing things at you?' he asked. 'What a shame! I believe I know who it is! I spied them hiding behind a bush just now. Brer Bear, you just tiptoe round behind that clump of bushes over there, and you'll see who it is hiding! Take a few apples with you, and throw them hard at *him!* That will teach him to play tricks on you.'

Brer Bear glared at Brer Rabbit. Then he picked

up a handful of apples and went on tiptoe round the clump of bushes. Brer Rabbit followed close behind, grinning to himself. When Brer Bear spied Brer Fox crouching low down on the ground he nearly burst with rage.

'So it was Brer Fox who threw things at me!' he growled, deep down in his throat. 'Well, I'll teach him how to throw!'

And with that Brer Bear flung an apple at Brer Fox as hard as ever he could! Brer Fox got the apple in the very middle of his back, and it hurt him. He sprang up in rage and turned to see who it was. When he saw Brer Bear just about to throw yet another apple at him, he shouted angrily and ran towards him.

'So it was you who threw apples at me when I was waiting for you under the tree! That's a funny thing to do to a friend! Weren't we going to catch Brer Rabbit! And you go and spoil everything by flinging apples about! Wait till I catch you!'

'I'll teach you to throw apples at me!' roared Brer Bear, who was now in a fine old temper too. 'I was sitting under that tree waiting for you, as quiet as could be – and plonk, along came an apple and hit me hard! I'm just getting a bit of my own back now. Take that – and that!'

Brer Fox got the apples on his head, and he gave a shout of rage. He sprang on Brer Bear and got him down. They rolled over and over on the grass. Then Brer Bear got on top and bit Brer Fox on the right ear. Brer Fox was so annoyed that he tried his very hardest to get hold of Brer Bear's little tail and pull it out!

Well, the one who enjoyed that fight most of all was old Brer Rabbit. He just sat and cracked his sides with laughing! Then a great idea came to him. He ran to fill his pockets with the rottenest apples he could find.

And soon he was pelting Brer Fox and Brer Bear

with them as hard as ever he could! Plonk, splish, plonk! Those apples hit them hard and then burst into juice all over them.

Brer Bear and Brer Fox got up and stared round. They saw old Brer Rabbit sitting on the fence, almost falling off with laughter.

'It must have been Brer Rabbit pelting us with apples!' said Brer Bear. 'What sillies we are! Here we came along to catch him and eat him for our dinner – and all we do is to fight one another and roll on the ground whilst he throws his rotten apples at us! Quick – catch him!'

But Brer Rabbit didn't wait to be caught! He was off and away long before either Brer Bear or Brer Fox had reached the fence. And by the time they reached his house the door was bolted and all the windows were shut.

'Go and make yourselves into apple-pie!' yelled Brer Rabbit's voice from a window. 'I'll make some custard to go with it!'

But he didn't, of course, though he would dearly have liked to! Cheeky old Brer Rabbit!

# Brer Fox Goes to Market

Once Brer Fox and Brer Rabbit very badly wanted some money, and they tried to plan how to get some.

'We could go and dig in Mr Man's field and earn some,' said Brer Rabbit.

'Pooh!' said Brer Fox. 'That's too much like hard work! Think again, Brer Rabbit, think again!'

'Well, we could find a bee-tree, collect the honey, and take it to market,' said Brer Rabbit.

'And get stung all over,' said Brer Fox. 'You are not very bright today, Brer Rabbit.'

'Well, you take a turn at thinking, then,' said Brer Rabbit crossly. 'I'm getting a headache with thinking so much.'

'I've got a fine idea,' said Brer Fox. 'What about going along to Brer Bear's house when he's gone out and taking a few things to sell at the market?'

'But that's stealing,' said Brer Rabbit, quite shocked.

'Well, it would do Brer Bear good to lose a few of his things,' said Brer Fox. 'But if you think it would be stealing from him, what about going to Miss Goose's house and taking a few of her things? She's got some nice sheets and towels we could sell at the market.'

'But that would be stealing too,' said Brer Rabbit. 'Don't be silly, Brer Fox.'

'Now if you're going to call everything stealing, I shall stop thinking of plans,' said Brer Fox, and he showed his teeth.

'All right, all right,' said Brer Rabbit in a hurry. 'We'll have your plan. But who does the taking? I don't want to.'

'Of course you'll have to,' said Brer Fox. 'I'll do the selling – and you must do the taking.'

'Well, does it matter whose house I go to?' asked Brer Rabbit.

'Not a bit,' said Brer Fox. 'Go to anyone's you like.'

'And you are quite, quite sure it won't be stealing?' asked Brer Rabbit.

'Quite, quite sure,' said Brer Fox. 'Now see you get into someone's house, choose a few things, bring them to me here – and I'll go to market with them. I'll sell them, and you shall have half the money. I promise you that.'

'Thank you kindly,' said Brer Rabbit. 'I'll go straight away, Brer Fox. But mind you stay here till I come back, so that I will know where to find you!'

'I'll stay all right,' said Brer Fox with a grin. 'Hurry now.'

Brer Rabbit hurried off, grinning away to himself. He didn't go to Brer Bear's. He didn't go to Miss Goose's. No – he went to Brer Fox's own house. It was quite empty, of course. Brer Rabbit pushed open the door and looked around.

He took all the spoons and forks out of the drawer. He took all the clean white towels out of

533

the cupboard. He took six pots of jam from the larder. He took a brand-new kettle from the stove. That was enough for him to carry, so he hurried back with all his goods to where Brer Fox was waiting impatiently.

'Good!' said Brer Fox, taking all the things. 'Now I'll be off to the market and sell all these for as good a price as I can get.'

'You are quite, quite sure it wasn't stealing?' said Brer Rabbit.

'Oh, quite sure,' said Brer Fox. 'You make me tired, asking that question over and over again. Stay here till I come back and I'll give you your share of the money.'

He went off to market. He stood there and offered the spoons and forks for sale, the nice white towels, the brand-new kettle, and the six pots of jam.

He wasn't long in selling them, for he didn't ask very high prices. Soon he had ten shillings in his pocket, and he hurried back to Brer Rabbit.

'Look here!' he said. 'Ten shillings between us! Five for you and five for me.'

'Thanks very much indeed,' said Brer Rabbit, putting his money into his pocket. 'I'll walk home with you, Brer Fox.'

So the two of them walked back to Brer Fox's
house together – and, of course, as soon as Brer
Fox got indoors, he saw that six pots of jam had
gone from his larder, that his kettle and spoons and
forks were missing, and that there were no nice
white towels in his cupboard.

'Hi-yi!' he yelled in a temper. 'Someone's been
here and taken my things! Wait till I catch the thief!
Just wait! What else has he stolen? Oh, the scamp!
Oh, the robber!'

'What has been stolen?' asked Brer Rabbit,
keeping the other side of the gate. 'How strange,
Brer Fox – just the very things you sold at the

market this morning! Now don't you think that's really VERY peculiar!'

Brer Fox turned and stared at Brer Rabbit, who was grinning all over his whiskery face! Brer Fox went quite green. He spoke to Brer Rabbit in a shaking voice.

'Brer Rabbit – whose house did you go to for those things I sold at the market?'

'Why, yours,' said Brer Rabbit. 'You said it didn't matter whose house I went to. Didn't you mean what you said, Brer Fox?'

Brer Fox gave such a dreadful yell that Brer Rabbit thought it was time to run, and run he did! My, how he ran! But when he got to the top of the hill he stopped and turned round.

'Hie, Brer Fox!' he called. 'Are you still quite sure it wasn't stealing?'

And old Brer Fox hadn't anything to say to that!

# Brer Rabbit and the Guy

Once Brer Wolf and Brer Fox put their heads together and laid a plan to catch Old Brer Rabbit.

'It will be Guy Fawkes Day soon,' said Brer Fox. 'What about me dressing up as a guy, and you wheeling me through the streets till we see Brer Rabbit. He's sure to want to come and look at the guy – and I'll pounce on him straight away!'

'That's a good idea, Brer Fox,' said Brer Wolf. 'We'll do that!'

So when Guy Fawkes Day came, Brer Wolf dressed Brer Fox up in old clothes, and put a mask on his face. It was a funny mask, with a broad smile on it. Brer Fox's sharp eyes looked through the holes, and how he grinned to himself to think of Brer Rabbit coming up close to him! Wouldn't he pounce on him!

Brer Wolf put Brer Fox into a chair with wheels

on it, so that he could wheel him easily through the streets.

'Now don't you sit up too straight,' he warned Brer Fox, 'else you won't look like a guy. Go all crooked in the chair, as guys do. Try to look as if you are stuffed with saw-dust.'

So Brer Fox slumped himself down in the chair, and leaned all crooked to make himself look like a real guy. And Brer Wolf took the handles of the wheel-chair and wheeled him away to the village.

Pretty soon they met old Brer Terrapin, and he raised himself up to have a look at the guy. But he was too small to see much further than the guy's feet. He stared at those for a long time. The guy had on a pair of very old boots, and one boot had a hole in it – and through the hole Brer Terrapin felt sure he could see brown fur.

'Brown fur!' thought Brer Terrapin to himself in surprise. 'That's strange. That guy isn't a real guy. It's somebody dressed up to look like one.'

Old Brer Terrapin ambled on his way, and pretty soon he met Brer Rabbit skipping along as merry as a blackbird in spring.

'Heyo, Brer Rabbit,' called Brer Terrapin. 'Have you seen the guy that Brer Wolf is wheeling around?'

'No,' said Brer Rabbit. 'I haven't. I'll go and have a look at it.'

'Well, don't you go too close, that's all,' said Brer Terrapin. 'That guy had got brown fur on his ankles!'

Brer Rabbit grinned. 'So old Brer Fox is up to tricks, is he?' he said. 'Well, you come along with me, Brer Terrapin, and we'll see what we can do about it.'

So the two of them went along to where Brer Wolf stood behind the guy's chair. Brer Rabbit called out to him.

'Brer Wolf! You're wanted at home for a minute! I'll take the guy for you till you come back.'

Now this sounded good to Brer Wolf. If he left Brer Rabbit in charge of the guy, what could be easier than for Brer Fox to jump out of the chair and catch him!

'Right!' said Brer Wolf. 'I'll go home and see what's wanted. I'll be back in a few minutes, Brer Rabbit. Just stand quietly by the guy. That's all you have to do. And remember to shout, "Guy! Guy! A penny for the guy!" when anyone comes by. That's my cap down there on the ground for people to throw pennies into.'

'Right!' said Brer Rabbit, seeing that two or three people were coming along. 'You go now, Brer Wolf. Hurry!'

Brer Fox didn't like to jump at Brer Rabbit with Brer Goat and Brer Possum coming by. So he just sat slumped down in the chair, waiting for them to pass.

'Heyo, Brer Goat!' cried Brer Rabbit. 'Can you help me with this guy? He can't sit up properly, and I'm afraid he'll fall out of the chair.'

'Yes, I'll help you,' said Brer Goat, and he came up. 'What do you want me to do?'

'Oh, just hold him for me whilst I get him fixed,' said Brer Rabbit, winking at old Brer Terrapin who was standing not far off, splitting his sides with trying not to laugh. Brer Rabbit whipped out some rope from his pocket and Brer Goat took hold of the guy to pull him straight in the chair.

And before Brer Fox could do anything about it, he found himself tied tightly to the back of the chair so that he couldn't move!

'Thanks, Brer Goat!' said Brer Rabbit. 'Now he's all right!'

Then Brer Rabbit began to wheel the guy down the street shouting, 'Guy, guy, a penny for the guy!'

Brer Fox didn't like it at all. He began to struggle and wriggle for all he was worth, and the passers-by stared in surprise.

'It's a live guy!' they said in astonishment; 'Who have you got there, Brer Rabbit?'

'Oh, I've got Brer Fox!' said Brer Rabbit. 'He's been a bit of a nuisance to me lately, so I thought I'd pay him back. I'm making him into a guy – doesn't it suit him!'

Well, Brer Fox was simply furious. He struggled with all his might to get free, but the rope held him tightly.

People laughed to see Brer Fox trying to get away. They thought Brer Rabbit was mighty clever to catch him like that! They threw pennies to Brer Rabbit and he sent Brer Terrapin to buy some rockets at a shop.

'We'll take him to a bonfire and send him up in the air with the rockets,' grinned Brer Rabbit. Brer Fox was very frightened to hear this.

'Help ! Help!' he yelled. 'Brer Wolf! Where are you?'

Well, Brer Rabbit wheeled Brer Fox to a big pile of rubbish, and he tied four rockets to him. 'Light the bonfire,' he said to Brer Terrapin, with a wink. 'We'll make things hot for Brer Fox, so we will!'

Brer Rabbit didn't really mean to burn Brer Fox, but Brer Fox didn't know that. He yelled so loudly that Brer Wolf heard him. Brer Wolf had been home and found that he wasn't wanted at all. He had guessed that it was a trick of Brer Rabbit's to get him away, so he had hurried back. But by that time Brer Rabbit had wheeled away Brer Fox, and

Brer Wolf didn't know where.

But when he heard Brer Fox yelling, he ran to save him. Brer Rabbit saw him coming. He quickly lighted the ends of the rockets and then he and Brer Terrapin scurried away behind a bush.

'Save me, save me!' squealed Brer Fox, hearing the rockets sizzle behind him, where Brer Rabbit had tied them to the chair. He wriggled hard and the chair fell over on top of him. The rockets went off with a loud bang, and two of them flew straight at Brer Wolf.

Ker-plunk! They hit him and bowled him over. What a shock they gave him! He got up, turned and ran with all his might, yelling out, 'Brer Fox has shot me! Brer Fox has shot me!'

The rope that bound Brer Fox broke and Brer Fox was free. But did he go chasing Brer Rabbit? Not he! He had had enough of that rascally rabbit

for weeks to come. And my – you should have heard
Brer Terrapin and Brer Rabbit laugh! It would have
given you a fit of the giggles too!

# Brer Rabbit and the Little Girl

Once day, after Brer Rabbit had been tramping all around to find some salad to make his dinner good, he came near to Mr Man's house. He went along until he came to a little gate, and near the garden gate he saw a little girl playing around in the sun.

Well, Brer Rabbit looked in through the garden-gate, and saw cabbages and lettuces and carrots and all kinds of other greens growing there, and his mouth began to water.

He took a walk up to the little girl, bowed politely, and talked mighty nicely to her.

'Howdy, Little Girl,' said Brer Rabbit. 'How do you feel this morning?'

'Howdy, Brer Rabbit,' said the little girl. 'How are you feeling yourself?'

'Poorly, Little Girl, poorly,' said Brer Rabbit. 'Tell me, are you the little girl whose Pa lives up in the big white house?'

'Yes, I'm the little girl whose Pa lives in that big white house you can see yonder,' said the little girl.

'Then I'm mighty glad to hear that,' said Brer Rabbit, 'because I've just been to see your Pa, and he sent me to tell his little girl to open the garden-gate for me so that I can go in to get a few greens.'

'I'll open the gate now,' said the little girl, and she ran to open the gate, and with that Brer Rabbit hopped in, and got a fine armful of greens and then hopped out again.

He bowed politely when he left the little girl, and said he was much obliged to her. Then he set out for home, and made himself a fine dinner that day.

Well, the next day Brer Rabbit hid near the garden gate again, and when he saw the little girl come out to play he ran up to her, told her the same tale as before, and she let him into the garden. He picked all he wanted of the greens, and then set out for home again.

This seemed a mighty easy way of getting greens, and Brer Rabbit, he went up to the garden every day for a long time and the little girl let him in. Things went on like this till Mr Man began to miss his greens, and he kept on missing them, and got so angry that he began to blame everybody on the place for taking them.

When the little girl heard this she went to him and said: 'My goodness, Pa, didn't you tell Mr Rabbit to ask me to let him into the garden each day to get some greens, and haven't I done it every day since!'

When Mr Man heard that, he was mighty wild. Then he began to laugh, and he told the little girl he had forgotten all about Mr Rabbit.

'Now, Little Girl, next time Mr Rabbit comes along, you take him into the garden as usual, and then you run as fast as you can and tell me he's there, because I've got some business to do with that young fellow that must be attended to.'

So the next morning, when Brer Rabbit came up, the little girl let him into the garden, and then she ran up to the house and shouted: 'Oh, Pa! Pa! Oh, Pa! Here is Brer Rabbit, in the garden this minute! Here he is, Pa!'

Then Mr Man rushed out and grabbed a fishing-line that was hanging in the back-porch, and he ran to the garden and when he got there he saw Brer Rabbit trampling round on the strawberry bed and smashing down all the tomatoes too. Brer Rabbit saw Mr Man and squatted down behind a cabbage, but it wasn't any use. Mr Man saw him all right, and before Brer Rabbit could count three Mr Man had caught him and tied him up hard and fast with the fishing-line. After he had got him well tied up Mr Man took a step back and grinned at Brer Rabbit.

'You've tricked me lots of times, Brer Rabbit, but this time I've tricked you! I'm going to give you such a whacking! And then I'm going to skin you, see? And to make sure you get the right sort of whacking I'm just a-going to step up to the house and fetch my little red cowhide whip!'

Before he went to get his whip Mr Man called to the little girl.

'You watch Brer Rabbit for me whilst I'm gone,' he said.

Brer Rabbit didn't say a word till Mr Man was

out of the gate. Then he began to sing. And in those days it was a real treat to hear Brer Rabbit sing.

The song he sang went like this:

*The jay-bird hunts for the sparrow's nest;*
*The kestrel sails all around;*
*The squirrel, he jumps from the top of the tree;*
*Mr Mole, he stays in the ground;*
*He hides and he stays till the dew drops down;*
*Mr Mole, he hides in the ground!*

When the little girl heard this song she laughed, and asked Brer Rabbit to sing some more. But Brer Rabbit began to cough, and he shook his head.

'Seems I've got something in my throat,' said Brer Rabbit. 'I can't sing any more.'

'Oh, do, do, do!' begged the little girl. 'Please do, Brer Rabbit. That was a beautiful song.'

'I can dance much better than I can sing,' said Brer Rabbit.

'Well, dance then, do dance,' begged the little girl.

'Now tell me, how in the name of goodness do you think I can dance when I'm all tied up like this!' said Brer Rabbit.

'Well, I'll untie you, and then you can dance for me,' said the little girl.

'All right, you do that,' said Brer Rabbit. 'Then I can do a fine dance for you.'

So the little girl untied him, and Brer Rabbit, he sort of stretched himself and looked all round.

And then he began to dance! Yes, old Brer Rabbit put his feet together and he danced a mighty fine dance! He danced down the path, he did, and he danced right out of the garden gate. And old Brer Rabbit didn't stop dancing till he got home. My, that was a mighty fine dance Brer Rabbit did that day!

Another enchanting story collection from the world of

*Enid Blyton*

## *Mr Galliano's Circus*

It's a dream come true!

Jimmy is so excited when Mr Galliano's famous travelling circus comes to town. Jimmy loves animals and they trust him. Soon he's spending all his time with the elephants and monkeys, the riders and acrobats – and the magical Mr Galliano himself. If only Jimmy could be part of the circus forever . . .

Another enchanting story collection from the world of

*Enid Blyton*

## *Fireworks in Fairyland*

They're naughty, they're clever – are you ready for
the magic folk?

Life in fairyland is fun but unpredictable. Some fairies
are hard-working, but some just cause trouble. Pixies
can be full of mischief and surprise. And if you've never
met a brownie, you won't believe the scrapes Hop,
Skip and Jump get into.

# Enid Blyton

is one of the most popular children's authors of all time.
Her books have sold over 500 million copies and have
been translated into other languages more often than
any other children's author.

Enid Blyton adored writing for children. She wrote over
600 books and hundreds of short stories. *The Famous Five*
books, now 75 years old, are her most popular. She is also
the author of other favourites including *The Secret Seven*,
*The Magic Faraway Tree*, *Malory Towers* and *Noddy*.

Born in London in 1897, Enid lived much of her life in
Buckinghamshire and adored dogs, gardening and the
countryside. She was very knowledgeable about trees,
flowers, birds and animals.

Dorset – where some
of the Famous Five's
adventures are set –
was a favourite place
of hers too.

Enid Blyton's
stories are read
and loved by
millions of children
(and grown-ups)
all over the world.
Visit enidblyton.co.uk
to discover more.